DAVID GILBERT is the author of the story collection *Remote Feed* and the novel *The Normals*. His stories have appeared in the *New Yorker*, *Harper's*, *GQ* and *Bomb*. He lives in New York with his wife and three children.

From the reviews of *& Sons*:

'Gilbert's sharp wit runs from the caustic to the metaphysical, recalling Andrew Marvell one minute . . . and Edward St Aubyn the next . . . richly entertaining . . . a book that has the rare quality of being funny without being silly, serious without being solemn, and powerfully moving without being either sentimental or coercive.'
JAMES LASDUN, *Guardian*

'Hugely energetic . . . On one level, *& Sons* is a conventionally gripping read . . . It's all engrossing and superbly done, the characterization alive and convincing – sprinkled with catchy image-making . . . His novel's 400-plus pages zip by in a rush of accessible, high-browish pleasure.' ROBERT COLLINS, *Sunday Times*

'Wonderfully energetic and perceptive, exceptionally vivid and a tour de force. Look out for it.' JUSTIN CARTWRIGHT, *Observer*

'*& Sons* is a sophisticated, compassionate novel, very much more than a clever take on the vicissitudes of the writing life. Funny and smart, it is lit with the kind of writing that makes the reader break into a smile.' ERICA WAGNER, *Financial Times*

'Superbly written, wonderfully entertaining and often outrageously funny . . . the verbal firework-display is relentless.'
KATE SAUNDERS, *The Times*

BY THE SAME AUTHOR

The Normals
Remote Feed

& Sons

A Novel

David Gilbert

FOURTH ESTATE • London

Fourth Estate
An imprint of HarperCollins*Publishers*
77–85 Fulham Palace Road
Hammersmith
London W6 8JB

This Fourth Estate paperback edition published 2014
1

First published in the United States by Random House, an imprint of The Random
House Publishing Group, a division of Random House, Inc., New York in 2013
First published in Great Britain by Fourth Estate in 2014

A catalogue record for this book is available from the British Library

ISBN 978-0-00-755281-8

Grateful acknowledgment is made to Alfred Music Publishing Co. Inc. for permission
to reprint an excerpt from "Salt of the Earth," words and music by Mick Jagger and
Keith Richards, copyright © 1968 (Renewed) ABKCO Music, Inc. All rights reserved.
Used by permission of Alfred Music Publishing Co. Inc.

Designed by Simon M. Sullivan

Printed and bound in Australia by Griffin Press

Find out more about HarperCollins and the environment at
www.harpercollins.co.uk/green

For Max & Eliza & Olivia

Sometimes Louis saw in his sons a mirror that reflected the best of who he was and he was in awe; other times he hoped to see nothing of himself and would insist on molding the opposite, by force if necessary. Fatherhood is the bending of that alpha and that omega, with the wobbly heat of our own fathers mixed in. We love and hate our boys for what they might see.

—A. N. DYER, *The Spared Man*

ONCE UPON A TIME, *the moon had a moon. This was a long time ago, long before there were sons who begged their fathers for good-night stories, long before there were fathers or sons or stories. The moon's moon was a good deal smaller than the moon, a saucer as compared to a platter, but for the people of the moon this hardly mattered. They maintained a constant, almost mystic gaze on their moon. You might ask these people—not quite people, more like an intelligent kind of eggplant, their roots eternally clenched—What about the nearby earth, with its glorious blues and greens and ever-changing swirls of white? Surely that gathered up some of their attention? Actually, not at all. The earth to them seemed a looming presence, vaguely sinister, like something that belonged to a sorcerer. This brings up another question: how did the creatures of the earth feel about its two moons? Well, to be honest, life at that time was rather pea-brained, though recently scientists have discovered a direct evolutionary link between those moons and the development of binocular vision in the Cambrian slug.*

But one day—for this is a story and there must be a one day—the moon's moon appeared bigger than normal in the sky, which the wise men of the moon chalked up to something they called intergravitational bloat. Regardless, it shone with even more brilliance, only to be outdone the next evening, when the circumference had quintupled. Nobody was yet frightened; they were too much in awe. But by the tenth day, when the moon's moon resembled the barrel of a train bearing down on them, the people started to worry. This can't be happening. What they loved more than anything suddenly seemed destined to kill them. Oh mercy. Oh dear. A resigned kind of panic set in, as they gripped their roots extra tight and prepared for the inevitable impact, which would have come on the twenty-first day except that the moon's moon passed over-

head like a ball slightly overthrown. Thank heavens it missed, the people sighed. Then they turned their heads and followed its course and soon realized its true path: the distant bull's-eye of earth. It seemed they were not the players here, merely the spectators. On the twenty-fourth day, roughly sixty-five million years ago, the moon's moon traveled its last mile and a great yet silent blast erupted from the lower hemisphere of earth. And that was it. Their moon was gone. In its place a cataract of gray gradually blinded all those blues and greens and swirls of white.

The sky where their moon once hung now seemed dark and injured, its color the color of a bruise. A new kind of longing set in as they stared at earth. Someone was the first to let go, likely the most depressed. To his amazement, instead of withering, always the assumed prognosis, he began to float—not only float but rise up and drift toward the distant grave site of their beloved moon. "We've all been holding on," he shouted down, newly prophetized, "all this time just holding on." Was this suicide or deliverance? the wise men of the moon debated while someone else let go, and then another, three then five then eight rising up into the sky, their eyes casting a line toward earth and a hopeful reunion with their moon. Before any opinion could be agreed upon, the horizon shimmered with thousands of fellow travelers, the moon like a dandelion after a lung-clearing fffffffffffffff. The surface grew paler until eventually only one soul remained behind, a child, specifically a boy. Every second he was tempted to join the others, but he was stubborn and mistook his grip for freedom. Friends and family slowly faded from sight, their pleas losing all echo, and many years later, when the sky no longer included their memory, this boy, now a young man, lowered his head and contemplated the ground. Soon he took his first steps, dragging his cumbersome roots across dusty lunar plains, certain that what was lost would soon be eclipsed by whatever he would find.

But that will have to wait until tomorrow night.

I

ANDREW DYER

June 24, 1942

Dear Charlie,

Thank you for the Inkless Stainless G-men Fingerprint Set. I like it very much. I have already made a record of my family's dirty mitts. I'm dusting old Mr. Piggybank daily just in case Daddy Desperado gets any ideas. And I'll be dusting for you too. Hands off the baseball, bud! Thanks for coming to my birthday though it wasn't half as fun as yours. Normally I hate magicians and their corny tricks but Mr. Magnifico was right good. Where did that bird go? I bet he had two, maybe three of them. Maybe he was all bird. Anyway, see you tomorrow at school, before this letter sees you.

Finally your fellow eight year old,

I.i

AND THERE HE SAT, up front, all alone in the first pew. For those who asked, the ushers confirmed it with a reluctant nod. Yep, that's him. For those who cared but said nothing, they gave themselves away by staring sideways and pretending to be impressed by the nearby stained glass, as if devotees of Cornelius the Centurion or Godfrey of Bouillon instead of a seventy-nine-year-old writer with gout. Rumor had it he might show. His oldest and dearest friend, Charles Henry Topping, was dead. Funeral on Tuesday at St. James on 71st and Madison. Be respectful. Dress appropriately. See you there. Some of the faithful brought books in hopes of getting them signed, a long shot but who could resist, and by a quarter of eleven the church was almost full. I myself remember watching friends of my father as they walked down that aisle. While they glimpsed the Slocums and the Coopers and over there the Englehards—hello by way of regretful grin—a number of these fellow mourners baffled them. Were those sneakers? Was that a necklace or a tattoo; a hairdo or a hat? It seemed death had an unfortunate bride's side. Once seated, all and sundry leafed through the program—good paper, nicely engraved—and gauged the running time in their head, which mercifully lacked a communion. There was a universal thrill for the eulogist since the man up front was notoriously private, bordering on reclusive. Excitement spread via church-wide mutter. Thumbs composed emails, texts, status updates, tweets. This New York funeral suddenly constituted a chance cultural event, one of those I-was-there moments, so prized in this city, even if you had known the writer from way back, knew him before he was famous and won all those awards, knew him as a strong ocean swimmer and an epic climber of trees, knew his mother and his father, his stepfather, knew his childhood friends, all of whom knew him as Andy or Andrew rather than the more unknowable A. N. Dyer.

All this happened in mid-March, twelve years ago. I recall it being the first warm day of the year, a small relief after months of near-impossible cold. Just a week earlier, the temperature sulked in the teens, the windchill dragging the brat into newborn territory. Windows rattled in their sashes, and the sky resembled a headfirst plunge onto cement. After a long winter of dying, my father was finally dead. I remember standing up and covering his face, like they do in the movies, his bright blue socks poking free from the bottom of the comforter. He always wore socks with his pajamas and never bothered to sleep under the sheets. It was as if his dreams had no right to unmake a bed. I went over and opened both windows, no longer cursing the draft but hoping the cold might shelter his body for a bit. But on the day of his funeral, the city seemed near sweltering, even if the thermostat within St. James maintained its autumnal chill, the Episcopalian constant of scotch and tweed.

Churches are glorified attics, A. N. Dyer once wrote, but now he resembled a worshipper deep in prayer—head lowered, hands crammed against stomach. His posture reminded me of a comma, its intent not yet determined. People assumed he was upset. Of course he was upset. He and my father were the oldest of friends, born just eleven days apart in the same Manhattan hospital. Growing up, this minor divide seemed important, with Andrew teasing the older Charlie that he was destined to die first—it was just basic actuarial math—and Andrew would bury his friend and live his remaining numbered days in a glorious Topping-free state. "The worms and creepy-crawlies will eat you while I swig champagne." This joke carried on until the punch line became infused with intimacy and what once made young Charlie cry now made him smile, even toward the end. "You really are milking this," Andrew muttered during his final visit. "I've had the bubbly on ice for a month now." He sat by the bed, like a benched player witnessing an awful defeat. My father was no longer speaking. That bully with the scythe straddled his chest and dared him to breathe, c'mon, breathe. So Andrew decided to give his friend the last word by leaning closer and stage-whispering in his ear, "This is where you tell me to go look in the mirror, with all my pills a day and my ruined joints and unsalvageable lower midsection; this is where you point and say with the awful knowledge of those who go first, 'You're next.'" Andrew was rather pleased with this comeback. He wondered how far back his dying friend could reach, if apologizing was worth all the dragging up, but really he decided the important thing was that he was here, A. N. Dyer in the flesh, today's visit no small feat considering the state of his big toe. It had been a two-Vicodin morning. Charlie for his troubles sported a morphine drip. "Just look at us," Andrew started to say when Charlie's right hand took unexpected flight and flopped like a dead bird onto Andrew's knee. His fingernails were thick and yellow, and Andrew recalled from his more macabre youth the keratin that keeps growing after death, which raised his eyes to that weedy Topping hair and how in the coffin Charlie would miss his monthly trim and turn bohemian, like Beethoven conducting his own decay. Unnerved, Andrew gave his friend a gentle pat. His own hand seemed hardly any better. Then Charlie tried to speak, he tried and tried—clearly he had something to say—but all meaning remained locked up in his throat and what rattled free sounded like one of those cheap Hollywood scarefests where the living transform into the contagious undead and you had best run. To his credit, Andrew refused to look away. While he was obviously upset, he also seemed embarrassed, perhaps more embarrassed than upset, as if dying involved a humiliating confession. Please let me go, he probably begged to himself. Release me. After a minute of listening to this hopeless rasp he interrupted by saying, "I'm sorry, pal," and he placed his hand on Charlie's chest and kissed him softly on the head. That was good enough, right?

Charles Henry Topping earned a respectable if pictureless two-hundred-word obit in *The New York Times*—lawyer, philanthropist, trustee, world-class decoy collector, and lifelong friend of the novelist A. N. Dyer, who often wrote about the blue-blooded world of the Toppings and the Dyers. Wrote? I'm sure Andrew marveled at that particular choice of tense. It likely surprised him that my father even warranted a mention in the *Times*. How little a life required nowadays.

The church organist played the last of the Mendelssohn prelude.

Andrew curled farther forward in his pew, as if pressed by the world behind him. If only Isabel were here. She would have known what to say. "Enough thinking about your miserable self." She could cut through him like no other. All day yesterday Andrew had sat over his IBM Selectric and found little to recall about his friend except that he liked bacon, liked bacon tremendously. Charlie could eat a whole slab of it. BLTs. Bacon burgers. Bacon and mayonnaise sandwiches. Liver wrapped in bacon. Disgusting. Of course there was more to say (after all, the *Times* managed two hundred words) but it seemed that so much of the Dyer-Topping friendship was based on those early years when action trumped language and bacon was as profound as anything. Since birth their relationship was as fixed as the stars. That was a large part of its charm. Like many men who keep friends in orbits of various length, a month, six months, a year might pass without talking and yet they could pick right up again, unfazed. The two of them were close without question so why bother searching for answers. Talk centered on the trivial, past and present, on summers and schoolmates, those earnest memories of youth, while the stickier issues, like disease and divorce, death and depression, occurred on the subatomic level: they had their fundamental effect, their important interactions, but they had no identifiable consequence when having a pleasant meal together, a meal likely pushed upon them by their ever-attentive wives.

Charlie sure loved his bacon.

Andrew removed the eulogy from his suit jacket.

How can I read this crap in public? he wondered. How will I even manage to climb the lectern without my gout igniting a thousand crystal-cracking explosions? My bedrock is nothing but chalkstone. From his pocket he retrieved then popped his just-in-case Vicodin, the lint-covered backup to his post-breakfast Vicodin. Just swallowing the pill seemed to hurt, as if ground-up glass were part of its pharmacology. The organist approached her tonal amen. Behind the altar loomed that massive golden screen with its carved miniatures of important church figures, once memorized by Andrew and Charlie during their Sunday school days, with that cow Miss Kepplinger insisting on a metronomic recital of names—*St. Polycarp, St. Gregory of Nazianzus*—

a pause and no snack for you—*St. Michael, St. Uriel*—and while Andrew had a strong memory—*St. Raphael, St. Gabriel*—if old Miss Moo were tapping her clubfoot today—the fifth archangel up top, um, the patron saint of all who forgive, um, the angel who stopped Abraham's Issac-slaying hand, um—he would have gone graham crackerless. But there was no tapping. Not today. Mendelssohn was done and Charlie was dead and Andrew was a few minutes away from mortifying his more famous self in front of all these people.

Just leave right now, shouted in his head.

Pull the old fire alarm and bolt.

He blamed the whole mess on the second Mrs. Topping, my stepmother. Lucy had the unique ability to corner a person on the phone. "He did love you," she told him the day after my father died.

"Yes," Andrew said.

"So so much."

"Yes."

"So proud to have you as a friend. So proud. Just plain proud of you."

"And I he," Andrew said, wondering if he was speaking English or Mandarin.

"And the boys, and Grace, they love you too, like a second father really."

"Their father was a good man."

"You have such a way with words. As a matter of fact . . ."

It was ridiculous, her flattery, or perhaps mockery since her lips often pursed the thinnest of smiles, passed down from a particular brand of suburban housewife who could appear both dense and all too wise, like any service industry veteran. Yet somehow by the end of the conversation the divorcée from Oyster Bay had nabbed her prized eulogist. A goddamn eulogy? What could be worse? Maybe a graduation speech. A wedding toast. Andrew had said yes despite the clearest of professional and private intentions, had said yes despite the fact that his last novel, *The Spared Man*, was published ten years ago and most of that was cribbed from something he had abandoned twenty years before—since then nothing new from the celebrated author of *Ampersand* and *Here Live Angry Dogs and Brutal Men* and a dozen other books, not even a letter of decent length. Sometimes it seemed a vital piece had gone loose in his brain and he could feel the bit rattling around, a temporal gear that had slipped its carriage and no longer stamped thoughts into proper words and sentences. He was, in effect, broken. Often he wanted to jam a screwdriver into his ear. Like last night, in his study: he was sitting at his desk distracted by the recent reissue of his books, with that stupid business on their spines (if arranged chronologically they revealed a red line that traced the peaks and valleys of a cardiogram), which, while clever enough, did not take into consideration the random heart conditions after midnight, the arrhythmias and shortnesses of breath and implied flatlines, the irrational fear of sleep, the old friend recently dead and only a few hours to sum up his life. Four-thirty in the morning and chest-deep in his own grave, Andrew reached for that most loathsome and inguinal of writing instruments, the laptop computer. He lowered himself into the underworld of the Internet. Almost as a lark he did a Google search (was he the only one who noticed in its logo a babyish connotation, a sort of infantile infinite?) for *eulogy* and *help* and *please*. Within an hour he found his Eurydice:

My dear friend,

    I am here to offer you my very deepest sympathies for the loss you have recently suffered. In this time of grieving it can seem overwhelming to deliver an eulogy in front of an audience of friends and family and clergy and strangers let alone writing said eulogy with all the care it so obviously deserves and all in a matter of a few fraught days. What can you give but tears? Believe me I know what you are going through. I myself was beyond bereft and scared when my brother-in-law asked me to give the eulogy for my much loved but tragically deceased sister and while I was afraid I might not do the lovely part of her life justice I preserved and there were such good feeling and warmth for my words that since then I have written and delivered eulogies for my father, my cousin, my uncle, two of my aunts, my grandmother, countless dear friends, even poor newborns abandoned I have remembered. If you want to skyrocket your confidence and

save precious time and rest assured in delivering a memorable
tribute to someone who once meant so much to you, then www
.eulogiesfromtheheart.com is the most important website you will visit
today. My Instant Eulogy Package will give you everything you need to
stand tall with appropriate and meaningful sorrow. Let me help bring
forth the loss that is struggling within you.

Sincerely and again with deepest condolences,
Emma Norbert

Yes, Andrew thought, Emma Norbert understood. Her photo was
front and center, her face soft with the sweetest kind of intelligence,
even if the eyes were punctuated with too much makeup, like unnecessary quotation marks. But you could tell she was an honest if dyslexic
mourner. Emma had the real words while all Andrew had was artifice.
Drunk with scotch and swirled with Vicodin, he considered the fourteen books that would stand as his testament, a handful of older critics
giving their kind words, a handful of younger critics challenging such
weary opinions. Oh Emma, Andrew thought, what would you say
about me for $29.99? He plugged in his information, his credit card
number, then pushed ENTER. In five minutes he had his choice of fill-
in-the-blank eulogies.

They say that at the end of our time on this earth if you can count a few
good friends you are a fortunate person. I know that I am fortunate
because I could always count on _[insert name]_ to be the truest friend I
ever did know, and today I am sick with despair, doubly sick because
[insert name] is not here to repair me with his/her kind words and loving
heart . . .

Andrew clapped his hands, maybe even cackled. The idea that he or
Charlie could repair anything was laughable. Their mothers, and then
their wives, did all the repair work, often literally, while their sons, and
later their husbands, bungled even the easiest of household chores and
came to depend on a general air of domestic incompetence for a sense

of well-being. They were hopeless without their women. Andrew rolled a sheet of paper into the Selectric, always a satisfying action, like adding memory to an empty head. As he copied the words he allowed himself a brief fantasy with Ms. Norbert, Emma in leather and high heels, pushing his face down and riding him like a run-on sentence. Nothing rose from her whip but there was some solace in the harsh slap of keys.

> I just hope I was half the friend that _[insert name]_ was to me, and in the end, when my time is up, God willing I will once again find myself with him/her and we can (a favorite shared activity) again. The sun might set, but there is always the promise of a new day, always the promise, always.

But in the gloom of this day Emma floated like stone. Andrew slipped the eulogy back into his suit jacket and bunkered himself farther into the pew, hoping perhaps that old Miss Moo would forget to call on him. He wondered about Andy—he had escaped outside for a quick smoke but that was four or five cigarettes ago. Then again, what did twenty minutes mean to a seventeen-year-old? Or an hour? Even a year? All that future ahead was a bright light shining under the door, the present just a narrow peephole. Still, Andrew wished he could reach over and touch the boy's knee and maybe settle himself with a self-confirming glance. Andy was the answer to that late-night question: Am I alone? No. You have him. But where was he? Andrew thought about turning around and looking but the idea of wading through the collected crowd, the various social connections, the past that grew thin but never snapped, if anything grew more elastic, exhausted him. It was a history he couldn't deny. Like an Appalachian boy who done good, the entire Upper East Side had embraced his early success, even if his novels tended toward the Upper West, with friends of his mother and stepfather praising the reviews and magazine articles and asking about sales and potential awards and if Darryl Zanuck had come calling yet, these same hands congratulating him decades later when he ripped them apart in the Henry Doubleday diptych (*American*

Ligature and *The Gorgon USA*), but by then there was no cause for outrage. A. N. Dyer was famous. Andrew cleared the ever-prolific phlegm
from his throat, a thirty-second job nowadays. Yes, the pews behind
him carried the junk DNA of his life, useless perhaps but within their
folds he might glimpse his mother, long a ghost, making her giddy
rounds and he might overhear a kind word said about his father, who
died the day after Christmas when Andrew was just eight. But rather
than turn he continued to peer ahead, disoriented, like somebody mistaking a mirror for a way out.

The organist roused into the first chord of the processional hymn,
"Thine Be the Glory." The congregation stood and angled toward the
back, though A. N. Dyer remained seated, seemingly too distraught to
move. First came the boys choir, followed by the clergy, the coffin, and
finally we Toppings, led by the Widow Lucy. No doubt her black en-
semble with fur trim and fat satin buttons caused a stir among a few of
the ladies who expected no less from Mrs. Oyster Bay. The original
Mrs. Topping, aka Eleanor, my mother, would have been understated
to the point of high style, a woman, like so many of her generation,
who took her cues from Jacqueline Kennedy, to the point where you
could imagine all these women the survivors of some public assassina-
tion. But in Lucy's defense, she had drawn the short straw, having been
tied to my father for all the difficulties—the first bout of esophageal
cancer, the mental confusion, the heart failure in conjunction with the
second bout of cancer—and she had made his last years as comfortable,
as happy, as possible, even if she droned on about thwarted trips to
India, to Cambodia, to Xanadu, I swear. Only the cruel would have
criticized that ridiculous Halston knockoff hat. She deserved this big
wedding of a funeral, in full choir.

> *Thine be the glory, risen, conq'ring Son;*
> *Endless is the vict'ry, Thou o'er death hast won*

Andrew, still sitting, thought, or sensed, sort of breathed in the air
and comprehended the years within the particulates of this church,
where nothing changed, not even the smell, which was similar to his

father's closet, and how as a boy he could stay huddled on top of sharp-heeled shoes, not quite hiding but not quite not hiding, almost wanting to be found though he'd instantly feel foolish—yes, winged within this constancy were numerous past weddings and christenings and funerals, God knows how many times sitting in this church and Andrew hardly believed in God.

Make us more than conq'rors, through Thy deathless love:
Bring us safe through Jordan to Thy home above.

Boys like pocket-size men passed by in their red and white frocks. This slow-moving, high-pitched train startled Andrew, and he realized, Oh crap, I should be on my feet, the service has begun. He grabbed the pew and eased himself up, hobbled only by a memory of pain, thanks to the Vicodin. Some of us gave him a weary grin as we entered our reserved pews. Lucy and Kaye Snow, her daughter from her first marriage, slipped in beside Andrew. Kaye was an unmarried breeder of Wheaton terriers, though seeing her you might have guessed Pomeranians. But her true profession was aggrieved yet devoted daughter, a career she had thrived in for nearly forty-seven years and from which she would never retire. Kaye smiled at Andrew. She must be very talented with dogs, he thought.

Lucy reached over and touched his forearm. "How are you feeling?"

"What's that?"

"You look peaked."

"No, I haven't," he misunderstood. "Have you seen Andy?"

"No. Is everything all right?"

Andrew assumed she was asking about the eulogy. "Oh, it'll be fine."

"It's hard, isn't it?"

"What?"

"All of this," she said, her hands spreading as if the human condition were roughly the size and weight of a melon, then she fixed his collar and brushed a bit of dandruff from his shoulders. "I wish I had a comb."

Daughter Kaye grimaced, a sentiment that seemed tattooed on her lips.

"Anyway"—Lucy waved to a friend—"thank you for agreeing to do this."

The hymn concluded and Rev. Thomas Francis Rushton stood before the congregation and spoke those familiar words "I am the resurrection and the life, saith the Lord . . . " though there was nothing particularly immortal about his delivery, just the words themselves in intimate soliloquy " . . . and whosoever liveth and believeth in me shall never die . . . " the Reverend reminding Andrew of an Astroff from a production of *Uncle Vanya* he had seen many years ago, when he hated the theater a little less " . . . I know that my Redeemer liveth, and that he shall stand at the latter day upon the earth . . . " Andrew trying to remember what Sonya said during that last scene, something about the futility of life and how we must play the hand of our remaining days " . . . and though this body be destroyed, yet shall I see God . . . " where in Christ's name was Andy and how many cigarettes did the boy need " . . . and no man dieth to himself . . . " Andrew himself a pack-a-day smoker until he was fifty and still he yearned for the morning smoke " . . . whether we live, therefore, or die, we are the Lord's . . . " seventeen years old and smoking, just like his old man " . . . Blessed are the dead . . . " Andrew breathed in and imagined his lungs in harmony with the boy's " . . . for they rest from their labors . . . " and that's when he shuddered, terrified by what his next breath might bring.

Reverend Rushton declared, "The Lord be with you."

"And also with you," replied those in the know.

"Let us pray."

In the pause before the Our Father began Andrew whispered, "What have I done?" loud enough for some of us to hear.

I.ii

BEFORE CHARGES OF NARRATIVE FRAUD are flung in my direction, let me defend myself and tell you that A. N. Dyer often used my father in his fiction. Not that my father seemed to care or even notice much. But I certainly did, ever since I was a teenager and first read *Ampersand*. I spotted the immediate resemblance to Edgar Mead's best friend, Cooley, the awkward but diligent student who was raised in a household of athletes, crazy-haired Cooley who rejected sports for study except in the case of Ping-Pong. That was my dad. His zeal for Ping-Pong seemed to belie his nature until you realized it was his way of telling you he could have been a sportsman himself, as great as his brothers and sister, as his own father, who was the last gentleman amateur to reach the quarterfinals at Forest Hills. Using the abbreviated language of angles and spin my dad would lecture you on not wasting your talents—match point—on silly pursuits. Historically speaking, he probably missed being sensitive by eight to ten years, depending on where you date the New Man era; rather, he grew up shy, then aloof, then distant, his feelings best relinquished from the palm of his hand—a firm grip, a pat on the back, a semi-ironic salute. He was the master of the goodbye wave. Closing my eyes, I can still see him, an unspoken sorrow on his face—"Oh well"—as he lowered his hand and propped that small racquet over that small ball, embarrassed by even the smallest victory.

Reverend Rushton took us through the opening prayers.

I myself was beyond tired.

Up front, the coffin glowed with extreme polish. Inside was nothing but a gesture of the man. Per his wishes, he had been cremated, half of his ashes to be scattered into the Atlantic of eastern Long Island—our summer getaway—the other half to be tossed from the church tower at Phillips Exeter Academy—our collective alma mater. These instructions were a surprise to us, his children. Dad was not one to swim in the ocean, or sail, or poeticize about its vast blue canopy; in fact, he quite publicly disliked sand. And while he was a generous supporter of Exeter and a longtime trustee, he was hardly nostalgic about his prep school days and never touted its pedigree or insisted that his children follow in his footsteps (though we all did). So it seemed odd, these final resting places, as well as inconvenient. New Hampshire? How delightful. But the mahogany coffin with its satin finishes and interior of champagne velvet (dubbed, I believe, *The Montrachet*) was our stepmother's doing. She wanted something to bury, something to visit, even if that something was just a scoop of her third husband.

"A ten-grand ashtray," my sister muttered during the arrangements.

"She also bought a plot at Woodlawn," my brother muttered right back.

"Hate to think how much that cost."

"Fifty thousand, not including annual upkeep."

"Unbelievable."

"And then there's the headstone."

The prospect of an inheritance had made them both accountants.

I was—or am—Charles Henry Topping's second son, the youngest of three. Grace and Charles Jr. were ahead of me respectively and literally: Grace commanded the second pew, her whole family jammed together, the six of them sour yet insistent, like the richest people flying coach, while behind her sat Charles Jr., never Charlie or Chuck, with his two girls, the ever blond and blonder copies of his wife, who was six months pregnant with what I could only imagine was a blinding ball of blazing white light. Then there was me, Philip, the momma's boy without his momma. I was bookended by my five-year-old son and seven-year-old daughter, both of whom dressed like tiny adults mourning their lost childhood. I hadn't seen them in a few weeks. I always suspected that I could be a bad husband, a bad son, but I always assumed that I would be a good father. Rufus and Eloise were so well

behaved as to be almost offensive. This was the consequence of their
angry yet polite mother, who was somewhere in this church waiting for
the service to end so she could swoop in and whisk her babes back
home. Ashley was probably crying herself. She was fond of my father,
and in his quiet way he was fond of her. "She is well built," he once told
me, the opinion having nothing to do with her figure but rather with
her overall form. And maybe Ashley was thinking of my mother, a
woman she got along with spectacularly well (my mother had an ease
with making people feel warm and welcome, though her children were
often dubious of her actual impressions), and of course seeing all of
these people, the old Topping crowd, many of whom had attended our
own wedding ten years before—well, it must've been hard for her. We
were the ridiculous subplot: the cheating husband, the betrayed wife,
the poor poor children. Yes, Ashley was probably crying while all I
could do was stare at that coffin and picture the closed mouth of a giant
clam, a charred bit of irritant within its velvety folds. As the Exeter
motto states, *Finis Origine Pendet.*

But where was the beginning?

I have no idea what my father was like as a boy, or a teenager, or a
young man. Even today I find myself poring over the novels of A. N.
Dyer in search of possible clues to his other life: the aforementioned
Cooley from *Ampersand,* but also Richard Truswell from *Pink Eye* and
Killian Stout from *Here Live Angry Dogs and Brutal Men.* I'll study
these characters and I'll think, Maybe that's him, in Truswell's tragic
decency, in Stout's oppressed desires, both their lives slowly collapsing
under the strain until a seemingly minor act brings them down. But
my father never buckled. He was consistently unsurprising. But just
last year I learned he had a stammer growing up, and this news hit me
hard, like adding pastel to a police sketch. Fathers start as gods and end
as myths and in between whatever human form they take can be ca-
lamitous for their sons. I have no first memory of the man, only a mild
impression of him sitting safely behind a newspaper, the back of his
head leaving an ever-present mark on the chair, his oily shadow. I first
learned about current events by staring at him silently, waiting for the
paper to twitch down. Those poor expectant sons. And who knows
what my son sees when he closes his eyes around me? The trip to the

natural history museum, where he caught me weeping? But this story, however poorly realized, is not about me or my father or my own son, though we make our appearances; no, this story is about the man in the first pew, the important man, the man who will live on while the rest of us will fade under the raised arms of a Reverend Rushton somewhere.

"You may be seated," he said.

The eulogy came first. It took nearly a minute for A. N. Dyer to trudge up to the lectern—even my youngest strained for a view—and I remember thinking, What's happened to him? His spirit no longer seemed to reach his extremities but pooled around his torso and only fed the essentials. I had last seen him a month earlier, when he visited my father on a Saturday in mid-February. He showed up at the apartment in a knit cap and a wool overcoat and still resembled one of those timeless preps, ruddy and lean, who wore their old age the way a mischievous boy might wear a mask.

"Philip," he stated solemnly as I opened the door. It forever amazed me that he knew my name, even if he was my godfather. "Freezing out there," he told me.

"I know, unbelievable," I said.

That February was an ice age in miniature. Andrew asked if I had a fire burning, I said no, so he clapped his hands and requested a drink. We went into the library, where he browsed through the brown offerings before pouring himself a glass of Glenfiddich. A moment was spent admiring the complete set of miniature ducks and shorebirds carved by Elmer Crowell and lovingly displayed in specially crafted vitrines. Crowell was a master decoy maker, though neither my siblings nor I had any idea of his name let alone his reputation until three years ago, when we put the entire collection up for auction. It was, in certain circles, a big deal. I myself always found them embarrassing, a notch above toys; where other families had real art, in some cases serious art, we had a Very Plump Black-Bellied Plover by Obediah Verity. And my father didn't even hunt.

"I've always liked this room," Andrew commented. "So very marshy."

"I suppose."

"You know your grandfather was quite the shot."

"That's what I've always heard."

"Famous for it really. Practically his career. That and tennis and golf and fishing and drinking. And don't forget the women. He was one sporty bastard, always on the lookout for something to catch or kill or thwack." Andrew stopped in front of a black duck carved by Shang Wheeler, its surface worn from years of working the water, a half-million-dollar patina. He touched its smooth head. "It does seem an honest art form, in terms of endgame." He mimed a shotgun and blasted the air. "I for one always missed. They told me I was wrong-eyed, whatever that means, plus I tended to aim too low." His arched mouth wrapped a certain drawl around his words, a lockjaw that stretched back to the earliest Dutch diphthongs. It was a handsome if easily ridiculed voice, a fellow writer once claiming that A. N. Dyer spoke as if he had Quaaludes stuffed in his ears. "Sorry I haven't visited as much as I should," he said.

"Please."

"Been busy."

"I'm sure."

"How are the wife and kids?"

"Fine," I said, which at the time was true.

"And are those Buckley bums still sucking their thumbs?"

I nodded, privately ashamed of my fallback career though publicly proud of my noble profession. A few years had stretched into an almost unfathomable fifteen of teaching fifth grade at that most patrician of New York elementary schools, three generations' worth of Topping and Dyer boys on its rolls. I would soon get fired.

Andrew lifted his glass. "Life as an educator, very honorable."

Perhaps too defensively I told him that I was still writing, stubborn despite the rejections, that I was working on a novel about the Cuban Missile Crisis and the dawning generation gap, that in fact I was taking a sabbatical next year so I could get a good solid draft down. Like a stage mother I pushed my other self forward.

"Good for you," Andrew said, politely uninterested.

Full disclosure: I entertained vivid if laughable notions of an A. N. Dyer blurb—*A huge talent, my heir apparent*—for this hypothetical novel of mine. I already had a title, *Q.E.D.*, which was hands down the best part of the book, and I knew the perfect image for the cover: a William Eggleston photograph of a long-haired redhead sprawled on a lawn as if felled in combat, in her right hand a Brownie Hawkeye camera like an unemployed grenade. But beyond the exterior heft of the book, beyond my name written in Copperplate Gothic Bold—**PHILIP WEBB TOPPING**—beyond the dedication and acknowledgment pages, beyond those summer months where a teacher must justify his existence, *Q.E.D.* hardly proved anything at all. Over the course of two years I had written maybe fifty pages, yet still I dreamed of A. N. Dyer's approval, the book a frame for his signature. I have always had an unfortunate tendency to spin myself into alternate universes. Growing up I had a regular fantasy of an accident leaving me orphaned and the Dyer clan taking me in as one of their own. It seemed so obvious that I was born into the wrong family—a suspicion of many a teenager, I suppose—and I knew I could be a good son, the right son, the proper son to this great man, certainly better than his actual sons. Absurd, my imagination. And it lingers. Even nowadays I can find myself turning in bed and trying to will into existence a time machine. Please let me go back, I'll plead to the darkness, please let me guide my younger self away from this present mess, let me unlink him from my past so I might fade from his view, a retroactive suicide. The stupid things I've done, the outright bad things. My memory is like a series of kicks in the gut, including this beaut: my father on his deathbed and here I am a foundling on my own doorstep.

"A fire would be nice," Andrew said again.

"Should I?"

"No, no, just speaking in old code." He went and refilled his glass. His drinking hand trembled in an almost rhythmic meter, like a seismograph registering the effects of nearby destruction. "I feel for you," Andrew said. "It's impossibly hard, a father's decline. You both want to say so much but you're both so afraid of saying the same thing, something like, I hope I wasn't a terrible disappointment, or some variant on that theme. Of course in the end the only decent answer is a lie." With that he took a satisfied, almost ceremonial sip.

Maybe in the back of my mind I took offense. After all, the brutal truth was dying down the hall and I, the weaker truth, was simply doing his best. But I was mostly intrigued by this intimate disclosure and decided to lawyer through the opening and ask about his own father, if he remembered him, since I knew the man had died when A. N. Dyer was quite young. Was this a conscious jab? Not at all. I was just curious and if anything wanted to ingratiate myself and express an understanding of his biography without revealing my absolute dedication. But Andrew's eyes fell onto the floor as if he spotted a nickel that was hardly worth picking up. "You're right," he said, "I don't know what I'm talking about."

"I didn't mean—"

"And it was a car accident. There was no big goodbye between us. I remember almost nothing about him, in fact. Maybe I could claim my stepfather but he seemed fully sprung from my mother's single-mindedness and didn't need any words from me when he died. Yes, Philip, you have exposed me." Andrew opened his arms, a lick of whiskey sloshing over the side. "I am exposed."

"But—"

"Even worse," he said, "I think I was cribbing those words of wisdom from one of my books, can't remember which."

"*Tiro's Corruption*," I told him, "when Hornsby dies in Formia."

"God, not even one of my better attempts."

"Oh, I like that one."

Andrew made a displeasing sound and put down his drink. A heavy gust hit Park Avenue and for a moment the windows belonged to a small hunting cabin in the middle of nowhere. Later that afternoon and all night it would snow and tomorrow school would get canceled and I would email my mistress (forgive the word but all the others are worse) and arrange an afternoon tryst while my wife took the kids sledding. Bad weather always makes me horny. Christ, the recklessness.

"I should go see him," Andrew said.

"I know it means a lot to him, you being here."

"I suppose, I suppose," he said in a defeated tone. What with his boyish mop of white hair and his bygone Yankee exoticism, his meter and repetition, Andrew put me in mind of Robert Frost and his poem

"Provide, Provide." I always did like that poem. *Some have relied on what they knew / Others on being simply true.* While Frost as a man exists in our head as eternally ancient, A. N. Dyer stands in front of us as forever young, peering from his author photo, the only photo he ever used on all of his books, starting with *Ampersand.* In that picture he's pure knowing, his darkly amused eyes in league with a smile that edges toward a smirk, as if he's seen what you've underlined, you fiend, you who might read a few pages and then pause and glance back at his face like you've spotted something magical yet familiar, a new best friend waiting for you on the other end. Fourteen novels written by a single, ageless A. N. Dyer. No doubt this added to the mystery, along with his total avoidance of fame. The photo is credited to his wife, Isabel. This marital connection was sweet early on and a possible clue as you imagined those newlyweds in Central Park, in the middle of Sheep Meadow, Andrew reluctantly posing while Isabel framed Essex House for its maximum subliminal message. Click. Hard to believe that was fifty years ago. © Isabel Dyer. The photo remained even after the affair that produced Andy and finished the marriage and secured the final estrangement from his already distant sons. I suppose nothing keeps the end from being hard. But for most readers, A. N. Dyer was forever twenty-seven, so when he took the lectern in that church and looked as old as he had ever looked, the congregation practically gasped as if aging were a stunt gone horribly wrong.

Andrew flattened his eulogy. Hands frisked pockets for reading glasses, the microphone picking up a few grumbles, all vowel based. "Okay," he said, after which he cleared his throat and pinched his nose clean. "Okay," he said again, the sentiment towing an unsure breath. Finally he began to read. He was like a boy standing in front of class trying to get through an assignment without a possibly catastrophic lull. "What are we in this world without our friends if family is the foundation then friends are its crossbeams its drywall its plumbing friends keep us warm and warmhearted friends furnish and with a friend like Charlie Topping I was never without a home." Andrew paused for breath, which was a relief for all our lungs, until he glanced up and asked if everyone could hear him. A handful nodded while a few of us lowered our heads. He went back to reading. "Whenever I was in need of succor—succor," he repeated the word as though surprised by its appearance, "I could count on Charlie." From here he started to read slower. "He was an unlocked door with something smelling good in the oven. He was the fire in the fireplace, the blanket draped over the couch, the dog at my feet. He was the shelter when I was the storm." Andrew paused again, interrupted, it seemed, by higher frequencies. He turned around and pointed to the top of the gilded altarpiece. "Zadkiel," he said with newfound authority, "that's the name of that angel up there, the fifth from the left. Zadkiel. Kind of like a comic book character, that's what Charlie always said to his audience. Mandrake the Magician. Zadkiel the Absolver. Faster than a speeding regret." Andrew turned back around. "Sorry," he said to his audience. "I am the storm, right, that's where we were, me as the raging storm." Watching him was like watching Lear forget his lines on the heath. He removed his glasses, shielded his eyes from the glare of the inner dim. "Has anyone seen my boy?" he asked. "Andy Dyer?" He searched the crowd as if every face were a wave and there was a small boy overboard, possibly drowning. "It's important, please," he said. No answer broke the surface, though I could imagine the whispers of bastard, the giddy apostasy of gossip. "Is he even here?" Still nothing. "Are you here, Andy?" Silence. "I need to find him. Please."

Somewhere within this infinite realm of being, or potential being, I'm the one who stands up and approaches the lectern, who gently takes A. N. Dyer by the arm and guides him back to his pew, rather than my stepmother, who did the charitable thing while I just sat there and waited for my name to be called.

I.iii

OUTSIDE ON THE STEPS, Andy Dyer smoked cigarette number five and watched the well-heeled walk up and down Madison. The newly minted warm weather offered an exuberance of flesh, women the main demographic on this avenue, their shopping bags swinging on a spring harvest of clothes. Many of them circulated through the nearby Ralph Lauren store, and I wonder if Andy realized or even cared that old Ralph was originally Lipschitz from the Bronx. Oh, the ironies of American reinvention: we appreciate the striving, the success, the superior khaki, while also enjoying the inside joke. The store was situated within the old Rhinelander mansion, a fabulous example of French Renaissance Revival, its insides decorated with horse and dog paintings, portraits of precious boys and athletic men, sailing scenes, candid snapshots from the club. It was enough to make any self-respecting WASP queasy if also a tad envious. We should all still live like this. But Andy hardly cared about such things. No, he was busy sitting on those church steps, smoking cigarette after cigarette, waiting for one of these mysterious New York women to stop and smile and take possession of the name Jeanie Spokes.

He had no idea what she looked like, even after numerous Internet searches. She refused to friend him on Facebook and the only picture publicly posted on her page was of Ayn Rand photoshopped onto a beach volleyball player, her right hand powering through a self-determined spike. All he knew about her physically was her age: twenty-four years old. As he sat there the air between shirt and skin puckered with extra humidity. Twenty-four. That number came like rain down his back.

"How will I recognize you?" he had asked during their last IM chat.

"When you see me, your heart will skip a beat," Jeanie pinged back.

"That scary?"

"Absolutely frightening."

"You're not a dude, are you?"

"Um, no," she pinged, "I swear," she pinged, "Really." Her words fell in a series of seductive rows, like dialogue in a sexy comic strip. "Wait," she pinged, "Define dude." Jeanie Spokes had impeccable timing.

"I'll be on the steps of St. James, 71st and Madison," Andy typed.

"You sure you want me to come?"

"You sure you want to come?"

A pause.

"Cum?" he typed.

"Nicely done, Cyrano."

"Don't tell me you weren't thinking the same thing."

Andy waited, waited, waited, until "No cumment" pinged back.

What was it about instant messaging that invited this kind of innuendo and pun, this straight-up dirty talk, as if a transcript of future sin? It was all very tilted, of course, in the vein of a separate identity, the Internet's lingua franca, but sometimes the tilt straightened and a high-speed intimacy entered the exchange. Suddenly you start bouncing your innermost thoughts back and forth just to see if those feelings can be caught.

"I can't wait to see you," Andy wrote.

"Me neither."

"Seriously."

"Mean either."

"Circe."

"Man eater."

Andy knew only a few concrete details about Jeanie Spokes: she grew up on the Upper West Side; her mother was an architect, her father an editor at Random House; she attended Dalton, then Columbia, with a year abroad in Paris; she graduated magna cum laude with a degree in comparative literature and presently worked as an assistant at Gilroy Connors, A. N. Dyer's literary agency; she lived in a studio apartment on Riverside Drive, the rent outrageous, but she was a Manhattan girl to the core and anywhere else gave her vertigo. Many of these details were analogous to Andy's own biography: Trinity to Exeter; Central Park West to Fifth Avenue; Sharon to Southampton. He was, in concept, familiar with this type of girl, or woman, and that's where the whole business got tricky: Jeanie Spokes was a full-fledged adult while Andy Dyer hovered around 83 percent in terms of development and experience and areas of skin without acne and even grades, which could ruin his chances for Yale and screw up his equivalency with this Columbia grad, dooming whatever outside chance he had beyond a mere online flirtation.

Andy lit his sixth cigarette. He wanted her to find him smoking, that seemed important, but she was thirty minutes late and he was light-headed and almost done with his pack. Organ music murmured from behind the church doors. The previews were over and the feature was about to begin, with its cheesy special effects and tired script and ludicrous, entirely unbelievable character named God. Andy wondered if Jesus was once a supreme embarrassment to his Father, this hippie carpenter who ran around with the freak crowd until finally he gave up on his dreams and stepped into the family business, probably to his mother's regret. What a sellout, Andy thought. A truly kick-ass Jesus would have said, Go forsake thyself, and remained a humble builder. Now that would have been something to worship: the son of God rejecting God in favor of life, meaning death. Andy glanced back at the church, suddenly reminded of why he was here. Charlie Topping had been a nice enough man, formal without being too serious, like a pediatrician, though Andy often caught him staring like he could spot hidden symptoms of some terrible future disease. Every Christmas and birthday he gave Andy a set of vintage tin soldiers—dragoons, grenadiers, hussars, highlanders, whole battles, whole wars, the American Civil War in ten deluxe boxes. The least Andy could do was go inside and pay his respects.

But where was she?

Andy checked the distances, north and south, for potential Jeanies. Every one of these women seemed awash in extra light, as if throughout the city young men awaited their arrival. But none of them noticed this 17 percent boy with the zit goatee and the shaggy hair and the stubborn baby fat around his middle like he was halfway through digesting his younger softer self, or if they did notice, they thought— who knows what they thought of this half-boy, half-man, though one older woman did do a double take as she rushed up the church steps, late for the service. She was almost attractive, for seventy-plus, tall and slender with a handsome face and one of those I'm-no-granny haircuts. And her shoulders. They were a reminder that the collarbone could also be called a clavicle. Andy imagined himself a lucky old man.

Recently he had become more conscious of the female form, or not so recently, since in his early teens he had noticed the obvious—breasts, backsides, a certain leanness he found intriguing—but nowadays he noticed something else, noticed what he couldn't see: the mystery of the girls at school and the women on the street, how under their clothes lay secrets by way of particularity, the variety of style and shape and color, the Platonic ideal of Woman falling to the ground and breaking into a thousand pieces. A hint of nipple under a shirt was like discovering a hidden safe, the combination unknown but the lock visible, and he would speculate over the pubic hair sealed within, the areolas and freckles and moles, the rifts and gaps. Those tantalizingly fine hairs on cheeks and arms and how they caught the sun killed him. But it wasn't like he was a sex fiend or anything (though he could be a bit of a perv), it was just, well, you witness a woman naked, like truly witness her naked, like up close and in full natural light, and you almost want to cry, an instant martyr to the cause. Maybe because you're offering so little in return.

In total, Andy had kissed fifteen girls, tongue-kissed twelve of them.

Of those twelve he had felt up nine.

Of those nine he had fingered five.

Of those five, four had touched him in return.

Of those four, four had given him head.

And of those four, just three weeks ago, one had let him go down on her—Felicity Chase, his girlfriend since October. Five months as a couple and she was happy giving him blowjobs, which was certainly great—blowjobs in the library bathroom, blowjobs in the nearby woods—but she never seemed comfortable with the reciprocal side of the proverbial coin. "I prefer your hand," she'd tell him, much to his frustration. Andy was ready for the next logical step, his rather misguided instinct telling him he had to go down on a girl before he could get laid, that there was a natural progression, an order, and you had to graduate from one act before you could move on to the next, even if you were dry-humping in the basement of the Phelps Science Center and Felicity was moaning and edging down her pants and undoing your zipper and saying something porno about how your schlong would feel deep inside of her—Andy probably could have lost his virginity right there and then but he was too focused on crossing cunnilingus from his list and Felicity muttered something about soccer and no shower and not now and Andy got upset as if he were dealing with a prude who presently had his dick in her mouth. But finally three weeks ago she said yes. Andy took his time going down, his tongue skiing on powder until he finally hit hair, just a forelock, and he spread her legs. He found the taste interesting, sort of sour, like a stale lemon drop, and he assumed he discovered her little nose of a clit though it was dark. Much too dark. He wanted a flashlight. But he made do and tucked in as if he were reading a thin but important book, like *The Great Gatsby*, relishing each sentence, even as Felicity's hands tried to pull him back up.

"Everything all right?" she asked.

"Sure. Was I doing something wrong?"

"I guess not."

"Can I go back down?"

"That's all right."

"Why not?"

"I'm kind of weirded out right now," she said.

Three days later Felicity broke up with him, and a month later she was having a full-blown fuck-a-thon with Harry Wilmers, one of Andy's best friends. "Hope you're not pissed or anything," Harry said.

"No, it's cool," Andy told him, which was true.

"I've always liked her."

"Yeah, she's great. You ever notice how her nipples are kind of puffy, like a Hershey's kiss except pinker. Kind of European, I think."

"You're a total fucking freak," Harry said, and not in a nice way.

The problem for Andy was that his birthday was in a few short months (June 24) and the idea of losing his virginity at eighteen seemed like a lifelong disaster, whereas seventeen, well, seventeen seemed perfectly respectable. He imagined Jeanie Spokes: meeting her, grabbing a quick cab back to her apartment and in a matter of minutes going through the preliminaries of kissing, feeling, fingering, sucking, licking, all above the sheets and with the shades wide open, and then jumping into the historic act. Andy rose a minor boner on those church steps. Even if she was unattractive, he would fuck her, because he kind of loved her.

"How many guys have you slept with?" he once IM'd her.

"Andy," she pinged back.

"Yes."

"None of your business."

"At least send me a picture."

"Noooooooooo. Let's keep the

"M

"Y

"S

"T

"E

"R

"Y," she pinged.

The two of them had met by accident. It was after his father had mailed him the latest reissue of all his books with a note attached: *Pretty slick, huh, maybe too slick, missing you, always, me.* Of the fourteen, Andy had only read one in its entirety, *Ampersand,* which he was now reading again, this time for English class. He was a bit of a celebrity around campus, having the inside scoop on the famous alumnus author. All of Exeter was obsessed with the book. And not just Exeter. Most high schoolers who dove into A. N. Dyer and his Shearing Academy found themselves head over heels. When *Ampersand* was first published, the Exeter community denounced the book and its barely disguised portrayal of their beloved school. It was as if a turncoat had taken *A Separate Peace* (the previous favorite and only a few years old) hostage, and tortured it, and brainwashed it, until it emerged from the darkness as a less forgiving version of *Crime and Punishment*. This fiction was not their beloved school. They did not abide such behavior in their students or faculty, even in prose. The headmaster went as far as to insist on a statement from the twenty-eight-year-old author attesting to this fact, and A. N. Dyer, claiming contrition, decided to compensate the school with a percentage of the book's profits. He sent them a check for fifty thousand dollars, made payable to the Shearing Academy. Once the Pulitzers were announced and he became the youngest winner ever, the check turned up framed and on permanent display in the library, where it still hangs today.

Twenty years after its publication, *Ampersand* became a part of the school's upper-year curriculum and soon led to an ongoing tradition, Exeter's version of Bloomsday, where on May 4 an upper-year student is whisked away by five seniors and taken to the student-run used bookstore, to that closet hidden behind bookshelves, the actual real-life spot where in the novel the headmaster's son, Timothy Veck, is held captive for fourteen days. But in this literary reenactment Veck is detained for only a few hours, with bathroom breaks, and afterward he, or nowadays she, is released and marched up to the school assembly, where they announce the winner of the annual A. N. Dyer award in creative writing (an award I myself almost won). To be chosen as Veck is in its way an honor, and this particular year was noteworthy: not only was the namesake of the author an upper-year student, but get this, Andy was an upper-year student on the fiftieth anniversary of the book. It was a happy coincidence that even the oldest, most skeptical faculty member, Bertram McIntyre, commented on one afternoon in mid-February, "We think your father should come up this year and release you as Veck, and then the two of you can announce the winner of his award."

Andy just grinned. As with so many questions about his father, he had no answer.

"It's a good idea, don't you think?"

"I guess," Andy said.

"I guess," McIntyre aped back, his mouth appropriately slack. They were sitting in his office. If time held true, it was covered in books, stacked up in columns, some as tall as four feet, like a reconstruction of a Roman temple with Bertram McIntyre as its resident god. Eighty years old and head of the English department since he was thirty-seven, Bertram was one of those asexual educators who used teenagers, in particular teenage boys, as his own rickety altar. During your years at the school he might strike you as most impressive, impossibly well-read, an intimidating and occasionally inspiring teacher, but after graduating, his status would shift and your recollection of him would wane into an absurd character, likely a closeted queer, all those books his folly, and he was scary as a garden gnome. You would mock his old-fashioned insistence on reciting poems, with all those hours spent on memorization. What a worthless endeavor. But like Wordsworth, who is wasted on the young, decades later you might wake up one morning thankful for a few remembered lines that lie too deep for tears. All things have a second birth, even old high school teachers.

"You know, your father's never been officially feted by Exeter, and we've tried, particularly when your brothers were here. Christ, how we tried."

"Half brothers," Andy corrected.

"Full sons to him. He could have come up here and attended a class, could have said a few words about writing, a lecture perhaps, but for whatever reason, he refused. We just want to celebrate our esteemed graduate. We're not looking for a commencement address. All they want is a goddamn picture for the goddamn alumni magazine. A. N. Dyer smiling. Is that so much to ask?"

"I really can't say, sir."

"That wasn't a question. I for one think *Ampersand* is an emotionally dishonest, self-satisfied, cruel, overly schematic, cynically adolescent exercise in pseudo-European pretensions with a dollop of American hucksterism thrown in. But that's just me. The rest of the school swoons. But his attitude toward this place is ludicrous for a man his age. It's as if he's still a teenager, mistaking pigheadedness for principles." A pause and that famous McIntyre tongue poked free like an alien finger reaching up from occupied depths and searching for leverage. "But maybe you could ask him to come up for a little visit?"

"Me?"

"You are related to him, aren't you? Not to put words in your mouth but you could tell him it would mean a lot to you, a short visit, no big fanfare, just you and him and good old Exeter. One day is all we—all you ask. An afternoon really, though a dinner would be fantastic. Nobody is getting any younger. A hard wind blows and some of us, sadly, can hardly breathe, but Exeter, Exeter will outlive us all, so let us stand together in this most fleeting of moments and celebrate our shared history. You understand what I'm saying, right, or should I quote from *Henry V*?" The famous McIntyre tongue now investigated the inside pocket of his left cheek, always the second move in any student's impersonation.

"He'll say no," Andy said.

"Well maybe you should insist then. What did the school do to him except provide an excellent education and a setting he put to good, if overdetermined, use? I think he owes us something—that's just me to you, not you to him."

"I promise, he'll say no."

"Just ask him."

"He'll say—"

"Just ask him, for Christ sake, with sugar on top. And maybe do that trick with your eyes when you don't know the answer to one of my questions, all recoil and droop, dereliction and dismay, like a poem with its title not yet fixed. And after that, maybe beg." Unlike some other people in this book, Bertram McIntyre is still alive, nearing an amazing ninety-two years old and retired in Maine. He's one of the reasons why I became a teacher, without his success, of course, and when my father died, he wrote me a condolence note (. . . *I always enjoyed his visits during those trustee meetings, his good company, his love of old-fashioned poetry, a nice nice man, your father. I shall miss him.* . . .) that warranted a reply (. . . *My father loved old-fashioned poets? Which ones?* . . .) and developed into an unexpected friendship. You call a man Bert and everything changes. But enough of the future past. Bert must remain Bertram glowering behind that book-laden desk, at least until the very end.

Back in his dorm room, Andy thumbed through the fourteen books his father had recently sent. While he was embarrassed to have only read *Ampersand*, he had skimmed the others and for the most part enjoyed the writing. The man on the page seemed so confident, so sure and settled, unlike the man in the flesh, who could stare at Andy like he was the only route toward salvation. "You are a wonderful boy," his father would say. "I just want you to know that I love you, very much." Maybe it was sweet. Maybe it somehow repaired the damage of his own upbringing and shored up the ruin of his first go-around as a father (classic fatherhood, the sequel, behavior). But for Andy the neediness was exhausting. His dad called him multiple times a week, always on the verge of stumbling into tears. He had no true friends. He couldn't sleep. He was anxious. He was old. He missed his wife and his other sons. Christ, the guilt. Oh, and he was in constant pain. "Thank God I have you," he'd conclude. "Otherwise, well, what's the point?" It was no fun being someone's reason to live. Andy hungered for the A. N. Dyer of the blurbs, of the precise prose and biting humanity, who began *Dream Snap* with

R ather than one of those seed-filled tubes with holes and perches, his wife insisted on a miniature bird pavilion, two hundred dollars plus installation, which in her perfect world would attract Blue Jays and Cardinals, but in reality only charmed the crows who screeched like witches until Avery Price, on the sixteenth of July, chopped the fucking thing down.

Where was that man with the axe? Andy flipped the book over and read the familiar quotes, the snippets of reviews. Was his father really so different thirty-plus years ago? "Dyer is savage and funny and oh-so-human, and this book might be his knockout blow. Ladies and gentlemen, we have a new champeen, perhaps the greatest of his generation," said Anthony Kunitz from *The Washington Post*. How was the man in that author photo even related to his father? Whatever sly humor had dried up and what was left behind was a husk. Even his best days seemed like a nervous performance from an understudy. Of course, Andy knew the backstory; knew his status as the result of a May-December affair; knew his birth was a secret until his mother's untimely death forced the issue of paternity; knew his sudden arrival as an eight-month-old wrecked the Dyer marriage and resulted in a minor scandal—he knew these things, he was spared no detail, but a long-dead mother, bitter half brothers, a frail and increasingly unstable father, was nothing when compared to his normal, everyday emotions, which had all the qualities of spin art: thrilling in movement, uninspired at rest. Andy stared at the old photograph of his father. A. N. Dyer was good-looking in the style of those vintage pictures where everybody shimmered by dint of their bad habits, and while Andy had similar dark eyes and shared the same thin lips, the rest of his features seemed lumpy with adolescence, as if every night a pair of tiny fists pummeled him raw.

Near the bottom of *Dream Snap* he spotted an Internet address: www.andyer.com. Discovering this seemed as reasonable as discovering a tattoo on his father's neck. Computers were hardly his domain, and the idea of his own website was beyond laughable. Andy plugged in the URL. The loading icon was a cardiograph and after the red line had fulfilled its journey the screen formed into a Saul Steinbergian view of A. N. Dyer's world. Every landmark was a link, to his novels, to his biography, to his awards, to his upcoming events (an almost sardonic blank), to a handful of essays, even to that rare interview in *The Paris Review* that Andy had read in his early teens, when he was first curious about his father's career:

A. N. DYER

I don't believe in the romance of writing, in inspiration, in characters taking over, in any of that sham magic. I know exactly what I do. I sit alone in a room all day, those days starting mostly at night, and I chip away until there's a likeness of a book on my desk, about yay high.

The website was an obvious selling tool, so there was some sense here, but the email address that popped up after clicking on the contact moon seemed plain silly. As a joke, Andy sent him an email:

To: andyer@andyer.com

This can't be you. Last time I mentioned email you thought I was talking about a boy named Emile. Anyway, hello whoever you are. Your unrelated son, Andy.

Later that day, he got a response:

To: andrewdyer-13@exeter.edu

The question is: Is that really you?

To: andyer@andyer.com

Yes, it's me. Notice the Exeter address. But this can't be you. I imagine you trying to write an email right on the screen, with a ballpoint pen, then stuffing the whole computer into a manila envelope. Technology, huh? Amazing. Anyway, still me and still can't be you.

To: andrewdyer-13@exeter.edu

No, it's me. I have embraced your friend Emile, if gingerly. I guess at this stage it's nice to know that people still care about my work, that it means something to them. You tend to forget, especially as you get older and forget so much. Mostly they ask what I'm working on (none of your business) or if I might sign some books (no chance) or be interviewed (god no) or have a quick cup of coffee (you've got to be kidding). People are so lonely. A few ask about specifics in the books. Misogyny has been mentioned. One person thought I was dead. Another claims I stole all of his ideas, which is likely true. A vast majority simply tells me how much they love this or that or they parrot a favorite line or tell me I wrote their lives, that I must have installed a tiny listening device in their brain. It's been so long since I've been faced with, dare I say it, fans, that I failed to remember the reason I stopped responding in the first place—you very quickly start to despise them. Odd, how it works. They compliment you and you want to strangle them with their tongues. Anyway, how's school?

Andy read and reread the email, even printed it out twice, the first time not quite sharp enough. It must be him, he thought. This was by far the longest piece of correspondence he had ever received from his father, who normally preferred Post-it notes attached to an article or a book. In the writing he heard the echo of his authorial voice, strong and unsentimental and, best of all, for Andy alone. It was like a first game of catch.

To: andyer@andyer.com

You have your fans here too. People come up and ask me about you and I don't know what to say and I just kind of stand there and mumble and hope they'll lose interest and walk away. I think they must think I'm a jerk. Or possibly brain damaged. You can't win. Like with your name. Sometimes I feel like I'm dropping your name even if it's my name too and I feel like a loser, like I'm using you, like I'm so insecure I need a hit of your fame. You become a means instead of a plain old Dad. Even worse, everyone assumes I must be a genius like you.

I still don't like Exeter much. In fact, I hate it more.

I'm glad you have email now. Have you heard of instant messaging? My God, do you text? Blog? Facebook? Tweet and Tumble and Flickr? Pittypat? (I made that last one up.) A

It was exciting, and scary, to communicate with his father in this way, but it also seemed safe and self-contained, without the fear of a quick rebuttal or a stupid thing said, just the words themselves. And maybe for the first time in a long time Andy enjoyed writing. He spent an hour on the above reply, tinkering with the style, the voice, the rhythm, trying to re-create himself on the page, this son who might stand before his father. And he liked this Andy. This Andy seemed smart and funny and open. And then, this Andy was crushed.

To: andrewdyer-13@exeter.edu

I need to stop this. I am not your father (forgive the reverse Darth Vader). My name is Jeanie Spokes and I work with your father's agent. I am so sorry. I thought you were joking. Not true. I thought if I could fool you, I could fool anyone. I've been in charge of your father's email for the last couple of months, creating a master list of his readers for marketing and publicity purposes, and sometimes, well, I answer a few. I know it's wrong wrong wrong, it's downright fraud, but I'm very respectful and people seem to appreciate the replies and I have to say there's a real hunger out there for your dad. I'm sorry, that's no excuse. I really like this job and I'm only twenty-four but if you need to tell someone, I understand and I won't hold a grudge or anything. I should get fired. BTW, I went to Dalton. I hear Exeter is like crazy hard unless you're a brain. I love your dad's books. You sound sweet. Again I am so sorry and whatever you do, I totally understand.

Forever ashamed,
Jeanie Spokes

PS. I love IMing. Pittypatting as well.

What an idiot, Andy thought, to mistake his father for a girl, probably an intern, probably one of those literary groupies, even if she did do a decent job of capturing his voice, or what Andy imagined his voice might sound like in email form, but instead his father was a spoiled brat from Manhattan who enjoyed toying with the vulnerable, which doubly sucked because it seemed like he was getting somewhere with his dad, really talking, like a friend instead of a reflection. Andy was pissed. Who did this girl think she was and what did she mean by sweet? He reread her emails and between the lines emerged a sneaky yet apologetic and perhaps beholden twenty-four-year Dalton grad, a school known for its attractive, progressive-minded girls, a likely bookworm who thought Andy was a genius and might not frown on his seventeen years of virginity. Pittypat indeed. He decided to email her back. His response was only seven words but it took three days to compose and one day to send, and though it was nothing like the real Andy, it was truer than anything he had ever written.

To: andyer@andyer.com
Dad, you are a very naughty girl.

The next day, they were IM'ing. And the rest is, well, Andy sat on those church steps and saw no point in leaving. Why walk away now? Time's gamble had already proved him to be a loser, might as well be the biggest loser possible. He had left school a few days before the official start of spring break just so he could attend this funeral with his dad. Another spin of the wheel. Most of his classmates were going skiing or hitting some tropical clime, while Andy was staying put. Another spin. He was going to see a bunch of movies and hang with his fellow New York captives but mainly, hopefully, have sex if Jeanie Spokes ever—

"Andy?"

He heard his name rattle into a slot and turned and saw her standing near the steps, grinning awkwardly. She had reasonable good looks, like many a reasonable girl at Exeter, the product themselves of reasonable mothers, always with dark hair never cut too short and surprisingly bad teeth—if not crooked, then yellow; if not yellow, then with large gums—and naturally UV-protected skin, glasses almost mandatory but stylishly framed (their most overt fashion choice), bodies solid but never fat, athletic from those reasonable genes that had survived past feminine hardship and now chased field hockey balls instead of wayward sheep, this type of reasonableness not necessarily smart but often very focused, and not guaranteed plain Janes because there was plenty of sex appeal and humor in that reason, a sharpness that stood in contrast to the groundless swell around them, so that these girls, these women, with their chunky jaws and dirt-brown eyes and honest opinions of themselves, held the secret of their own common sense, which, if discovered, would shock you blind. These women often work in publishing.

"Sorry I'm late," she said as if towing a heavy piece of luggage.

Andy smiled and got up. "That's okay." It was strange. Here she was, a voice, a face, a context, Jeanie Spokes as a specific presence in front of him, breathing in the same air, warmed by the same sun, all of his previously imagined shapes and forms and fantasies, those liquid details—and there were plenty, many of them more beautiful than this version—leaking into her and filling her with everything he ever wanted, leaving him with the peculiar sensation of feeling both drained and overflowing.

"Traffic was crazy," she said. "I had to jump on a subway."

"No problem."

"And the subway took forever."

"No problem."

"Just a mess."

"No problem."

"You look a lot like your dad," she said, tilting her head.

"Well, we are related, you know."

She—success—smiled, her lips rolling under like she was hiding something in her mouth, a small round pebble, and Andy could sense her flirty enthusiasm, which is by far the greatest aphrodisiac, knowing that your smile is being returned, possibly twofold, in that lovely escalation of mutual assurance, and he thought, This is really happening, the happening part still undefined.

"It's nice to finally meet you," she said.

"Same here. Really nice."

"I almost didn't come. Still not sure if this is such a good idea."

"Oh, it's a great idea," Andy said. "I bring all my first dates to funerals."

Jeanie flinched.

"What? Date?" he asked, confirming his possible miscue.

She nodded without affirming.

"How about something in the fig family then?"

"I should just go."

"No, no, no, unfair, you just got here, and we're conversing, and this is pleasant, right, this is nice, and informative, don't forget that, and I'll stop with the crazy fruit talk, no dates, no figs, I promise you, unless you're looking for a tasty kumquat 'cause I know a guy."

She seemed to swallow that pebble. "You're seventeen."

"That's like a hundred and fifty in dog years. It's a miracle I'm still alive."

She smiled.

"Enough of the ageism," Andy said. "Hell, my father and mother had like thirty-five years between them, not saying there's a comparison. We're just getting to know each other, right, face-to-face, in that old-timey analogue, and hey, I like your face, you have a very nice face, Jeanie Spokes." She blushed, or her neck blushed, or flushed, went all blotchy, which Andy hoped wasn't an allergic reaction.

In perfect Topping timing, the coffin burst through the church doors, guided by professional pallbearers who quick-stepped toward the hearse as if the commercial residents along Madison insisted on a low-corpse visibility.

"Oh no," Jeanie said, turning, "you missed the entire funeral."

"We should just leave, go for a walk or something."

"But isn't your father here?"

"It doesn't matter," Andy said. "I don't need to see him."

"I should've gotten here earlier."

"Trust me, you've done me a favor."

The congregation started to filter through the doors, us Toppings first, Lucy holding A. N. Dyer by the arm. I spotted Andy as he spotted his father, and I recognized his look from the look I get nowadays from my own son: a certain instant exasperation mixed with historical mortification, like I've blown another easy save. As more people spilled from the church, their numbers grew into a spontaneous sidewalk social. A tight grip of admirers gravitated toward A. N. Dyer, some holding books protected by Mylar, which seemed more fetishistic than archival, but for the most part they were a polite group, like servers offering up trays of unwanted canapés.

"I think I see your father," Jeanie said, pointing.

"Let's just get out of—" And that's when his father caught sight of him and unhooked from Lucy and waved both hands, almost yelling, "Andy! Andy!" as he headed clumsily down the steps. I feared he might trip and break his neck, so I left my children with my sister and offered Andrew the crutch of my shoulder, like a good son, I thought, present in this world. Andy noticeably sagged upon our arrival. It was a gesture that threw me back to high school—oh great, here's Philip Topping. Meanwhile, Andrew placed his hands around Andy's neck and sort of did the inverse of strangling him, like he was trying to repair his breathing. "Thank goodness," he said. "I was getting worried. I had you injured and bleeding, dying on the street alone. Swear I heard ambulances. Bells ringing."

"Good to see you too," Andy said.

"If I had known the proper medical procedures perhaps I could have saved you."

"What a shame," Andy said.

"I can't help where my mind goes."

"But why does it always go to where I'm dead?"

"When you have children you'll understand."

"It's only been like twenty minutes."

"No, almost an hour."

"And that means I'm dead?"

As they bickered I shared a look with Jeanie Spokes, her name as yet unknown. She was obviously older than Andy and the probable cause of all this trouble. She grinned at me like we were seconds in a bitter yet humorous duel. The hair on her arms was dark and obliquely sexy and I noticed a few moles brailled on her cheek and neck, which I had an instant desire to touch. My dowsing stick told me it was going to rain. I was curious when the time came if Andy would introduce me fondly, since old teachers, particularly old elementary school teachers, exist in the underworld of nostalgia, stuck in the eternal loop of whatever grade you've long passed. To this day I close my eyes on Andy as a ten-year-old, a peculiar boy who struggled to control his body, swinging his arms wildly and running into corners, tripping over his big feet, forever falling backward in his chair. In sixth grade this developed into a particular brand of shtick. You never knew if his accidents were on purpose even if the blood was always real. But in sixth grade everything gets complicated. That's why I preferred fifth graders. They struck me as the best versions of themselves, middle-aged children effortlessly straddling their youth. Soon the gap would spread too wide and they would have to leap to the other side, but while I had them they were safe and merely curious of the divide.

"I just hate the idea of you being alone," father was saying to son.

"But I'm the one dying."

"Enough with the dying."

"Yes, please," Andy said, "enough." He mimed a patient grin, the sort of exasperated condescension seen by parents immemorial, and that's when he took the opportunity to turn to me and ask, not without fondness, about Buckley. While honesty was my new goal, I refrained from telling him the whole truth and simply explained that I was taking an extended leave of absence, to recover from my recent loss. The young woman, this Jeanie Spokes—hello, nice to meet you—gave me a grimace of woe that seemed almost exaggerated, and I half-wondered if she had heard about my sordid tale, if my shame had somehow gone public. I mentioned how very difficult these last few months had been and that I was no longer living at home but had taken up residence at the Hotel Wales, "just like your short story," I said to Andrew.

"What's that?"

Had he been listening? "My wife and I are having a bit of a break, and so I'm living in the Wales, like Asher in *Hotel India*, but so far no Morse code tapping on the pipes."

"Jesus, Philip, don't live in my stories."

"No, no, no, in the Hotel Wales. On Madison." I pointed north.

Andrew tried to track but his eyes were like hands in the dark. "I'm sorry," he said, "but I think I need to go home. I just need to go home. The idea of a reception after my performance in there, I just can't. And my feet. My head. My fingernails, I swear. Philip, I loved your father—of course I loved him, he was my oldest friend—but I need to go home. I'm starting to feel, I don't know, in my teeth even, which can't be good. If I had proper use of my body I'd fling it out the window. I didn't say that. Beckett did. I don't have much to say anymore. Except I need to go home. But Philip, living in the Wales, that's no good. It ends poorly, if I recall. You could always move in with me—with us, we have the room, until you get settled or work things out with your wife. But Jesus Christ; not the Wales. I can still see those rugs with those stains that could eat you alive."

Perhaps this invitation was offered in a moment of morbid duress, fueled by a tenderness for my father, ignited by guilt, stoked by a certain softness in the head, but regardless, I was thrilled with the offer

and told him so right then and there, trying my best not to jump up and down. I think Andy embraced the arrangement as well, figuring I might lessen the filial load—Mr. Topping, Philip, he can sit around the fireplace with pain-in-the-ass Dad while I try to bed this diffusely provocative woman. The truth is, no matter how beloved, a fifth-grade teacher is only truly beloved in fifth grade. After that we are like dioramas.

"I need a taxi," Andrew said.

"It's only a few blocks," Andy said. Cruel boy.

Newly adopted and determined to heed all calls, I took the initiative and rushed onto Madison, past the limousines and the hearse, where a fragment of my father lay nestled in satin. I hailed a cab easily, like in the movies. Just wonderful. The church was now fully unpacked, with more and more of the A. N. Dyer faithful lingering near their hero, but only their eyes rioted, tugging and jostling for an autographed view. Did they wonder who I was? Did they mistake me for a son? With anxious yet dutiful purpose I went over and led the great man toward the waiting cab while Andy remained unmoved. It seemed he was making a stand. But not for long. Jeanie Spokes reached down and curled her fingers around the low-hanging fruit of the boy's left hand. How her touch must have thrilled him. She pulled him toward the cab and into the backseat, where she positioned herself in the middle. Touché. I said my goodbyes, my see-you-soons, like maybe tomorrow, early evening, yes, yes, great, nice to meet you, Jeanie, who looked at me as if the duelists had retired and we seconds now held their aim.

I closed the door and the taxi pulled away.

I probably should have climbed into the front seat.

The funeral reception was at the Knickerbocker Club, on 62nd Street, and people were already on the move, commenting on the pleasant weather and the reemergence of a stroll. I caught my wife glaring at me from the top of the church steps. Ashley had lost weight and was as beautiful as ever, a perfect self-portrait, damaged yet determined, a newfound survivor. Her confident future was already being extruded through my unfortunate past. She stared at me and then gestured toward Rufus and Eloise, abandoned with their aunt. Recriminations radiated from her knuckled lips. *You jerk, you asshole. You've ruined our life, you pig.* This was all true, and I tried to acknowledge the sin on my face, but to be honest I was more focused on my impending move to 2 East 70th Street. Had the Dyer apartment changed much since I was last there? Which bedroom would I sleep in, Richard's or Jamie's? Would I share meals with the man, conversations, favorite books and movies, latest pages of our writing? Would we drink and smoke and talk late into the night? My mind raced along old track. I was a foundling found. All told, or totaled, I would spend a week under A. N. Dyer's roof, which is how I became a witness, the primary witness despite some feuding claims, to everything that happened.

Ashley grabbed the children and started up Madison.

My son waved goodbye to me, or so he told me years later.

"You were looking right at me and you just stood there, like I was nothing."

It's the little things they remember, like a raised hand, or the lack of a raised hand.

"Like I was less than nothing."

How are we meant to see everything?

By late March we would all return to this church.

II

H-3990   FROM NEAR EL TOVAR HOTEL, GRAND CANYON NATIONAL PARK, ARIZONA

POST CARD

Dear Charlie. The Grand Canyon really
is quite grand, despite the poor
reproduction. The reverse looks nothing
like the real thing, believe me. Imagine
Dorothy in Oz and all that crazy color
and realize we live in a black and
white world. In an hour were taking
mules down to the bottom for three
nights of camping. I've named my
ass after you! He is a stinky ass!
I hope my ass doesn't step in any
holes for there are plenty of ass
holes here! The sky at night is so
dark & clear, the stars so starry
you can't believe what were missing
in New York. It's like a firecracker
vs fireworks. Next stop the Hoover
Dam for a bit of manmade glory.
Hope you're doing well in Canada.
Caught any big ugly fish? Looking
forward to the lies.

Echo... Echo... Echo... Andy

MESSAGE   7A-H2930   **ADDRESS**

Master Charles Topping
12 East 72nd Street
New York, New York
USA

Oh Christ. Richard hadn't seen the movie, not yet, which was stupid since it was their most successful release, both critically and commercially, their obvious pride and joy, and he should have at least watched it before the meeting and been prepared to talk about it and tell them how much he love-love-loved it. Typical. His big chance and he had already sabotaged himself, like the loser he was and the loser he would forever be, from clueless boy to idiot teenager to delusional adult. *Who are you fooling, you motherfucking shithead?* The old Richard could have gone on like this to the point of running to the parking lot and doing complicated crack math in his head, but the new Richard (5,475 days sober) took a fair-minded, even-keeled breath and pushed his shoulder against that banging door. "Oh yeah," he told Curtis, "I see it now. Such a wonderful film."

"You remember Daniel Dupont's office. Well"—Curtis let his expression hang for a moment, almost like a boxer's taunt—"here it is, exactly the same, except for the rug. The rug had to be changed. Obviously."

Richard nodded *Of course.*

"We don't believe in props."

"Oh."

"For us, reality is the key."

Richard—"Absolutely"—whatever the hell that meant. In a flash he pictured punching this Curtis guy in the nose—*pop!*—his knuckles perfectly designed for the bloodying of seersucker. The thought calmed him down. But he winced at how he started kicking the poor man in the head. His fantasies always turned into felonies.

"I tell you, *The Erasers* was an amazing project to work on," Curtis started to say, his hands impatient, as if he constructed balloon animals in his spare time, "because I'm a huge fan of Robbe-Grillet and I remember reading *Les Gommes* at Brown with Coover and thinking even then that with the right tweaking this could be a terrific film. Very strange, very compelling. I'm the one who brought the idea to Rainer, just like I'm bringing you to him, or him to you, but that's my job. I'm a facilitator. A connector. I thought it was going to be a hard sell—Robbe-Grillet, not you—but Rainer understood the potential immediately." Hands in need of something heavier than air, Curtis picked up a small wooden sculpture, a modernist totem carved from ebony. He could have been Yorick if Hamlet were the skull. It was clear that Curtis was part of that Ivy League crowd that Richard called the Moveable East, innately privileged yet no longer happy with the idea of simply making money, these pseudo-creatives embracing the business of Los Angeles, with its ease of living and its lifestyle of plausible deniability. Curtis smacked the sculpture against his palm. "This Noll right here is what Wallas used on Dupont's head. It's probably worth thirty thousand, but as a piece of movie memorabilia, who knows, maybe fifteen more. Rainer doubled the value like that." Curtis put the sculpture back on the credenza, readjusted it numerous times as though its proper alignment would guarantee him a sleek afterlife. "But that's what we do," he said. "Attention to detail, Integrity toward the material, Respect for the artist." Curtis stepped back from the sculpture. Perfect. "That's the kind of place this is."

The place in question was called Aires Projects, a production company under the umbrella of Sony Pictures. Aires had declared an interest in one of Richard's screenplays, which was amazing, not the screenplay but the interest, amazing because Richard had basically given up on the screenwriting experiment. Over the last eight years he had written four and had landed an agent and a handful of meetings but that was about it, the *it* losing its meaningful referent, which was fine. Richard was perfectly content with his twelve-plus years in the trenches of substance abuse counseling. It was a good job, a sane job, a job he thrived in, bringing a particular brand of tough love to the process, breaking the body and its wants down to base mechanical function, emotion and ego the unwanted fuel. He preached a form of Radical Honesty and Personal Transparency. Some people even told him he should write a book on the subject, and though the idea of self-help literature turned his stomach, he often found himself coming up with imagined titles—*The Lasting View*—and perfect first lines—*When darkness falls, the window becomes a mirror.* These thoughts usually hit him during the first few miles of his normal eight-mile run, when his body preached the importance of exercise, his breathing a perfectly composed pop song, verse-chorus-bridge, but by mile five started to go atonal with all the deceptions, all the rationalizations, the near-manic extremes, the nineteen vitamins a day, the regimented breakfast of blueberries and kale, his confidence splintering near the seven-mile mark as he considered his career helping fellow fuckups, his sense of accomplishment losing its wind, his wife and children falling behind, until his father invariably peeked in, disappointed at the square footage and the limited scenery—this is your life?—but by mile eight, as Richard made his final sprint across the Santa Ana River and headed home on South Street, all these old feelings that chased him shifted into action, a building about to explode, a killer stalking his house, the love of his life leaving on an airplane, one of those scenes in which our hero has to run, and it was here, in these cinematic equivalencies, that Richard became happiest. As many people know, or know by way of cliché, everyone in L.A. has a screenplay in their back pocket. Whatever the dubious truth of that claim, the idea can settle on your shoulder and whisper dialogue in your ear until you're touched by the spirit and born into believing again. Hollywood, like God, needs constant feeding.

The thing is, Richard did have talent. As a boy he wrote comics that Jamie illustrated, stories like "The Destructor" and "Fealty Blaze," which we all read with great gusto. I was a particular fan of "The Coarsers of Bedlam" and its tale of Random Coarser, who had to kill a person every week in order to keep Death from his terminally ill son. The ending, with Random's suicide and the older son's awful new responsibility, still unnerves me. Later Richard devoted most of his writing energy to his journal, which he maintained with teenage vigilance; whenever anyone came over, he made a show of Shut the fuck up until he had finished a particular entry and if you called him a pussy or a fag, as my brother once did, he'd slug you in the stomach hard enough to raise tears. All of this changed when one day his father asked if he could read some of his entries. Most kids would have said, Are you insane? but Richard had been waiting for this moment, had essentially been writing for this moment, and not only did he hand over his journal but he ran upstairs and retrieved his previous journals as well. He was fourteen years old. For three days his father read without comment, and Richard waited. It was like a tight-lipped confession, a silent unburdening of self. There were long passages concerning the man and his literary fame, how Richard was proud yet tormented, wishing their relationship was better though also wondering if either of them really cared, or if maybe they preferred the easier distance. *Sometimes I think we should talk exclusively by telegram,* he wrote, *with its helpful shorthand and stops.* August 21 was a long-imagined eulogy to his father. April 5 was a make-believe suicide note. There were other things, feuds and crushes and the overall grind of Exeter, drinking beer and smoking pot in Central Park, Whip-its and minor shoplifting, a bit of sex on the weekend, in particular December 19 with Abigail Hunter, but years later Richard was struck by how father-focused these entries were, how every word seemed crafted for the old man and how even today that lone entry on February 9 (and who knew the cause) could stagger him: *Am I a cherished thing?* After three days his father finally returned the stack. "You have a good strong voice," he told him, and gave Richard a tap on the back, like a doctor diagnosing good health without bothering with the stethoscope. Richard might have hoped for more, but this seemed enough, and for a while his lungs took in mellower air and he only slugged someone when they really deserved it.

Jamie recalled this short-lived period as the storm before the shitstorm.

A year and a half later, *Percy, By Himself* was published.

The novel won the National Book Critics Circle Award, which some considered a consolation prize. The judges praised the story of Percy Sr. and Jr. and their silent struggle for connection, citing in particular the journal entries of Percy the younger and their uncanny adolescent verisimilitude (a word Richard had to look up, thinking it had something to do with vivisection). You have a good strong voice indeed. What a crock. Unbelievably his father pled ignorance to lifting so many of the entries word for word. "I swear I was just trying to get a sense," he said. "I guess the writing stuck, which is a compliment in a way. There was nothing I needed to improve." Isabel came down hard on him, calling him selfish and clueless, insensitive to the world outside his own head. And she tried to comfort Richard by telling him that it was a good book, a really good book thanks to his writing, and that Jr. was the rooting force of the story, certainly the more likable of the two Percys. But Richard disagreed. If anything he thought the character was an apprentice idiot, confirmed by the last lines of the book:

> Sr. secretly watched Jr. eat his lamb, and he wondered if they both wondered the same thing, the two of them unspeakably quiet as they managed the tough business on their plates. Pauline was going on about daylight savings and how quickly the afternoon slipped into dusk. Amazing the difference an hour can make. Then she asked which time was the real time, that she forgot? Neither father nor son had an answer. They hardly bothered looking up, between the chore of cutting and chewing. But maybe, yes maybe they shared a thought on that first Sunday of falling back: Am I a cherished thing?

Curtis gestured for Richard to sit, please. "I really like your script," he said.

"Thank you."

"It's smart, it's funny, the ending sneaks up on you." Curtis remained on his feet as if playing a game of charades, trying to get you to guess his future success. "We're all very excited."

"That's tremendous," Richard said.

"Where have you been hiding? Do you have other scripts in the top drawer?"

"Actually—"

"Because we want to be in business with writers like you." Curtis checked his phone. "That's the short answer to what will be a longer conversation. We usually don't go for movies about movies, I mean *Day for Night*, sure, *The Player* maybe, but mostly they tend toward the solipsistic and too clever by half, and the satire, because it's always a satire, the satire tends to be a snooze. Actors are self-involved pricks, wow, alert the media. But you've done something different here. The setting is both real and absurd, and the characters, well, your Martin

Forge is right up there with Geoffrey Firmin in *Under the Volcano* and every other loon from *The Day of the Locust*. Reading these pages I kept on thinking of Brando toward the end, in one of those junk movies he did, Brando as played by Richard Burton stooping to the level of the gruff but lovable grandfather in—sorry, what's the name of your movie-within-the-movie again?"

"*Dog Daze*," Richard said.

Curtis flexed a smile, his bow tie the dumbbell. "Right right right right right right right. I love it. The whole man-switches-places-with-his-dog story is so perfectly high-concept I'm sure half a dozen studios would green-light your fake movie in a heartbeat. I'm almost tempted—it's crazy, I know—but I'm almost tempted to push Rainer to do both movies and have you write the fake one and we release them simultaneously. How excellent would that be? *Dog Daze* and *A Louse and a Flea* on a double bill, like, like, like a diptych, a *mise en abyme*. Forget sequel or prequel, how about"—Curtis tossed the word forward with both hands—"metaquel? Maybe that sounds too much like a cough syrup. I'm sure we could come up with something better."

The funny thing was that Richard had had the same thought when he first toyed with the idea. It usually came to him right before falling asleep, during those moments of pre-dream seeding, where he would start to think about Martin Forge, the once-in-a-generation actor praised for his intensity and admired by the younger set for barreling into life like a bullet, right up until the last stupid movie to pay another stupid debt, and Richard, eyes closing, would imagine both movies intertwined, tragedy and comedy, playing side by side in the same multiplex. Fully awake, he gave Curtis a nod and a grin. Was there smugness in that grin? Richard hoped not, he despised smugness, but here was this Curtis guy, smart and successful and seemingly conjured from a world that finally understood just how special Richard Dyer was. "Yeah," Richard said, "that would be ama—"

Without warning, the office door flew open and in came Rainer Krebs, the head of Aires Projects. Meeting Rainer was the obvious goal. Curtis was all talk, but Rainer was the action, and Richard was ready. Last night he had practiced the pitch with his wife and thirteen-year-old daughter (his sixteen-year-old son found Dad, the script-writer, to be its own lame sort of a movie). Richard had even rehearsed the small talk and was willing to reach back and go down the unpleasant road of growing up in Manhattan and how he always passed the Dietmar Krebs Gallery on 76th and Madison, with all those Schieles and Klimts inside—just spectacular—and from there maybe he'd ask Rainer where he went to school—Collegiate, he believed—and then might fish up a few names they had in common—his cousin, Henry Lippencott—even if Rainer was a few years older and part of that Euro crowd who cared more about clothes and clubbing than baseball, who even in eighth grade reeked of sexual boredom. They all ended up at Brown, it seemed.

Richard rose to his feet with East Coast propriety, but Rainer had company, a boyish man expertly casual in Converse sneakers, a machinist union T-shirt, and a baseball cap pulled tight to the brow. This guise belonged to a familiar species of L.A. duck. One could imagine all the young white males in this city migrating from the wetlands of various Midwestern malls, flying west when the weather turned boring and gray. Rainer and his guest were in mid-conversation, oblivious to anything but the room itself.

"So . . . ," Rainer said, pleased.

The young man froze with stagey admiration.

"Amazing, huh?"

"You took the paneling too?"

"The paneling is Prouvé; so is the door."

"Of course, the portholes."

"I liberated them from a technical school in Algiers."

"Fucking insane." The young man continued with the drama, pressing his palms and face against the wood as if his touch could transduce the grain. "When I get to the right age I want to play Le Corbusier. I already have the perfect Charlotte Perriand in mind."

"Actually that would be a good project," Rainer said.

"Hell yeah it would. Bring in Pierre Jeanneret and we have *Jules et Jim* but with an architecture, French Resistance vibe. Total slam dunk. I even have Le Corbusier's glasses, like his actual glasses glasses. Cost me a hundred grand. I'm told it's the second-most-expensive pair of modern eyewear ever sold at auction."

"Very nice."

Richard stood there, at first annoyed, smiling like a photograph waiting to be taken, but then the young man, his voice, his face—think of the three phases of matter, of a solid heating into a liquid heating into a gas—finally conveyed the steamy presence of Eric Harke, the actor, the movie star, the teen heartthrob. Richard tried to act nonchalant within these strange thermodynamics of celebrity, but being the lesser actor, his posture stroked into a stiff approximation of cool. Eric Harke was taller than expected and less pretty, thank goodness, since onscreen he appeared summoned from the baby pillows of a thousand pubescent girls, including Richard's own daughter, who was presently screaming Oh-my-Gods in his head.

"You remember Curtis," Rainer said to Eric.

"Oh-yeah-sure-absolutely-hey."

Rainer then turned toward Richard and smiled like an oven revealing a loaf of bread. "And it's really nice to finally meet you," he said, taking Richard's hand. "I think our mothers know one another, from the Chamber Music Society or the Cos Club or something small-world like that." Rainer was huge without being fat, his six-foot-eight bulk belonging to an antiquated class of male who by dint of size exist on another, arguably greater plane. "And aren't you friends with Henry Lippencott?" he asked.

Richard was thrown by the stolen small talk. "He's my cousin."

"Oh, okay. You get back much?"

"To New York?"

"Yeah."

"Never."

The oven opened again. "And said with conviction. I hear you. I have my issues with the city as well, mostly family related, ex-wife too, that and my built-in cynicism doesn't quite jibe with the place anymore. I get there and just turn mean, you know, wonderfully mean but mean nonetheless. Out here my cynicism seems, I don't know, seems somehow jubilant. I can relax enough to hate the world with a tremen-

dous amount of affection." Though raised in New York, Rainer spoke
with a vague European accent that seemed rucksacked to his shoulders,
the straps pulled tight, giving the impression of an overweight boy who
had spent long, over-enunciated summers with his grandparents. "I
still manage to go back at least once a month," he said.

"I'm buying a loft," Eric offered, "in the Meatpacking District."

"Of course you are," said Rainer, who, rather than roll his eyes,
practically threw them toward Richard as if Richard would find this
rush into nouveau trendiness risible. But Richard didn't. Or not in the
way Rainer imagined. Because in Richard's memory the Meatpacking
District still existed as the capital of sex clubs, with roving bands of
transvestites sucking five-dollar cock. "You see poor Eric is from Min-
nesota," Rainer added, as if this further explained his choice of neighborhood.

"Go 'Sota," the actor fake-cheered. He was not known for his com-
edies.

"Son of ice farmers, I believe."

"Fuck you, you kraut."

And they both laughed. Richard tried to join in by adjusting his lips
and eliciting a ha-ha sound, but he was nervous and sweaty and desperate to please as well as thrown by the image of this teen heartthrob
cruising the Mineshaft on Little West 12th, his pockets stuffed with
fivers, and this killed his sense of humor, which in many ways had been
killed years ago. What remained was a hard-earned optimism that he
could survive almost anything, even extreme opportunity.

Rainer sat down. Everybody else followed suit. "Curtis, where are
we?"

"We love the script."

Rainer turned to Richard. "We love the script. It's funny, it's smart,
it has depth. Whoever plays the lead could well win awards. Don't get
me wrong, it's not perfect. It still needs work. It's too long, the middle
sags, the individual character arcs could be clearer, the females are
weak, but those are small fixes in what is otherwise an outstanding
piece of screen prose. We can give you proper notes when and if the
time comes, but essentially what we're saying, Richard, is that we want

to do it. We want to make this film. But we want to make it the right way, with the right people and with the right budget." Rainer lounged back in his Rainer-sustaining chair. The color-field painting hanging behind him was mostly white with a red slash going down the middle. It made him appear newly born. "So what do you think?" he asked.

Richard was the opposite of numb. When your biggest hopes are realized in an instant and childish fantasy transfigures into fact, into the life you only dared imagine, well, numbness is nowhere in the picture. If anything there's an overabundance of feeling as you finally let go of all that history so tightly gripped within, to the point where Richard experienced an epic, almost literal whoosh throughout his body and for a moment nearly turned liquid. A sense of relief was the first emotion to settle in. After fifteen years of near-constant pressure, of willing himself sane, of focusing on the steps but never the climb, finally, after all these years, he could stop for a moment and turn around and see what he had achieved: possibly the best view in town.

Eric Harke asked who his agent was.

"Um, Norman Peltzer," Richard said.

"Who the fuck is that?"

"Head of the Norman Peltzer Agency," Richard said.

"Of course he is," Rainer said. "Maybe we could hook you up with someone we know. Maybe Koons at CAA. He might be a good fit. Or Vartan at UTA."

Curtis took the note.

"Koons is really fucking good," Eric told Richard, his feet keeping a bass drum beat. "You can trust him a hundred percent, well actually ninety percent, the other ten going into his own pocket." It was beyond bizarre to have this celebrity suddenly play the role of confidant; Rainer and Curtis struck Richard as dubious, with their high-gloss professionalism, but Eric Harke was different, Eric Harke was endearing, which was probably a function of his skill as an actor, the way he could come across as likable, but Richard guessed he was responding to something else, judging by the manic exuberance and the chorus of facial tics and those baby blues with the chewy center: Eric Harke was definitely coked up. Richard figured he had had a pick-me-up before the meeting—snort left, snort right, and in we go, the hologram of a secure young man. "But Vartan's your guy if you're looking for someone to take your phone calls and show you around town, if you want some of that old-fashioned agent cheese."

Rainer requested champagne via phone. "Hope I'm not being presumptuous," he told the group. "More than anything, I like the ceremony."

"Yes, yes, yes, yes, yes," Eric agreed, nodding to his new best friend. "Absolutely we should celebrate. We should all go to my house for dinner tonight and we can really celebrate and discuss the project. I could even call Donal Fenster because I know he'd be interested and we can brainstorm and just fuck around. You married, Richard? Well, bring the wife. Bring the kids. I have a huge fucking pool, a basketball court. You play? Do you bowl? I got every shoe size imaginable. Bring everyone, hell, bring the family dog. The goldfish, the hamsters. We'll barbecue. Not your fucking pets I promise. I've got prime rib you can't believe."

"Fenster's interested?" Rainer asked.

Donal Fenster was the young director recently robbed of an Academy Award.

"He could be. We're desperate to work together again. You know," Eric turned to Richard and said without pretense or pause, "I know people, I mean, I know Rainer knows people, but I know people, and people want to know me, that's just the way it is, no matter how shallow, presidents, dictators, holy men, billionaires, they want to know me, ridiculous, I know, not my value system, but they hear my name and they get interested. It's a weird kind of power, I tell you, and it's not like I can ever hide and be Clark Kent or Bruce Wayne, no, no, no, I'm always wearing the fucking cape, which is exhausting, but if I'm in your movie—and I'm seriously considering it, Richard, like seriously— but if I'm in your movie, you can land a healthy budget and book some hard-core talent and schedule a start date for July, like this July, man, and movies are hard, hard to get made and getting harder by the minute. How amazing would that be, the two of us working together during the summer on a big old film written by you and starring me, I mean just plain old straight-up cool." Eric Harke spoke as if the last ten minutes equaled their lifelong dream.

Richard sat back in his seat. The force of future success started to slam into the humble present, and years later, during those times when he replayed this meeting in his head, he would wonder if his initial reaction somehow dictated all that followed, since his first active thought was, Now I can go back to New York and shove this in my father's face. Did that impulse trigger what happened? If instead he had thought about his wife and children, of sharing the good news with them, would things have turned out differently? Who knows? But maybe thoughts, their synaptic charge, maybe they bump into surrounding particles and change their direction and spin and help shape some of that spooky action at a distance. We are all socially entangled, especially on the Upper East Side. How often does a random thought generate a coincidence, like the one presently vibrating in Richard's pocket?

"You all right?" asked Rainer.

"Just my phone." Richard checked the screen. It was Jamie.

"Go ahead and answer," Rainer told him.

"It's just my brother. Believe me, I can ignore him."

"Never ignore family," Rainer said with Teutonic sternness. "I insist."

Richard was in no position to disagree.

"You gotten a call from Dad yet?" Jamie asked, his voice sounding stoned.

"No. Can I call you later, I'm kind of—"

"Well, you will."

"I seriously doubt it."

"Oh, you will. He's all mortal coil since Charlie Topping died."

Richard lowered his head into a more discreet angle. "Charlie Topping died?"

"Like a week ago."

Richard was shocked. Though he refused all contact with his father and for half his life had lived successfully removed from the man and his city, forsaking everything, even financial help, the loss of wealth in some ways enduring longer than the loss of love, saying no to those Dyer trusts, no to those yearly tax-exempt gifts, taking nothing on principle (unlike his brother), even when money was scarce, even when his son, age seven, was diagnosed with acute lymphocytic leukemia and for two years the hospital bills piled into an economic record of despair, even then Richard held firm (and accepted help from his mother instead), still, the death of Charlie Topping hit him hard, not the death so much as the lack of news concerning the death. No one bothered to call or email him? Like many people who have escaped their past, Richard assumed his absence was suffered on an almost daily basis. But really no one missed him much.

"Did you go to the funeral?" Richard asked.

"No," Jamie said. "It was yesterday and I'm not in the city."

Richard didn't bother to ask where he was since it was likely somewhere annoying. "Can I call you later?"

"Sure. Just heads up, Dad's going to beg you to come home."

"Right, okay, whatever." And with that Richard hung up. After a deep breath he gave the room a where-were-we grin, and for a moment it seemed like the office had reverted back into a film set, a perfect reproduction of false reality, where brothers chatted with brothers and fathers called sons and Richard might actually be successful.

"Everything okay?" asked Rainer.

"Yeah, fine."

"If you need to go . . . "

"A friend of my father's died. My godfather actually."

"I'm so sorry."

"It's okay, he died last week."

"Well he's still dead." Rainer rose from his chair, like Oscar Wilde playing Winston Churchill getting bad news from the front. "And dead is dead." He pointed to the painting behind the couch. "See that, that's a Clyfford Still. He's dead too. My father was good friends with him and he told me when I was a boy that this was a portrait Still had painted of him. A Still life, he called it. My father loved pulling our legs. Despite that, I believed him and I can't help but see his face in the brushstrokes, his tight-lipped smile, his droopy left eye. It might as well be a photograph of the man. He's also dead. When we were div-vying up the estate, it was the only thing I wanted. My siblings thought I was insane. They gravitated toward the more valuable work, the Schieles, the Klimts, the Kirchners, while I went for a then-unfashionable Still."

All eyes rested on that Still, embraced its outer stillness. The red slash seemed to record the saddest kind of sound wave, where silence is the only possible response. Richard, ever the literalist, tried to spot recognizable features in the paint and thought he caught a disapprov-ing frown coming from a streak in the upper right corner. "It's quite something," he told Rainer.

"Of course it's a reproduction."

"Oh."

"I couldn't keep the real one here. A Still nowadays is worth a for-tune. It's a decent reproduction, though the original has a browner red." Rainer turned back to Richard. "You know I used to see your fa-ther walking around Central Park, around the boat pond. I'd watch him do his laps and I'd try to imagine what was percolating inside that head. It seemed such athletic thinking. I never had the nerve to actu-ally stop him and tell him how much I loved his books. I think I was"— a knock on the door—"around sixteen"—an assistant came in with champagne and four glasses—"when I first read *Ampersand.* I still have that cheap paperback copy, all underlined and dog-eared." Rainer started unwrapping the foil. "I lost my literary virginity to that book."

Eric Harke accompanied the sentiment with some phantom drum fills against his chest. "So cool that he's your dad, just so fucking cool. I mean, A. N. Dyer. Hello. I've read *Ampersand* four times and I don't even read menus more than once, but the book, it speaks to me, yeah, yeah, yeah, actor boy goes blah-blah-blah, but it does, it recharges me, makes me want to do great art." In his excitement Eric balled his fists into exclamations of FUCK and YEAH. "It seems to me you have *Catcher in the Rye* people and you have *Ampersand* people, and I definitely, ab-solutely, one hundred percent fall into the *Ampersand* camp. I mean *Catcher* is excellent on a lot of levels, but it's basically a character piece which stays stuck in the muddy bog of adolescence. That's part of its

charm, for sure, but that's also its limitatio
ity. But *Ampersand*, man *Ampersand* explode
existential parts and it keeps on expanding
right up until your last breath. To me, Saling
to adopt, but A. N. Dyer is a different beast al

Yeah, a tick, Richard thought.

The cork popped, and Rainer began to fill gl
this interesting, Richard. You know how many copies *Ampersand* has
sold since its publication? Over forty-five million. That's a nice big
number. And every year it sells about a hundred thousand more. Or
used to. The sales are slipping. Did you know that, Richard?"

"No," Richard said, wishing the topic would spit up blood and die.

"It's down about thirty percent over the last six years, while *Catcher*
has maintained its sales. Some of the problem is high schools, that they
have to choose between *Catcher* and *Ampersand*, and *Catcher* is three
hundred pages shorter and not nearly as difficult, so *Catcher* wins with
two hundred and fifty thousand copies sold a year and *Ampersand* falls
further back into the rank of unread classics."

The bubbles in the champagne shimmied up the flutes, a hundred
phony smiles breaking the surface, like some Esther Williams routine,
Richard thought, a memory of stinging sweetness flooding his mouth.

"I should tell you up front," Rainer continued, "that for the last ten
years I've been courting your father, more like courting his agent,
about getting the rights to *Ampersand*. I know I'm not alone in this.
Every decent producer has given it a shot, going back fifty years, big-
time people too, much bigger than me. I know Robert Evans got close,
at least that's the story he tells. Your father has made it abundantly
clear that he's not interested and never will be interested in seeing any
of his books, let alone *Ampersand*, turned into films. Maybe he's still
competing with Salinger, I don't know, but I respect the impulse. Movies of great novels, for the most part, are disasters. Give me a flawed
story anytime. That said, I do think we at Aires have a strong track
record as well as the right kind of sensibility for this kind of project. I
mean, look at *The Erasers*. Robbe-Grillet bringing in two hundred and
fifty-four million worldwide, that's a medium-size miracle, let alone

...response and the awards and the boost to book sales—
...d get you the numbers if you'd like."

Richard could feel his body shrinking.

"So I have a proposition."

Or maybe everyone else was getting bigger.

"I want to make your movie, Richard, I want to make it right, with good people involved, like Eric here, and I want to get a proper budget, but satire is a tricky game, especially, no offense, from an unproven writer. You have to appreciate there are numerous strikes against this project from the get-go."

Richard was yet again the boy who understood life far too late.

"But a package deal, that's another thing. Maybe you could talk to your father about giving us a chance with *Ampersand*, just a chance, and based on your script as a writing sample, I think you should do the adaptation. Who better than the son? The publicity alone. And it would certainly pay well, and of course we would pay your father well, very well. It would be a nice windfall for the Dyer clan, not that money is the issue, of course. But if you could deliver *Ampersand*, just a twelve-month option, I could guarantee you *A Flea and a Louse* with all the bells and whistles."

"*A Louse and a Flea*," Curtis corrected.

"What's that?"

"*A Louse and a Flea*."

"Oh, yeah, right right right right right. It's a total win-win, Richard, with Eric doing both films. Just imagine this guy as Edgar Mead."

"Man-oh-man-oh-man," Eric said.

"But in five or six years, he'll be too old, no offense."

"None taken."

"Nobody's getting any younger, Richard, and heart-on-sleeve time, I'm desperate for this to happen. I love this book more than anything and I know it can be a great movie. So have a talk with your father and see if you might sway him toward us. Minimum, try and get me—"

"Us," Eric corrected.

"Us a meeting."

The champagne glasses were passed around and Richard took one. It seemed huge in his hand, the liquid vaguely laboratorial.

"To beginnings," Rainer said.

What is the exact science of failure? Richard wondered.

Then Eric Harke stood up and after lifting his glass, did a curious thing: he sort of tossed a grin over his shoulder as if whatever deity that had so blessed his life was giving him a congratulatory pat, after which Eric froze and squinted, spotting a shape, it seemed, a person approaching, possibly familiar, yes, yes, I know this person, his face suggested, his brow treading deeper, his mouth momentarily hitching on the proper weight of the words before giving them voice,

"You know those games, sir, that start off innocently enough,"

his delivery obviously practiced in front of the mirror, along with every interstitial stammer and twitch, those tricks of authenticity, as well as the false naïveté of a mid-century American boy,

"or almost innocently enough, like a game of catch or tag, and you're all in it together, in the beginning, you're all in cahoots, but things sort of evolve on their own, suggestions are made, rules are changed, and suddenly hitting is allowed and that area over there is out of bounds. You know those games, sir? Well, those are the kinds of games that can only happen once. They can never get repeated, no matter how hard you might try. When the game is over, the game is over. Maybe that's why you don't want it to end. Maybe that's why you keep on playing even if the next rule is harsher, maybe even unreasonable. You know what I mean, sir? It's like those games in the quad, the games you can probably see from your window right now. There's a moment, who knows when, but there's a moment when it's too late and you're left with nothing else to do but to keep on playing, even if it's not fun anymore, even if you know it's stupid, you keep on playing, even if you know someone's going to get hurt, seriously hurt, you keep on playing because the only way the game can end is with blood, and when that happens, sir, well, it's not really a game anymore, is it?"

Eric paused to allow for his earthly return, then he smiled that famous smile as if invigorated by a dip in one of his native ten thousand lakes. "I hope that wasn't too ridiculous."

"Could there be a better Edgar Mead?" Rainer pronounced. He raised his glass in artistic salute, while Richard tried to anchor his insides, unsettled by the personal effects of gravity, and though he did lift his glass along with the others, he never took a sip. No, after cheers Richard put the glass back down on the table without comment, just like he let the phone keep on vibrating in his pocket without saying a word.

II.ii

L ET'S NOW TURN to the second son, Jamie Dyer, sitting in a
rented Honda Odyssey parked across the street from the
Riverbank Cemetery in Stowe, Vermont. It was two in the morning,
the temperature outside in the twenties. Jamie sat there and waited—
I can picture him, sitting perfectly still, beyond still, pretending to be
a lizard-like creature either on the hide or on the hunt, that motivation
forever uncertain. I am nothing, he thought. Nobody sees me. He sat
there and he waited and after some minutes he broke the pose and lit a
joint. Because of his fondness for marijuana people assumed Jamie was
a relaxed individual, one of those semiprofessional stoners in high
school and college and beyond, but in reality he was often anxious, not
in ways fearful or troubled, certainly not neurotic, but more like a jug-
gler with too many thoughts tumbling through the air. Most of those
thoughts tended toward the innocuous yet deeply felt, in the realm
of I should learn how to fly an airplane, or I should run a marathon
next year, or I should really pick up the guitar again, which he
had only played for six months in seventh grade, but a few of those
thoughts were machete-sharp, as in issues of personal worth and failed
promise—oh man, that was a buzzing chain saw—but after a cleansing
hit of dope a small pure sense of self seemed to open up—here he is,
ladies and gentlemen, the man you've been waiting for—and Jamie
settled onto the stage, the minivan's dash his footlights. All of those
previous doubts were reduced down into brief soliloquy: I am me.
Three hits quelled him, the fourth he wisely denied. After all, there
was hard work to be done tonight. The windshield çarried the grimy
aftereffects of snow, the wiper blades describing an arc similar to an

open book, with this chapter landing on a full moon, a cemetery, a quiet country road, a setting evocative of madmen and axes. Jamie lowered his eyes to the navigation screen. He imagined a dot creeping up from behind, a crazed bloody dot dragging its left foot. Jamie locked the doors. He smiled. For distraction and fun, he pushed the button on the steering wheel and asked the minivan for the nearest Friendly's. In seconds a Friendly's popped up ten miles away. Maybe afterward he'd have a burger. "Nearest ATM?" There were four within two miles. He pushed the button once more. "Tell me, O muse, what the fuck am I doing here?" The computer asked him to restate the question. "Never mind," he said.

Evidently there were four never-minds in the state of Vermont.

Since yesterday the minivan had doubled as Jamie's temporary home. It was a rather comfortable nest, even if this morning a layer of frost covered the inside: an ice palace of his own breath, he reckoned, pleased that this metaphor from *Here Live Angry Dogs and Brutal Men* mingled with his own life (despite Dennis Dormin's fate). Jamie scraped the glass with his fingernail and wrote his name, just like Dennis did. It's a small moment in the book, and a lesser writer would have wrung the image of every sniff and snore, but A. N. Dyer simply let the scene play, with Dennis late for work and waiting and waiting— "Goddamn it!"—waiting for those vents to defrost the despair of last night. It was a lovely bit of writing, Jamie recalled, as he watched the physical record of his sleep melt under that rising Vermont sun. He wondered which of those drips belonged to his dreams and which belonged to his father.

"I need to see you." That's what Dad said on the phone, his voice catching with improbable yet unmistakable emotion, like hearing a middle-of-the-night train whistle in Manhattan. "I need to see you, you and your brother. I want all of us together again, not like old times, of course. I'm not pretending there were old times to be had, though there were more old times than you care to remember, but how about new times, the three of us, you and me and Richard, and Andy, of course, you need to get to know Andy better. He's a sweet boy, a caring boy, a good boy, hardly a boy anymore but a young man, a young man who needs more family than just me. Whatever happened between you and us and me was hardly his fault."

"Um . . . "

"Please."

"Ahh . . . "

"Please."

Unlike his brother, Jamie had constructed a pragmatic relationship with the old man, even if the fix was rather leaky. They talked maybe six times a year, which seemed right for the both of them, and once in a while they shared a meal but always under an air of formality and obligation, as if documents were to be signed after dessert. Maybe Jamie would have preferred a closer bond with his dad—we all have our optative moments—but in his heart he understood that the man was ill-equipped for the task. Being a good and attentive father was neither in his nature nor in his nurture, and that was fine, even a relief as he became older and feebler and there was no reciprocal pressure on Jamie to be a good and attentive son. Jamie didn't suffer over the relationship, not like Richard. Plus Jamie had his mother. Isabel quite obviously favored her youngest, who was the spitting image of her own adored brothers and a happy reminder of her scrappy male-dominated childhood, right down to her own mannish mother, a swimmer of some renown. Yes, Isabel saw in Jamie a certain charm she admired (whereas Richard just exhausted her) and with this maternal affection securely in pocket, Jamie the boy often preferred his father's absence, not only as a means to spend more time with Mom, but also as a means to a greater end, which were those novels he admired from an early age, first as mysterious totems with a strange, tangible mass, their smell and touch evocative of stubble and cigarettes, all those words inside with their slow hatchings—d-o-g in *Ampersand*, h-o-u-s-e in *The Bend of Light*—until whole paragraphs were born into meaning, their exact significance unclear but the hope of significance present in their cries and squirms, in all those paragraphs and all those pages that pointed both to the future and to the past, the length growing longer as Jamie hit his teens and imagined writing a ten-page term paper fifty times over—what Herculean effort lay bundled in those books, his father's quiet yet aggravated labor, and when Jamie in his late teens, early twenties, sat down and read all the books, they were better than any bullshit father-son bonding even if he only grasped half of what was being said, which became clearer over subsequent rereadings and opened up deeper understandings and engendered a different kind of awe—how funny and smart his father could be, how human, how moral, even after he carelessly broke Mom's heart and rubbed all their noses in his bastard namesake, regardless, the books, these amazing books, they spoke to Jamie and he knew they would continue to speak to him, the author a far greater father than the man. Plus the residual fame helped with a certain kind of girl.

"Come and visit, please," his father said. "I'm feeling . . . like dust."

"Like dust?"

"You know what I mean."

"Um—"

"I've never asked for much."

That's true, Jamie thought, and you never gave much either. Of all the Dyers, I knew and know Jamie the best. Friendship was imprinted upon us from the start, despite our obvious differences. We were born five months apart (me first) and were nurtured side by side by adoring mothers who embraced their youngest extra tight, though, more important, our nannies were from the same Caribbean island. There are photo albums filled with pictures of Jamie and me in Central Park, at the beach in Southampton, at the zoo holding hands. I was always taller than everyone, until ninth grade, when I stopped growing and soon became the shortest. We matriculated through the same schools in the same years and part of our education was learning that, like our fathers, we could be friends without all the fuss. We were probably closest in fifth grade, when Jamie briefly flirted with my Transformers obsession (I worshipped Megatron), but by upper school it was obvious that he was destined for cooler things, and with each matriculation our relationship became more asymmetrical, so that by the time we finished with Yale our years together had a funhouse-mirror effect. I was the type of student who reinvented himself with each new school, never satisfied with my status as both person and peer. I took the change of environment as an opportunity to fine-tune my persona, until junior year abroad, where I hit upon earnest dilettante and returned from Paris newly found. I graduated from Yale with a degree in English literature, my senior essay focusing on A. N. Dyer and the kidnapping of identity. It received a passing grade. But Jamie was one of those rare exotics who emerged fully formed, without pretense, it seemed. Everything was always possible for him, so why bother changing. From an early age he stood apart as the most striking in any group, man, woman, or child, blessed with perfect skin and mink-brown eyes and a smile that revealed crowded incisors but crowded in a way that Walt Whitman would have celebrated. You might have guessed he had some Cherokee blood. He was the first to swim in the ocean, the first to ride a ten-speed, the first to break his arm. Parents called him wicked, though they all adored him, teachers included. Jamie was the mirror that brought back the most alluring aspects of youth and everybody wanted to see themselves in his glow. A day in his company invariably produced uncalculated adventure: start in Chinatown searching for fireworks and end up in Queens watching a cockfight with three Chinese kids and a Russian switchblader named Stahn. I myself found these adventures exhausting (and always frightening), but for Jamie it was just another Saturday afternoon. Nothing was out of the ordinary, certainly not a cemetery in the middle of the night.

The almost full moon shone against the snow and created a drift of ghostly light. The last time Jamie was here, the trees were doing their best advertisement for autumn in Vermont. He had stood on that hill and watched his old girlfriend, his first real girlfriend, get planted into the ground. It was like Sylvia was a seed and cemeteries were gardens in reverse. Her daughters, Delia and Clover, had painted flowers and butterflies on the coffin, sentiments of *I'll Never Forget You*, and *I'll Miss You*, and *Love* and *Peace* in heartbreaking purple and green, a family portrait done on the lid—the girls, the house, the horses, the dog, Mom and Dad standing hand in hand—the backdrop of Green Mountains rendered by Sylvia herself over the course of a week in August. It seemed a shame to bury such a lovely thing. Nearly everyone was crying as two friends played "We Bid You Goodnight" on mandolin and violin. Delia and Clover leaned against their father like ponytailed two-by-fours holding up an unsteady wall. Jamie tried not to stare. Ed Carne did not like him. Jamie knew this because Ed told him so. "I don't like you," he said. "I don't like you being here, I don't like what you and Sylvia are doing, but this is her call, and whatever makes her happy, you know." At 12:01 P.M. Jamie started to film, discreetly, he hoped. The coffin would stand as the final shot.

"Me going into the earth," Sylvia had said.

"You going into the earth," Jamie had said.

But here he was, six months later, checking for a sprout.

Jamie sat in the minivan, waiting on Myron Doty, who was late, but who could begrudge a man named Myron Doty, particularly when the man resembled the Myron Doty type, unimagined until the moment of introduction. Myron operated a ski lift in the winter and buried bodies in the summer. "I take 'em up. I take 'em down. I'm cold when they go up and I'm warm when they go down." Jamie liked Myron, but then again Jamie provided favorable weather conditions for people like Myron to thrive, much like the panhandle of Florida. During our sophomore year I remember when Jamie quit painting (he was quite talented) and picked up a video camera instead. Almost instantly his weekly Sunday night Ecce Homo movies attracted a cult following, the screenings migrating from dorm room to coffee shop to midnight showings at the York on Broadway. His piece on Lord God, the New Haven street preacher/celebrity impersonator, created a minor stir around campus. Was this exploitation of a poor deluded black man or a happy vehicle for creative self-expression? Who knew and who cared, because it was funny and it was real and soon after Jamie found a white actor to play Lord God and he did a shot-for-shot remake and spliced the two together, like a Siamese double feature. More outrage followed—this was Yale, after all—but the movie became a hit on the festival circuit and even won an award at Telluride. For a brief moment Jamie Dyer, filmmaker son of the reclusive novelist, was the school's most famous undergrad, until an actress took his place. During his senior year Jamie began to investigate the rougher neighborhoods around New Haven in search of similar characters sporting harder truths. He had this vision of a reenacted documentary titled *The Pin Tumblers*, using a Yale lock as his visual metaphor, but somewhere in the process, maybe when he saw that teenager get stabbed or watched that mother stare at her crying baby, stare without doing anything, something in him shifted, something infinitesimal yet essential— a matter of perspective, I suppose—and whatever life Jamie was trying to capture became stuck in his own head. He started to consider himself a professional witness, a type of superhero bystander, powerless yet unblinking. To me it seemed he was overcompensating for his natural optimism, which he distrusted. The films became darker. Fewer and fewer people attended those Sunday night screenings. I remember once telling him I no longer understood the point.

"What do you mean?" he said.

"I just watched ten dogs get euthanized and for what reason?"

"What reason? Maybe because it happens."

"But to what end? It's not cathartic, it's just sad. Toss in some narrative. Interview the ASPCA guy. Give us a sense of his job, his daily routine, his coping in the face of all that death. Denounce the practice. I don't know, but say something I can hang my hat on."

"But that's a lie."

"No," I said. "That's life without the *f*."

"I know what you can do with that *f*."

"I'm almost serious," I said.

"Almost, huh? The safety of qualifiers. So what do you suggest, Philip, that we follow this guy home, that we see him make dinner, feed his kids, walk his own dog, see him wake up the next morning and start his day all over again? Is that what you require, oh audience? Because that feels ridiculous to me, feels like a device, a filter, even worse, a manipulation. Should we also follow the dogs on the street, or in their loving homes, humanize them as well? I'm not looking for art here. I want the opposite. I want the world without the person behind the camera constructing the scene. This is how dogs die, period."

"Charming," I said, lighting a Gauloises.

Jamie sighed and packed a bowl. "You know that famous photograph from Vietnam, the one of the soldier shooting the guy in the head, like the war photo of all war photos. It was taken by this guy Eddie Adams and he captured the exact moment the trigger was pulled. *Boom.* These two men, one in profile, in uniform, middle-aged, the other in full view, in casual wear, young—it's almost like a wayward son meeting his disappointed father—anyway, those two men are forever connected by that bullet. An absolutely iconic image, almost beautiful in its true expression of horror. But do you know there's a video as well? An NBC News crew filmed the whole thing, from almost the same exact angle, but there's nothing iconic about that fucking footage, nothing artful about that man getting shot in the head, no innate drama, no arche- typal story, just a cap-gun-like snap followed by the guy falling to the ground, a brief fountain of blood spraying from his head. Whatever sense of timelessness is destroyed in four seconds flat. It's just plain horrible." Jamie lit the pipe, the act carrying a certain native intensity, as though the smoke told the story of prehistoric man. "Look," he said, after exhaling, "my goal is to fight that easy art-making instinct. Peo- ple die. People suffer. This is how they die. This is how they suffer. It's unspeakably small yet unspeakably big."

"But the 'art' of that photograph is pretty effective," I offered.

Jamie disagreed. "The 'art' of that photograph plays into our voy- euristic inhumanity, to artistically empathize with the horror, to transfer all our own dread into the image, turning a person's death into a personal metaphor."

Despite the college-worn earnestness, I did understand the motiva- tion: the almost incandescent urge for the dreadful thing. When you are a decent person and you have grown up safe and comfortable, with parents who themselves have grown up safe and comfortable, in New York, no less, the Upper East Side of New York, no less, you often find yourself admiring the poor and desperate as if they are somehow more honest, more legitimate, than your tribe, Buddhists to your Capitalists, and you want to prove yourself conscious with a capital C by dipping into hardship—lower—into degradation—lower—into self-abasement. There is liberal guilt and there is liberal sin, where you go slumming, the most cheerful of vagrants. I know I was guilty of this. The stories I wrote in my creative writing classes always gravitated toward seedy locales, dive bars and trailer parks, with low-down folk in the dirtiest of circumstances. Ugliness seemed to signify emotional authenticity. Half of my characters had problems with heroin, and I had never seen heroin before but please give me a hit of that tragedy so I might swim in more human waters. This desire thankfully passed after graduation, when genuineness was no longer an issue for debate. The concrete had hardened. But Jamie, he became worse, turning into a tourist with forensic intent. He started to travel to ridiculously dangerous places and videotape whatever he came across. The siege of Sarajevo. The red-light district of Mumbai. The civil wars in Algeria and Sri Lanka and Sierra Leone. The everything in Palestine. Why did he do this? Maybe he was rebelling against his father. This, right here, this is the real world, Dad. This is true tragedy. Or maybe he was rebelling against his own artistic tendencies, which tended toward the glib and too clever by half. Nobody was sure what the point was, least of all Jamie. He didn't work for the press; he didn't ask questions; he didn't pursue stories; he just shot video like he was on vacation in Venice, hours and hours of video, animals, children, women and men, trees on fire, houses in ruin. Every few months a box of videotapes arrived in New York and his roommates added it to the stack in his otherwise empty room, Jamie Dyer growing in cardboard form. What are you going to do with all this stuff? was a regular question, and Jamie would just shrug. He had no plans to expose these miseries to the less miserable. He even turned down a few news agencies that were interested in his Darfur footage. His mother begged him to stop. You're thirty . . . thirty-four . . . thirty-eight . . . forty-one, enough of this lunacy. What could he tell her, that it made him feel something in his gut, as though feelings were a rare substance formed only in places of high pressure and heat?

A *rap-rap-rap* on the minivan's window.

Jamie startled, then smiled. It was Myron.

"You almost scared me to death."

"Just trying to drum up business," Myron said. "Me late?"

"Not really."

"I feel late." Myron slid into the passenger seat and proceeded to remove his gloves, his hat, his left shoe, his left sock, his hands enclosing his left foot, his toes like a nest of deformed baby mice. "Once you get frostbite you always got frostbite," he said.

"When did you get frostbite?"

"Shit, I don't have frostbite, thank Christ, but you gotta stay on top of it." Myron Doty was a twice-divorced, thrice-incarcerated father of three who carried a certain nobility of failure that seemed passed down from a long line of disreputable Doty men, probably all the way back to the *Mayflower*.

"How're things?" Jamie asked.

"Fine, as in fine print, as in always read the."

"What happened?"

"I'm not privy to all the details yet."

"Good winter though?"

"Winter is winter. You been running through the high grasses?"

Jamie handed over his half-smoked joint.

Myron cleared a path in his beard. "I will tell you I'm ready for the living to return to the dead. Don't need to see another fucking skier, with his hollering and his whooping. It's like I'm stuck on an assembly line manufacturing kick-ass fun." Myron took five quick hits, pinkie splayed like he was sipping hot tea, then he put his sock and shoe back on. "You think your project worked?"

"Hope so. Reminds me." Jamie handed over an envelope, the other half of the agreed-upon sum, which Myron counted, smiling like the cash was a real lifesaver, though his eyes twinkled with the opposite impulse. "You ready?" Jamie asked.

"Yup."

Back outside, into air made material by breath, they crossed the road and stopped by Myron's truck, where Myron handed Jamie a flashlight and a shovel and grabbed for himself a bigger flashlight and a better shovel. They started up the unplowed road, aptly named Cemetery Road. The earth seemed lit by the television moon and tonight's episode was a doozy about the wackiest kind of grave robbers. Every footfall broke through a crust of melt and freeze. Only the taller headstones poked through the snow like something forgotten, and Jamie had the sensation of apocalyptic doom, of backyard archeology below his feet, tricycles and soccer balls, Frisbees lost, a place where everybody was once a child.

"That strong pot?" Myron asked.

Jamie nodded.

"Guess I'm really fucking stoned then."

Jamie gave vapory shape to an uncertain sigh. Then he heard the opening riff of "Whole Lotta Love"—one of his all-time favorites—and after a pause where Robert Plant seemed to whisper in his ear *You need coolin', baby, I'm not foolin'* Jamie snapped back and recognized his ringtone. "Just my phone," he confirmed out loud, in case Myron was in danger of floating away. It was Richard, and he was on a tear. "Like you said he called and asked me to come home, like my home isn't my home, like I'm living a make-believe life or something. Come home. What an asshole. I should have hung up right then. Why do I have to be the better person? I know, I know, it's not about him, right, it's about me, about what's healthy for me in the long run, but to make that kind of phone call when he's an old man and it's too late for anything, you know, too late for me to scream at him, to be functionally pissed, it doesn't seem fair."

Jamie was accustomed to these rants. His brother was most comfortable when angry, preferring those depths where the world squeezed. God forbid if you were stuck in line with him; then again, he moved things along nicely. Jamie only half-listened as he trudged through the snow and admired the stars above. A random line of poetry dropped into his head—*The stars are mansions built by nature's hand*—its origin unknown. Regardless of these distractions, he could hear the hurt his brother could never hide. Sometimes Jamie wondered whether his own happy childhood was partly to blame.

"Why are you breathing so hard?" Richard asked. "Where the hell are you?"

"In Vermont."

"Where in Vermont?"

"Outside, walking through snow."

"At two in the morning?"

It was typical of his brother not to notice his side of the offense. "Yes," Jamie said, "at two in the morning, thank you, and it's cold, and I'm tired, and I'm in a graveyard visiting Sylvia Weston."

"Sylvia Weston?"

"Yes."

"Sexy Sylph died?"

"Yes."

"Jesus, how?"

"Breast cancer," Jamie said, the shovel and flashlight awkward in his other hand. "I don't really want to talk about it right now."

"I always liked her. She was my favorite of all your girlfriends."

"Mine too."

"Fucking terrible," Richard muttered. "Between Sylvia Weston and Charlie Topping. Anyway, I'm calling to tell you that I am going to go to New York, arriving late Monday, with the whole family. The kids will miss some school but I figure they can finally meet their grandfather. He didn't sound good on the phone, out of it, you know, not all there. Sounded kind of desperate. It was weird. Certainly not the dad I remember. You need to come home, he kept on saying, like he had swallowed someone else's voice. But I was hoping, I don't know, I was hoping we might catch up as well. I know Candy and Chloe and Emmett would love to see you. But we can talk details later. How many years did you and Sylph date?"

"What?" Jamie asked, struggling over a snowdrift.

"How long did you date Sylvia?"

"Almost three years," he said, though the truth was a little over two.

"Can't believe she died."

"I know."

"She was so sweet. Dad had such a crush on her. We all did."

While Jamie was always considered to be the more sensitive of the Dyer boys, Richard the rougher, mainly because of his teenage years of fighting and bullying, his general troublemaking, in truth Richard was the one who teared up easily, who consistently found the world unfair, who, especially after having children, flashed almost daily on images of Emmett and Chloe's demise, terrified and helpless, seeing them in planes falling, in bird-flu epidemics, in futile moments of save-me-Dad-please, Richard doing the eggshell walk across fate, while Jamie, forever half-stoned and fortunate, poked his fingers into the sores, like a scientist more curious about the symptoms than the cure.

"Give my condolences to the family," Richard said.

"What? Oh yeah sure." And with that the brothers hung up.

Up ahead Myron planted his shovel into the snow. "Here we are."

"Positive?"

"As positive as a poorly educated guess."

The two of them started digging through a winter's worth of weather, like airy dirt, Jamie mused, descendant of clouds. Yes indeed, I'm stoned, he thought. After shoveling up great wedges of this non-earth earth, they scraped against something hard. A headstone. SYLVIA CARNE · MOTHER · WIFE · SISTER · DAUGHTER. Jamie knew her primarily as *Girlfriend*. She was perhaps the most beautiful girl he had ever known, Sylvia Weston, blond but not obviously blond, with permanently chapped lips and a flinty nose, her smile the smile of someone who has found you first in a game of sardines. Sylph, as she was known in those days, was a bit of a hippie. She ate all her food using a single wooden spoon and laughed at herself for doing so, a raspy laugh, a great-grandmother's laugh, Oma of some sturdy Nordic stock, Jamie would tease, as they smoked pot in those surrounding New Hampshire woods. Even then Jamie understood that her face was a face he should remember, kissing her forehead, her neck, tossing all those details forward like Hansel with his bread crumbs, so that decades later he might find his way back to her Finesse-scented hair and her love-bead necklace and her peasant skirt exposing a single black freckle on a sea of inner amber. Jamie and Sylvia dated until the summer after graduation. They loved each other yet were realistic and put their relationship on hold for college (she was heading to Middlebury), which soon became permanent except for a few brief but never very happy returns.

Many of my Exeter classmates still shake their heads at the mention of Sylvia Weston. She's like an old high school injury that flares up during semi-erotic play. Back then we all knew she was having intercourse, more than intercourse, every kind of course with Jamie, from sophomore spring until graduation, sex and more sex, Jamie and Sylvia holding hands in the quad, yet we knew, the sweaty undercurrents of those public displays. They were magical in that way, adults among us children, the hopeful examples of what we might achieve if we ever fell in love.

Myron hit the coffin earth.

It was last July when she tracked Jamie down. He was in Caracas, in its outlying child-infested slums, when a mutual friend managed to get in touch with him. Sylvia Weston needs to talk, that was the message, and Jamie's first reaction was, Oh shit, she's pregnant. "I swear that's what I thought," he told her when he finally reached her by phone, "like my sperm was lying in wait all these years, a sleeper cell suddenly activated."

"Funny."

"I was a teenager again."

"If only."

"Well, yeah," Jamie said, unsure of the subtext.

"It's amazing I never did get pregnant," Sylvia said. "We were hardly careful."

"Totally."

"You realize most of our fooling around happened outside the comfort of bed."

"We made due."

"Yeah, all over the place."

"The Latin room," he said.

"Oh jeez, the Latin room. And upstairs in the library."

"Don't think I've ever been more scared. You realize next May is our—"

She—"I know"—interrupted before Jamie could say "twenty-fifth reunion."

"I don't think I can go," he told her.

"Yeah, me neither."

"Really? I would have thought—"

And that's when she told him. She spoke in unflinching terms, well versed in the broader conversation, its grimmer meaning, to the point of annoying Jamie, as if she owed him some shudder and tears, as if he were still the first instead of the hundredth, the thousandth, the old boyfriend in the far back row of her life. He offered her words of support, which sounded hollow, then he offered her a few battlefield sentiments, which she brushed away with a single statement of fact: "I'm going to die soon."

"Oh, baby, I'm sorry."

"Me too," she said, hinting at the strain behind all this restraint.

"So so sorry. If there's anything I can do . . . "

"Actually, that's why I'm calling. I need help with something."

"Of course, anything."

"I have this idea for a video project that maybe only you would appreciate." She went on to explain how she wanted to document herself answering the question, How are you? every day at exactly 12:01 P.M. right up until the very end. "I know it sounds ridiculous but it's something I want to do. Just answer that question with complete honesty."

"It's not ridiculous at all," Jamie said.

"And I want you to direct it."

"Me?"

"It won't take up too much time," she said with sobering common sense.

"It's not that, it's just that you don't need me. It's basic stuff. Any video—"

"Please."

"I'll just be in the way, Sylph."

Silence on the other end.

"Sylph?"

"I just really want you to do this," she said.

"I'm in Venezuela."

"We can catch up."

"Did my mother put you up to this?" he said, hearing his narcissism too late.

"Jamie, I'm dying, okay, and I just want you to help me, that's all."

And of course he said yes—how could he not—and within thirty-six hours had gotten himself back to New York and in another twelve hours found himself in Stowe, Vermont. He took a room at a local motel and for the most part stayed away from the family and spent his days hiking and swimming and sleeping, and more sleeping, and reading, rereading a few of his father's books, even *Eloise and Tom*, which had always been his least favorite though this time he quite enjoyed it, what with its bitter takedown tour of Tuscany by Sebastian and Louise, the non-eponymous main characters, who by the end confess a long-standing hatred of their best friends. All in all, an aspect of vacation settled into those strife-free days, except for the late mornings when Jamie would rendezvous with Sylvia and at the predestined, God-knows-the-reason time would push RECORD and feed her the line, "How are you?"

Sylvia: "I'm all right."

Sylvia: "I'm fine."

Sylvia: "Okay."

Sylvia: "Hanging in there."

Sylvia: "Good, thanks, and you?"

Day in and day out, she gave these standard answers to that most banal of questions, and Jamie began to get annoyed. Because he had expected something more, a philosophy, a struggle toward the profound. Was this her version of irony? He didn't think so. That wasn't in Sylvia's nature. Plus she was sincerely dying—her face, long ago his lodestar, was collapsing under its own diminishing weight, her eyes growing denser yet brighter, white dwarves of luminous demise. It seemed Jamie was stuck watching from the lowly earth, wondering what any of this meant. Why did she bring him here? Did she still love him? What was she really saying?

"I'm good."

"All right, thanks."

"Good, and you?"

He tried to steep the question—"How"—with as much significance —"are"—as possible—"you?"

"Pretty decent."

"Getting by, you know."

A month passed and he considered going off script and blindsiding her with "Are you scared?" or "Do you believe in God?" or "Can I kiss you?" but come 12:01 P.M. he'd lose his nerve and stay on message.

"Super, thanks."

"No complaints."

That's what Sylvia said a few days before she took that nasty turn. The whole family was at the Trapp Family Lodge, the Green Mountains standing in for the Alps. It was a special event where a few of the original cast members from *The Sound of Music* had gathered for a weekend with the relatives of their factual counterparts. There was Heather Menzies (Louisa) and Charmian Carr (Liesl) and Duane Chase (Kurt), even Daniel Truhitte (Rolf), who took Charmian's hand, to the delight of everyone. These former child stars seemed swollen with age, as if stung by a very large bee, and Jamie found the whole thing pleasantly meta. After filming Sylvia, he wandered about, and when he saw little Gretl (Kym Karath) signing autographs, he lingered for a moment and tried to find in her eyes the memory of sitting in his living room during the holidays and watching *The Sound of Music*, a true story, his mother always stressed. "They escaped Austria during the war and now live in Vermont, in a Tyrolean-style lodge," she told him and his brother, amazed by the tale, and of course by the songs too, which she knew by heart. Jamie was around six when he first saw Maria open her arms and spin in those hills, and he remembered thinking, These people are real, this all happened, a hundred percent true, even as he recognized Brigitta as Penny from *Lost in Space*. Was Mom disappointed that Dad never surprised the crowd by sweetly warbling that famous, age-old Austrian folk song? Oh, the days when families fled the Nazis together. Before Jamie knew it, he found himself in the front of the line, and Gretl (Kym) looked up and smiled, a black marker perched over a picture of her younger dirndled self. "How are you?" she said, and Jamie froze, the question snapping around his ankle, forever ensnaring him.

With the snow cleared, Myron banged his shovel on the turf until he received a hollow reply, after which he bent down and removed the square piece of sod that camouflaged a wooden trapdoor. Attached on the other side was a rope, which descended into that dark, surgical hole. It was only six feet but might as well have gone a mile underground. Myron pointed his flashlight down. The sides were braced with wood.

"Hardly a bulge," he said, admiring his work.

Over the last few months Jamie had had misgivings over this particular direction in the project, especially since this part was his own idea and done without permission from Sylvia or her family. It was meant to be a coda. A recapitulation. But as he stood over that hole, he lurched into full-blown What-the-fuck-have-I-done terrain. How did this ever seem like a good idea? Jamie remembered when she became bedridden and talked to her family with terrible, if sometimes incoherent, purpose, as if the rest of existence were last-minute stuff, and he sneaked in a few minutes before 12:01 P.M., sheepish yet determined to fulfill her wishes, and the girls dutifully moved aside, and big Ed glared, and Sylvia, even in her heavily opiated state, understood the time and she sat up, curling a stray lock of hair behind her left ear, just like she did in high school, her secret message to him, but what was she saying now, as she gathered up her breath and answered the question with force-of-will clarity, "I am fine, thank you, and how are you?" maintaining the pose until he stopped recording and exhaustion dropped her back onto the pillow—Jamie, near tears, knew he had to continue with this project, just for a little while longer, just to keep her, if not alive, then not totally dead.

Five days later she was gone.

By then Jamie had called a friend who shot nature documentaries, and he asked him about filming in dark, confined spaces over an extended period—"For a weird time-lapse thing I'm working on"—and the friend told him he had the perfect rig, a reconfigured Sony PDW-700 with all the bells and whistles, enclosed in a weatherproof housing with an exterior Li-ion polymer battery and lights—"We call it the crab pot: load it, lock it, leave it. It's how we did the hibernating-bear thing." The friend overnighted the camera to Vermont, and two days after the funeral Jamie returned to the cemetery with his new pal Myron. The first night they dug a hole and built a shaft over the coffin; the second night they carefully sawed away the mountains on the lid and replaced it with a piece of plexi; the third night they installed the crab pot. After a few tests to set the lighting and frame the, well, frame the face properly—Jamie could barely look—they returned Sylvia Carne to darkness, except for six seconds a day.

"You need to check on it once in a while," Jamie told Myron.

Myron saluted.

"You sure you can do this?"

"Absolutely."

But the question was more self-directed, and over the following months, Jamie thought about paying Myron in full and leaving the camera and letting its memory run down to nothing. What an excellent find centuries from now: these crazed Americans even filmed themselves dead. The initial How-are-you? footage consisted of seventy-four consecutive responses, time- and date-stamped from late July to early October. In total, it was less than eight minutes of film, and Jamie had yet to watch a second. It didn't seem complete to him. Not yet. He wanted the entire loss. At least this was his rationalization, that he wanted to peer into the absolute truth, to once again push boundaries. This is what happens, he would have told you, this is the final, not-so-stupid answer to that most banal but brutal question. But if you looked closer, you might have noticed a darker grip to his eyes, as if he was hauling a heavier load within. How are you? I'm confused, baby. I'm barely surviving. I'm a fucking mess. He moved back to New York and rented his own place in Cobble Hill, landing a job teaching videography at the New School, thanks to an old professor from Yale. He reconnected with friends (we even had a drink). He dated around. He thrilled his mother with his mere presence and managed an occasional meal with his father. Jamie did all of these things in hopes of— well, he wasn't sure except to say that when the hour and the minute were in the range of 12:01 P.M., he hoped he might give that lifting darkness a decent response.

Myron grabbed the rope. He waited for Jamie to grab hold too.

What sort of witchy thing had she done to him?

On three they pulled.

"I'll come back in the spring and fill in the hole," Myron said.

The camera was heavier than Jamie remembered.

"You have to promise to send me a copy," Myron said.

As he pulled, Jamie had the sensation of bringing up something from the bottom of the sea, a trap loaded with creatures, crustaceans with multiple legs crawling all over the cage, bottom-feeders feeding on thoughts of his father, his mother, his brother and half brother, the familial bait of one-way entrances, the forty-three years with nothing to show, nothing to feel, but the recorded evidence of this suffering world, right down to the first woman he ever loved, dying and dead and—

The camera reached the surface.

Once free and clear, Myron aimed his flashlight down into the hole, but before his curiosity could be answered, Jamie swatted his hand. The flashlight, knocked loose, landed with a thud on the Plexiglas, briefly swaying back and forth, its sideways beam seesawing over paint still bright and vibrant: part of a small house, smoke curling up from its chimney.

II.iii

I T WAS WELL PAST EIGHT when I showed up at 2 East 70th Street carrying two suitcases and an old backpack, a weary traveler of twenty blocks. The doorman announced my arrival via intercom—"Philip Topping is here"—but the permission to rise took longer than was comfortable. I stood there, forcing a smile, thinking I should have called ahead and reconfirmed, while the doorman—Ron was his name—waited for the answer like a noncommissioned officer serving the higher ranks, prepared to stop even the best-dressed bullet. Across the street was the Frick, and I surveyed its exterior as if appreciating the opportunity to reacquaint myself with its architecture. Truth is, I've always loved the place, with its collection of Turners and Titians and Vermeers. It's a grand home but a small museum, its economy multiplying its pleasure, much like a play without an intermission. Each visit yields a new favorite: Bellini's *St. Francis*, I'll think, then months later, no, no, no, El Greco's *Purification of the Temple*. Right now Jan van Eyck's *Virgin and Child* holds the title, its finely considered details, like the brocade Oriental carpet, the crisp backdrop of a cityscape, the blond Christ child with his round belly, like my own boy at that age, Ashley taking on the bodeful Mary role, they restore me. Art seems to be the only thing that makes me happy nowadays—*happy* being the wrong word, less miserable, perhaps. Staring at that van Eyck I can feel my eyes peering into the murk of creation, at the glimmer down near the lower depths. We all live. We all die. Even the great ones. Funny how that can be a comfort. The shifty-looking donor in the painting might as well be me. Tonight the Frick was in party mode. Town cars shadowed the properly parked Civics and Corollas, and a clutch of young smokers clouded the front door, costumed in high

Belle Époque style: men in top hats and waistcoats, long white gloves for the ladies in silk evening dresses trimmed with embroidery and a velvet fringe. I was once one of these people. I hate them now.

After seven minutes Doorman Ron got the okay and let me up.

"Thank you," I said.

I would have waited a month.

The Dyers had lived here for as long as I could remember, a sprawling duplex on the sixth and seventh floors; the elevator opened onto a private vestibule, the orchid-themed wallpaper losing its hold along the edges, like a slow change of seasons. Before I could decide between knocking and ringing, the front door swung open and there was Gerd Sanning. Her grin was both polite and distrustful, like a character in an Ibsen play receiving an unexpected visitor. "Mr. Topping," she said.

"Please, Gerd, call me Philip. It's been a long time."

"Yes, yes, yes," she said, flushed. "Sorry to keep you waiting." She was dressed in a white T-shirt and pajama bottoms, obviously ready for bed, though I always imagined her sleeping in the nude, on a bed of straw. Gerd was in her late thirties, blond and blue-eyed, of solid proportions, hardly a curve on that slab, yet despite this, she managed a sneaky allure, as if within that plain box lay a wonderful ergonomic piece of Scandinavian design. She had begun her career as the baby nurse for Andy but then evolved into nanny, into cook, into secretary, and finally into official woman of the house, a sort of secular feminine spirit. At Buckley she attended every one of Andy's school functions: the plays, the performances, the athletic events, even the parent-teacher conferences. "She might as well be the mother," Andrew insisted, all matter, no fact. I think this employed maternity made Andy self-conscious, and brought up the question, What did she do for love and what did she do for money? Was there a line? The feudalism of fourth grade in fifth gives way to latent capitalism.

"I'm sorry to hear about your father," Gerd said.

"Thank you."

"He was a very nice man."

We walked into the main entry. The parquet floor was long neglected, strips of wood cracked or missing, loosened by that first set of heavy-footed sons. I saw the curving staircase that stood in my mind as a prop for a series of stuntman falls, Jamie throwing himself down with annihilating grace—backward, forward, shot, stabbed—until Richard came along one day and decided to ride him like a sled and busted Jamie's chin on the bottom. I tried to recall when I was here last. Twenty years ago? Nothing much had changed except for the added burden of time, which colored the atmosphere with uncertain guilt, the furniture sitting about like characters in an Agatha Christie mystery. The divan in the living room looked particularly suspicious. We all know how memories of a place can tower over us but when revisited decades later might barely reach our knees, yet here was the opposite effect: what once struck me as normal-size now struck me as grand. Upstairs had four bedrooms with three bathrooms and an attic's worth of closets, while downstairs had a living room, an eat-in kitchen, a maid's room, where Gerd lived, a pantry that led into a dining room, and finally, down a short hall with a bathroom on one side and a wet bar on the other, behind a thick mahogany door, A. N. Dyer's inner sanctum, with wood paneling and built-in bookcases, an Aubusson rug, two club chairs posed around a fireplace, and an old partner's desk, all these things conjured by his mother, who closed her eyes around the fantasy of being a writer and decorated the room accordingly. The apartment was her wedding present to Andrew and Isabel.

"Is he around?" I asked Gerd, peering down that hall.

"Yes, but he's working."

Did she notice the change in my posture, like a dog listening for his master?

"He doesn't like to be disturbed when he's working," she told me.

"Of course. I understand. I'm the same way with my writing."

"He's been working very hard lately. Too hard, if you ask me."

"Really?"

"He barely eats, barely bathes, barely leaves his desk. I'm forbidden from entering. I hate to think of the mess in there, and the smell. I've been trying to get him out and about, especially with Andy home, but he refuses, just stays in that room, typing away, even sleeps in there."

I was intrigued.

"If he refuses to see you, don't take it personally."

"I won't."

"Also if he gets mean for no good reason."

Gerd led me upstairs to my room. What with the late hour and with A. N. Dyer locked away in his study, my gothic mind imagined her ascending those steps with a torch in hand. I recalled the second-floor hallway as being chockablock with family photos, thanks to Isabel and her ever-present camera: Richard and Jamie hung salon-style, babies, teenagers, toddlers, on vacation, during holidays, the summers on the beach, the winters on the slopes, Andrew and Isabel making their rare appearance, Andrew always posing like his author's photo, as if he had only one look to give. I even had a place up there, posing with Jamie at our Exeter graduation, the two of us buddied together without conviction. Between the tremor of my smile, the fire of my acne, the tidal wave of my hair, I resembled the Lisbon earthquake, whereas Jamie was Candide. But I was touched to be included. Or once included. Only their silhouettes remained. Isabel must've taken them.

I asked if Andy was here.

"No," Gerd said, sounding pained, "he's met a girl."

"I think I've met this girl. Jeanie Something," though I knew Spokes.

"She's older," Gerd mentioned.

"I know."

"Not sure if I trust her."

"Luckily Andy's not looking to invest money with her."

Gerd stopped in front of Richard's old room. "I hope this is all right."

It was scrubbed of all things Richard except for the bureau, which was almost entirely spackled in Wacky Pack stickers. I gently recalled the era of Crust Tooth Paste and Rinkled Wrap Aluminum Fool. It was like a piece of folk art.

"This used to be my room," Gerd told me, "before Andy got older. He had terrible night terrors as a boy. Wake up shrieking and I'd have to run in and try to settle him down. He also sleepwalked, or crawled, like he was looking for something, something tiny but important, like a screw. He still does that, rarely now, thank goodness, but if you see him on his hands and knees just guide him back toward his room." As she talked, Gerd struck me as someone too accustomed to the whims of man, like Eve if she had arrived in Eden first and formed Adam from her own rib, but after a few weeks Adam abandoned her, and so she offered up another rib, without condition, and soon enough this second Adam disappeared as well, and so another rib was plucked and she stooped a little bit further hoping this one might take. She asked if I needed help unpacking.

"I'm good, thanks."

"Well, good night then," she said, tugging at her fingers.

I know some biographers—actually just one in particular and hardly a biographer but rather an opportunist who has spun herself intimate with this tale, which, while technically true, is true in the way the evidence of wind can be gathered by its effect on trees without ever stepping outside and feeling its force against your cheek, yet this person, watching from her closed window, wants you to imagine Gerd Sanning and A. N. Dyer intertwined in storm and stress, all because they lived under the same roof for all those years. But Gerd Sanning was no concubine. Her part in this tale is a hundred times more interesting.

After squaring away my clothes, I washed up and peeked into Jamie's old room. Most of the furniture was gone, replaced by cardboard file boxes piled high and arranged with an almost Stonehengean precision, as if on certain days the afternoon sunlight explained their meaning. While I was curious what was inside—there must have been fifty of them—I refrained from looking, but I did notice a specific year written on the side of each, the years stretching over six decades. I turned off the lights. I noticed that those glow-in-the-dark stars were still stuck to the ceiling, its Milky Way spelling FUCK YOU.

I went downstairs under the guise of a drink of water. The kitchen was one of those New York kitchens that predate the use of stainless steel and marble, and seem, in their lapsed luxury, almost quaint, as if a butter churn could have been in the corner. I opened a cabinet and found a glass, opened the fridge and found a pitcher, poured, and as I performed this basic task I suffered a brief but intense moment of crisis, puzzling over what I was doing here and what I had done, panging for my wife and kids, mourning for my father and his long-drawn-out death, missing my mother, cringing over Bea, absurd Bea, my huge screw-up, in general indulging in a wave of hopelessness and helplessness, the everythinglessness of my current existence. I thought about calling a friend, but it was late and being separated from my wife I suddenly realized my woeful lack of social connections. It was a pitiful drink of water.

As I stepped back into the vestibule an inevitable force drew me down the short hall toward the closed door. I could hear the typewriter going, the keys never pausing, like how writers write in the movies, typing and typing, never napping between sentences, or staring at their own faces in the mirror, or picking up random books and reading random passages, feeling briefly inspired and then mortally defeated. The temptation to knock was undone when I touched the door and sensed the heat of my own infatuation. Step away, Philip, the great man knows you're here, and obviously he has no desire to greet you. Either way I had no problem being the eavesdropper, imagining in that persistent clatter the opening lines to *Ampersand:*

An alarm sounded, shrill and insistent, and we boys of Moulder rushed from our rooms for the nearest exit and once outside lined up as a rank shadow of our dormed self. Some had smudged burnt cork on their faces though they didn't extend the theatrics by coughing. Absolute silence was the rule. Others, athletes mostly, imagined themselves caught mid-shower and emerged fully lathered and covered in just a towel. Newbies were forced to brave the outdoors in skivvies alone. As always, a few glum students recused themselves from all comedy. I myself wore my father's WWII gasmask, a prized possession rarely employed for its original use. Then there were Stimpson, Harfield, Matthews, and Rogin, our prefects, their names already incorporated into Shearing legend. They stood at attention in front of their command with smoke billowing from their blazers. They were men on fire if fire were the most casual of elements. I remember thinking those smoke bombs in their pockets would ruin their clothes, and I think that's what impressed us most, their absolute dedication. Willetts the dorm master called roll. He refused to acknowledge the joke, as he did every year, a sign of his high good humor, and with all present and accounted for, he dismissed us with a limp salute. Thus ended the first fire drill of the school year.

I heard my name and for a moment wondered if A. N. Dyer had set an elaborate trap to catch me spying. I turned. It was just Andy home for the night. "I didn't know if I should interrupt," I tried to explain.

"He wouldn't hear you anyway," he said, grabbing at his pants like an overgrown toddler.

"Oh."

"So you're actually staying?"

"Not for long."

"Like upstairs?"

"You'll hardly know I'm there."

I followed him back into the main entry. His shirttail was untucked in a sort of a preppy mullet, and I wanted to reach forward and give his shoulders an affectionate squeeze, like any old teacher or family friend, to break through the distance and reconfirm our shared past. But his posture did not invite easy companionship. He seemed a veteran of— I don't know, adolescence, I suppose, which like all wars is particular to the combatant. I was closest with Andy when he was in my class, a sincere boy filled with nervous tics, always fiddling his fingers, always squinting even though he had perfect vision. Can you see this? I was always asking him. For most of fifth grade his number-one priority was learning how to juggle, which he did to stunning effect, thanks in part to my encouragement (I bought him these special beanbag balls). His blend of awkward grace and extroverted shyness led you to believe he might have a career in mime. As a teacher I was perhaps guilty of favoring him over the others. I gave him extra help and provided him with those spiral notebooks made for lefties and in general took on the role of father figure, since I knew his own father was not in tune with normal boyhood concerns. In some ways I was his best friend. Then he moved on to sixth grade and fell in love with Mrs. Hawes. They all fall in love with Mrs. Hawes.

"Did you really get fired from Buckley? I mean that's what I heard tonight."

It was obvious that Andy had been drinking.

"Sort of," I said.

"Why?"

"Sometimes you become unmoored."

"I heard it was a girl."

"A woman," I countered.

"And she like worked at J.Crew."

I imagined the *New York Post* publishing my daily humiliations.

"Sounds totally excellent," Andy said, swaying.

I tried changing the subject. "How about you? How's Exeter?"

"Was she cute?"

"The woman?"

"Yeah."

"Sure, she was cute," though *cute* was hardly the word unless used sardonically, like when Bea tied a necktie around my balls and asked if she should blow my nose. In that way, yes, she was cute. Very cute. But more than anything I was in terrible awe of her vampish, almost anachronistic youth, like a silent film star straddling me with her eyes. The truth is, sex can make you fall in love. It might not be the deepest love imaginable, but it's the kind of love I can grasp with both hands, even as I'm sinking. "What house are you in?" I asked, trying to steer Andy back to Exeter.

"She live nearby?"

I can't say I enjoyed the direction of this conversation.

"I'm not really sure," I said. She lived in Staten Island.

"And which J.Crew?"

"Um."

"Were you like her best client? Are there like a hundred pairs of chinos in your closet?"

I have to say it was hard to refuse this teenage admiration. "Where you been?" I asked.

"Nowhere interesting. Had some drinks, I bet you can tell, but just a few and I'm not drunk or anything, just buzzed on sparkling wine because I'm an idiot. I thought I'd be out later, thought I'd be out for the whole night. Dare to dream." He glanced toward the hall and its buffet of continuous typing. "You know he sleeps in there. Says his feet are too messed up for the stairs, and his breathing, you know, the up and down, the hassle of it, so he sleeps on the couch. Eats in there too, just sandwiches, cream cheese on white bread. Says his stomach can't handle color anymore. If Gerdie weren't here, he'd be homeless in this apartment. It's gotten that bad. I can't wait to get back to school and I hate school."

I nodded sympathetically. "I feel for you," I said. "It's impossibly hard, a father's decline. Because you both want to say so much but you're both so afraid of saying the same thing, something like, I hope I wasn't a terrible disappointment, or some variant on that theme. The only decent answer is a lie."

"Like with your dad?" Andy asked.

"Well, yeah."

"What'd you say to him when he was, like, I don't know, near the end?"

I wasn't expecting the question. "Um, I told him I loved him," I said.

"And that was a lie?"

"No, no, not at all."

"So what's the lie then?"

"That we weren't disappointed in each other, I guess."

"Sounds like too much unnecessary blame, you know."

"Well—"

"Death isn't a gift to complain about," Andy said, tugging at his hair as if testing its hold.

"You think death is a gift?"

"Kind of. Sure. Maybe *gift*'s the wrong word, maybe life is the gift, right, but death is like opening up the box and seeing what's inside, like the meaning part, what the dead give to those of us still alive. But I'm spewing. Spumanting," he said, grinning. "I just wanted to say I'm sorry about your dad."

"Thanks."

"I still have all the tin soldiers he gave me."

This interested me since I certainly remembered my father's collection preserved in the library in Southampton, shelves upon shelves of squadrons and legions and corps, a miniature world carefully displayed as if couch and chairs were disputed territory. Not even my normally indulgent mother let me touch them, which made me a frustrated Gulliver. These were toys, after all. "But not toys for kids," she told me. She always took my father's side, not out of agreement, it seemed, but out of maintaining some sense of balance, as if the world pressed hard on him. My father and his collections. Besides decoys and tin soldiers there were inkwells, and vintage mug shots, and books with unique bindings and/or rare fonts, and six meteorites of varying size, and my personal favorite, a steamer trunk filled with examples of fossilized rock, their surface cast with ancient insects and plant life, the occasional small fish. He once walked into an antiques store and spent the next five years tracking down Edwardian sporting medals. My mother embraced these eccentric accumulations, perhaps because otherwise he was so conventional, and if I were to sink into a favorite image of their life together it would be the two of them walking on the beach, my father in his blue Keds, my mother in her floppy straw hat, both looking down like heads of state discussing pressing matters, in this case the geopolitics of sea glass. My mother had jars of the stuff, gathered since she was a girl and organized by color: the greens and browns and whites and blues and the oh-so-rare reds and yellows. The pursuit seemed to fit her Protestant idea of repair, that something broken could become lovely again if given enough time and touch. In my teens I would sometimes tag along, mostly to escape my peers sunbathing and flirting on the beach. The three of us could walk for miles. I pictured us as a line of police officers, British for some reason, systematically searching the ground for the smallest of clues, a shell casing, a tear of fabric. Whenever my mother found a piece, she oohed like she had captured a sliver of firework. I think these were moments my father and I both collected. But as for those tin soldiers, they disappeared once Lucy entered the field of battle and insisted on redecorating the house. I never wondered what had become of them, till then. "Did he give you a lot?"

"Of what?"

"Tin soldiers."

"Sure, yeah." Andy glanced toward the stairs. "I should head up."

"You know if you ever want to talk about things."

"Like what?"

"I don't know. Your dad. Anything really."

Andy shrugged before starting up.

"Maybe in the morning I can quiz you on medieval history," I said.

"Oh jeez."

"Charlemagne. The Magna Carta. You remember the dates I hope."

Andy stopped halfway up the stairs. "Do fifth graders still read *Alice in Wonderland*?"

"Of course."

"And do they still memorize 'Father William'?"

"Absolutely, it's Buckley tradition."

" 'I am old, Father William, and my hair has become very white.' "

"That's right," I said.

Andy was never my best student.

He scurried up the rest of the stairs, hopefully in a better mood, and I wandered into the living room in search of a television and the panacea of late-night TV. Finding none and hearing unbridled whoops coming from the street below, I drifted to the window for my fill of distraction. Being New York–born, I'm a natural Peeping Tom. God bless that woman in the building across the street from my childhood bedroom who seemed allergic to shades, and God bless those binoculars gifted under the pretense of bird-watching. The Dyer living room had a nice view of Central Park, the trees still dormant, their bare canopy like a rendering in graphite. From this perch Richard and Jamie Dyer used to toss soggies on the people below, in particular on me when they were bored and in need of game. But I was a willing target. Never sure of my position between the rails of affection and disdain, I was just happy to be invited over, running down Fifth, wet clumps of toilet paper exploding around me.

Outside the Frick the cotillion of smokers had grown, a few of them talking anachronistically on cellphones. Their old-world couture improved their posture and I thought again of my mother, who put such tremendous stock in appearances and the power of personal grooming. She would have loved this sight, especially in people so young. To her all was fine in the world if you tried your best to look attractive. "I know it sounds silly," she would tell me, "but it rubs off." In her eyes you were likely depressed if you went a few days without shaving, if you let your hair grow loose around the edges. Holes in pants were grounds for an intervention, and God forbid if you put on a few pounds. Her daily toilet was analogous to church, her bath a baptism, her makeup table a confessional. It was often exhausting for her children, especially my sister, but she arrived at this philosophy genuinely, without pretense or motives of covering up the messy truth, except, that is, when she became sick. But even toward the end she remained well put together and was undeniably pleased by the weight loss. Good appearance was her core belief. I know my adolescence was practically hard on her as hormones split her handsome boy and turned him inside out. Home from Exeter and I could see the horror on her face (and perhaps the commiseration in my father's turning away). She bought me special soaps. She took me to a dermatologist, to a hairdresser. She sent me back to the orthodontist who had already tried to straighten my teeth in fifth grade. "Don't worry," she would tell me, ever the fixer, "we'll solve this." For a few weeks, a month, her handiwork might hold, but then—"Oh, honey"—I would return to my natural unruly state. It wasn't until my early twenties that I finally settled into my face, not bad-looking though nowhere near its earlier promise. I think it took a few years for my mother to recover from the head-on collision of my getting older.

Down below a young man emerged from the Frick; he was in white tie and gloves, a cane in one hand and an impressive fur cloak in the other. He gave his friends a bow, elegant even if exaggerated, and his aspect seemed both ironic and fully invested, as if he would die for the sake of a good pose. Even from this height I recognized him: the mustache curling at the ends, the hint of a goatee, the high-society Musketeer who was Comte Robert de Montesquiou. His portrait hangs in the Frick, *Arrangement in Black and Gold*, one of Whistler's less facile attempts, simple, austere in its palette, the subject emerging from a haze as if the paint had been mixed in an opium den. Montesquiou also famously inspired Proust, in his construction of Baron de Charlus, while Whistler took on the role of Elstir, the painter who sought to re-re-create the world. The Frick must have been having one of their *A la Recherche du Temps Perdu* parties. Every five years or so they choose this tired theme, and the benefit committee becomes giddy with their delicious inventiveness—we can serve madeleines!—and people raid attics and costume shops and in some cases employ stylists (in my day I went as Swann, though I still regret not going as Scott Moncrieff).

A horse carriage pulled up to the Frick and this—

"Andy?"

Startled, I spun around and saw A. N. Dyer standing in the doorway. Shirt unbuttoned to his navel, pants rolled up around his knees, he resembled a castaway.

"Not Andy, no, it's me, um, Andrew, Philip." I confused even myself.

"Philip?"

"Yes," I said.

"So you are here, as in here."

"Yes."

"Away from the Wales."

"Yes," I said, like some chastened Jonah.

"And is Andy here too?"

"Yes, but he's just gone up to bed."

"Goddamn I hate this," Andrew said.

I didn't dare ask what he hated.

"Was he okay? Was he in fair mood or foul?"

"He seemed fine," I said.

"He seemed fine," Andrew repeated, insinuating that my answer, while acceptable, was weak. He listed to the left and put more weight against the doorframe, like he was remembering the shipwreck that had brought him here. I assumed he was drunk. "I thought I heard something," he muttered, and he grew distant and silent, still listening, it seemed, until a cough tore through his lungs, its color both pink and black. Andrew lowered his head and—I couldn't quite believe what I was seeing here—spat, letting the phlegm meander from mouth to floor. It was quite a performance, reminding me of a schoolboy's provocation of gravity, something the younger Dyers used to call snicker-snagging. Andrew stared at this newborn presence near his feet and said either to me or to it, "They'll be here soon," after which he turned and hobbled back to his study.

Who were they?

And where was here?

And how soon was soon?

A ghost seemed to linger in his place, roughly the size of that glob of spit, but my attention eventually returned to the window and a car impatiently honking its horn. The young man playing Montesquiou playing Charlus climbed into the back of a waiting, horse-drawn carriage, bound for Jupien's, I imagined, and after holding up traffic a bit longer, three other characters, none of whom I recognized, joined him. Once all were on board, they trotted down Fifth, their youth a jealous, if ironic, echo.

III

July 12, 1948

Dear Charlie,

Just got back from the big Lake Sawamaui canoe trip and my arms are spaghetti without the meat sauce. I can barely hold this tiny paddle of a pencil, and my eyes see nothing but water, water water everywhere. But the trip was great. No injuries this time though there was a massive mosquito attack and we were without any proper ack. Poor Jeremy Foskett almost got sunk. How's the leg? Does it still hurt? I can still see you fall and hear you scream and you're still lucky nothing worse got broken, like your head. It must've hurt like hell. Everybody here says hi and get well soon and watch your step and beware of the lemonade. You're not missing much. I'm jealous you can go to the beach. How are the waves? Charlie buddy I didn't mean to laugh when you were crying, honestly but the sound you were making was funny in an awful sort of way. If you saw me laughing I am sorry. When I get home you can throw rocks at me. By the way I found some more stromatolites for you. I have to go now. Tonight's the epic campfire. I'll write your name on a log. Can't wait to get home and sign your cast.

Your pal,
Andrew

III.i

A. N. DYER MANAGED TWENTY-ONE PAGES before finally re-
tiring to the couch. Nowadays he preferred naps to
more defined sleep, even if those naps lasted many hours and stretched
the semantic bounds, still Andrew held firm to the notion of temporary rest. It was three in the morning. Sleep was sponsored by Vicodin,
with a two-finger assist from Dewar's. All the previous typing had
imprinted on his eyelids the residue of motion, sheet after sheet of
Eaton twenty-pound stock rolling behind his tired platen brow. Eaton
had been his brand since the beginning, its rag like onionskin but
thicker, its overt quality as pleasing as a fountain pen with his signature. As a young man he could produce eight, maybe nine pages a day,
an average of four hundred words per page (he always counted), which
on a yearly basis would yield roughly six reams and still allow for five
weeks of vacation. Oh, to dream such math again. Tonight he had
ground through an entire chapter, the twelfth. The pages measured a
quarter inch of hard linear labor. It was impressive work, regardless of
the dubious task, and after he had finished he jumped right into the
editing and took care to imbue his handwriting with as much youthful
vigor as possible, striking the deliberately overblown words, refashion-
ing the clumsy sentences, x'ing an entire wayward paragraph, and
scribbling its correct version in the margin. This part was fun, almost
like painting: Andrew put red pencil to manuscript and gave his brush-
stroke to the canvas—lines, arrows, swirls, in some cases well-practiced
doodles, even a mysterious phone number for a man named Roberto
Lupe, just for kicks. Make it messy, he thought, make it real. He imagined himself as twenty-seven again, an age that still seemed sadly

within reach, just yesterday really, before everything went wrong, before his biggest regret turned into his greatest success—Andrew flinched as if startled from a thirty-second, decade-spanning dream, the type that can snag you when sitting through opera. Lying on the couch, looking for sleep, Andrew's body seemed like a house with a possible intruder inside—what was that? that noise? His study certainly appeared ransacked. Earlier that day he had been searching for something to read, something special, something of worth, please, give me something to help me through the night. Good old Coleridge finally tempered the panic:

> The Frost performs its secret ministry,
> Unhelped by any wind. The owlet's cry
> Came loud—and hark, again! loud as before.
> The inmates of my cottage, all at rest,
> Have left me to that solitude, which suits
> Abstruser musings. . . .

But now the abstruse had turned to crap. Books were all over the floor, papers too, file cabinets practically dumped, newspapers, mail, mostly unopened, dirty plates, coffee mugs, clothes, all the clothes, the socks and the underwear, pants and shirts woefully overemployed. Just close your eyes and think of those twenty-one pages, he told himself, eight thousand words, fifteen thousand individual keystrokes. He had always been a decent typist. (Thanks to Exeter, we were all decent typists.) *The quick brown fox jumps over the lazy dog.* Instead of sheep he tried counting foxes, the image of fox inspired by the crafty Mr. Tod. Andrew loved Beatrix Potter as a boy, the fond memory of being read to aloud, the words coming on trails of smoke and scotch, his father's wonderful voice. He decided the lazy dog would be his own, a cocker spaniel named Smear. One of his other clear memories of his dad was the delight he took in calling the dog. "C'mere Smear!" He had promised a Smudge and a Splotch some day. Oh, all the numberless goings-on of life, inaudible as dreams. Almost asleep—or so he hoped—Andrew's attention fell heavily on the fireplace. It took only eight months to write *Ampersand*. Amazing the speed. Just eight months to give up his soul. He closed his eyes and found something warm and wriggling inside.

Tomorrow Richard and Jamie were due to arrive.

Andrew would continue his writing in the morning.

The goal was to get the book finished in the next week or so. It was a self-imposed deadline, with death running hard in the line, outpacing all other thoughts and expanding its ever-expanding lead. After all, this was the man who wrote in *The Bend of Light:*

> Take a look. There's a black hole smack dab in the middle of your eye, a reflection of what looms ahead, of what you can never peer around no matter how much light shines. The fix is in. God dies a thousand times a second.

And that was thirty-five years ago, when he was in good health. Imagine him now. Or imagine yourself if your lifelong obsession was no longer in the distance but in the same room; imagine the sepulchral couch; imagine the strange anticipation, its sad sort of achievement; imagine the blackness, the eternal nothingness, which of course is unimaginable. We the living might appreciate our mortality, but no matter how deep we delve into the subject, of our bodies as our sieves, death is just wordplay. We all have something to steal.

In *The Bend of Light* Hardy Rohem dies of skin cancer and he dies alone. "I love you all" are his last words. The Tin Man is given his illusory heart. A. N. Dyer struggled for months over that line. He typed pages and pages of potential last words, veering among the faux philosophical, the absurd, the spiritual, etc. Whatever the choice, these words would end the novel, that was obvious, but the heaviness of the situation, even in the shallowest of characters, overwhelmed him. He gave the manuscript to Isabel, always his first and best reader, to see if she had any ideas, and while a few of the female characters were given a better shake and a subplot was tightened and those Isabel-averse words were circled (*drapes* and *sofa* had become their private joke), she had no explicit answer for the dying Hardy. "He can say almost anything and it'll be moving," she told him. "All this time he's been searching for a sense of his own meaning, but essentially he's incapable, he's just a polished surface, but now meaning is forced upon him and whatever he says will be powerful, I think. Nobody dies a worthless death, at least in my view. We all die together." As she talked Andrew rubbed her right foot as payment for her critique, his thumb planing the arch of her serious size-elevens. How he loved those feet, missed those feet, the way they existed in harmony with her shoulders, as if she stood balanced on generations of big-footed, broad-shouldered Isles women. That smile completed the picture, dimples like tiny fists pulling you in, catching you within its net.

"You should go."

Those were her last words to him, seventeen years ago. Could he have said anything differently, done anything differently beyond the obvious, like craft a story that would have made it right, that would have repaired this injury and broken this terrible spell? Of course, a few months later he did come up with something, but by then it was too late. On the day in question he remained tongue-tied in the doorway of the living room while she sat unmoved on the couch, reading some thick and redolent magazine. The narrative part of his brain had been so sure that she would forgive him, eventually, and she would help him raise the boy, the combination of resentment and perverse pride too great for her to pass up. Even if this was miscalculation on his part, his miscalculations often ended in success, his thoughtlessness bringing on his greatest triumphs. No doubt about it, his life would have been happier with less luck.

You should go.

And the sweet everything slipped from his hands.

Now Isabel was remarried and living in Litchfield, Connecticut.

Andrew, trying to fall asleep, wished his cramped arms could detach.

He wondered what A. N. Dyer would say when it came time for his last words?

James Joyce had asked, "Does nobody understand?"

And Heine had requested pencil and paper; Goethe more light.

Emily Dickinson had muttered, "I must go in, the fog is rising."

We all have our last words, no matter our status. A week before my father labored through his, Andrew had visited the Morgan Library on Madison and 36th Street. Arthur Sinkler, its director, was courting him in hopes he might secure his papers, and he was showing Andrew a few of the library's treasures, such as the original manuscript of *Lady Susan*, in Jane Austen's lovely hand. But all Andrew could think of was poor Jane dying in bed, only forty-one years old, her beloved sister Cassandra asking if she needed anything, anything at all, and Jane answering, "Nothing but death."

Arthur Sinkler mistook this silence for appropriate awe. "Fabulously immediate, isn't it?" His enthusiasm was honest yet annoying, like a seller of high-end men's apparel. Andrew assumed he came from nowhere, one of those self-made intellectuals who modeled themselves on the type of Ivy Leaguer Andrew so disliked: the premeditated WASP. That said, it was hard to rage against his dedication to form and pedigree; people like Arthur Sinkler gave meaning to these small implications, like an archeologist fitting together the shards of an ancient trash heap. "The ink still seems wet," he practically gushed.

Andrew removed a handkerchief and coughed.

They were sitting around a table spread with various manuscripts, and if Andrew and Arthur were cordial at eleven and one o'clock respectively, an impatience negotiated the quarter-tos, with Sidney Garrow, the Morgan's curator for literary and historical manuscripts, on one side, and Dennis Gilroy, A. N. Dyer's literary agent, on the other.

"Never heard of *Lady Susan*," Dennis said.

"It's certainly not her finest work," Sidney Garrow confirmed. "But it is the only surviving full manuscript of one of her novels, so in that way it's quite important."

Arthur frowned at this opinion. "Oh, I think the book's quite wonderful, almost subversive. Lady Susan is this wicked Venus flytrap of a woman who catches these charmed men. It's early Austen, and it was never published in her lifetime, but you can see her honing her craft and working through her eventual themes. It's more novella than novel, an epistolary novella."

Sidney Garrow slumped closer to twenty-to-whatever while Dennis Gilroy tried to smile without his usual smirk, which resulted in an approximation of good humor, like one of those rigged carnival games involving a water pistol and a clown's open mouth. "An epistolary novella, hmm," he said. "I'm sure her agent was pleased with that, and yes, I know dear Jane didn't have an agent, only her brother Edward, and I know there's a long, proud history, from *Pamela* to *Les Liaisons Dangereuses* to her own *Sense and Sensibility*, my personal favorite, but my God, talk about a hard sell." This was classic Dennis Gilroy: to offer himself as a buffoon, a mere moneyman, then undercut that impression with an offhanded display of scholarship, thus deflating all pretension and leaving only cash, great piles of it, on the table. Many a writer owed him their second home. Dennis wooed A. N. Dyer after his longtime agent, Teddy Moran, retired to Greece so he could get pickpocketed by the local boys. "I've cut holes in all my pockets," he wrote to Andrew from Naxos a few years before he drowned, "and glued a drachma to my inner thigh." Teddy was a functional if expansive drunk who started his career as a copyright lawyer with a penchant for verse. "Give me the fringe rather than the infringement," he would pronounce with a loony Irish accent by way of New Paltz. But Teddy had an eye for young talent, as well as a sharp editing pen, and even if you only understood 80 percent of what he muttered, the remaining 20 twisting around a warped and non sequiturial universe, you were charmed by his obscure delight. Once as a favor to Andrew (who was doing a favor for my father ((who was pressed by my mother to do a favor for me (((whom I begged not to ask for any favors)))))) Teddy Moran read my first unpublished novel, a miscarriage of deformed autobiography, and he was nice enough to treat me to a midtown lunch like a real writer. "You have the look of the dog chasing you," he told me near the end of our meal, "and that dog won't tire so you better grab a big fucking stick and start swinging. Do that and then give me a call." Evidently Teddy Moran was obsessed with dogs. A. N. Dyer dedicated *Here Live Angry Dogs and Brutal Men* to *TM and his drugged honeycakes.*

"She was in terrible pain when she died," Andrew said of Jane Austen.

Arthur and Sidney Garrow dipped their heads, ever respectful, but Dennis hoisted his smirk to full sail. "Oh, thanks for that fun thought."

"They think she had Addison's disease," Andrew continued. "Suffered terribly, just terribly, severe vomiting and diarrhea, awful convulsions." He picked up a pair of white conservator gloves and held them like a memento from the days when girls wore white gloves, dancing school days, debutante days, fifty years ago or two hundred years ago, the good old days. The gloves seemed tiny yet they fit his hands rather easily. Andrew regarded them theatrically. "Maybe ending that pain is what makes the end bearable."

"You feeling all right?" asked Dennis. "Or is this just a mood?"

"I feel fine," Andrew said, the words dank with disgust.

Arthur Sinkler changed subjects by reaching for another manuscript, wisely passing over Keats's *Endymion* and Poe's *Tamerlane* and Wilde's *Dorian Gray* before landing on Trollope and pushing forward *The Way We Live Now*. "Have a look," he said. "Hardly a revision on the page, the absolute cleanest working draft you will ever see. The man just wrote and wrote and wrote, finished *Ayala's Angel* in the morning and after lunch started *Dr. Wortle's School*."

"I always hated his titles," Andrew said. Without much enthusiasm he turned a couple of the pages housed inside a clamshell box, like a secret book hidden within a fake book. The words flowed free of second thought, not even an inky pause. Trollope wrote for money, hence the speed and output, and sometimes Andrew envied that motivation and was curious if he himself would have written more books, looser, faster, funnier books, if he had lived more hand to mouth and needed a real job, not in the postal service like Trollope, but maybe in advertising, with its brainstorming and sloganeering, its hard-to-please clients, its everyday exotic camaraderie. Andrew realized this was an absurd fantasy. Advertising? Please. And who could ever feel sorry for him? By all rights, A. N. Dyer's life was enviable. Success came fast with *Ampersand* and, combined with a supportive and loving wife and a generous trust fund, he no longer had to pretend to have a job and could focus all of his attention on writing. A real privilege. Whatever baseless torments he suffered from he kept to himself, the amorphous misery that stagnated into self-fulfilling loneliness, like an affection that turns into a twitch. Hearing a kind word about one of his books was like going through a seppuku ceremony with his insides acting as the blade. Was it shame? Guilt? We all know how meeting a favorite writer can often be a disappointment, but imagine being that favorite writer who understands the disappointment intimately, who might manage to charm you by signing your book with one of twenty time-tested witticisms but who in the end knows the truth all too well, that this thing of beauty, this kind solace in a dying hour, is nothing more than a well-crafted ruse.

Arthur Sinkler reached for *Our Mutual Friend*. "Now look at Dickens. . . ."

Andrew had hoped that spending the morning at the Morgan would somehow push him away from the oncoming bus of his own head, plus Dennis had been begging him to take this meeting, since this was an opportunity to finally mint some real money from the A. N. Dyer name. But being in the presence of these manuscripts just made Andrew feel, well, to use a humble word, sad. The handwriting seemed too personal. Here were these people beyond their undying name; here was the evidence of their brief human existence. Where John Harmon was an abstraction, the hook of the *J* and the double cruciform of the *H* was pure Dickens, with his mess of revisions, his revisions of revisions, the unwieldy scratch and scrawl of a man more than a century dead. Andrew peeled off the gloves and let them drop on top of *Our Mutual Friend*. Arthur Sinkler was going on about the Trollope Society and how they pointed to the sloppiness as evidence of Dickens's inferiority, but all Andrew heard was his own breath, innocuous yet terribly evident.

It was mid-morning.

The sunlight slanting through the window seemed delivered mid-dream.

He needed another Vicodin, maybe three.

In an office nearby a telephone rang.

Dennis Gilroy, sensing the drift, suggested moving the conversation forward, and after a nod from Arthur, Sidney Garrow removed his glasses, as if speaking and seeing were exclusive acts. "Over the course of a week I made a cursory, and I do mean cursory, inspection of Mr. Dyer's papers. I very much enjoyed my time in their company, and I thank you, Mr. Dyer, for your hospitality."

"I hardly knew you were there," Andrew said.

"Before I start I want to stress that in no way is this a proper catalog of your papers, which is something the Morgan can do and do extremely well. But let's start with your letters. I made a rough count of three hundred twenty, which span six decades. Within that grouping there's a very nice and full correspondence with your mother where we have both sides of the exchange. There's also a complete but smaller correspondence between you and your stepfather."

"Can't believe I wrote to him at all," Andrew said.

"Excuse my prying," Sidney Garrow said, either grinning or cramping, "but are there any letters between you and your first wife?"

"First and only wife," Andrew corrected. "If she hasn't burned them, yes."

"Any idea the number?"

The number? Well, there was a letter a week for five years, when he was in college and in the army, the letters short and superficially charming, giving Isabel a brief rundown of their time apart, all romance buried in the very-sincerely-yours and the hope-to-see-you-soons, once going as far as thinking-of-you. Only a few kisses had been exchanged and he was using these letters as more of a bookmark, hoping Isabel might remember their place when she ran into him in New York and maybe kiss him again. Which she did. Her lips were thin but strong and always tasted of the ocean. During his military service at Fort Jackson in South Carolina (he was trained in demolitions) Andrew began to fear her loss of interest as she attended Smith and came in contact with all types of Williams and Amherst men, God forbid those Harvard asses. His letters took on more incident, with the day-to-day labors embellished, such as blowing up the latrine or witnessing the sapper lose both legs, a few of them turning into outright fraud, as in the duck hunting trip to Meccapeek Plantation, where Charlie Topping made an appearance since Andrew knew Isabel liked Charlie and maybe liked Andrew for liking Charlie; in that letter Andrew had

Charlie chasing down a crippled teal through a flooded corn field, tripping all over and getting soaked and generally ruining the hunt, all in
pursuit of a dying bird. As Andrew grew more confident with his writing, the truth became shorter, the bulk of the letters taken up by short
stories he enclosed for Isabel to read, love, cherish, and possibly obey,
secretly proposing to her with his first published piece, *Miserable Army*,
though it took another two years before he went on bended knee and
unscrambled those letters. "I have no idea," Andrew said to Sidney
Garrow.

"Maybe we can talk to her."

"Good luck."

"Of all the letters in the present collection," Sidney Garrow continued, "the most noteworthy are the correspondences from Mr. Pell at
Random House, and from your original agent, Mr. Moran. It's great
material, very apropos in terms of process and career. I particularly
like the exchange concerning the cover of *Ampersand*." Sidney Garrow
turned to Arthur. "It seems they originally wanted an image of a tightly
knotted school tie rather than the red schoolhouse door we know so
well. Amazing to think. There's also a small but strong batch from
other writers, artists, figures of the day, but I wouldn't say it's an extensive grouping. Then we have friends, in particular Charles Topping.
Now, three hundred twenty letters isn't necessarily a large archive, but
perhaps it's not indicative of how many letters you yourself actually
wrote."

"I'd be shocked if I wrote half as many," Andrew said.

Sidney Garrow—and always Sidney Garrow and never plain Sidney
or Sid or even Mr. Garrow, his deep yet meek intelligence needing the
brace of every syllable to prop up what seemed a delicate presence—
straightened the single sheet of paper acting as his notes. "To be honest, the letters are not the strongest part. Which brings us to the
notebooks. The notebooks, Mr. Dyer, are wonderful. I counted
seventy-three, big and small, some full, some half-full, some barely
full, but all loaded with terrific material. There are no journals or dia-
ries, as far as I saw. I estimate over a thousand index cards and loose
sheets of typescript, and those are jewels in terms of methodology and
nuggets of prose. I also found six sketchbooks."

Dennis gave Andrew a reappraising look. "You draw?"

"And draws quite well," Sidney Garrow remarked.

Andrew grimaced. "In my youth. My mother saved everything."

"That kind of ephemera is great," Arthur told him.

Ephemera. Andrew imagined the most capricious of Greek goddesses.

"This brings us to the manuscripts," Sidney Garrow said. "First, the short stories, mostly written early in your career, quite a few unpublished, which is always thrilling. I counted thirty-eight; that's including the fourteen that were in the collection *M*. And then we have the novels. For the most part it seems that three drafts have been preserved for each book: the original draft, with the author's notes and edits; the working draft with the editor's notes and edits, for the most part Mr. Pell's; and the corrected draft, first proof pages, with additional notes and edits from the author. I have to say it's a real boon to have all these drafts together, to get a sense of the evolution. It's really quite wonderful." Sidney Garrow liberated a handkerchief and half-blew, half-wiped his nose. Andrew guessed that this man's love of books started from a defensive position, a palisade in the palm of his hand. "But there is one issue, a discrepancy really. I couldn't find any drafts for *Ampersand*. Nothing. Otherwise the manuscripts are very complete. We even have scrapbooks of reviews and articles."

"My mother again," Andrew said.

"Maybe there's an explanation, but it is an issue since we would want *Ampersand* included, unless of course for whatever reasons the drafts are nonexistent. But it is your best-known work, and we would be foolish to make a significant investment only to see *Ampersand* turn up elsewhere."

"Say in Austin," Arthur Sinkler added. "It'd be institutionally embarrassing."

The Andrew inside Andrew curled up in the corner.

Dennis shot him a sly-old-fox grin. "Let's talk significant investment."

"With or without *Ampersand*?" Arthur asked.

"Let's say with."

"Okay, but first let me give you my quick pitch for the Morgan. As a citizen, a devotee of this city, I feel that it's incredibly important, Andrew, that your papers remain here, among, well, among your people. You're a quintessential New York writer and if your legacy were to end up somewhere else, that seems like a shame verging on a crime. You need to be on the East Coast, near East Coast scholars, near East Coast readers, and when I say East Coast I mean smack dab in the middle of Manhattan."

"What's the offer?" Dennis asked. "I mean there is a non–East Coast reality."

"Yes, reality. Thank you, Mr. Gilroy, for keeping us grounded. I don't need to tell you that the Morgan is a special place. You know that. In my biased view, we are the intellectual heart of this city. A visitor from another planet would do well to visit here first in order to understand our human narrative. We also have a tremendous gift shop. That said, we don't have unlimited funds. We can guarantee you the institutional respect and support you deserve, but money, alas, is always tight. Regardless, these papers are of exceptional value and with *Ampersand* firmly on the table, we can go to three five."

"For everything?" Dennis asked, almost offended.

"Even the paper clips."

"Full disclosure," Dennis said: "I've talked to Ransom."

Arthur smiled. "Such an evocative name."

"And they offered double that."

"Dennis, if money's the bottom line, we can't possibly compete. Ransom and their ilk will always win. And they are a fine institution and Austin is a fine central Texas town. But if you want to maximize profits, may I suggest breaking up the archive and selling the pieces in lots. But if respect, sensitivity, geo . . . "

As this polite haggling persisted, the Andrew within Andrew drifted behind another thought that began with a glance at the ceiling and its impressive plaster molding and then freewheeled to cake frosting and weddings, to Isabel and her glass blown neck—she triumphed in turtlenecks—to her lean and sharp features, her generous tongue, her body unfolding again and again in his imagination, tilting back-back-back into a kind of aggregate sexual act that also included their honeymoon in a few short shifts, Isabel naked and willing, the willingness forever the sweetest part and overpowering every other sense, like he was a teenager again where every intimate thought was siphoned through skin, through the funnel of her sideways recline, those thoughts becoming more powerful as he got older, as his need for solitude tightened into a stubborn grip and they—or more specifically he—had difficulties with the mechanics of touching without feeling disgusted with himself, like he was watching from afar, thrusting and grunting, and in his late forties and fifties he lost all sexual fortitude yet still clung to fantasies of her naked and on top of him, like a masochist wishing himself insane. Then the thought of Andy opened up, as if their memories were conjoined. He wondered if the boy had tucked away his virginity yet. He hoped he was screwing a lot of girls, nice, bushy-tailed boarding school girls. On a handful of occasions Andrew tried asking about girlfriends in an attempt to recast himself as the kind of father who had frank conversations with his son, who imparted wisdom concerning the opposite sex, but maybe it was his tone or his advanced age, maybe it was his blatant lack of useful knowledge, or maybe it was just fathers and sons immemorial, but the question made Andy squirm—"Well, sometimes, um, you know"—which in turn caused Andrew's happy retreat—"Okay, yes, that's wonderful"— though he could clearly hear what he wanted to say, about how he had lost his virginity to that Miss Porter's girl, Emily Stackhouse, who only required three dates before giving up her prize, as many a boy could attest, old three-date-Stackhouse from Garden City, a dinner, a movie, a dance, any combination of these three and she'd end up on her back, Emily thick and plain but lovely in her thickness and her plainness, like something born in a stable, a thought he thought only later because at the time she was simply plump and he wanted the ride over with as soon as possible, Emily not moving much but she did hum and she did wrap her arms around his shoulders and she did hold him tight and he realized that this was his reward for his dubious company, the fat girl gives you a fuck, and while he knew this going in, under the waxing of her skin he had to conclude things as gallantly as possible by faking his finish into that ridiculous rubber reservoir. My God, what son would ever want to hear that?

"Respect is a two-way street," Dennis was saying, "and this—"

That's when Andrew broke from the ceiling and spoke up.

"I want my youngest involved," he said.

Arthur gave a foot-in-the-door smile. "What's that?"

"If I give you my papers I want my youngest involved. All permissions would have to go through him, all research queries, all publication requests, everything, and I mean everything. That's my condition."

"Plus real money," Dennis added.

"Yes, of course, plus gobs of money," Andrew said. "Now, I realize Andy might not care for this particular responsibility, especially given his age, but he can do whatever he wants with it, rubber-stamp every request for all I care, or let someone in the library handle the bulk, but he has to be made aware of what's happening. The entire archive can be opened let's say eight years after my death."

"Assuming the money issues are settled," Dennis said.

"Yes, yes, money." Andrew struggled to push back his chair. "You can pick everything up in a month."

"Including *Ampersand*?" from Arthur Sinkler.

"Including *Ampersand*. But I only have the original draft."

Arthur nodded like a hummingbird was held captive in his mouth. "Perfect."

Andrew stood up, which required a bit of balancing. His life nowadays seemed lived on a plank. "I'll let the three of you figure the details out, but right now I'm tired and if I stay any longer I might have to lie down, on the ground." Arthur Sinkler did the honor of accompanying him downstairs, going on about how pleased he was, how absolutely thrilled, overjoyed really, Arthur later recalling how the great writer responded with silence, as if words were mere sound and smoke. "I put him in a taxi and he finally said something, in that voice of his, he said, 'I think I need to buy a goddamn cane,' just like that. Probably so he could whack me on the head." That line in concert with Arthur's poor impression always procured an abiding laugh.

While Andrew was riding back uptown from the Morgan, I was likely on duty watching my father breathe. That's what I did, I watched him breathe, watched his chest rise, watched his chest fall, ready to call my siblings and stepmother when the end seemed truly near. I rubbed his shoulder and said sorry, which meant sorry for everything, I suppose, sorry for what you're going through, sorry we never really talked, sorry if I was not the son you wanted, or needed, or deserved, just plain sorry. I was too scared to kiss him. But I did hold his hand. At times it seemed he was newly born and I was both father and son to the man. What with these eerie similarities with that scene from *Tiro's Corruption*, I decided to call Andrew and give him an update.

"It's not looking good," I told him.

He seemed startled. "With what?"

"With Dad," I said. "It's not looking good."

"Jesus, I thought you were calling to tell me he died."

"No, not yet, but it's not looking good."

"And what do you want me to do about that, Philip?"

"Um—"

"What do you want me to do? I visited. I was there not so long ago. I said my goodbyes as best as I could. But I'm not family. I'm not supposed to be there for the absolute end. I've gone as far as I can go."

"I'm sorry," I said, mortified by my overreach.

"You know I'm not well myself," he told me.

"Oh."

"Ever since I saw your father I've been very weak."

"Anything I can do to help?"

"No, no, no. It's viral, I'm sure. In my lungs. In my feet. I'm a disaster."

"I'm sorry."

"But your father, he's in my thoughts." And with that he hung up.

What were those thoughts exactly? Did Andrew see my father as a young man or an old man? Our oldest friends, their faces, never really change, as we both travel at the same speed of life. Parents and children are different. They help us measure our existence, like the clock on the wall or the watch on our wrist. But old friends carry with them a braided constant, part and whole, all the days in the calendar contained in a glance. When Andrew went to the bookshelf to retrieve the fresh copy of *Ampersand*, did he remember the seventeen-year-old Charlie who had sought the safest path through those boarding school halls, head down, focused only on homework and Ping-Pong and the choir and his best friend in the whole world? Charlie had a lovely singing voice, though most of his classmates only recalled his high-pitched screams. Did Andrew think of wedgies and towel snaps and uncle crackers when he retrieved his second-to-last ream of Eaton twenty-pound stock, the company having discontinued that particular brand years ago? He rolled a sheet into his typewriter and typed:

Ampersand

by

A. N. Dyer

It was always going to be called *Ampersand*. The title came before the story. But using his initials, that started back in sixth grade, when he first toyed with his signature, pages and pages of different autographs, searching for the right architecture to house his sure-to-be-famous name. Andrew Dyer never scanned well. And Andrew Newbold Dyer just seemed pretentious. But after seeing E. F. Benson and L. P. Hartley in his parents' bookshelf he gave A.N. a try. It rolled across his pen beautifully, like a baptism in ink.

"I like it," Charlie told him after seeing the practice page in his notebook.

"Do you always have to sniff through my stuff?" Andrew said.

"I was ju-just, it was right here, open. But I think, it sounds, um, sounds sharp."

"Just shut up with your Listerine breath."

Andrew let the title page fall to the floor and rolled in a fresh sheet.

Ampersand

by

Andrew Dyer

Like hot newsroom copy, he ripped the sheet from the Selectric and placed it facedown on his desk. He could always come back and edit the Andrew part (having forgotten the earlier short stories already published under the auspices of A.N.). Maybe it would turn into something scholars would debate in academic books and journal articles that nobody would ever read. *The Denial of Self in the Works of A. N. Dyer*. Charlie Topping had it right. It did sound sharp.

In went another sheet and Andrew opened the book and started to retype the first chapter, re-creating what had been burned fifty years ago. The first page. The second page. The introduction to the boys of Shearing Academy. Back then he was so sure of its failure but now he was surprised he ever wrote so well. The third page. The fourth. With gaining momentum, he returned the book to its primal state, running the publication process in reverse. His own line edits long forgotten—God knows the state of that first draft—Andrew crafted new mistakes and corrected them. The fifth page. He noticed bits he wished he could have changed in the original, small revisions mostly, excising that one phrase too many. On the sixth page, almost as a lark, he typed *sly* instead of *slick* in his description of Nick Rogin, and let the change stand without amendment. It was thrilling, in its way. And on the eighth page he experimented with something bigger: the woods around Shearing no longer seemed *possessed by the wolves of fairy tales* but rather *whooped with the ghosts of the Wampanoag*. Andrew stopped, caught his breath. If this were a tale of magical realism, these revisions might have some effect, Andrew slowly replotting his past and correcting his future in a few weeks' worth of edits, but of course nothing changed. He thought of Andy at Exeter, reliving his life, and he thought of himself all those years ago burning every scrap that had to do with *Ampersand*, a ridiculous piece of melodrama since the novel was on the verge of publication. Those flames signified less than nothing; they were a fire without warmth. Andrew continued his transcribing. On the tenth page he came to the headmaster's son, Timothy Veck:

> . . . like a fondly remembered book from childhood left in the rain, what was once sweet and compelling was now bloated and spotted and, even less forgiving, corny. Poor Timothy. At present he was running from a bee. It seemed Timothy Veck was always running from a bee. Maybe he thought his high-pitched terror was somehow funny.

Last year, I tried to feel sorry for him and even defended him on occasion, but this year I decided to let the world sting. Timothy saw me. His eyes—and I still see those eyes, breaking against my studied detachment—popped wide, and he smiled and waved. He began yelling my name. He practically did an Edgar Mead dance. My reply wasn't negligence per se.

And so ended the opening chapter. By the time of my brief stay A. N. Dyer was well into his reconstruction project. My first night in the apartment I didn't sleep well, unaccustomed to the sounds of buses roaring down on Fifth. And Central Park seemed to holler as if lit with rape. I also half-expected a visit from a sleepwalking Andy. But most of my restlessness no doubt stemmed from a certain night in this apartment when I was a teenager, but let us focus on the clear bright morning of the next day, when I was in the kitchen pouring a glass of orange juice and toasting some bread. That's when Andrew limped in. After a brief recalibrating pause—What the hell is Charlie Topping's son doing with the butter?—he tried to speak, to say good morning, I presume, but his throat was knotted with phlegm, which, after a series of hacks, finally cleared. "Sorry," he said.

"That's okay."

"Every morning it's like I swallowed a cork." He poured a cup of coffee, and I grabbed a cup as well, even accepted the milk and sugar though I preferred mine black. His mysterious pronouncement from last night, that they'll soon be here, was solved when he told me that Richard and Jamie were visiting tomorrow. "Richard's coming all the way from California," he said. "He has two children, a boy and a girl I've never met. Do you know if I have to come up with a nickname, a 'Gramps' or a 'Pops' or something? What did your children call your father?"

"Grandfather," I said.

Andrew smiled. "Of course."

"If you have a full house, I can . . ." I gestured the *leave* part.

"No. I'm putting Richard up at the Carlyle. A nice big suite. Killing him with kindness. And Jamie has his own place, in Brooklyn of all places. I thought the two of them should have some dim sympathies with Andy before I complete my journey down the drain."

I nodded, uncertain what to say. I was so nervous to be in his company, doubly nervous at such an intimate hour, seeing A. N. Dyer in need of fresh clothes and a comb. A strange, inexplicable sorrow welled up within me, like a call for tears, as if the future were tapping me and telling me to pay attention right here, that this was sadder than I could presently understand. Andrew must have assumed my wobble was linked to my father and he told me that he missed him. And maybe he recognized some fellow foxhole feeling in my eyes, because he asked if my father had said anything before he died.

"Like what?"

"Like last words," he said.

The question took me by surprise. I'm sure we could go back and trace a final conversation, but in terms of proximity, my father was silent. I know this because I was the only family member with him when he died. My brother and sister and stepmother had all done their bedside best, remaining with him as he weakened, his pillow like a sponge absorbing his demise, and we all sat there, and we waited, and we said our goodbyes, and we waited, and we sat there, and we told him that we loved him, something we rarely did when he was not dying, and we waited, and we sat there, pressing around him and telling him, you can go now, it's all right, we'll be fine, because frankly we had other things to do, but we continued to sit and say our goodbyes, for days, for weeks, stewing in our own healthy company, and after a while my brother had to get back to work, and my sister had to take care of her children, and my stepmother had to resume her lunches and Pilates and bridge games and gallery tours and Italian lessons. Me? By then I was full-time free. So I took on the job as a monk takes on a calling, vaguely addicted to the mortal codependency. To borrow a line from *The Bend of Light:*

Nobody knows who is stationary and who is orbiting.

When I was a boy I could die multiple times a day in a multitude of styles, but once older I stopped with the playacting though I continued to imagine myself getting run over by a car or crashing in an airplane or suffering through a terrible disease—half the fun, I think, was proving myself still alive. But as my father's breathing grew more shallow and inconsistent, divided by low tones like the upwelling of the soul, and the hospice nurse said soon (but she was always saying soon), I could tell that this time was real and I took in the details of this ultimate performance. I noted his eyes staring at the ceiling like a nasty word problem had been scrawled up there. I studied the nest of his mouth, the straining chick-like tongue. I was shocked by the smell. The overall reek I anticipated, but the hint of stale water in a vase full of lilacs, my mother's favorite, spooked me, and I stared at him and tried to make sense of this metaphysical association, and he stared back just as hard, unblinking, unbreathing now, his left hand gripping the sheets like he was slipping, like he was going to fall, and I remember reaching over and holding his arm, this lifelong presence I barely knew, and I held his arm and I said again and again, I love you, like Lamaze in reverse, I love you, hoping this sentiment would fall side-by-side with the man rather than Why can't my stupid son save me? And that was it. There were no last words on his part, only mine. But rather than tell this to Andrew, instead I lied and told him that my father did say something, he said, "What a world, what a world." I have no idea why that popped into my head. If I had more time I would have reached for poetry and really impressed the man, but *What a world, what a world* was what lay within my immediate grasp. It was something I used to squeal at my children when I was trying to both frighten and thrill them.

Andrew seemed shaken. "He said that?"

"Yes," I said.

"Exactly that?"

"Yes."

I was curious if he realized the origin of the phrase, or if I should explain its provenance, but I was already in the hole for lying so I kept quiet. After nodding a few times he went back into his study and I imagine that he rolled in another sheet of that precious Eaton stock. I myself have a piece of that paper, sent to me a few weeks after this story ends. The original folds are now cut into a razor-thin sharpness, the edges framed by my constant handling. I'll admit I even licked the corner once. I keep it in my wallet and often check it, like a traveler with a passport, just to make sure those six words are still there.

Tell me please what he said.

Behind that closed door, A. N. Dyer started on the thirteenth chapter of *Ampersand*. It was the midpoint of the book. The opening letter of each chapter corresponded with its position in the alphabet, though no one ever picked up on this particular detail. It seemed so obvious to Andrew, unlike the other secrets in his books. The pattern was meaningless beyond its own sense of play, a symbol of symbols, the letters forever married to that preliterate song with its lonely, almost pleading coda: *Next time won't you sing with me.*

CHAPTER XIII

Me? Maybe I should've said something....

Andrew typed.
Andy slept upstairs.
I ate my toast.
I wonder how many of us were keeping our mouths shut?

III.ii

T HE ALARM CLICKED on to WFMU, in midstream of "I'll Be
Zeus" by Bionic Love, which slowly tilted Andy awake, his
vision falling on his clothes, disposed on the floor near his bed like a
chalk outline. A goddamn crime scene he thought, what with all the
stupid things he did last night. Like the way he said, "My father, well,
he's A. N. Dyer, the writer," to that bookish girl from Brearley whose
father was probably a billionaire and partied with rock stars. And the
way he got stoned and insisted that everyone listen, like really listen, to
"Jupiter" from Holst's *The Planets*, a choice even the morning radio
seemed to vote against. Oh shit and the way he demanded Martini &
Rossi Asti Spumanti, and the way he pretended to trip and fall and
actually did trip and fall into a bunch of girls from Chapin, spilling
their red wine and giving their pants a menstrual pantomime, which
he himself pointed out, and Doug Streff laughed because he laughed at
all Andy's antics. "You one silly bastard," Doug said in a big hug of a
Greek accent, totally made-up. But everyone was in a festive mood. It
was the first night of spring break, the New York tribes of boarding
school kids and private school kids gathering in a neutral setting (the
host was booted from St. Paul's for writing bad checks and now went to
Poly Prep) before they all left on their family vacations. Why the hell
did he invite Jeanie Spokes to this low-roller affair? She had been un-
reachable since visiting the apartment after the funeral, and he was still
suffering from the blue balls of showing her around, of having her
briefly in his room, right near his bed, which he pointed to and said,
"Welcome to Hogwarts," hoping this was clever and funny, but she left
soon after and since then had responded with total electronic silence,

like maybe she had wised up and decided that seventeen was way too young. Hogwarts? Jesus. And what does he do to convince her otherwise? He emails her an invite to this lurkathon of seventeen-year-olds, and not cool cinematic seventeen-year-olds but seventeen-year-olds who remind you that being seventeen actually sucks. Fucking Muggles. During the entire party he hoped she wouldn't show, and when she didn't, he was devastated.

On the floor his shirtsleeve seemed to stretch toward the bed in a last-ditch plea of Save me please! Andy would have sunk further into the evening's postmortem except he was happiest waking up in this room, in this bed, the sheets cool and clean, impossibly clean compared to the Exeter papyrus. What did Gerd use, some special Scandinavian flakes? He rolled over and pushed the snooze button mid (*"Dip back your head, into my shower of gold, feel no dread, I'm a swan and I'm cold"*) chorus. It was 10:46 A.M. He had no reason to be awake. The alarm was set so he could roll over and fall back asleep, without worry yet still conscious of time. It was like floating in an ocean of untroubled purpose. Maybe this is how babies exist in the womb—fetuses, he supposed, if being technical—and we, or me, maybe I still carry a link to that primal buoyancy, to that great grand whatever of my warm watery beginnings. Andy readjusted the pillow under his stomach. Maybe, he thought, this is a trace memory of my mother.

Her name was Sina Astreyl, and she was twenty-three and Swedish, originally from the town of Mora. All Andy really knew about her came from three photographs: Sina on a snowy street; Sina with a poodle; Sina in the doorway of a yellow house with green shutters. In all three photos Sina was smiling, revealing deep-rooted teeth that proclaimed joy as both a natural phenomenon and a fierce pursuit. Her eyes seemed alert, like an athlete parsing the split-second differences between success and failure. The photos had no dates, no inscriptions, but whatever their circumstance they were taken close together: all three Sinas wear the same blue parka and all three Sinas seem lit by the same affection for the photographer. Gerd once told Andy that they were likely taken during something called Vasaloppet week, a popular cross-country ski marathon that finished in Mora. "You can see the

128 · DAVID GILBERT

banners and the crowds. It's a great big party," she said, scratching his scalp the way he liked. "She's lovely. I can see her face in yours." But Andy wished he had more of her blond hair and blue eyes, her easy Nordic complexion. He was determined to visit Mora and someday investigate his maternal side, but in the meantime he just had these photos of a woman who looked as if she were speeding downhill.

The story goes that Sina Astreyl was working as an au pair when she slammed into A. N. Dyer with her charge's stroller. It happened in Central Park, by the model-boat pond. "She was practically jogging and she clipped me in the ankle," his father once told him. "There was blood." *Blood?* "Not much, a scrape's worth." Over the next week the two discovered that they were on the same park schedule, and when he saw her he teased her by carefully stepping aside. "She was adorably embarrassed." *Did you like her?* "She was much younger, so liking never really crossed my mind." But after a few weeks of these fellow transits they began to hitch up in synchronous loops. "It was nice company, that's all." *What did you talk about?* "She liked poetry, Rilke, whom I once adored. She shined her youth against my darkening age." And then one Thursday, her free day, she appeared unburdened by stroller and "We started on our usual loop but halfway through we sort of moved closer, more for warmth than intimacy." *Did you kiss her?* "Listen to you. Let's just say our walks grew longer." But all this walking and talking and other things only lasted a few months, maybe seven discrete Thursdays in total, until one day, a Monday, she failed to show. "I waited and waited." *Where was she?* "I don't know. I never saw her again." *Never?* "Never." A year later a lawyer from way upstate contacted him with news of her death. "Seemed she had a cerebral aneurysm." *What's that?* "It's like a heart attack in your brain." The lawyer also informed him that there was a child, a five-month-old boy, and the boy was—"Me?" asked Andy, cheerful to be finally included in this tale. His father nodded. Sina Astreyl had no immediate family and since he was listed on the birth certificate, he agreed to take custody. At the age of sixty-two became a father again. "Were you glad?" Andy asked.

"Was I glad? Of course I was."

"And what was she like?"

"Your mother?"

"Yeah."

"Hmm." His father seemed to listen for a hint of song through the static. "Well she was wonderful. Full of life. Always swirling about, always busy. But tough too. Brave. She made the best of a difficult situation, that's for sure, and she loved you very much, would have done anything for you. I'm sorry you don't have that kind of person in your life. You just have plain old me."

"C'mon, Dad."

"I'm not much of a parent."

"Stop it, okay." Even at ten Andy knew where this was going.

"I'm not a good person," his father said. "It's not like I'm evil, but I'm not good."

"Stop, please."

"It's just the way it is."

"Dad—"

"But you're different, you're all good."

"But if you're not a good person why should I believe you?"

"That's clever," he said, tapping Andy's chest. "See, you're a clever boy, which you'll need to watch, that cleverness, because it'll come easily to you. But what kind of father talks to his ten-year-old like this? It's insanity. And I'm not a terrible person, of course, I'm just saying you should have friends, lots of friends, and find a girl you love, and find a job you like well enough but focus your passions on hobbies. Those are the happiest people. Try to do something beyond what's inside your measly head. Be a citizen of the street rather than the ruler of your own world. I'm speaking as a cautionary tale." Cud-like material started to mortar the corners of his mouth, like even his insides wanted him to clam up. "Do you understand?"

"I guess so," Andy said.

"Don't be a ghost haunting your own life."

"Yeah, okay, thanks." Anything to make him stop.

And that was just one of many good-nights.

Andy repositioned the pillow from under his stomach to between his knees. Would he be a different person if he had had his mother in his life? Well, sure. But it wasn't like something he missed, plus he had Gerd and a certain amount of nonmaternal freedom, with a touch of demi-orphan appeal, that brought back to mind last night and the Brearley girl and her thick caterpillar eyebrows, their fur a hint of the butterfly between her legs. "Have you read *Ampersand*?" Had he really asked her that? Was he so desperate for a little sway?

"No," she'd said.

"Well, you should. It's like a total classic."

"And that's your dad?"

"Yep. His name is my name too." Then Andy had half-sung, half-shouted, "a na na na na na!"

The girl had frowned playfully, those caterpillars arching their backs. "A John Jacob Jingleheimer Schmidt reference?"

"That's right," Andy had said. "All the cool kids are singing it nowadays. Very addicting. Once you start you can never stop. And speaking of jingle and heimer . . . "

From floor level, tucked within his pants, the Hallelujah chorus sounded, courtesy of Andy's new ringtone, which was probably the most awesome ringtone ever, with its high holy majesty, even if it interrupted a half-asleep-semi-erotic trending-toward-full-blown fantasy involving a girl with metamorphic eyebrows. Andy dragged his pants up. It was proba—Jeanie Spokes?

"Andy?"

"Oh, hey, yeah, hey. Howdy." *Howdy?*

"Sorry I missed you last night."

"Oh yeah, no problem, just a flier, you know. A reach-out." *A reach-out?*

"I've been in a weird mood lately," she told him.

Hmm, weird? "No need to explain."

"I'd like to see you," she said.

"Yeah, sure—"

"Like now," she said.

Andy sat up as if barged in on.

"Where are you?" she asked.

"Um, in bed."

The agreeable noise she made wavered between a sigh and a purr, with Andy caught in the middle. "Do you know where I am right now?" she said.

"At work?"

"No."

Andy's pulse rate was like an elbowing friend. "Outside my building?"

"Try a museum."

"Okay, a museum."

"Try guessing which one."

"Um, MoMA?"

"Nope." *Nope* never sounded more bilabial.

"The Frick?"

"Nope."

"The Whitney? The Guggenheim? El Museo del Barrio?"

"Nope, nope, *ni siquiera cerca*. You're missing the obvious."

"The Tenement Museum?" he said, proud of his flirty misdirection.

"Andy."

"Hey, it's a fine museum."

"I'm at the Met, you loser, and I'm standing in front of my favorite work of art, practically blushing, Andy, like I'm the secret inspiration for this artist. I feel positively pinned between rough hands."

"Oh," Andy said, suddenly feeling very young.

"Now listen, I'll be here for the next, let's see, hour and thirteen minutes. I'm not going to move an inch. I'm just going to stand here and wait and see if you can find me. Think of it as a game of hide-and-seek and like any game there's a prize for the winner. You think you're up to the challenge?"

After a pause that unpacked many thoughts,

. . . get moving asshole . . . should I take a quick shower . . . Monet . . . there's no way I have time for a shower . . . this is kind of cheesy . . . do I need a condom . . . damn, I'm so comfortable here . . . Cézanne . . . minimum brush my teeth . . . just get up . . . I'll screw this up some-

how . . . badly . . . going to have to run . . . I might get laid . . . to sprint even . . . maybe it's more sexy than cheesy . . . Degas . . . does "prize" perhaps mean anal sex . . . this bed is crazy comfy cozy . . . Renoir . . . I'll get sweaty with all that running . . . jump in a taxi . . . Georgia O'Keeffe . . . Fifth goes the wrong way . . . why did I drink Asti Spumanti last night . . . could swing up Madison but that's a pain . . . feeling kind of horny . . . need to pee . . . could I pee on her . . . Spumanti . . . Manet . . . man am I tired . . .

the ball-peen of significance shattered all deliberation into core instinct—*Just fucking move!*—and launched Andy from bed and once launched put him into a state of panic, his hourglass head leaking sand into his empty, increasingly anxious, stomach.

"Somewhere in the Met?" he clarified.

"Yes."

"Like the Met on Eightieth and Fifth, with the knights and stuff?"

"Yes, doofus, that Met."

Andy reanimated the clothes from last night. "That's a big place," he said.

"It is."

Andy stepped-wiggled-stomped into his shoes. "Any hints?"

"No."

"No hints?"

"No."

"Like maybe it's a painting?"

"No hints."

"Because it's a big place."

"And getting bigger by the second." And with that Jeanie hung up.

Andy stood there, bogged down by a quick strategy session concerning art history and the feminine spirit and the geography of the Metropolitan Museum and Jeanie Spokes's possible position within that geography, Jeanie waiting for him, Jeanie perhaps ready, willing, and ableing for him in European Paintings; in Modern and Contemporary Art; in the Temple of Dendur; in Greek and Roman Art; in Arts of Africa, Oceania, and the Americas; Arms and Armor; Ancient

Near Eastern Art; Asian Art—Andy shook himself free and rushed from his room, nearly barreling into me, kneeling by his door.

"Everything all right?" I asked, pretending to tie my loafers.

"Can't talk," he said.

"Where are you going?"

But he was already halfway down the stairs.

Who could begrudge this virginal enthusiasm? Certainly not me. I myself was twenty-one, a full-fledged adult, when I finally unloaded that burden. Her name was Helen Dieter. She was stout and freckled, a soccer player, I recall, a fixture among a certain boisterous group of Yale women, Helen deemed the funny one though funny seemed defined by flashes of public nudity. I always assumed she was a lesbian. We were acquaintances our first year, classmates and coursemates sharing nods and hellos in hallways but never lingering for conversation, but by our last year we had progressed to minor speaking roles, our relationship based on being competitive English majors. Late spring she knocked on my door. It seemed she was celebrating a perfect mark on her senior essay, something about George Eliot and George Sand titled "By George" (I remember laughing at that asinine title), which went on to win her the Paine Memorial Prize for best senior essay and the Steere Prize for feminist theory and the Tinker Prize for Outstanding Senior in English, this half-drunk girl right here, who leaned into my room like a sister sticking out her tongue. Before I knew it, she was inspecting my bookshelves and my desk, where my own senior essay, "The Hostage Taker: The Kidnapping of Identity in the Works of A. N. Dyer," lay blindfolded and gagged. I was on my third and final extension; another week late and I would fail. Papers, drafts, books were scattered everywhere, along with various forms of caffeine and desperation. Seeing this, Helen surprised me with a few supportive words—"You can do this, Philip, you can finish"—and then she was on me like a squirrel on a tree, with her small, sharp claws and nibbling teeth and evident love of nuts. Thankfully she did most of the work, since our styles were ill-suited (particularly since my style was all bluff), but I did have a sense, whether right or wrong, of her laughing at me, as I kissed her neck and blew into her ear, of her laughing with friends later in a bar, as I thrust, and came, and rolled over on my back, helplessly ashamed and pitifully transformed.

Helen Dieter is now a managing partner at Goldman Sachs.

And Yale still talks about the Dieter trifecta.

But Andy, seventeen years old and thrilled with possibility, hustled from the apartment in hopeful pursuit of art. Dix, Bonnard, Poussin, Klimt, Munch played a game of innuendo in his head, and as he waited for the elevator he called Doug Streff, who lived not far from the Met and could easily wander into another person's misadventure.

"Where are you?" Andy quickly asked.

"You are never taking command of the stereo again."

"I need a favor. Where are you? Doug? Doug?"

He lost the call in the elevator. Floors ticked down, every number firing a plosive *fuck* from Andy. Doug had been his best friend since Buckley, though Doug had departed in sixth grade for Indian Mountain and now went to Millbrook and if his highest academic dream came true he would finish up in Boulder. Considered a terrible influence by parents, he bore the brunt of much vestigial blame, like an overweight, overbred golden retriever with a minor drug habit. But he was always good company. All of your ideas were excellent ideas to Doug Streff.

"Doug?"

"So what was up with that music?"

"I was stoned."

"You were such an asshole about it."

"I know, I know."

"You were like the listen police, listen, listen, listen."

"It's a very influential piece of second-rate music, like every movie score—"

"There you go again."

"Whatever, where are you right now?"

"I'm in the park, watching kids in the playground—remember that playground on Eighty-first where I broke my nose? I'm sitting here watching the kids not break their noses and I'm sitting next to this guy named London, right, like the city, but his last name isn't England, or

I don't think it's England—is it England? No, it's not England, it's Williams, London Williams, which is a cool fucking name, and he has a son named Manchester, Mani for short, six years old and Mani is definitely not breaking his nose today because Mani is a careful little kid, right Mani."

Andy blew past the doorman and hurried north. "Have you been smoking?"

"Perhaps."

"It's not even noon."

"High noon."

"Jesus."

"And the big deal is? I believe last night you were fairly levitated. You certainly had your head up Uranus."

"It was Jupiter and was I that bad?"

"Besides the whole Mein Stereo thing you were a hundred percent outstanding. At one point you had us all believing we were part of your massive déjà vu and you told us exactly what we were going to do next, and we believed you, or some of us believed you, or maybe just one of us, but it was fucking genius."

Andy cringed. "Oh God."

"No, no, it was superb. And you kept the ball rolling way longer than anyone thought possible. People started to walk away and you'd describe them leaving like you were five moves ahead."

"I shouldn't smoke."

"You kidding me? You should smoke more. Just avoid the stereo."

From 75th Street, through the trees on the western edge of Fifth, came a partial view of the Metropolitan Museum, and Andy remembered the point of this phone call. "I need your help," he said, "if you're not too incapacitated."

"I'm in. Excuse me, London; later, Mani."

"Can you like meet me in front of the Met, like right now?"

"Like *now* now?"

"Pretty close to now, yeah."

"Got it, chief."

The Met slowly revealed itself, low-slung yet massive, intimidating in its grand bureaucratic design, as if the world's most important mail was being sorted inside. But all Andy saw was a hiding place. He rushed past the fountain and up the broad steps where tourists mingled in a strange kind of order, like notes on a sheet of music. Looking for Doug, waiting for Doug—where the fuck was Doug?—Andy grabbed for his cellphone when he heard his name and spotted his friend approaching, arms pumping faster than legs, like a salesman selling hurry.

"Hey."

"We have an hour—"

"I packed you a bowl." In his palm was a pipe the shape of a small wooden bird.

"I can't."

"It's the Met, man. I'd be scared to go in there not stoned."

"We don't have time."

"It'll take two seconds."

"I need to be focused."

"On what?"

"I have like an hour to find this girl, a woman really, she's twenty-four, brownish hair, hair to here, chunky glasses, cool chunky, though; kind of looks like Heather Topol from Chapin, but better-looking, Heather Topol if Heather Topol had a fairy godmother, but the same sort of features, sort of the most attractive version of the Heather Topol type."

Doug stared at Andy.

"Fuck it," Andy said.

They sidled to the shady, less populated side of the steps.

"So we're looking for a Heather Topol–like girl," Doug said, newly enthused.

Andy nodded as he took a hit.

"And what happens when we find this Topolian girl?"

"I get laid" from Andy with a smoky smile.

"Laid as in bow-chicka-bow-wow?"

Andy nodded, took another hit.

"Right there in the museum?"

Andy squinted. "No, you fucking idiot. Or I don't think. Shit, that would be nuts. No, no way. Look, all I know is she's standing in front of her favorite work of art. That's the hint she gave me. I find that, I find her."

"You fuck her."

"That's my guess."

Doug refortified himself.

"I'm assuming European Paintings," Andy said.

"Definitely. Like Renoir, Monet, Manet."

"Might be too obvious."

"Balthus. Modigliani."

"I'll check that area. But I need you to cruise Greek and Roman, Egyptian—"

"All those vases," Doug said.

"Exactly. It's a big museum."

"The American Wing."

"A really big museum." Andy started to feel the task's thin air.

"Okay."

"Okay."

Uncertain with how to start exactly, they both took one last hit until a hazy if genuine purpose sank in and they marched into the museum, past security peering into bags, into the great hall where pods of people crowded the information desk and the coat check and the circular seating areas, so many people, class trips, group tours, a dozen buses cracked open and whipped up in this inverted bowl, everyone's clothing just a little too bright, everyone's shoes just a little too comfortable, people of every stripe, visitors from other countries, parents with children, families on vacation, tri-staters in for the day, college students, couples in love, voices, accents, languages traveling up and around the rotunda and swirling in a batter of half-understood echoes—Andy rushed past them, disdainful of their blocking ways. He played the role of detective and these folks belonged on the other side of the crime-scene tape.

"So I'm looking for a Heather Topol type," Doug clarified one final time.

"Standing in front of whatever she's standing in front of."

"Got it. I'm hitting Greece."

Doug broke left, toward Greek and Roman, while Andy flashed his membership card and bounded up the central staircase toward European Paintings, Tiepolo's *The Triumph of Marius* greeting him on the second floor, Andy pushing straight through the glass doors, excuse me and sorry to a bundle of Asian women, into the first gallery of nineteenth-century French (David, Ingres, Delacroix), Andy paying no attention to the paintings, only to the crowds around the paintings, *The Death of Socrates* getting the most eyeballs, but no Jeanie among the mourners, so on to the next gallery, more French (Boucher, Greuze, Fragonard) and a fruitless search for a gauzy portrait of a twenty-four-year-old brunette with a crooked smile, titled *You Find Me, You Fuck Me*, so Andy continued on, speed essential, though this time he was presented with a choice of staying straight or turning right and Andy chose straight (Clouet, La Tour) but no further female illumination here, only more galleries, more possibilities, straight, left, right, the galleries opening up onto a maze of human-made beauty, but no Jeanie, no hot-breath hello, and the enormity of the situation, as well as the THC streaming through his blood, panicked him, there's no way, just no way, this place is too huge, as he tripped into sixteenth-century Florentine and Bronzino's *Portrait of a Young Man*, which drew a swell of high school girls, Catholic judging by their uniform, who watched Andy scurry past and giggled in his wake like he was a boy in need of the nearest bathroom, Andy landing among eighteenth-century British (Reynolds, Gainsborough) and then backpedaling into seventeenth-century Flemish (Rubens, van Dyck), then more French, and Spanish, with Goya and some hopes for *Don Manuel Osorio Manrique*, with that bird and the three cats, surely a potential favorite, but only a few grandmother types gathered around as if descendants of those de Zuñiga felines, and Andy kept moving, his stomach churning excitement into dread, as Vermeer delivered no other girl interrupted and Rembrandt's Aristotle seemed to sigh as if Homer had nothing on this poor kid's plight, and now Andy was almost running, stumbling back on Bronzino's *Young Man* again and muttering "fuck" loud enough for a guard to notice, Andy fast-walking into the Italian Renaissance, with its altarpieces and annunciations and lamentations, spotting three galleries away, rather incongruously, Sargent's *Madame X*, another good chance, he thought, but no *Mademoiselle S*, and hope started to lose meaning as Andy turned left (Watteau), then right (Raphael), and found himself, once again, in front of Bronzino's *Young Man*, who mocked him like he was as die-hard a virgin as that Virgin of virgins who hung on the wall opposite.

Andy's phone went Hallelujah.

It was Doug.

"You have to come and see this bronze of a veiled dancer, Greek, like third century B.C., a boatload of time ago and they were doing this kind of shit."

"Is there a Heather Topol–like girl standing in front of it?" Andy asked.

"No, but she should because this is profound."

"Doug, keep looking."

"Nothing in the Impressionists?"

"I'm lost in the Old Masters."

"Every door is like a wormhole in here."

"Doug."

"Yeah?"

"Stay focused."

"I'm on the move."

After a roomful of El Grecos, Andy wandered into a large central arcade packed with oversized genre pictures, and he was relieved to be free of Old Masters. It was around here that he noticed the crowds more, despite their Jeanieless nature, the tour groups and the school groups and the senior groups regrouping in this area before entering the late nineteenth century, by far the most popular section in the museum, the galleries within bustling, two rows thick in front of some paintings, and Andy stared at these people and his distraction grew until it gained the power of unexpected thought, of these strangers here admiring paintings he had known since he was a young boy, these Manets and Monets and van Goghs, their familiarity breeding a certain kind of intimacy, almost like this was his living room and Degas's

Dancers hung over his couch, Andy standing in the middle of the gallery like he was its secret patron and he thought, Enjoy, please enjoy all of this, and yet he wanted to give more, so much more, wanted to touch shoulders and slap fives, I want to give you more, he thought, watching the people turn slow circles clockwise, slow circles counterclockwise, a clockwork divided into pictures (half past Pissarro) of time compressed and composed by art, and suddenly and totally Andy understood the human impulse toward expression, the primary need after food and shelter, even before religion, this desire for creation and just then he thought, rather grandly, I am art, knowing he was super-stoned and this was nonsense, but still he thought, I am art, and maybe for the first time he appreciated what his father did, overhearing in front of Seurat's *Circus Sideshow* a stooped woman shouting to her too-cheap-to-pony-up-for-the-audio-guide friend, "The luminous shadows endow objectively observed forms with mystery," and the friend nodded and repeated "mystery" as if hoping to make the word her own. Andy watched and listened for who knows how long before Hallelujah rang him back to earth. It was Doug again. He was in the sculpture court, freaking in front of Carpeaux's statue *Ugolino and His Sons.* "It might be the scariest slab of marble I've ever seen. Any luck on your end?"

"No."

"You mind if I go and hit that hot dog cart outside?"

"No," Andy said. "I'm basically out of time anyway."

"You wanna join me?"

"Think I'm going to wander around a bit more."

"Good luck with this Heather Topol–like girl."

"Yeah, thanks, man."

A great affection for Doug Streff welled within Andy. Right then he would have died for his friend, not that this sacrifice was called for, or even a possibility, but a fantasy bubbled up in his head of foiling a bullet with his chest, and as he drifted through the Astor Court and the American Wing, the Jain Meeting Hall, this fantasy escalated until Andy was checking the ground for possible grenades, searching for annihilating grace. I could die for you, he thought rather extravagantly, for all of you, death existing as gesture rather than extinction. That's when he stumbled upon Medieval Art, my old teaching grounds, with its Reliquary of Mary Magdalene that supposedly contains her tooth. All ten-year-olds love that tooth. I wonder if Andy heard traces of our fifth-grade class trip, the boys without fail having a hundred questions? Molar or incisor? Does it have a cavity? Did the Tooth Fairy come? Why a tooth? Why not the eyes? Or the tongue? I remember Andy asking, "Did they rip her apart after she was dead or was she still alive?" A few boys laughed, but I could tell he was serious.

Did he remember, even subconsciously, Christ of the Living Dead? Or me grinning and ruffling his hair?

A tooth. A relic. Like a pair of old wingtip shoes.

As Andy's head loosened into a more specific view, he thought about leaving but feared leaving would usher in forgetting, or worse, would reshuffle the experience into a funny story about an older girl and the Metropolitan Museum of Art, which would be a shame because right now this seemed like something more, though the something was already losing its ripple, like that last solid notion before falling asleep.

Every act of memory is an act of imagination.

Would Andy have recognized the opening of *Eastern Standard*?

> The more Rand Finch remembered the stairs, and the door, and the light under the door, the less true the memory seemed. The sharpest truth is in the heads of those who have forgotten.

I myself can recite the entire first paragraph. My guess is that Andy had probably read a few pages but grew bored when Rand starts piecing together his postcollegiate trip abroad, traveling through Europe with his two closest friends. Where's the promised sex? Where's the promised mayhem? And who cares about that door? Rand Finch sees his memories like heat lightning in the distance, the possible reflection of a long-anticipated war, until by the end he's unsure if he's the victim, the villain, or merely the viewer.

We can't really remember. We can only re-create.

And I myself have roamed these galleries looking into the eyes of impossibly young women as if they were waiting for me, as if they might recognize me, a late middle-aged man who wished himself young. I have roamed these halls until bone-tired and like Andy have stumbled into the Robert Lehman Wing. It lies hidden behind that Gothic choir screen like a futuristic escape pod latched to a church. It is a reward for the persistent, much like the Renaissance itself. With a second wind I have orbited the galleries inside with their Memlings and El Grecos and a rather spectacular Ingres, and I have taken in Christus's *A Goldsmith in His Shop, Possibly Saint Eligius*, and Di Paolo's *The Creation of the World and the Expulsion from Paradise*, and I have been stopped in my tracks in front of *The Annunciation* by Botticelli, though I'm less inclined to believe that Jeanie Spokes ever paused here. But Andy leaned in close to that small tempera. He swore there was some residual heat here, some traces of friction from her eyes. This is it, he thought. There was no irony in his conviction, no easy teenage joke—*Jizzus Christ*—only a sweet and lovely painting of Gabriel kneeling and God's light passing toward the bedchamber where Mary humbly waited. And Andy was right: it is a sweet and lovely painting. The label mentions that Robert Lehman gave this as a birthday present to his father. Imagine unwrapping that.

Andy's phone rang.

It was Jeanie. "You didn't find me," she teased.

"I think I did, just too late."

"Where?"

"I can feel you," he said.

"Where?"

"Like I'm standing outside your window, watching you."

"And what do you see?"

"Love as a sad kind of fate," he said, unembarrassed.

Andy might have located her among this profound company, but he was the one who prized the purity and grace, the uniting mystery, while I see Jeanie Spokes somewhere else in that museum, probably upstairs in the gloom of works on paper, among those Dürer prints, her eyes considering the block of wood and how the blade had to cut away whatever remained white, slowly turning flatness into relief: a woman sitting on a scarlet beast, full of names of blasphemy with seven heads and ten horns.

Find the doorknob and decide the brass is still warm.

III.iii

EVERYTHING WAS READY for the 6:30 A.M. departure. The *Los Angeles Times* had been suspended. The dog was in a kennel. The school, the after-school, the teams, the dance class, the band, the car pool, had all been notified of upcoming absences. Near the front door lay Richard Dyer's family in luggage form. But Richard himself, sleepless for most of the night, found his early-morning thoughts riffling through what he had packed, like a surgeon suddenly unsure of basic anatomy. Did he own a proper pair of New York shoes anymore? Were Brooks Brothers tassel loafers still the brand of choice? Maybe he should go shopping after they landed, since all his decent clothes were stylish in that questionable California style of casual meets designer meets high school visions of dressing up. Under normal circumstances Richard did not care about such things (he famously wore only one necktie during his Exeter days, a solid brown affair that everyone dubbed the Skidmark. After more than twenty years of living in L.A. he still considered himself a visitor to this world; whatever customs or fashions these natives followed, well, he would participate for the sake of camouflage. So bring on the V-necks, the too-tight T-shirts, the designer jeans, the absurd sunglasses. It was almost fun. Nobody in these climes knew his New York self. Here he was free. Despite this liberation, Richard quietly bore his pedigree like a trench coat in case of rain, his shoulders hunched, ready for an unexpected Northeast chill. This inner Dyerness gave him comfort despite his willful renunciation of the past. Oh, the contradictory nature of self. But soon no more of this secret identity. He was returning to the home planet, with a wife and two kids in tow who were thoroughly Angeleno and potentially mortifying. "Dad, these are my children." Maybe he should take them shopping as well. Richard tried to picture Emmett and Chloe in the clothes of his youth, Emmett who never met a button he liked, Chloe who insisted on wearing every color of the rainbow, claiming this as her "signature look." Then there was his wife, Candy, the former meth head who now worked the front desk at a veterinarian's office, lover of tight pants and turquoise jewelry, whose parents christened her Candy never thinking Candice was within reach, softly snoring by his side, naked and warm and fragrant, her arms and shoulders covered in a tattoo of meandering vines (while Richard had a hand grenade on his chest with the pin pulled). "Dad, this is, this is Candy." Richard hated his own knee-jerk snobbery. Defend her. "And I love her more than anything!" "And I don't care what you think!!" "I'm nothing like you!!!" That old familiar feeling took up construction in his stomach, and he thought, I am so fucking doomed.

Jamie Dyer lugged his backpack up three flights of crummy Cobble Hill stairs, the weight more abstract than concrete. He dug out his key. He hated keys. He hated having his own apartment, back in New York no less. It seemed like a defeat. After all the years of traveling, far removed from the mainstream of his roots, filming almost everything the human condition had to offer, Jamie the adventurer, Jamie the fearless documentarian, Jamie the envy of friends who remained stuck in cities and suburbs and careers and families, after all these years, here he was, slouching back to gentrified Brooklyn, like he was fresh from college. His apartment was a mess. He was seven weeks into an I'm-not-cleaning-a-fucking-thing binge and almost expected a homeless man to have been spawned. *Welcome home, asshole.* Jamie unzipped his backpack, retrieved the HDCAM SR tape with the solemnity of a stolen artifact. He placed it on the table. She was once so beautiful, he thought. Time stood still in her shadow. Jamie, exhausted, stripped down and headed toward bed. Back then sex had been unspeakably fun, the vigorous sweat, the silly sounds, the straight-up thrill of it. Her pussy—Jamie wondered if this was being disrespectful to the dead or if the dead begged for these memories—but her pussy was perfect, with its mitten of dark blond, its interior the impossible smooth of a conch—this was disrespectful, Jamie decided, picturing her spread on his bed instead of the books and magazines and random scraps of paper that surrounded him like a cat lady's cats. This was no way to live as an adult, but he was five days from reaching terminal disgust. Back to Sylvia. Sexy Sylph. Her breasts conveyed the incredible physics of being both heavy and light, the nipples small and specific, as if added later by a famed enamelist in France. Stop, Jamie thought. But memory pressed on. Her face, her lips, her tongue licking the tip of his cock, her hair swaying against rare, sun-deprived skin. All of this happened almost thirty years ago yet the sensation curled through him, and as Jamie worked the static darkness, he sensed something else on the other side, something else microscopic yet in this grubby atmosphere a thousand times its normal size, scrabbling along the walls and the floor, carrying its weight on eight bent legs, pointy and black, like nibs leaving behind terrible hieroglyphics. *Scratch-scratch-scratch.*

LAX appeared in the distance, and Richard was relieved. The traffic had been light and they were early, as predicted by Emmett, who had begged for another hour of sleep. "Great, two hours of lurking in the airport," he muttered from the backseat, his thumbs working a text. God knows what he was typing: *my dad sux.* Richard periodically checked on him in the rearview mirror, just to confirm he was still there. It was almost disconcerting how handsome and physically mature the boy had become. It seemed in violation of time. Six foot one and in need of a shave. Broad-shouldered with a narrow waist. A natural swimmer. And smart too, gifted in math and science. But whenever Emmett acted his age, which was often, Richard forgot that he came to this obnoxiousness naturally and wasn't impersonating a pain-in-the-ass kid. The car approached the Delta terminal. Chloe dug into her handbag and asked if she needed her passport. Passports were the new craze at school, all the seventh-grade girls carrying them as if prepared for a sudden whisking to St. Moritz. Chloe had begged and begged for one even though they had never cleared North America, but over

Christmas they relented and she spent an entire morning styling herself for her big photo shoot. You would have thought she was a citizen of Fauve. Already the magic of girlhood was being mediated through the complications of becoming a woman, a far less knowable state for Richard. In the car Emmett fake-laughed and poor Chloe bit down on the hook and asked, "What's so funny?" Emmett wiped his nose along the inner handkerchief of his wrist (the boy generated copious amounts of snot, which always made Richard worry about his possible blast count). "I can't wait until you're like nineteen," he said, "and you're like traveling to Estonia and some border guard checks your passport. You'll be so embarrassed your face will crawl under the nearest rock." Chloe gave a whiny rebuttal and Richard warned Emmett but Emmett was unapologetic. "I'm not allowed to get a small tattoo of a Chinese character representing strength and courage because I'm still too young, and hey, no big deal, I get that, I can wait until I'm eighteen, but Chloe here can dress up like a drag queen named Skittles for her passport photo?" Richard warned Emmett again as he searched for a place on the curb, but Emmett pressed further. "And I'm just saying that when she's older she's going to feel really really stupid." Richard had to double park. "What's that line from *Ampersand*, Dad?"—Richard hated the way Emmett said Dad nowadays—"*Give it time and shame eventually clambers back as pride*. So maybe when Chloe's thirty she'll laugh but—" Richard spun around and punched the back of his seat. "Shut the fuck up, please!" he nearly screamed. It was one of his zero-to-ninety outbursts. Instantly Chloe began to cry and Emmett sniffed as if ripping up a disputed contract, after which he opened the door and started unloading the bags with helpful spite. Candy smiled at Richard. "A good start to the trip," she said. But she knew his battles, knew how fraught both sides of fatherhood could be, and for the most part her sympathy outweighed any frustration. "Take your time with the car," she told him, squeezing his knee. Richard circled back toward long-term parking. As he drove he imagined heads exploding, which for some reason relaxed him while also confirming his general fucked-upness. The car went into the lot. Before leaving he gave the inside a quick look-over: there on the backseat near the crap-collecting seam was Emmett's cellphone. The kid must be freaking, probably too prideful to say a word. Maybe its recovery would spur amends. Hey man, you missing this? Oh, and I'm sorry. I'm kind of, well, anxious about going back to New York. Then, amid this fantasy, Richard thought, When had Emmett read *Ampersand*?

Jamie went up to the fifth floor of the Brill Building, to the offices of RazorRam and his old pal Ram Barrett. Ram had been a star at the Yale School of Drama, a promising actor and director and halfway-decent playwright, but somewhere in his jobless twenties he drifted into editing, specifically reality TV editing, and while he rode that boom into a very nice living, the career had taken its toll. Ram greeted Jamie awkwardly, as if five minutes earlier he had kissed Jamie's girlfriend or had changed alliances. "What brings you here, not that I don't love seeing you, I do, of course, I'm just, I thought you were eating peyote in Afghanistan, not to say you're not doing important work, unlike me, God knows, but I have a family, and bills, and do they even have peyote in Afghanistan?" Ram seemed to plead for a cutaway from his face. "I need a favor," Jamie said. He stacked the original mini-HD tape and the HDCAM SR tape on Ram's desk. "I need you to cut these two together. This the beginning, this the end. Clean up the transitions however you think best, do whatever you think best, and then burn me a master. It's maybe ten, twelve minutes of footage, all pretty self-evident, I think. I'd do the job myself but I'm too close to the subject matter. I need an objective eye, that Ram Barrett touch. And this tape here." Jamie picked up the HDCAM SR tape. "I have no idea how it looks. The quality might be crap. It also might be, I don't know, it might be kind of disturbing." Ram perked up. "Coming from you that means something," he said. "Do we have a title?" Jamie told him *12:01 P.M.* and Ram wrote it down on a Post-it which he headstoned to one of the tapes. "I'll get to it when I can," Ram said. "I mean sooner than that, not like I'm some big shot or anything, but I am busy, yeah, with the latest episode of *Wall Street/Main Street*, but hey, busy is busy. I'll try to take a look this afternoon." Jamie said thanks. Back in the elevator he checked his watch and though it was only mid-morning he wondered if he'd ever have a decent answer to that question.

. . .

Richard headed toward their meeting spot, one of those awful airport restaurants that reeked of disinfectant, as if Mr. Clean were decomposing in the corner. He passed people milling about the shops and food courts, a parallel world of in-betweenness that was both drab and exotic, the word *terminal* suggesting possible engine failure, of these people being the last people you would ever see. But Richard was mostly thrilled by the moving sidewalks. It was like the future promised in his youth. A brief vibration grabbed his thigh. Emmett's phone had a text—

> YWTDTM ;^@

—from someone named T-Bone. Richard tried to decipher the acronym but had no clue except that ;^@ seemed up to no good, and then Carson buzzed in—

> (*) + <=8 = (o)

—and before Richard could digest its algebra, Kelly checked in—

> OMFG did u open SUMiss E via b-door
> bcuz Barbed saying u a rude 2Q2C POS
> (LIDK) :{P

—but what the hell was b-door and 2Q2C and just when Richard was ready to stop a random teenager and ask his advice, Penny cleared things up—

> Ur a shit for doing what u did to Emma
> knowing sheda done anything for u.
> U slipped a nightmare into her dream.

—kind of. Richard read the text twice. Was this Emma, sweet Emma from school, with the brown eyes and the long brown hair? Richard was just wrapping his head around this information when he arrived at the restaurant. He slipped the phone back into his pocket and found his family sitting in a booth, minus Emmett, who was hanging by the gate. Richard went to find him so he could get rid of this damn phone now vibrating nonstop as more and more of Emmett's friends were waking up and exercising their thumbs. Zzzzzz. Zzzzzz. Zzzzzz. God knows the messages now. What had Emmett done to Emma exactly, cute Emma with all her shades of brown, a friend of Emmett's since forever. Zzzzzz. Zzzzzz. Richard was ready to hand over the phone without ceremony or teasing, without any paternal condescension whatsoever (every Zzzzzz was like a poke at Emma), but then he spotted Emmett sprawled across two chairs reading *Ampersand*, no doubt in anticipation of meeting the author. And that was fine. That made sense. Of course he'd be curious. There was no need for permission to be granted. But Richard stopped short, and Emmett looked up and seemed to measure the distance between them as if space and time were defined exclusively by confrontation. Or was Richard putting across this view, remembering his own teenage years? Regardless, a father's memory is longer. A few feet is merely a continuation of all those previous steps from infancy to—Richard's pocket gave another nudge. Just give him the fucking phone, he thought, and walk away. He must be missing it. "What?" Emmett finally said full of accusation, and Richard answered with "Nothing," thrusting his hands into his pockets and turning back toward the restaurant.

After the Brill Building, Jamie called Alice because Alice lived nearby, in Hell's Kitchen, or what was once Hell's Kitchen, and Alice was his girlfriend, or almost girlfriend, a girl he saw on occasion, an actress you might recognize from a Xerox commercial ("So real it's almost . . . real?") and a short-lived Apple iMac campaign (she played Eve) but mostly you would know her if you ate at Orso on West 46th Street since Alice had been on the waitstaff there for eighteen years and was well known to its regulars, her presence representing a sort of Kuleshov effect, whether a barometer of consistency in New York—*Alice at Orso*—or an uncomfortable reminder of dreams gone stagnant—*Alice at Orso*—or the flat progress of other people's timelines—*Alice at Orso*—or the disappearance of once-lovely youth—*Alice at Orso*—and if you mention Alice at Orso to certain people, first they smile—she's *the best*—then they grin—she's been there forever—then they just grow quiet. We all know Alice. It was early afternoon when Jamie stopped by for a cup of Sanka. This was their code for sex. Sometimes it was Folger's, sometimes it was Maxwell House. Once he made her laugh by asking if she cared for a Brim job, her laugh sustaining him for the rest of the day. He was saving Chock full o'Nuts for a special occasion. Alice wanted more than just casual coffee—Jamie knew that—but Alice had forgotten how to ask for more and nowadays just took what she could get without much complaint. She was a forty-three-year-old waitress/ actress who tried her best. As they drank their coffee, across town Ram Barrett grew more curious about what his old friend had brought him, so he put aside his work and watched this pretty woman answer "How are you?" over and over as if Ram had asked the question, which seemed almost cruel when gauged against her obvious decline, and Ram's stomach, or not quite his stomach but the area within his belly where that weepy boy took cover, tightened as the question gave its final answer with a funeral and a husband and daughters and a coffin going into the ground, the time code confirming the silence of 12:01 P.M. Then Ram put in the other tape. It took a moment to understand what he was seeing in that tidal light, the stillness of the face and its terrible but affecting reality, as the darkness rose and fell like waves and this woman was made of sand. Jesus. It was hard to watch. But it also inspired Ram, like he was in college again, and he went about assembling the footage long into the evening, tweaking the visuals to enhance the oblique liquid movement, putting in a haunting temporary score (*My*

Neighborhood by Goldmund) and trying to give every cut and transition a particular tone. No doubt about it, the man had talent. As he worked he thought about his younger sister, who had died ten years ago, and when he was finished he emailed the short video to his older sister— *Just wanted you to see this*—who after crying for an hour forwarded it to her best friend—*Warning, the ending is rough but ain't that the truth.*

Richard and family were thirty thousand feet in the air, three hours into a five-hour flight. Candy and Chloe were watching a romantic comedy about time travel, one of those eve-of-marriage plots where the bridegroom-to-be gets confronted by his older divorced self. They were enjoying the movie, the two of them laughing—too loudly, thought Richard, who was busy pushing aside notions of impending death, convinced the plane was going down—now—now—now—and wondering if he had the wherewithal to say the things he should say, like "I love you" to his family, rather than scream or shit his pants or reach over and give Candy's boobs a quick squeeze. That was still his go-to impulse when presented with the concept of disaster: find nearest girl, squeeze boob. When do those stupid urges go away? Adolescence seems to open a small hole in which the rest of our lives drain. Emmett was sitting in the seat in front of him, and occasionally Richard pretended to search through his carry-on so he could peek through the gap at his 2Q2C POS son. He was a third of the way through *Ampersand*, roughly the section where Stimpson, Harfield, Matthews, and Rogin begin to plot their senior prank. Should they steal the license plates from the faculty cars, dress the statue of John James Shearing in a nurse's uniform, remove the clapper from the church bell, all pranks committed by previous classes? Then Edgar Mead, lowly but accepted junior, gives them an idea:

"I told them they should kidnap the headmaster's son." Of course it was a joke, one of those things you say thinking you've said nothing at all, but when a silence follows you realize, good or bad, you've said something. In my defense I was still recovering from my spring vacation with the Vecks, still roiled that my own family had neither the money nor the will to bring me back to San Francisco, still offended that some kids hit the slopes in Vermont and some kids hit the beaches in Florida and all I hit were the books with Mr. Veck, who tutored me so I might limp through junior year without flunking. "The man is doing you a tremendous favor," my father said via letter. All these favors and opportunities from the Vecks, the stories from Mr. about how my father had saved his life in the war, the half-mast glances from Mrs. like she wished a white cross stood instead of this windbag here. You would have thought the Battle of the Bulge was last week. And then there was Jr. Two weeks of a muddy New England March with Timothy Veck. Who was the one doing the favors? Give me Bastogne any day. So I said it again, seconding that silence. "Absolutely kidnap Veck. I bet he would even enjoy it."

Richard thought about reaching through the seats and tapping Emmett and saying, "Pretty good, huh?" But esteem for his father seemed a zero-sum game. Rather, he leaned back and rehearsed the next twenty-four hours in his head. "Dad, I need *Ampersand*." Nobody knew about the quid pro quo proposal from Rainer Krebs and Eric Harke. "You owe me this." They were simply going to New York so Emmett and Chloe could meet their grandfather. "It could be a real opportunity for me." Candy could meet her father-in-law. "I'll make it a good movie, I swear, and we can write it together, if you want." They could all meet Andy and get to know him, just like his father wanted. "It's a win-win." And maybe Richard and his father would reconcile and shake hands and who knows, maybe even hug. "I'm glad I came." The plane's engines—was that sound normal? And the flight attendants—did they look nervous? "Give me *Ampersand* or I swear I'll fucking kill you."

So much happens to us without our knowing. People might talk about us, whisper and judge, and those whispers and judgments are forever in our company, a groundless shadow. Let me defend myself, we might plead, if we were aware of the charges, but they only smile at us and we smile right back. Who knows what about whom? And then there's the undeniable role of coincidence, the thousand chances in a day. Good fortune. Bad fortune. How many times have we almost died without our realizing it? Life, I'm convinced, is filled with far more near misses than we dare to imagine. Late in waking up, missing a train, not answering a phone, going down 79th Street instead of 80th Street—how many of those moments have spared our life? Until, of course, the blade drops, reverse engineered, it can seem. Like that morning when a bus driver in Queens—let's call him Stan, Stan Mocker—was tiptoeing to the bathroom so as not to wake his wife, which Stan had done numerous times without incident, but today his right foot slammed into the bureau and he viciously stubbed (in hindsight broke) his toe, and because of that and a few other choice bits of happenstance, at 9:12 A.M. on a Friday near the end of March he would be a few seconds slow in noticing the distracted person stepping from the curb and—*boom!* The sound would travel with terrible speed. All hearts within hearing would hold a beat, all lungs would gasp, as the world briefly constricted around a newborn center, as if a noise could describe the radius of a soul. Then the sirens would come. All because of a toe. There might be no gods but we are still their playthings. So while Jamie was having his kaffeeklatsch in Alice's apartment, he had no idea that *12:01 P.M.* was being uploaded, forwarded, linked, liked, and shared a hundred, a thousand, ten thousand times, until it quickly became one of the top-rated and most-viewed videos on YouTube with user comments like *This is devastating* and *What an amazing woman* and *@#$% nasty* and *I've never seen anything like this, thank you, thank you, thank you.* It crossed generational lines since it combined the sentimental with the macabre, wrapped up in mothers and wives and tied together with cancer and that greatest of universalities, decay. By the time Jamie mustered the strength to return to RazorRam to pick up the edited version, two days and almost two hundred thousand views had passed. Jamie's brother was arriving later that afternoon, and that, plus the situation with his father and his uncertainty over the video's extreme postscript, gave Jamie a distracted air, which Ram Barrett read as soon-to-be-unleashed fury. Ram was ready with an explanation and an apology—"I swear I never thought it would go viral"—though mostly he appreciated the exquisite reality of the situation. When Jamie finally broke the silence and said, "I'm not going to watch the thing so just tell me the truth," Ram searched for the proper angle. "The truth?" "Yeah," Jamie said. "Like is it a total disaster?" Ram considered this for a moment. "No," he said, "it's pretty great." The things we don't know until it's too late.

Coming into LaGuardia, Richard was on the wrong side of the approach. The other windows gathered up the skyline view with its rows of razor-sharp buildings, like a shark bursting through water. Candy strained for a peek, as did Chloe, while Emmett remained stubbornly uninterested. He was nearing the final chapters of *Ampersand*, his attention periodically flipping to the back of the book and the photo of his grandfather. There was a definite resemblance, Richard thought, returning his seatback to the upright position, a resemblance in those eyes, like odds were being calculated, emotions dictated by a set of knowable rules. The boy was probably destined for a full ride at Stanford or Caltech, robotics one of his interests. The landing gear went down, its thump introducing the possibility of catastrophic failure, but Richard had moved into the acceptance phase of the flight, as if there were a special providence in the fall of a Boeing 737–800, and he almost dared a fireball. The last time he was in New York it was a mecca for a person in his line of abuse. He could give the family a tour of his humble chemical beginnings, sit them in a double-decker bus and start with the Red Dragon on 73rd and Third and the bartender who never carded and knew Richard as Jack-and-Coke, and after that head into Central Park, where pot and speed had their early reign, the dealers singing sense-sense-sensimilla and ice-ice as if a musical number were about to commence, and while in the Upper East Side be sure to peek into the parentless apartments where Whip-its and poppers were the party favors of choice, and definitely go west and pass the natural history museum and mention how a tab of acid could put flesh back onto bone. Funny, he could think back on those days and blush at their innocence. The plane took its final turn, banking over the gray lake of a cemetery. "That's a lot of dead people," Candy said, and she gave Richard her hand. She hated the landing part. But Richard's gloom was lifting, even if he was wary of what hid under the sheet, something he discussed in his last meeting—that excited feeling of return. His chemical tour would continue down in SoHo, where eighteen-year-old Richard discovered his true passion, cocaine in all its forms (imagine Lou Reed covering Lou Rawls's "You'll Never Find Another Love Like Mine"), like in that loft on Wooster where he dabbled with freebase (*viva la liberación*) and that other loft on Wooster where he pondered speedballs (picture a ménage à trois with Rogers and Astaire) and from there get your camera ready for the ex–ink factory on Grand where he met his number-one-true-love (do you take this rock to be your lawfully wedded wife) and after that stumble into Alphabet City (the ABCs of being fucked) into one of those near-abandoned tenements near Tompkins (no plumbing, no electricity) lit by the flicker of butane (oh, the multilevel thrill) revealing all you can imagine (a full-blown crackhead) and all you can never understand (this is the person I deserve to be). The plane touched down. Candy clapped. Richard always hated the people who clapped.

They sat around a table, ten of them, nineteen, twenty years old, six males, four females, none of them as attractive, as outright irresistible, as the nineteen- and twenty-year-olds of the imagination. Then again, this was the New School. These kids were the hand-me-downs from NYU, their sleeves longer than their reach. They stared at Jamie and probably wondered Who the hell is this guy and what gives him the right to teach our class? I mean, NYU has Errol Morris. And Columbia has Miloš Forman. Jamie Dyer? Ooh, a film course with *the* Jamie Dyer. Jamie drummed a fuck-you-too rhythm on his chest, a nervous yet enjoyable tic, and in terms of beat and tempo, one in which he excelled. He grinned at the class. Thirty thousand dollars a year for this chest-drumming maestro? Serves them right. They were foolish enough to sign up for something called Dramamentary: A Search for the Real in the Hyperreal. They had lost all credibility at the door. Jamie considered putting in *12:01 P.M.* and maybe getting their opinion (he was still unaware of its growing viral status, though his class was aware, was in fact buzzing about its strange effect and were curious who had made the uncredited thing and if it was even genuine), but Jamie wasn't yet ready to suffer through that memory. Since Sylvia was on his mind, he started to tell them about that time in college (and there was a point, he swore) when he went to Vermont for a ski trip: "I was driving with my high school girlfriend, like my first love, my first everything, and we were at that off-and-on-again stage, both of us at different colleges, but we were going on this ski trip together and I was really excited, not sure how she felt, but I was really excited, and we were driving on one of those almost too-perfect Vermont country roads, near Middlebury—she went to Middlebury College—and there wasn't a lot of traffic on this road, it was empty, and I remember seeing this dog up ahead, a brown Lab, he was sort of jogging along the side of the road, and I remember thinking, Watch out for that dog, you know, in case it makes a sudden turn, and my girlfriend, she wasn't really my girlfriend then, we had basically broken up because of the distance thing, anyway, she pointed at the dog because she was probably thinking the same thing, when from the other side of the road another dog bursts through the bushes and shoots out right in front of the car, like it was playing a game of how-close. Well, too close. I swear every tire rolled over him. It was the sickest feeling I had ever felt. I remember thinking, Oh no, oh no, God no. Did that really just happen? That moment of instant change. My girlfriend took such a deep breath that it was like she stole the air from my lungs. We stopped the car, quickly got out. The dog, it was some kind of collie mix, it wasn't dead but you knew it was not long for this world. All crumpled up. Blood was coming out of its mouth. All I could say was, Oh no. The dog tried to get up, but its spine must have been broken. But damn if it didn't try, again and again. Just terrible. By now the other dog, the brown Lab, he stopped and watched us from a distance. It must've been its friend, not to anthropomorphize. At one point it sat down. I tried to touch the dog, the dog I had hit, but it bit at my hand, like I was planning on hurting it more. That was hard. I didn't know what to do. This is before cellphones, mind you. I wanted to find the owner, obviously. So I tell my girlfriend, not really my girlfriend, to stay with the dog while I start running from house to house, but the houses around here aren't very close together and I'm running and I'm getting winded and I'm not in the best of shape and either nobody's home or they don't have a dog or their dog is by their side, it's all no luck until I get to a house and it's a nice house, like a gentleman's farm, and this woman answers, middle-aged but hell, I'm probably her age now, and I ask her if she has a collie-like dog, and she says yes, and I tell her that I think I just hit it with my car, that I hit it badly, that I don't think it's going to live. Now she's pretty cool and collected, calm and collected, even-keeled, whatever, maybe she's just reacting to my obvious panic, but, she gets her husband, they seem to be Boston transplants with some money, and the two of them jump into their car, a Range Rover, with me in the backseat, and it's like they're my parents and I've done some-thing very, very bad. We drive about two miles, I can't believe I ran that far, and we get to where my car's pulled over and where my no-longer-girlfriend-but-the-woman-I-still-totally-love is sitting with the dog, trying to comfort it, her jacket covering its body, keeping it warm. The second the couple sees the situation, they know it's hopeless. But the dog is definitely still alive. And the woman, it must've been her dog, and maybe the brown Lab was his dog, maybe this is their second marriage, their Vermont reinvention, anyway, the brown Lab goes over to the man's side, and the woman runs to the injured dog but at the five-foot mark she stops, because it is undeniably grim, and those last few steps she takes real slow, like she's walking down the aisle or something. By now I'm at the side of my car. I'm almost in tears. My girlfriend leaves the dog, to give this woman some space. I've never killed anything before. This woman kneels and puts her hands on the dog like she's going to heal it, like she still has that fantasy from child-hood, that you can magically heal something with your touch, but she can't, of course, no matter how much she tries, and she buries her face into the fur, and she's crying, weeping really, keening, and she looks up at the sky and stretches her arms heavenward in that classic pose of why, why, why—I remember thinking, Wow, that's dramatic—and she lets loose with this cry of pure lament, like it was scraped from the bottom of her soul, so real, you know, and almost beautiful, I thought, like this right here is the meaning of life, right here, and then she um, she um, she howls the dog's name." Jamie stopped, no longer sure what the point of the story was. He had lost his way, sidetracked by the unexpected pleasure of its active remembering. At eighteen it was hands down the worst thing he had ever seen, watching this dog suffer, watching this woman wail, watching it all and knowing it was all his fault. Sylvia seemed almost comfortable in the situation, like high emotion was a shared experience, two players or more. And Jamie thought maybe this will bring us back together, maybe this is what we needed. Then the woman cried the dog's name—"Mr. Bumpus, Mr. Bumpus, Mr. Bumpus!" Mr. Bumpus? Who the hell names their dog Mr. Bumpus? There he was, his whole world thrown open, like he was the key and the dog was the lock and on the other side he glimpsed life, or life as reflected through pain and loss, that must have been the point of the story, but then he heard "Mr. Bumpus" and it slammed the door shut and turned the whole story into a punch line, a goddamn joke. Maybe that was the point. The woman rested her head on Mr. Bumpus's chest, gathered up the fur around its neck and started to lull, "You're a good dog, you're a good dog." The class waited for Jamie to regain the story's thread but instead he apologized for this tangent and dove straight ahead into a discussion of their short film projects, which were uniformly awful.

The taxi drove over the Triborough-now-RFK bridge, the sunset an hour behind lower Manhattan, its vestige of light almost ultraviolet. Candy and Chloe and Emmett were in the backseat talking, or Chloe and Candy were talking, but the protective barrier and the Persian music made it impossible for Richard to hear what they were saying. For the first five minutes he kept turning around and asking, "What?" and caught the gist of their excitement—Bergdorf's and Tiffany's, *Friends* and *Seinfeld* and *Sex and the City*—but after a while Richard gave up and returned to New York, alone. He was feeling carsick. It might have been the music, with its electric oud and high-pitched singer, like Scheherazade on the dance floor. Or the foul perfume of that bottle stuck to the dash. Maybe it was just coming back that turned his stomach. This particular approach Richard knew well since it was how they drove back from Southampton every weekend, Mom behind the wheel, Dad doing the Sunday crossword, Richard and Jamie in the back playing Twenty Questions. "Is he dead?" "No." "Is he famous?" "No." "Do I know him?" "Yes." "Is he me?" No, Richard told himself, I have a life beyond my old life, the family in the backseat a testament to that fact. At first Richard never wanted children. "I'll fuck it up," he told Candy when she told him she was pregnant. "I'll fuck it up and you'll hate me for it and that'll fuck us up and then I'm back to being a fuckup instead of a fuckup who's trying his best to be less fucked up." And he was trying his best, albeit unsuccessfully, unlike Candy, who was two years sober and dating him against the advice of everyone. "I have faith in you," she said in a way that was never annoying, "and I'm feeling all this love and I want to share it with whatever's brewing inside me." But Richard didn't rise to the occasion. Instead, he disappeared. For seven months. But near the end he tried his best again, and he was in the delivery room for the arrival of eight pounds' worth of shrieking, shaking, light-blue-shading-to-pink boy. "He's lovely," one of the nurses told him as she wiped clean the gunky mess. But all Richard could see was a stranger, or worse, an intruder, or even worse, a fellow addict suffering through detox. "A future heartbreaker," another nurse said. Richard wanted to throttle them. Because his first thought, his forever first thought was, I could so easily pick this thing up and smash it to the floor. The taxi merged onto the FDR Drive, and Manhattan was underfoot again. But feelings for the boy did come, haltingly, every month Emmett carving a slightly bigger space within Richard. It was almost like Richard's own pregnancy; the extra weight might have gone unnoticed but by the first year it was there, not entirely pleasant, and Richard delivered himself into the world of fathers, powerless but clean. But for the sin of that first thought, Richard had to imagine the boy always hanging on by a thread. The taxi turned onto

96th. "This is my old neighborhood," Richard told the backseat, and he realized that the whole way in he never once looked for the missing twin towers.

Released from the subway at 77th and Lexington, Jamie headed toward the Carlyle on Madison. It was almost ten o'clock. The weather was chilly, winter still in control of night despite the day's advances. Jamie wore an inadequate corduroy jacket, but he was meeting his brother at Bemelmans and no matter his low-down fantasies he wanted to look presentable, hence the shave and the shower and the lack of his warmer but grubby Carhartt. He passed Lenox Hill Hospital, people loitering around in a sort of 1970s tableau of New York. He remembered when Richard had done some time here, when he was twenty-two, a fuckup beyond measure, and ended up at the emergency room after a harrowing night, the details of which he never discussed with anyone. "I need to die," he told the admitting nurse. "I'm trying my best but it's just not working." Up to the psych ward he went. Jamie visited a few days later, went through those locked doors on the eighth floor and wondered what he was going to say. People milled about the central common area. It almost seemed as if the visitors were the ones afflicted, as if in here the world was reversed, the sad and suicidal, the psychotic, in total understanding of the truth, that they were lost, while family and friends and lovers tried desperately to find their way home. There was no screaming, no oddball behavior. Voices whispered and hands rummaged for something to do. Jamie saw Richard sitting by himself at a table near the back. He was pale and skinny, dark around the eyes but otherwise intact, like a house gutted by fire. Richard made no sign of noticing Jamie even when Jamie touched the table and said, "I'm glad you're safe." There was silence until Richard finally spoke. He spoke slowly and calmly. "I'm not sure I like you," he said. "I think maybe you're full of shit. But hey"—Richard lifted his arm to the scene around him—"look at the triumph I've made. But for the last six years I've pretty much wanted to hit you in the face." Typical of his brother to lunge rather than embrace. "I don't know why I don't let myself like you. Maybe one day I will. Or I hope so." Jamie nodded, neither shocked nor amused. "I'm just here to show my support," he said. "To tell you I love you and I'm glad you're getting help again." Did he mean this? Did he care? Or *was* he full of shit? Jamie crossed Park. The last time he saw Richard was two years ago, when he visited L.A. for Christmas. As a gift he drew pencil portraits of Emmett and Chloe, and Candy overreacted to their artistry, though Jamie did put in extra effort, hoping they might get framed and Richard would have to pass them every day. Near Madison "Whole Lotta Love" sounded and Jamie checked the caller ID and its accompanying photo: Sylvia smiling, snapped a few months before she died. Who was this ghost? Jamie stared at those eyes in sad retrograde, and instead of answering and breaking the spell, he allowed himself to be haunted.

Bemelmans was New York in its heyday, whatever heyday you might conjure, say when the city was really fun, yes, back then, when money and smoking and drinking were part of the great grand implied, when men looked great, women looked greater, and everybody was having sex on the sly. All of this happened before our time. Even our parents lamented about what had been lost, as if we all peeked from the banister and watched the grown-ups mingle downstairs. Our someday never quite came. Except at Bemelmans. At Bemelmans the walls were decorated with charming murals by what's-his-name of *Madeline* fame, his Central Park inhabited by dapper cats and dapper dogs, which added to its storybook quality, the children's fantasy of where adults congregate after they kiss you good night. It was a place of mysterious low light and red leather booths and uniformed waiters serving cocktails with names like Whiskey Smash and The Valencia, and a piano player playing "As Time Goes By" every hour for all the new arrivals, like good old Ned Durango who bushwhacked through the crowd and planted his elbow on the bar like Balboa at the Pacific taking possession of all he surveyed.

Unlike Ned Durango in *Pink Eye*, Richard divided his twelve-dollar Diet Coke into fifty-cent sips and resented every plink of the piano that clogged the middle of the room. His brother, no surprise, was late. Every newcomer carried an expectation of Jamie but the truth was another couple overdressed or underdressed. Irving Berlin turned into Cole Porter. Candy and the children were upstairs in a two-bedroom suite courtesy of his father. A chilled bottle of champagne greeted their arrival—*love Dad*—which enraged Richard but made Candy laugh. "He's trying," she said. Chloe bounced from room to room eager for the morning curtain and its first showing of *New York!* starring Chloe Dyer. And Emmett? He complained about sharing a bedroom with his sister. "It's not like we're ten anymore," he told Richard, and Richard gave him an anachronistic, out-of-the-blue "Dem's de breaks, bud." The stupid things fathers say to their sons. Cole Porter turned into George Gershwin. These songs brought to mind more glamorous people leading more glamorous lives and underscored Bemelmans as a movie set in search of a proper star. This is for you, the piano player lied. Finally the door delivered Jamie—thank God—his eyes blinking as if darkness were the brightest of lights, and Richard practically jumped and waved, Jamie touched by his enthusiasm. The brothers smiled and shook hands as if a net divided them. Despite everything they were the only ones who knew how to play certain games. History receded into a gentler past. Or was it the past that receded into a more gentle history? Either way, they shared that old conspiratorial Dyer air. I watched them from a corner booth, the best in the house. I wish I could claim some Dickensian coincidence in my being here, but that afternoon I had overheard Jamie talking to his father on the phone, mentioning Bemelmans and meeting up with Richard, and I decided to take the opportunity to bump into the brothers. Richard? Jamie? Oh hey, wow, long time, et cetera, et cetera. Quite the gamut of conversation chased its tail in my head. I would run into them with Bea on my arm, Bea who sat next to me in the booth, drinking her Carlyle Punch and looking almost thirty in her hydrangea-blue Anita dress, though the silk choker rendered her neck grade school. No doubt my lawyer would disapprove, and my wife, my children, my dead father, my dead mother. But I didn't care. I reached under the table, unrestrained by order. If only this was the worst thing I'd ever done. George Gershwin turned into Harold Arlen. Bea perked up. This song she recognized. I readied myself to get up, slightly disappointed that the brothers hadn't seen me first, and I was almost on my feet when Richard and Jamie started to laugh and shake their heads, and I wondered if maybe they had seen me—*Don't move, Philip Topping at five o'clock!*—if maybe I looked like a joke. Was the velvet jacket a mistake? The pocket square? Those brutes. With a certain kind of fury I tossed a hundred-dollar bill on the table and grabbed Bea, who protested, but I prevailed. Near the door the waiter rushed over and stopped me. It seemed I was sixty dollars short.

IV

April 25, 1951

Dear Charlie,

I feel really bad about what happened. I am sorry. Truly. I was still mad about that grade on my Coleridge paper – I deserved better, it was a good paper, well thought out and perfectly executed. Zeus forbid if you don't constrict yourself to the Exeter mold. I put a lot of effort into that paper and tried to write like that old opium-eater and it was fifty times more interesting than your run of the mill term paper with its tired thesis statements and conclusions. I did something different and now I am rolling the rock back up the hill. And then I got your letter and I thought maybe it was a joke. It was all bad timing. You were just trying to make me feel better. I know that now. And it was late and I was tired and when you came into my room and said those things and maybe you were starting to come down with whatever you have now and that would explain a lot but I lost my temper and I am sorry. I over-reacted. I should not have hit you and said the things I said. That was wrong. I was just so bloody upset about that paper. I am the best student in English class. Everyone knows that. Mr. Halley has it in for me, if that's not obvious. And you were just trying to make me feel better and you were tired and sick and I was tired and frustrated. How are you feeling now? Are you coming back to school soon? I certainly deserved my suspension and was lucky I didn't get expelled. You said what you said only meaning the nicest thing in the world. We are the oldest friends after all. I should have never gone as far as I did and called you the things I called you. You are nothing like that, Charlie. You're a good man, an even gooder friend (that's a joke, Mr. Halley). You were exhausted and feverish. I should have been more understanding but I had to write that damned paper all over again, make it boring just to satisfy the way it's done. So forgive me, Charlie. I hope you feel better and come back to school soon. You are, as Coleridge might say, a companionable form. Unlike Mr. Halley, bells his only music.

Your friend forever,

Andrew

IV.i

WHEN ALL OF THIS HAPPENED I thought of myself as old. Amazing. Every day I am more and more convinced that we can only use time to measure our own shadows, and while we might think of memories as the sun, they are at best a torch. In terms of Bea I was certainly old. Much too old. I should have known better. After losing my family and my job and my good name—whatever that means—I still called her and still took her to Bemelmans and still brought her back to the Hotel Wales where, despite everything, I still kept a room. Absurd. Amazing and absurd. But Richard and Jamie had put me in a mood. I hoped for a reunion but all I found was the old flickering, and me feeling around for a path. The Dyers perform their secret ministries, and we Toppings, or this Topping in particular, strains to catch his name on their lips. I remember summer beach picnics organized by the Dyer and Topping women, the mothers curating our good cheer; Isabel took the photographs as Eleanor posed the players, the two of them hoping that these happy pictures might stand in for how we looked back, a prefabricated nostalgia. If fathers are unknowable, then mothers are all too visible, a reminder of our earthly attachments. At some point between the swimming and the exploring of dunes and the tossing of various discs and balls, I would gravitate to the doldrums, hoping for sympathy. My dad was always quiet yet genial, like a foreigner who could only respond with a few common expressions. By the age of twelve I had pretty much given up on him and even told my mother so in a moment rife I'm sure with Freudian overtones. "I don't think I really love him," I said. She looked at me as if I had handed her something homemade and easily broken. "That's

okay," she told me, touching the back of my head. "You will someday."
During these family get-togethers my attention would wander over to
A. N. Dyer, and I swear I could read my own discomfort in those inkwell eyes. I'd watch him toss a stick for one of the dogs, his right arm
cranking it a good distance, my legs tempted to give chase. Absurd. At
the Wales I ordered room service—champagne and strawberries,
shrimp cocktail, crème caramel—since I had shortchanged Bea on the
glamorous portion of the evening. She stretched herself on the bed, on
a duvet of faded florals, geraniums mostly, and began to answer texts
on her phone, thumbs flying, feet heeling away shoes, a youthful gravity spreading her legs, like branches wet with snow. In my defense, I
loved her. Then again, I'm guilty of easily falling in love, of confusing
the abstract with the concrete, hoping those words might cast me as a
caring individual and dispel my notions of a sinister center. I believe in
love at first sight so that I might be seen.

I went over and touched her.

"The Bea's knee," I said.

She grinned but continued with her texting.

There were no other affairs before Bea, though I had become prone
to late-night wanderings into the seamier side of the Internet. To my
eyes at least, a new sexual revolution was taking place. Self-exposure
now seemed a rite of passage, a flash of breast carrying the weight of a
wink and full frontal nudity nothing more than a big warm hello. So
many women, barely women, were allowing themselves to be photographed in all sorts of compromised states. And every day more flesh
was added to the rolls. Were these amateurs or pros? Was this the way
of the world or simply the way of the World Wide Web? I honestly had
no idea. But regardless, these youthful exploits went begging at my
fingers. In my day pornography was a pleasant if offensive joke, strictly
the province of professional creeps and dirty uncles. At Exeter and
Yale I was a good citizen, a thoughtful man, certainly better than I am
today, marching in Take Back the Night rallies, volunteering at
Planned Parenthood, reading Luce Irigaray and Julia Kristeva and Hé-
lène Cixous. I would have spat on anyone using the word *bitch*, let alone
whore or *cunt*. My world had no fucking. Maybe people screwed or got

laid. They banged on occasion. But even one-night-stands went through a certain due process. Between Helen Dieter and my wife I had seven sexual partners, only three of whom I dated for any length of time. This is no excuse, I understand. Nine is a fine number. And I was happy with Ashley, happily married, happily entangled in parenthood, the love functional yet consistent. But then came the second blush of middle age, which, in combination with the discovery of Internet porn, roused my hibernating adolescence, who realized all that he had missed and all that he was missing, one naked girl at a time.

I unzipped for Bea.

Many a night grading papers was spent intermittently clicking onto another couple fucking, ass fucking, cock sucking, double cock fucking, fist fucking, *click-click-click*, yet still I needed more. I couldn't rest until I had seen it all and please God let me see it all so that I may rest. Hell is other people fucking. To allay myself of the virtual, I began to dabble in the consequential and created a secret email account (Larrymacawber@yahoo.com) and trolled Craigslist and joined an on-line dating service. I never moved past the most superficial contact and more often scared myself into three or four days of abstinence, that is, until one afternoon in mid-January. I was in SoHo shopping, hoping the J.Crew down here had a hipper edge than the J.Crew uptown, when a dark-eyed woman came up to me as I thumbed through a stack of chambray utility shirts and asked if I needed help. I said yes, please, and she took me around and updated my wardrobe to the tune of two thousand dollars. Somehow during the exchange I charmed her—I remember teasing her about her almost hidden tattoo—and by the end I signed her up as my personal shopper. That's when the emails began. Of course, when I came home loaded down with bags, Ashley praised my self-reliance—she usually bought my clothes—though a few of my fashion choices she found dubious.

Bea started rubbing me while finishing her text one-handed.

I'll spare you the details of that night and all the nights before, non-nights really, nights stolen from the middle of the day, like the two hours at the Sheraton near LaGuardia, or the hour and a half at the Howard Johnson's in Brooklyn. It's all too easy to imagine. Nothing new there. But on occasion I find myself crouching down and shining my light in her direction, seeking a great and passionate affair instead of a twenty-year-old girl making shadow puppets with her hands. Forgive me. And forgive me for the next morning when I waited outside my old building reeking of cocktail sauce and sex. I knew that Ashley would soon be down to walk Rufus to Buckley—he was in kindergarten—and then taxi Eloise to Chapin—she was in second grade. Except for the funeral, I had been dodging them, too mortified to deal with the situation, though I did have the excuse of my father dying. Strange, I was at my best as a son when I was at my worst as a father. A. N. Dyer would have had a field day with the likes of me.

> Look at Philip Topping, gathering up the morning sun like a cormo-
> rant in herringbone, while the better-formed flocks of Upper East
> Side bird passed by, their stomachs full of grain rather than the
> squirmier aspects of life.

Ashley was unsalvageable. She was forever devastated by my actions, as she told me, rather dramatically, early on—"I will never get over what you've done to me! Never!"—though soon she discovered her survivor's instinct, her ability to plow ahead, that sharp McCracken chin the furrowing blade. She began to exercise every day. She ran a marathon. She got back into graphic design and rekindled an interest in experimental theater (whereas I was an opera man). A year later she met an Irish expat and remarried and had another child, a girl named Charlotte. Funny how life has a way of justifying itself. Thanks to her misery, she was never happier. Plus she had the pleasure of watching me curl into a small turd-shaped ball, my destiny guided by a dung beetle. But as of that morning her happy prospects still seemed an impossibility, and I was the asshole king finally making an effort with his kids. I would take Rufus to school, the logical paternal choice; I would lift him onto my shoulders and bounce him to Buckley, show my face to the teachers, to the administration, to the parents: Philip Topping, guilty yet resilient. I grew Hollywood hopeful. But when 8:10 A.M. passed and there was still no sign of them I went over to Carlos the doorman and asked if they had come down yet. He told me they had left two days ago for spring break. Fuck me. Of course they had. A week in Lyford Cay. I even said, "Fuck me," and Carlos, fuck him, grinned, and I slipped further into A. N. Dyer's world.

> Philip turned from the building and started to creep south, a journey of twenty-two blocks that might as well have taken twenty-two years. Time streamed forward and backward, with Park Avenue as the opposite of Lethe—every street brought a damp realization of what he was and what he would forever be.

When I returned to the apartment Gerd was frantic. Richard and Jamie were due in thirty minutes, and Andy was still upstairs in bed while Andrew was in the bathroom downstairs, the shower running for twenty minutes, like maybe he had slipped and broken something, like maybe he was trying to yell but instead was drowning, "like maybe he's getting poached," Gerd said to me. The poor woman. Bagels and cream cheese and smoked salmon and a variety of muffin and morning pastry and fruit overwhelmed the kitchen, the sink bunched with an assortment of flowers in search of vases, and on top of this, on top of the squeezing of oranges and the brewing of regular and decaf coffee, Gerd was trying to resuscitate the apartment, to shock the living room into breathing again, to peel open the eyes of the dining room and let it glimpse once more a table spread with food. "I just want it to be nice," she told me as she straightened the chairs, "for Andy."

I took off my overcoat and helped with the flowers.

I knew flowers thanks to my mother. In Southampton we had wonderful gardens, in all states and styles, which she constantly tended to in green clogs, an oversized button-down shirt, a tennis visor. She snipped at whatever needed snipping, never pleased with the lilacs near the tennis court or the rhododendron around the cottage, dreaming of a greenhouse, a gift my father offered every year but which she poohpoohed as too expensive. She was wary of ever appearing to try too hard, which of course took great effort. She was a believer in the natural graces, and when she got sick, she never once thought of putting up a fight. But she was famous for her gardens. And I was her faithful assistant. I deadheaded, I pruned (there is a difference), I weeded, I mulched. By the time I was nine I could identify most varieties of flower, whether in the field or in chintz, and my older siblings accused me of sucking up, as if being a loving son was the same as being a teacher's pet. Typical. The teasing was particularly merciless when I won best of show for juniors at the Southampton Garden Club's annual flower show (won it three years in a row, in fact). Once married, I forsook Long Island for the McCracken family compound in upstate New York and gave up gardening, without regret. But as I stood over the sink and rushed through arrangements, I must have remembered my mother somewhere in the task, a loss briefly filled, an illusion of a life maintained, like water for those stems. I placed the vases around the apartment and was putting the last one on the table in the front hall when the doorbell rang.

Andrew was still in the bathroom.

Andy was still upstairs.

Gerd was changing in her room.

I was near the door so I answered.

Richard stood front and center, the bow to the family ship. When he saw me, his expression ran aground. "Philip?"

"Hi, Richard."

My hands were still wet from the flowers.

"What are you doing here?" he asked, wiping away the moisture.

"I'm staying here."

"Here as in here, in this apartment?"

"Yes." I smiled at the family behind him. "Please, come in."

Richard remained stuck by the door as the rest of the crew abandoned ship. I introduced myself and told them I was an old friend, like since forever, but then I noticed Richard flinch so I clarified the relationship. "Our fathers were very old friends, like from day one."

"How nice," Candy said, sharing with me her undeniable warmth. She wore tight embroidered jeans and furry boots, a coat more in tune with ski slopes than sidewalks. I half-expected her to whoop and come to a sliding stop. It was odd to think of Richard's family as tourists here in New York, but that's what they were, and for that reason their faces lacked a certain patina, of the city in their blood, I suppose, which made them seem extra shiny, untainted by the everyday corrosions of ambition.

"Let me take your coats," I said.

Richard refused the offer. "Where's my father?"

"He's still getting ready," I said. I brought them into the living room, improvising my duties as host. Thankfully the glob of spit from a few nights ago had been cleaned up or had dried into nothing. Or was it my imagination? I did my best to advertise the furniture as if great comfort lay ahead rather than mild suspicion. Small talk commenced regarding their visit to New York—any sights? any shows?—with Candy taking on the role of spokesperson. Most of my attention wavered sideways, onto Richard and how the years had treated him versus how they had treated me. He was definitely winning. But his trim physique and solid good looks had no love for the competition, his eyes the veteran of—

"What?" he said with an accusatory tilt.

"Excuse me?"

"You were staring at me."

"No," I said. "Or I don't think I was."

Thank goodness Gerd walked in just then. She was wearing of all things a maid's uniform, which gave her the distinct impression of being swallowed whole by a leaping killer whale. "This is Gerd," I said, my tone not entirely sure.

Gerd smiled—I imagined teeth digging in—and mentioned food.

It seemed everyone had already eaten at the Carlyle.

"No food at all?" she asked. "I thought this was a brunch."

"I had waffles from Belgium," Chloe said. "They were beyond delicious."

Emmett rolled his eyes. "Yeah, and I had toast from France."

"Mom!"

"Emmett."

"You heard that, waffles from Belgium?"

"Not now, Emmett."

"You want her to be a waffles-from-Belgium kind of person?"

Richard stepped in. "Emmett, please."

But Emmett was pushed a little further. "Tonight I guess I'll have chicken from parmigiana."

I have to say I instantly liked the boy, the way he slung a softer version of his father's glare, like he was taking in a pleasant sunrise and not the heat of the day. I was on the verge of adding my two cents about veal from picatta when Richard, staring at me, toggled his head so that the past jibed with the present and I was once again a sign of uncomfortable humidity. "Why are you here, Philip? Don't you have a family?"

"We recently split, my wife and I."

Candy sighed her sympathies.

"And I lost my job."

More sighs from Candy.

"And I don't know if you heard but my father died last week."

Sighs verging on coloratura from Candy.

"Your dad nicely invited me to stay here until I get back on my feet."

"That's really sweet," Candy said. "Friends and family are so—"

Richard cut her off. "Yeah, we're very sorry. Where are you sleeping?"

I paused, possibly for effect. "Your old room, I think."

"My old room?"

"Yes."

"Really?"

"I'm pretty sure."

Richard's eyes seemed to sink until level with a watery horizon, miles of visibility turning into a few grasping inches. Even his children noticed, I think. They watched him like he was too far away to help. Candy went over and slipped an arm around the latitude of his belt and gave him a sexy equatorial squeeze. "Strange being back, huh?" she said.

Richard asked again where his father was.

Candy squeezed tighter. "Has it changed much?"

He muttered about coming all this way, about making an effort.

Candy jostled him hard enough to clear the skip.

"What?"

"Has the place changed?"

"I don't know." He looked around. "It seems emptier, that's for sure. And grayer. Depressing. Like crashing down into Kansas instead of Oz."

"And whose feet are under the house?" Candy asked.

"That's the million-dollar question, baby."

I couldn't help but grin.

"What?" Richard said.

"Nothing."

"No, please, I insist, what?"

And so I told him, smiling because it was a fond memory, how every time I thought of that movie I remembered how the Dyers came over to our house during that summer when the rain never stopped, and how my father had a 32 mm print of *The Wizard of Oz* and he would set up the projector in the living room and pull down the screen, and we kids would gather around and watch it over and over again. "Seems so prehistoric now," I said. "That was our VCR."

Richard shook his head. "That happened maybe once."

"It happened all the time, at least that summer."

"Once."

"That summer was like the summer of *The Wizard of Oz*," I said.

"I remember once and it was at someone's birthday."

"Yes, my birthday. But then we kept on going. It was like every day. I showed the movie to my kids a couple of months ago, a rite of passage, I think, and it really is quite fascinating," I said, perhaps slipping into teacher mode, "how we all see *The Wizard of Oz* when we're about the same age, like six, seven years old, right. We all share that cultural DNA, that Oz gene. And for the two of us"—I directed my attention to Richard—"it goes all the way back to our fathers, who saw it together when it first opened in August of 1939 at the old Capitol Theatre in Times Square. And afterwards Judy Garland and Mickey Rooney got up onstage and did a little routine."

"How can you possibly know that?" Richard said, *asshole* in the subtext.

It was a reasonable question. But first, a bit of backtrack: After my father died my brother was appointed the executor—more like executioner—of the estate while I took on the job of archivist. It was a task no one else desired or deemed important, since the value was sentimental and by then mourning had become monetized, but I needed something to fill my time, so I holed up in his library and began to sift through his papers, well maintained as befitting a good lawyer. There was plenty of surface: maintenance records for bygone vehicles; warranties for old appliances; invoices stretching back fifty years; decades of tax returns; letters, memos, notes involving assorted trustee duties; records of semiprofessional obligations; collections of expired passports and driver's licenses in which I could see him age in bureaucratic leaps; even a copy of my grandfather's will that had specific instructions concerning the distribution of his tennis trophies as well as his 1928 Davis Cup team blazer (it went to Uncle Jimmy, the eldest). None of these things were precious, but it is amazing how a bill of sale for a 1972 Ford Country Squire ($4,318.67) can surprise you with tears. But there were glimmerings below the surface: an accordion folder filled with letters my grandmother had saved, letters my father had written from school, well scripted and postmarked once a week, their content Soviet-style propaganda—*The varsity baseball team should be stellar this year*—though once in a while a flash of truth—*I am happy, or happier, but I am still lonely, but maybe that's just my lot, or should I say my lack of a lot*—slipped in. Then there were the letters from my mother, with her optimism for the future even if the future reached only a few days: *I just know we are going to have a lovely Saturday night together.* She was thirty-one when she wrote that, and thirty-three when she wrote, *In a week I become Mrs. Charles Henry Topping, but tonight I remain Miss Eleanor Garrison Gould, the troublesome Ellie, a stubborn EGG soon to be hatched. What kind of bird will I be? Hopefully not one your father will want to shoot!* Considering those times, my mother was old when she got married, older than my father, and though I never heard any reason why this was the case, there were whispers from an aunt that she had had her heart broken, terribly broken, and it was a minor miracle that she had recovered at all. Recovered? Had this aunt suggested something I was too young to understand? I never did unearth any letters from my father to my mother, which was a relief since I could only take so much intimacy. But the real find in terms of this story came from an old shoe box, Weejuns from Bass, size five, retrieved from the far reaches of the lowest drawer. Inside were twenty-two letters from A. N. Dyer, a few of them bearing the brunt of obligation, a mother's striving for manners, though most seemed inspired by actual friendship with my father. That said, I could never tell the tone of these one-way conversations. Defensive? Dismissive? Good old-fashioned ribbing? There were other things in that shoe box too: a pretty good drawing of a cocker spaniel; a half-full pack of Lucky Strikes; a gnawed number-two pencil; a red rubber ball; an unfired shotgun shell; a wrinkled Exeter tie; a handkerchief crusty with blood; a collection of brass buttons. I had no idea what to make of this mishmash, but they contained an energy, a consciousness of touch, that begged for my hands to complete the circuit. My father's secret stuff. Loose photographs were in there as well, snapshots of Charlie with Andrew in front of Buckley, in Central Park, at the beach in Southampton, the two of them side by side yet formal, like already veterans of the past, soothsayers who saw their own fate. Or maybe it was just my lack of imagination to view my father as a real living boy. Either way, among these photographs was one taken in front of the Capitol Theatre under the marquee for *The Wizard of Oz*, and as further proof, Richard, you eternal prick, my father had saved the ticket stub and the playbill that was autographed by Judy Garland and Mickey Rooney, but before I could lay down this trump the doorbell rang. It was Jamie.

Everyone was glad to see him, which was always his gift.

Richard let his family dive in first with hellos before stepping in.

"Where's Dad?" Jamie asked.

"I have no idea."

"But he's here?"

"Supposedly."

"And Andy?"

"Supposedly as well."

Jamie spotted—"Philip?"—me standing in the background, the

nervous spear-carrier in this royal house. His natural ease with the unexpected won the day, and he approached with a handshake at the ready. "Been a while. I am so sorry about your dad."

I was genuinely touched.

"And I'm sorry I missed the funeral."

"Jamie was just at Sylvia Weston's funeral," Richard told me. "Remember her?"

"Of course. But I thought she died in the fall."

"What fall?"

"I mean in autumn, not like in a tumble."

"It wasn't a funeral, per se," Jamie clarified to his brother.

"So she's been dead for a while?" Richard asked.

"Since late September."

"And I'm just finding out now."

"I guess," Jamie said.

"Such a lovely girl," I added, in the mood to remember and of late having a limited audience to remember with. "And totally down-to-earth. The two of you—the two of them," I said to Candy and the children, wanting to draw them in and maybe get them on my side, "they were the golden couple of high school, like one of the seven wonders of the teenage world, the Colossus of Rhodes holding hands in the middle of the quad."

"Calm down, Philip," Jamie said, checking my sentiment before breaking me down to size. "Why are you here exactly? Don't get me wrong, it's a pleasure to see you, I'm just curious."

"He's staying here," Richard said.

"Like *here* here?"

"Like here in my room here."

"Does Dad know or are you hiding under the bed?"

My insides rattled their old cage. "Your father's been very nice to me."

"Fascinating."

"I've had a tough few months," I said.

Jamie seemed to catch the rain forming within my clouds, and he frowned sympathetically and touched my shoulder, this taste of compassion nearly crushing me.

A distant fanfare of coughs sounded and we were drawn from the living room into the entry hall and this developing sight: A. N. Dyer emerging from his study. The coughing was bright enough to put the rest of him in shadow yet he managed to creep into view, wearing the same suit he wore at my father's funeral, minus the necktie, and sporting a pair of slippers that whispered an undertone of *shh, shh, shh*. We all leaned forward upon his approach as if reaching for ropes to help drag him forward, his hand lifting and forestalling hello for one final reach into his lungs, which was followed by a disconcerting swallow. That's when we noticed his face. He must have recently shaved. Or attempted to shave. Tears of toilet paper clung to his cheek, chin, and jowl. He was Santa with a bloody beard, the twinkle in his eye the gunk that stops the drain.

"If you think this is bad, you should see the bathroom," he told us.

The unexpected joke put everyone at ease, except for Chloe, who backed into her mother's arms. I'm not sure Richard even heard the humor; he was busy following his own, more sentimental script as he stepped forward and clasped his father by the arm, his expression leafing through a dozen readable emotions before landing somewhere between apology and forgiveness. It was one of those moments, thankfully rare, when you can spot another person's core needs, almost by accident—absolutely by accident since those needs are almost graphic when blatant, like seeing the musculature and tendon required to prop up hope. I could see the scene playing in Richard's head.

INT. A. N. DYER APARTMENT/ENTRY HALL—DAY

Richard is shocked by how old his father has become. His idea of the man, trapped in a yesterday of twenty-five years ago, lies shattered on the floor.

RICHARD
It's good to see you.

                    ANDREW

      It's been a long time.

Andrew trails Richard's gaze to the floor.

                    ANDREW

      I'm sorry for that.

                    RICHARD

      Me too.

Andrew looks up. Are those tears breaking in his eyes?

                    ANDREW

      I haven't been the best father. I know that. It
      might be too late but I know that.

                    RICHARD

      It's only 10:30 a.m. We have the whole day
      ahead of us.

Candy starts to cry.

                    RICHARD

      Dad, this crying woman here is my wife,
      Candy.

                    ANDREW

      What a wonderful name.

Candy moves forward and hugs Andrew unexpectedly. Andrew
is at first thrown by this show of emotion but then gives in
to the embrace.

                    CANDY

      It's so nice to finally meet you, Mr. Dyer.

                        ANDREW
            Call me Andrew. And you two—

Andrew glances at his newly minted grandchildren.

                        ANDREW
            —you can call me Grumps.

                        RICHARD
            Grumps?

                        ANDREW
            That's what I came up with. Is it okay?

                        RICHARD
                        (smiling)
            It's perfect.

Richard turns to his children.

                        RICHARD
            Say hello to your Grumps.

Emmett and Chloe rush into Grumps's arms.

Even if sickly sweet, how could anyone not wish for a version of this? But before Richard could say anything, Andrew ripped up the script by noticing the lack more than the gain. "Wait. Where's Andy?"

"I don't know," Richard said.

"Is he here? In the apartment? Have you seen him yet?"

Richard stepped back. "We've been waiting for the both of you."

Gerd appeared from the kitchen.

"When did you become a nun?" Andrew asked.

"It's my old uniform." She pulled at the fabric. "Guess I've lost some weight."

"Has everyone met Gerd?" Andrew gestured introductions with his hands, which looked heavy and unwieldy, knuckles like knots of lead. "She's a much more important person than this costume suggests. Put on normal clothes, please."

"Okay."

"And where's Andy?"

"Upstairs. Should I get him?"

"Please, and if he's still in bed, empty a bucket on his head, like my stepfather once did—twice actually. I used to sleep like that. You know what my first thought waking up would be? I can't wait to go back to bed. Now I can't sleep at all. Now my first thought is, Did I really sleep? Because if I did then my dreams are nothing but dreams of not falling asleep. How's that for cruel? The gout doesn't help either. I have gout by the way. Funny word. *Gout.* And *goiter.* I don't have a goiter, but *gout* makes me think of *goiter.* Sounds almost Victorian. Dickensian. Goiter & Gout. Now there's a law firm, with Rickets & Scurvy as future partners."

As Gerd headed upstairs, Richard and Jamie shared a look, which I tried to join since I had the inside track on the man and could convey his fragile state of mind with a simple furrow and tilt. But the brothers weren't interested in my insightful semaphore. "We should sit down," Richard decided, his hand returning to his father's shoulder.

Jamie agreed.

"No," Andrew said, "let's wait for Andy first."

"But Dad—"

"No, we'll wait."

"Sure, but—"

"We're going to wait right here, so enough." A pause. "Please."

Richard relented as if he could see the smaller man peeking around the larger façade, the man who was powerless to grant you your childhood wish, who could only push into your hands the desire to be an adult. "Um Dad, this is my family," Richard said.

"Yes, of course, your family. Hello." Andrew accepted the introductions. "Forgive my appearance, my reality as well. Glad to meet you. Thanks for coming. Hope you enjoy the show."

"Dad," from Jamie.

"What?"

"Nothing."

"And how old are the two of you?" Andrew asked Emmett and Chloe.

"Sixteen," Emmett said.

Chloe remained unnaturally quiet.

"She's thirteen," Emmett said.

"Sixteen and thirteen. Both good ages. Both difficult, in their way. I'm seventy-nine. Nearing eighty. I never thought I was going to be this old, thought I'd die middle-aged, like my own father. Coleridge, you know, the poet, of 'Kubla Kahn' and 'Ancient Mariner' fame—Do they still read him in school?—he would have been a greater man, certainly more famous, if he had died earlier, right up there with Keats, who if he had lived longer would have been discussed in the same breath as Thomas Lovell Beddoes. Who, you say? Exactly. Sometimes life can seem like an experiment gone wrong. But enough of that. My best days ahead are somewhere upstairs, coming down soon, I hope. Andy's only seventeen. You'll like him." As Andrew talked a few of the pieces of toilet paper loosened and began to wave in the word breeze, adding an element of suspense to his stream of consciousness, until finally one detached and helicoptered to the floor. "Uh-oh," he muttered, "I'm molting."

"Maybe we should get you to a chair," Jamie said.

"If anything I could use a bier."

"Kind of early for that," Richard said.

Andrew spelled "B-I-E-R" then asked if he required a definition. This brought a half smile to Emmett's face and gave Andrew his first taste of success as a grandfather. "Regardless," he went on, "you're right about it being too early for a beer. Emmett, my boy, do you think you could do your grandfather a tremendous favor and go down that hall to where there's a bar, really just a bottle of Dewar's, and pour me a drink in one of those stubby glasses?"

"No problem." Emmett disappeared, already his ally.

"Dad, he's only sixteen."

"It's not a particularly difficult drink to make."

"I want to make a Dewar's too," Chloe piped in.

"See what you've done," Richard said.

"I think I like having grandchildren around."

"Are you already drunk?"

"Not already. If anything I'm giddy from loss of blood. It's the Coumadin's fault. Either way, the match is about to burn my hand and I'm just thrilled at having company—not company, family, back in this apartment after too long a time, and perhaps I'm nervous, and I thought a drink might settle me down. I am also, Richard, quite old enough to be drunk at any hour."

Emmett reappeared with the scotch near the lip, every step a test of balance.

"Now there's a boy with a good solid pour." Andrew lowered his head as if taking communion, sipping a half inch before accepting the glass. "My compliments. The ratio of scotch to air is flawless. Yes, I really do like having the grandchildren around. Chloe, dear, there's a syringe in my desk drawer—I'm kidding, I'm kidding." Andrew suppressed a rare smile. "We are all agreed, I need to shut up. Maybe I've been working too hard."

"Working on what?" asked Jamie, curious. "Something new?"

"The same old same old really."

Gerd came back downstairs. "He's on his way."

"Excellent. The family reunion can soon begin." Andrew took a serious slug of his drink, then another. "We are all feeling happy, right?" he said, wiping his mouth against his sleeve. More confetti fell from his face, and I imagined myself falling as well, letting go of whatever bloody scrap I was holding on to and drifting away. What was I doing there anyway? Andrew put the glass down on a nearby table and commented on the lovely flowers, and before I could've excused myself, I was drawn back in.

"Philip did all the flowers," Gerd said.

"Forgot you were here, Philip."

I heard the smirks from Richard and Jamie in my head.

Faggot.

"A talent just like your mother," Andrew said. "What kind are they?"

Philip the fag.

"Carnations, monkshood, lobel."

Phaggot.

"Does the Southampton house still have those wonderful gardens?"

Phaggot flower boy.

"I'm not sure. I haven't been there in a while."

Roses are red.

"I remember that rose garden," he said.

Faggots are Philip.

"But no point in getting rolled by useless memories."

Hearing Andrew mention useless memories, I saw an opportunity to ask about *The Wizard of Oz* and perhaps educate Richard about our fathers' past, but once again I was frustrated by an entrance, this time Andy, who appeared at the top of the stairs, like some allusion to a fairy tale, and A. N. Dyer was determined to uphold the spell, practically applauding his arrival. "Here he is, in the flesh."

Andy, hair styled by his pillow, took in this tableau. He seemed dubious of whatever awaited him.

"Come on down," Andrew said.

"What happened to your face?"

"It's all the pills. They water down the blood."

"You look trapped inside a snow globe."

"See, he's funny," Andrew said to the group. "Very funny."

Andy came down the stairs, but before greetings were exchanged he rubbed his face as only a teenage boy can, investing himself fully in the task. "Hey," he finally said, blinking us into being, more pauper than prince.

"Of course, you know Jamie," Andrew said.

"Oh yeah, hey."

"And this is Richard and his family, Candy, Emmett, and Chloe."

"Hi."

"Hey."

"Nice to finally meet you." Richard extended his hand like a marine.

"Sorry about being asleep," Andy said. "Kind of rude of me."

"That's okay," Andrew told him. "A boy needs his sleep."

A brief silence followed, everyone smiling with no direction, one of those awkward moments where families realize they are essentially a collection of strangers with a few things in common, like this old, unsteady man here who looked around as though waiting for his offspring to notice the obvious.

"Well," Andy finally said, "what this boy really needs is a big cup of coffee. Anyone else?" Only Emmett took him up on the offer and they both headed into the kitchen. Emmett might have been a year younger but he seemed older by four, safely on the other side of adolescence while Andy struggled through chin-high water. But their faces were obviously stamped from the same Dyer mold—the wedge nose, that brow—that made its first American mark with Jacob Dierickx, who amassed a tidy sum in the manufacture of wampum, only to be outdone by his Anglicized descendants, in particular Peter Dyer and his foresight in repurposing a rope factory into the Union army's biggest supplier of fabric. It was odd to think of Andrew and Richard having teenage boys in common.

With the boys gone, Andrew seemed to instantly flag, like a man who had just missed his flight and whatever the pleasant destination had been lost. He turned to Richard and Jamie and told them that they needed to talk "sooner than later," he said, "like now."

"Sure," Richard said. "How about we all go and sit in the living room?"

"No, no, just you and me and Jamie, just the three of us in my study."

Richard smiled toward Candy and Chloe. "But Dad . . ."

"That's all right, you go and talk," Candy said.

Chloe looked toward the kitchen. "Can I have coffee too?"

"It won't be for long," Andrew promised. "I'll make it short. Or I'll try to make it short. And then we can all catch up. But right now it's important that I speak to these two alone. Philip, maybe you can entertain the womenfolk. I know Gerd has plenty of food. Andy can show Emmett Central Park. Walk around. Do whatever. We'll be finished soon enough. But we need to talk, right now, just the three of us." Andrew's tone suggested an offense, decades old, that was in need of airing. Why do we always expect our fathers to yell? Without further debate Andrew started to shuffle back toward his study, *shh, shh, shh*, his left hand balancing along the wall, while Richard and Jamie lowered their heads and followed along, like the plow behind the oxen churning up a stretch of long-neglected earth.

"I can't stay long," I called to them.

I'm not sure they heard me. But it was true, I did have things to do. Evidence to obtain. Later that day in my father's apartment I would liberate from his desk the box of Weejuns from Bass. Done with sharing, I would tuck this small treasure chest under my arm and would hustle to leave, my stepmother, two parts polite, one part nosy, stopping me near the front door, mindful of belongings being whisked from her possession. She would ask me what I had there, pointing to the shoe box, and I would tell her that they were for Rufus, his first pair of grown-up shoes.

"It begins," she'd say, trying to smile.

"It begins," I would tell her.

The door to the study closed.

The secret to being a good thief is being as obvious as possible.

IV.ii

IMAGINE A VORTEX, slow-turning but gaining steam, drawn together by lungs: Richard and Jamie sitting on the couch, breathing in the mildew of wet battling dry, while their father sighed near the window with more pose than purpose, rocking as if the expanse of Central Park were his Wailing Wall, the sons keeping silent behind him, waiting for him to say something, to give center to this respiring tension but also glancing around the room, always a mystery growing up, other fathers leaving in the morning for midtown or downtown, but their father simply walked down the hall and shut that always forbidding door, usually only working at night, which added to the mystery, as if this were his secret lair, his Batcave, his Fortress of Solitude, where he tried saving a world he himself created, Richard and Jamie sometimes setting their alarms for past midnight so they could sneak downstairs and kneel by the door and hear the *booms!* and the *pows!* and the *splats!* of the typewriter and envision the battles within, surely more than words put on paper, surely something epic at hand, though the truth was that their father could only relax in the early-morning wilderness, comfortably alone and industrious, unlike the daylight hours where real people had real jobs and he suffered through hateful meaninglessness—*I am nothing*—the definition of himself growing wobblier by the instant—*you are nobody*—the people on the street living a life he could only imagine, both alien and common, reaching all the way back to when he was a boy peering from the window in his bedroom and layering upon himself specific detail after specific detail—wearing one red sock, one blue sock, earmuffs, a baseball mitt for a hat, reciting "You Are Old, Father William"—until he was certain, or fairly certain, that he had reached a level of absolute distinction and he could unwind himself from the burden of everybody else, the same sort of freedom he found when sitting at his desk in the middle of the night, never suspecting his sons sometimes listened by the door, their entry forbidden without a knock and a very good reason, though eleven-year-old Richard once slipped in while his parents were eating dinner and he hid behind those emerald curtains—the velvet now moldy green—determined to catch his father in action, Jamie given the task of engineering a bad dream and rushing downstairs to pound on the door, thus allowing Richard's escape, and all evening long Jamie practiced his nightmare about quicksand and sinking into a belowground world, hoping he might impress with his imagination, but when the time came Jamie slept through the alarm—or so he claimed and would still claim sitting with his brother and waiting for his father to finally speak, but really Jamie wanted Richard to stew behind that curtain, already interested in his own passive effect, a shady witness at nine, and the well-thought-out plan turned into a boy trying his best to remain still to the point where even now Richard thought he could detect a tremor in the curtain as his father stood a few inches from that past and stared at the crushing blueness of the everyday world, broken only by clouds approaching from the west like a posse kicking up dust, Jamie and Richard and Andrew, the three of them trying to brace themselves against whatever might come next.

Jamie decided to toss in a few words, testing the current. "What is this, Dad," he said, arms expressing the shambolic state of the room, "the office of Dorian Gray?"

Andrew turned from the window. "Always with the clever comment."

"I try."

"You try, huh?" He smiled like a man watching a captured animal go free, all because of his benevolence. "You ever wonder why Oscar Wilde used *picture* instead of *portrait*? Because *portrait* seems more appropriate, sounds better too, at least to my ears. *The Portrait of Dorian Gray*. Those matching *-or* sounds. Maybe the painting is a portrait but the story is a picture. Or maybe he wanted us to do the correction in our heads, to misremember the title and get it wrong and in getting it wrong actually get it right. That crafty subtextualist." Another glance toward the window, giving the boys his nose-strong profile. "I've been thinking about my last words lately. Of course old Oscar had a bunch of them, all excellent, but who knows what kind of condition I'll be in? Quite unhappy, I assume, in pain, delirious. I don't trust myself to come up with something that's both extemporaneous and memorable, so let me tell you now, in case I forget. Okay. *Be kind, rewind.* Laugh if you want but I'm serious. I think it has a nice touch of the *levitas.* Non-sensical and yet still sensical. Vaguely Hindu. I always loved those signs in video store windows. Funny how a phrase can outlive its technology, a Christian sentiment, I suppose. *Be kind, rewind.* Now imagine what follows is my last breath." Andrew limped over to his desk and shook two Vicodin into his palm.

"What kind of pills are those?" Richard asked.

"Sorry, but I'm dead."

"Dad—"

"The truth is, boys, I'm dying and I'm dying soon, to the point where I feel already dead." Andrew paused, unsatisfied. "Whatever I say lately sounds like it's been said before by somebody else, like my, my—what do you call this area of the mouth again?" He touched the labial commissure, though neither of his sons knew the term. "Whatever it is, it feels like quotation marks." Andrew opened and closed his mouth.

"Have you been to a doctor?" Richard again with the asking.

"I should have written this out."

"We could go to a doctor," Richard repeated, "maybe tomorrow."

"My brain is like a game of chance."

"Is Dr. Harkness still around?"

"Stop with the doctor talk, plus he's long dead. I need to tell you things, boys. I need promises from you. I need—a lot of needs, I realize, but I need to know that you can still care for me regardless of who I am or who I was. And I don't mean forgiveness. I don't need forgiveness. Forgiveness, once spoken, turns into something else, something no longer trustworthy. I was what I was. I am what I am. And now I'm quoting Popeye." With unsettled effort Andrew lowered himself into his desk chair. In front of him two stacks of paper, one blank, one typed, bookended his Selectric. "I should have written this out for clarity's sake, but God help my writing nowadays. You should know my goal as a father—and I swear this is true—my goal was positively Hippocratic, to do no harm, and look where that got me. You could sue for malpractice. I am a reckless scalpel. But I honestly tried, or have tried better with Andy, I've tried to say the things I should have said to the two of you. But guess what, I think that's made things worse. I do. I think I did you a tremendous favor by being so absent. I was so different as a boy. Or I think I was different. I must've been different, before the writing took hold. I used to climb trees. I could climb the bejesus out of a tree. I loved the heights, the vistas spied through branches, the hiding. That, and I could spend all day in the ocean, the rougher the better, just bodysurfing. There's a word to hang your hat on. *Bodysurfing*. But then everything changed. Talk about a hackneyed phrase. Your dad, the writer. But everything did change. And I don't mean my father dying, though that obviously had its effect, the suddenness of it, and my mother on her own, but I honestly don't remember being sad. I must have been. But you forget so quickly when you're young—you forget so quickly when you're old too, the former because of the latter, the latter because of the former. The push and the pull and the ever-shrinking middle ground. Occasionally there's a convergence, a moment of balance all too brief where your idea of the future seems to vector with your sense of the past. But I'm off subject. Or ahead of subject. I've mugged the goddamn verb.

"The irony I would like to communicate to you boys is the fact that I never enjoyed writing very much. Oh, maybe I enjoyed the moments before writing, the thinking about writing, when the story starts to form around its cagey heart, a word, an image, like with bodysurfing: in a flash I know everything, the themes, the metaphors, five of the characters, the setting, the time frame, the beginning, the middle, the end. It's a strange kind of fission, where a single atom of imagination radiates all this energy, splitting and splitting and splitting, endlessly splitting until you get *Bodysurfing*, or *The Bodysurfer*, which is probably better if perhaps bumping elbows with Cheever. But then you have to write the goddamn thing and it's Chernobyl. Two-headed cows. Terrible birth defects. And I'm not being glib here. I'm not playing a role, despite resemblances to actual persons living or dead. I will grant you moments of satisfaction in the process, that this mess might make sense after all, that a random piece of filler, say the detail of an airplane flying overhead, might beget a man parachuting down to earth. Yes, there are moments. But it's not joy, just relief that the disappointment is manageable. Whatever satisfaction is the satisfaction of keeping up the charade. Yep, the old imposter syndrome. But it beats the coal mines, as they say. But the coal mines seem a more honest labor to me, where your life, your real life, is focused aboveground, and your job is simply powering the lights for home. Daddy's work. But your Daddy chose to be a writer and the two of you were frankly fucked. All because I liked how it sounded in my head—no office, no boss, no bureaucracy, no nine-to-five, no desk, he says, having sat behind this desk for the last fifty years. I'd travel the world. I'd meet interesting people. I would be bohemian. Me, bohemian? But that's what I pictured, boys. I wanted to be a writer and I jumped into the first cliché. How's that? Did I ever do it for the right reasons? Mostly I just wanted to steer clear of lawyering and banking and politicking, the normal trades of my people. I needed to be unique. An unpredictable line rather than another circle. But it wasn't in my soul. Maybe a little bit in my soul. Mostly it just seemed like fun to focus on imagined things. Of course it helped that I didn't need money, thanks to my father. By the age of sixteen I started on my path. It's all I did, with superficial stabs in the real world. The work never left me alone yet it always seemed just out of reach. I became insular. Isolated. Always dragging this malformed thing behind me. Even a great day of writing was somehow bad. I shook only the trees in my head. And I was stubborn, my God was I stubborn. I staked my claim on A. N. Dyer and chained myself to that person. Sorry if I sound like Prometheus and Sisyphus rolled into one. Poor, poor me. The only thing worse than a writer is a self-pitying writer. And guess what, we're all self-pitying."

Jamie interrupted. "If your writing is a charade, it's a world-class charade."

"I mean charade as a parody of living."

"Oh, is that what you mean?"

"It made me a miserable person, Jamie, is what I mean."

"And you blame that on writing?"

"It didn't help."

"So if you had been a banker, you would have been a great dad, like all those great banker dads out there?"

"Take it easy," from Richard.

"I'm just confused," Jamie said.

"Advertising," Andrew pronounced.

"What?" from the both of them.

"That would've been my sweet spot. Spitballing. Pitching ideas."

"Advertising?" Jamie was unsure if this was a comedy or a tragedy.

"But Dad, people love your books," Richard said, "like truly love them."

"And I hate them for that."

"Oh please," said Jamie. "Don't be such an ingrate."

"You're right, I'm an ingrate too, but that's not what I want to talk about." Andrew knocked on the desk as if calling for order. "The point of this conversation, of getting you two back here, is not me, but Andy. That's the X among all this noise. Because right now I'm his only family, and I want you two to get to know him, to be there for him. I can't stomach the idea of him being alone. But first I need to explain a few things, need to put you in my shoes, almost twenty years ago, feeling like a failure while being reminded of what a success I was. That can wear you down." Andrew's mouth went slack, and he appeared wan and hollow, lost to some indistinct memory of indeterminate youth. Then he snapped back. "I know you know the story of the Swedish au pair. Not very original, I realize. I forget the exact circumstances of her death, but I remember arguing against her dying in childbirth since that would have introduced an unnecessary psychological element. Of course, after she died, however she died, this baby, our Andy, he was thrust into my arms and everyone discovered the truth. Or lie. In hindsight I would have done that part differently. I think I was too focused on the classic narrative. The surprise was a terrible mistake. Your mother's a proud woman, properly so, and she was already dealing with the difficulties of living with me. I should have confessed right away. A moment of weakness, I'm sorry, forgive me, please. That might have worked. But the extended secret and the big dramatic reveal? Me and a Swedish au pair? That was flawed from the start. Minimum she should've been older, some older intellectual type from Toronto, and that's why she died, a freakish pregnancy in her late forties and she never could recover from the strain of childbirth. That might have been better. But the two of you have to know I never wanted to split this family apart. And I never—never!—wanted to be with anyone but your mom. That's the absolute truth. I was, I am, hopeless without her. I stand before you as demonstrable proof. But Andy, he appeared and our life together slid backward and sideways, your mother devastated, you two last-strawed. Maybe it was a relief that I finally proved myself such an obvious shit. No more doubts. No more blaming yourself for my seeming indifference. You were free of my scrutiny. And all of this is true except for the story itself. So many stories spinning. Like the one about an icy road instead of my father driving straight into a tree."

"What are you talking about?" Jamie asked.

Andrew raised his hand. "Bear with me, I have to just get through this. Forget the au pair story, the real story begins twenty years ago when I was quietly losing my mind and everything I did seemed a form of denial, of avoidance, dangerous anatomizing nostalgia. Pretending took on a different shape in my head. I wasn't living. Had I ever lived? What the hell was I doing? I was sick of being this person but I was trapped and I was too old to change, which is ironic because I felt the same way at fifty and at forty and at thirty I swear, too old to change anything. It's the worst kind of passive-aggressive self-destruction, too timid for anything florid. Cowardice really. I blamed your mother for letting me get away with so much and I began to believe she was ignorant and clueless of what I wanted and who I was all because she couldn't read my mind. By now you were in California, Richard, and Jamie you were God knows where. Thinking of the two of you just reminded me of my further failures. It was about this time that I was contacted by a group of Swedes, or one Swede in particular, a man by the name of Norde Bellaf, who wanted to meet me. I agreed since there were murmurs of Nobel attached to his name and, well, a Nobel would be nice before I finally stumbled into suicide like a good Dyer. Ha, a pun. Anyway, notice the hubris, boys. Like so many stories this is a story that involves hubris. I met Mr. Bellaf for lunch at the Four Seasons. It was late winter but that doesn't matter. I remember he ordered an elaborate meal but didn't eat a bite, like the food was some test of will. Over this meal, or nonmeal in his case, this Bellaf character told me that he represented an organization called the Palingeneticists. P-A-L-I-N-G-E-N-E-T-I-C-I-S-T-S in case you're taking notes. According to him this group was founded in 1890 and bankrolled by Alfred Nobel himself, hence the whispers of Nobel. This is six years before the man's death and subsequent will, which as you likely know established the prizes in physics, chemistry, physiology, literature, and peace. Notice, boys, science and art and history as defined by the great-man theory. Bellaf explained to me that the Palingeneticists were essentially the shadow to the Nobel's light, one very public, the other very private. Alfred never married, never had children. He was famously misanthropic. But toward the end of his life he started to regret leaving this world without a proper heir. Now he certainly understood the dangers of mixing unknown chemicals. After all every newborn is a chemical invention unleashed upon the world. He grasped the long odds of success, of true success, of genius, and he started the Palingeneticists with the sole purpose of perpetuating great men—and later women—and keeping their particular talents alive for the benefit of future generations. A forward-thinking man, you might say. At this time great discoveries were being made in the field of embryology, with the two Hanses—Driesch with his sea urchins, and Spemann with his untying of the Primitive Knot—doing their groundbreaking work. Nobel put his friend and confidant Ragnar Sohlman in charge and it was Sohlman who came up with the prizes in order not only to identify these important figures but also to enlist them so that Nobel's dream might one day be realized. Hans Spemann himself won the prize in 1935, though he had been a member of the Palingeneticists since 1892. It took eighty years before Nobel's seed finally bore fruit, the first attempts not perfect, particularly in matters of gastroenterology, but soon the process became near foolproof. This is decades before other institutions began touting their sheep and their dogs and their bulls. That's when Mr. Bellaf informed me that I had been nominated for their particular award, an award not made of silver or gold or glass but of flesh. I can see your faces, boys, and trust me my face looked the same. Pure science fiction. How could anyone believe this gothic nonsense? But Norde Bellaf did not seem the delusional type. And his eyes, it's hard to explain the awful conviction behind those eyes. It was as if he saw an abyss stretching before him yet he was obligated to try to build a bridge. He offered me no proof, no evidence, no references, none of the names of previous winners, not even their approximate number. These were all secrets closely guarded by the Palingeneticists. They kept no records, had no paper trail. All they had were six men with well-trained memories. My initial response was a fast *No thank you, check please*, but Bellaf told me he would contact me in five days. I could officially refuse him then. That's how the devil works, boys. He gives you time. Bellaf said that everyone had the same initial response, but by the end most accepted. Being naturally competitive, I started to wonder who else they had asked. Was there a teenage Salinger somewhere in this world? A toddler Bellow? God forbid another Roth? It seemed something concocted by Pynchon doing his best impersonation of Barthelme. But over those five days I grew curious and engaged with the idea. It didn't seem like a terrible concept, in the broader sense. Who would complain about having another Einstein in this world, another Salk, another Edison? I thought about myself, about starting over and doing things differently, about, well, bodysurfing in a way. Maybe I could draft a happier version of myself, a better person. I became excited again by the possibility of life. My only stipulation— and here I thought I was being terribly original—was that I had to raise the boy myself. I never even thought about the repercussions with you and your mother. My head was in too deep. I just assumed that she would stay with me, that she might even enjoy having another child, no less another me. Wonderful, the elasticity of my narcissism. Maybe I also didn't truly believe this Bellaf character, so where was the harm in saying yes? I'd take possible being over definite nothing. Bellaf smiled at my request, or attempted to smile but he didn't have the right lip strength for a proper smile. He told me everyone insisted on the same thing. Nice to know all of us are equally sick. Three vials of blood later and Norde Bellaf was on his way back to Stockholm and I had no idea what just happened and slowly returned to my silent funk."

Whatever filial restraint that had kept Richard and Jamie steady on the couch began to waver, at least for Jamie, who glanced toward his brother and tried to nudge him with his eyes, like a moviegoer confused by the plot and in need of whispering, What the hell is going on here? But Richard gave no indication of confusion, if anything seemed to follow along without any problem, which put Jamie in the unfamiliar role of gadfly. "What are you talking about, Dad? I mean I think I know what you're talking about, but what the hell are you talking about?"

"I never had an affair."

"Of course you had an affair."

"No, not with a Swedish au pair."

"You had an affair, Dad, probably not your first, and the girl got pregnant and she had a baby and here we are."

"That was just the cover story," he said.

"The cover story? Really? So this is now some secret mission we're talking about? C'mon, Dad, you had an affair and you were careless. It's an old story. Because otherwise what you're telling us is that Andy is a . . ." Jamie waited for his father to fill in this particular blank, but his father just nodded, forcing Jamie to carry on. "I mean I was with you for the whole bodysurfing thing, and with Mom, and regret, maybe lost me with the dreams of advertising, though I totally understand where you're coming from, but the Palingeneticists and Norde Bellaf and—what?—cloning, right, that's what we're talking about here, cloning."

"I hate that word," his father said.

"What would you prefer?"

"An autonomous reflection."

"Oh yes, that's much better." Jamie's irritation bounced between his brother's outward calm and his father's matter-of-factness, back and forth, like a ball searching for a goal. "Richard, help me out here."

Richard leaned forward. "Does Andy know?"

Jamie was hoping for a harder kick. "That's your opening shot?"

"Well—"

"Does Andy know his father thinks he's a clone?"

"Jamie—"

"That's your first question."

"Calm down, okay."

Andrew remained unmoved by this brotherly sidebar. "Andy doesn't know," he said to Richard, "and he can never know. I'm only telling you now because when I'm gone I want someone who can give him a sense of who he is, who he was."

"Him meaning you?" Jamie said.

"In a manner of speaking."

"So we'll never be free of you, is that what you're saying?"

"I know it's hard to believe—"

"No, Dad, it's fucking impossible to believe. Obviously you are"—*in the midst of full-blown dementia*, Jamie wanted to say, *your brain rewiring the past into pure fabulism, all in service of impending mortality and shattered ego and self-inflicted remorse*, but instead Jamie restrained himself and simply said, "confused."

"I'm not confused."

"I can sympathize. I'm presently being haunted by a dead woman's cellphone."

"I'm not confused," Andrew repeated. "What I'm saying is absolutely true."

"Let's do a DNA test then."

"We're not doing a DNA test."

"Why not?"

"There's no reason."

"Why, because you say it's true?"

"Jamie—" from Richard.

"No, because it is true. I wouldn't lie about this."

"I'm sure you believe it a hundred percent, but that doesn't make it true."

"In this case it does," Andrew said.

"So that greasy seventeen-year-old kid out there is my dad."

"He's not that greasy."

"My father, the teenager."

"I know it's difficult—"

"Enough with difficult crap," Jamie said. "I'm not a child trying to grasp some adult concept. This is pure—and I want to be kind, Dad, I really do, but this is pure nonsense. This is you spinning yourself into one of your alternate worlds. And I understand it. Or I think I do. I think I know where this impulse is coming from, and it's a totally human place in my book, and I feel for you. But to say that Andy is a clone—"

"But he is a clone."

Jamie frustrated his hands into fists. "Is this for a new book, *Fathers & Clones*?"

"Jamie—" from Richard again.

"Testing our reaction for the sake of homegrown veracity."

"You know cleverness is not an appealing trait, Jamie, despite what your mother might think. It's a crutch. Fifteen months after that visit from Norde Bellaf an embryo was successfully implanted into a surrogate, and nine months later Andy was born, without complications, at Landstinget Hospital in Östergötland, Sweden. Check the hospital records if you must. He weighed nine pounds, three ounces, a full pound heavier than me. His mother never died, because there was no mother. Or his mother was my mother, same with his father, and they were both dead long before he was born."

Jamie, shading red, turned to Richard. "Aren't you going to say anything?"

"I've been trying."

"Please, go ahead, speak."

Richard planted his elbows on his knees and proceeded to rub his hands together as though rolling a hunk of clay into a sensible sphere. It was a move he often took when leading a group session back in L.A., a coach trying to come up with a lifesaving play. Richard was obviously concerned for his father's mental well-being, but he was also jet-lagged and in need of a longer run than the three measly loops around the reservoir this morning, and while he wanted to take on the role of mediator, he professionally always sided with the sick, at least initially, to get them on his side, and his father was obviously sick and in need of support, and all that was fine and good but more than anything *Ampersand* turned tightly in his head, along with Rainer Krebs and Eric Harke, who were both in New York this week and wanted to supplicate themselves before the master—now masters, Richard thought, major and minor, and the absolute lunacy of the situation spun a moral debate of using his father's breakdown to his own advantage, which, after a few more rolls of that psychic clay, emerged into a charitable, if snake-like form, of honoring his father and allowing a confused old man to believe whatever he wanted to believe. Where was the harm in that? "There is an uncanny resemblance," Richard said.

Jamie nearly exploded. "What the hell?"

"I'm just saying there's a resemblance."

"Maybe because he's his father."

"And history has shown the power of secret organizations."

"History has shown, if anything, their incompetence."

"I'm just saying—"

"You can't possibly believe this."

"Let me finish. I'm saying maybe we should give Dad the benefit of the doubt."

"You mean the willful suspension of disbelief, his stock-in-trade?"

"I believe it's willing," his father said, "not willful."

Jamie's nerves gripped his stomach. After years of keeping his head down he dared to challenge a question with a raised hand. "Maybe I meant willful. I'm sorry, Dad, but you haven't earned it, to use another awful expression from your trade. You need some belief to suspend, instead of stealing meaning from other people's lives. And I can relate to that, oh man, can I relate, but I can't step into your particular narrative here. Not now. I think you must be feeling very alone and you want to connect before it's too late, and I can appreciate that, and I'm here to do that, if you want, but I can't pretend it's anything else, especially using poor Andy like that." Jamie surprised himself with his honesty, since usually he just caved knowing that would lead to a shorter conversation and a quicker exit. But here he was speaking almost like an adult.

"I'm mentally fit," Andrew said. "Physically, maybe not."

"Dad, you're an overall fucking mess." Maybe Jamie was enjoying this too much.

"C'mon," said Richard. "This isn't the time or the place."

"How is this not the time or the place?"

"Can we talk about it later please?"

"When you're back in L.A. and I'm stuck here with my two dads?"

"I'm just saying we need time to properly digest this."

"But I'm not swallowing it."

"I don't think you're understanding me."

"I think I am. I'm just not willing to soft-shoe it. You were checked out when the whole divorce happened but I remember. I remember what she went through, I remember the shock, I remember the phone calls. She was catatonic for a year."

"Please you were hardly around either," Richard said. "You were busy doing your Faces of Death tour."

"Faces of Death?"

"Whatever you call whatever you did, or do?"

"You're such an asshole. Still."

"And you're still incredibly dishonest about yourself."

"Richard the True rides again. Please tell me more about myself."

"You've never grown up."

"And your early promise has flowered beautifully."

Voices rose toward yelling until interrupted by the *snap-snap-snap!* of a letter striking paper. The brothers turned and saw their father eyeing them from over his typewriter, his index finger firing two more shots—*snap-snap!*—head shots judging by his squint. "I don't miss these fights," Andrew said. "Being an only child I was always frightened of your relationship, its sudden potential for violence. I probably would have been better suited to daughters. But if you don't believe me, you don't believe me. I just wanted you to know. Andy is a good kid and seventeen is a tough age and I just hope you'll try to make him feel like he isn't alone when all is said and done."

"Should we push him toward a career in advertising?" Jamie muttered harshly.

Richard threw an eyeful of *prick* at his brother before getting up with no other purpose than to gain authority: the standing man. "I'm here for him," he told his father, "and I'm here for you as well. I do think you should go and see a doctor if you're feeling the way you're feeling, but you don't have to worry about Andy ever being alone. I can promise you that. He'll have family." Richard found himself standing near the curtains that years ago harbored his younger self. Time seemed to bend back, like an eddy in a river caused by a rock, with Richard taking on the role of his father staring out the window all those four o'clock in the mornings ago, staring for a good hour. "It's going to be okay," Richard said, like he was speaking to the boy whose efforts at staying still were slipping along with his bladder. "We're here for you." Outside the clouds pushed further east, and though the room had been growing darker, the Dyer men recognized the change as if a sudden and ominous sign instead of a long-previewed piece of weather. The three of them grew quiet, listening for what would come next. It was like one of those brief yet endless silences after a car skids where ears are tuned for the impending crash and the possible sirens to follow.

IV.iii

CROSSING AGAINST THE TAIL END OF TRAFFIC, Andy played the old game of car matador, timing his stride with the last passing bumper, his leading knee less than an inch from disaster. The effect was near suicidal. Emmett still stood on the corner, waiting for the light to change; he had to hustle to catch up. I watched this little scene from the sixth-floor window, watched the boys head toward the park entrance on 72nd Street, passing the ever-perplexing, who-the-hell-is-Hunt Hunt Memorial. Andy and Emmett bobbed and weaved in sync, as if movement were a duet. Ten minutes together and they were already a familiar tune. It was Andy who suggested the trip outside, no doubt desperate to crack open his head and let some fresh air in, and Candy had to shush Chloe, who begged to be included, please, please, please, like a rainbow who never fathomed her previous effect on the weather. Once Andy and Emmett had moved beyond my visible range I stepped away from the window and excused myself, telling mother and daughter that I had errands to do. Was I being rude, leaving them here? Candy just smiled, and I imagined her at ease on the back of a motorcycle, and though my heart shared a few beats with put-upon Chloe—"It's not fair he gets to have all the fun while I'm stuck here with you"—my larger sympathies lay elsewhere.

Whatever you might think of me—and I am curious—I did not stoop to follow those boys. They had too much of a head start anyway. My guess is that Andy took Emmett to the model-boat pond, his favorite place in the park, perhaps in the entire city. Having just woken up he was probably hungry and there was that hot dog cart near the Alice in Wonderland sculpture, the hot dogs not terribly tasty—81st and

Fifth, near-right corner, were far superior—but the soft pretzels were excellent, the dough toasted to perfection, the twist salted with a light, sticky snow, the first bite nudging the soft palate and kicking the salivary glands in a rough but pleasant schoolyard greeting—*Yo!*—and don't forget the lasso of mustard, a touch of the exotic without its pretension, like cursing well in French, and *merde sur ma chèvre* if Andy's mouth wasn't already watering as he led Emmett downhill, telling his newfound nephew, "I'm getting two, minimum of two, and you get whatever you want, your Uncle Andy's treat." Emmett smiled, its cut tailored to fit Andy's warm feelings. Or maybe it was just Andy's first experience with family, a nephew like a cousin like a brother, even if Emmett was taller and broader of shoulder, with longish hair that was naturally cool without being annoying. No doubt the kid was at home on a beach, one of those California beaches, and he probably surfed and skateboarded and snowboarded and did some boarding as yet unknown to East Coast man, and who knows the number of girls he's been with, probably women too, horny mothers with hot baked goods, this stud, this dude, my blood. A tremendous affection welled up within Andy, as if Emmett were one of those songs he wanted to listen to over and over again.

"Fuuuuuck."

"What?"

"Guy's not here," Andy said, all slack and agape. "Typical after my big buildup." They walked around the model-boat pond, toward the unfortunate absence. The weather was cooling but still mild considering the date, the dark clouds showing the opening set of a cold front. Half a dozen children scaled the Alice in Wonderland statue, with a bratty boy on top raising his fists. "That's kind of famous," Andy said.

"What?"

"The statue over there."

"Oh."

"Or maybe just famous for New York kids. Climbing that thing is like entering the octagon, the amount of injuries it causes. I swear some psycho butters the thing every morning. The left ear of the white rabbit almost killed me once." Andy pointed to the scar near his eye.

"Nice," from Emmett.

"How tall are you anyway?" Andy asked.

"Six-one."

"Sixteen and six-one. What a tremendous nephew I have."

"Thank you, dear uncle."

"I'll be lucky to crack six-feet."

"My mom's tall."

Andy for a moment considered the height of mothers and then said, "I guess so." He stopped where the hot dog cart should have been and surveyed the area like a great white hunter searching for umbrella prey. "Where is that bastard?" he said, knowing exactly how he sounded. To his right was the oversized and homely bronze of Hans Christian Andersen, with his self-reverential Ugly Duckling staring up at his feet, in looks more duck than swan, a straight-up mallard, as if the sculptor had somehow confused the tale with *Make Way for Ducklings*, or, worse, had given the illiterate public the literal version of the tale, turning the story into a story of delusion. But Andy couldn't care less about this artistic choice. "There are usually a lot more people here," he said, "lots of action when the weather's warmer and less gray. There's like water in the pond and people sail these toy sailboats, not really toys, more serious than toys, you can rent them over there, like these remote-controlled sailboats. I've actually never done it. I have no talent whatsoever with wind. But I did fall in once, by accident. Or kind of by accident. It was stupid. I was like twelve and I was trying to be funny— actually I was being funny, if I say so myself, but then I got soaked. The water's super-gross. Oh, and there's a hawk, I think it's a hawk—a peregrine—no, that's a falcon—either a hawk or a falcon and people go crazy for this bird, I forgot his name, and he like lives in one of the buildings on Fifth, not in the building, obviously, like a resident, tenth floor please, but in the façade, like builds a nest in the façade and raises little baby hawks or falcons—chicks, right—and everyone oohs and aahs and lines up with cameras and binoculars, a real fucking fan club. Pall Mall or something like that—wait, that's a brand of cigarette. He might be dead now. Or he's moved somewhere else, downtown probably. Or Brooklyn. One time he perched on the ledge outside my bed-

206 · DAVID GILBERT

room window. Pretty amazing, seeing that kind of wildness up close. The pigeons and rats, they probably have no idea what's hit them. There they are, in this city, their main predators taxicabs and kids, and suddenly from nowhere *swoosh* and *boom*. Maybe it's almost thrilling, like, Oh yeah, this is how I should be living my life, too bad I'm now dead." For some reason Andy wanted to tell Emmett everything, but Jesus, put a cap on those emissions and get back on subject. "Where the hell did that guy go?"

"There's another cart over there," Emmett said.

"It's not the same."

"Maybe he knows where the other guy went."

"Why would the dude move from this primo spot?"

"Why don't we ask?"

"I don't know, asking seems—"

"I'll ask," Emmett said.

"Yeah?"

"It would be my pleasure."

"Okay, most excellent nephew, you ask."

Like a newly formed vaudevillian duo, Andy gestured for Emmett to lead and Emmett nodded and kicked toward the cart and its vendor, who seemed a veteran of the Crimean War, his expression so flinched as to be flinchless. Seeing these boys approach, he raised his eyebrows as if warmth came one punk nickel at a time.

"Excuse me." Emmett smiled a California sunset.

The man replied with a vista onto rubble.

"Do you know where the other hot dog cart went, the one over there?"

The man turned to where Emmett was pointing.

"It's very important we find him," Andy added.

The man regarded these two as another fleck of New York shit blown in his eye. "He in trouble?"

"Not that important. We're just curious."

"About what curious?"

"About where he went curious."

"And so back to why curious. If you want hot dog, soda, knish, I your guy, but if you want information, well, that make me informant and I not your guy."

"It's not like that at all," Emmett said.

"Do we look like feds?" Andy asked, desperately wanting to look like a fed.

"Who's Fetes?"

"No, feds, as in FBI."

"Don't pull bullshit on me, kid. You want a hot dog or what?"

"Not from you," Andy said.

"What that mean not from you? I got good dog, fine dog. Even better sausage."

"Way overpriced."

"My price same price as everybody else around here price."

"Yeah, and that's called price-fixing and that's un-American."

"My story make you weep it's so American."

"I'm sure it is, sir," Emmett said, trying to get back on track. "We're just looking for the other guy because we really like his pretzel."

"His soft pretzel," Andy clarified.

"His soft pretzel," Emmett reclarified more politely.

The man's top lip threatened to curl past his nose. "I got pretzel," he said, gesturing toward the bready concertina that rested on a pan.

"Yes, we know—"

"I got good pretzel."

"Yes but—"

"My pretzel as good as his pretzel."

Andy stepped in as if those were fighting words. "Sorry, but no way."

"Sorry but same exact pretzel. We all get same exact pretzel from same exact pretzel supplier and we all cook pretzel same exact way, not even cook, just salt, warm, and serve, the pretzel the same exact for all of us, no difference." The man paused. "So two pretzel?"

"Maybe we—" Emmett began saying but Andy went bad cop.

"Just tell us where the other guy is selling his pretzels."

"This no sensical. Have you ever try my pretzel?"

"Why would I try your pretzel when I can get one of his pretzels?"

"Because my pretzel identical."

"I beg to differ."

"But you never try," the man said. "And I hear what you say, my pretzel-loving friend, some carts no respect with their pretzel, just moist doughy blob, oversalted, three bites and you feed rest to desperate bird. No cart like to sell pretzel. No good profit with pretzel. Not many people eat pretzel. Pretzel take up space. Pretzel need to be toasted. And the fucking salt, people wanting certain amount of fucking salt, just right. Bullshit. Hot dog good, sausage good, knish good, soda and water good, all that good, but pretzel bullshit. Old-timey, they say. Still better than pain-in-the-ass roasted nuts. That I never understand. But me, like you friend, me, I like good pretzel, I respect pretzel and I want pretzel to shine. I mean look at my pretzel. It pleases the eye, my pretzel, no? And these pretzel just display pretzel, window pretzel. Real pretzel right inside here, in toasty box, the ready-to-go true pretzel." He lifted the lid and a cloud of twisting heat burst into the atmosphere. His hand, half-gloved in a napkin, sunk in and removed a knot of golden brown. "I am proud of this pretzel," the man said.

Emmett grinned. "I never realized how much I liked the word *pretzel*. Or maybe it's just your accent. It's like *pretzel* is a poem written by Pushkin."

"Pushkin?" questioned Andy.

"Okay, maybe not."

"No, no, I like that. Pushkin's Pretzel."

"Not that I've read a word of Pushkin," Emmett admitted.

"Me neither but I still like it."

"Pushkin was a queer," the man said.

"What, like gay?"

"Not gay, queer. Big-time queer. He and Gogol, queer together. Father of Russian literature and its weirdo uncle, both queer. But thank God for the queers. It is easy to love a woman, it is in nature, but art to love a man, and a profound art to want to put your horse in another man's stall. Now which of you queers going to give me two dollar and fifty cents for this pretzel?"

"We're not gay," Andy said. "At least I'm not."

"Me neither," Emmett said, unclear whether to nod or shake his head.

"We're related."

"Nephew, uncle."

"Which *is* kind of queer," Andy admitted.

The man shrugged. "Asshole is asshole if you don't buy pretzel."

Emmett started to reach for his wallet but Andy stopped him. "You can't."

"All this pretzel talk has gotten me hungry."

"No," Andy said with absolute gravitas. "We will find the other guy."

"He's not here, and these look good. Let's just try—"

"We will find him. It'll be worth it, trust me."

"Really?"

"Really."

"You one fucking hard-on," the man told Andy.

"Just tell us where he went."

"I offended."

"I'll give you ten dollars."

"You can buy four pretzel for that."

"Just tell us."

The man dropped his rejected pretzel back into its creel. The outstretched bill seemed a bribe against his honor, with both money and virtue in short supply, and after brief internal debate conducted via eyebrow, he took the bill, giving five dollars in change. "He got permit at carousel, the fucker."

"Thank you," Andy said, turning away.

"Yeah, yeah, yeah."

But Emmett, new to New York, had a harder time leaving. "What's your name?"

"Lensky."

"I'm Emmett. Nice to meet you, Lensky."

"I hope you choke on that fucking pretzel."

"Thanks."

Emmett turned and followed Andy, who was trying to get his bearings for the carousel, somewhere south and west, he knew, somewhere in the lower middle of the park, but where exactly he wasn't sure, wasn't even sure if he had been to the carousel before—he must have, right, as a boy ridden on one of those circus horses that went up and down and all around with the organ music churning and the small hands gripping and the bigger hands playing the worn leather reins as if on top of a bucking bronco or on Belmont dirt, mothers and fathers snapping photos from the sidelines, the more careful parents riding alongside, the spin just fast enough to thrill without bringing on vertigo, a perfect human calibration—yes, Andy must have been there before but the question put a bit of apprehension in his step, like he had stumbled on the origin of deficit.

"That guy was excellent," Emmett said.

"Yeah."

They charged up Pilgrim Hill and passed the humorless statue *The Pilgrim*, high and mighty on his plinth, with his musket and his wide-brim hat and his God-possessed eyes settling on the wilderness, though this Plymouth Rock was a popular spot for late-night hookups, the joke of de-Mayflowering too hard to let pass. Sunday mornings the used condoms were displayed up at the foot of those boots like game after a successful hunt.

"You have a girlfriend?" Andy asked.

"Not really," Emmett said. "Not now. I mean I have girlfriends and stuff but not like a girlfriend girlfriend. I'm kind of avoiding the whole girlfriend girlfriend situation at the moment. I do have a friend and she's a girl but it's all screwed up, thanks to me. I was rotten to her even though I was trying to be nice."

"California girls, huh?"

"No, Lithuanian," Emmett said.

"I just mean those California girls must be sweet."

"They're some decent ones for sure. I don't know, I'd take New York girls any day. Just walking around here is like walking in a wet dream, but more sophisticated."

"A sophisticated wet dream? What does that mean?"

"The girls have smaller tits."

Andy laughed. "I bet you do pretty well for yourself."

"I do fine, I guess. I don't even care anymore."

"That sick of getting laid, huh?"

"I've kind of made a pledge of celibacy."

"No way."

"I just want to clear my mind of that distraction and focus on other things."

"I hear you, I hear you," Andy said. "I feel like I'm constantly peering over a hard-on."

"It's been liberating."

"And how long have you been celibate?"

"Almost three days."

"Wow. No action in three days?"

"Not quite three days."

"You're like a fucking monk," Andy said.

The two boys merged onto a path heading south. The people sitting on the benches seemed a lower class of bench sitter, staring at them like they saw their mislaid youth wander by. Andy decided to try for a more direct route that cut west through a well wooded, unfamiliar dell. He was bewildered by his bewilderment. This park was his backyard, after all, but here the land seemed to slip into its prediscovery past. Bears could have come crashing through the trees.

"How about you, do you have a girlfriend?" Emmett asked.

"Um." Arrows could have zipped by their ears. "There is this older girl."

"Yeah?"

"Like twenty-four."

"Nice."

"And we've been like flirting, I guess. Pretty adult content, I'd say."

"Excellent."

"But we haven't fooled around or anything. Not yet. I tried to get her to send me a picture of herself naked but that was a no-go, so I sent her a picture of my junk instead."

"Uncle Andy!"

"Actually it was someone else's junk, a random image I grabbed off the Internet, though I paged through a lot of dick before I found an acceptable double, so there was a moment where I questioned my motivation."

Emmett grinned. "And she thinks it's yours?"

"I think so. And maybe that penis had more grandeur."

"Grandeur?" said Emmett, now laughing.

"I was adding room for growth."

"So it's a picture of your future penis."

"If my future is about yay big. I'm seeing her tomorrow night. She invited me to this big book party, which will probably be awful. You should come, you should totally come. You can rub shoulders with real New York assholes. It'll be ridiculous but the drinks will be free, and there's no fear of getting carded. You can meet this girl, this woman, and tell me what you think. It might be humorous."

"If my dad let's me, sure."

"Oh Jesus," Andy said, looking around.

"What?"

"Nothing."

Andy was getting giddy at the prospect of being lost within this facsimile of nature, Currier and Ives giving way to a spastic Lewis and Clark. But then he spotted Bethesda Fountain—there!—and posed like stout Cortez, misplaced but beautifully delivered. He guided Emmett onto the lower brick terrace and through the arches of the underground arcade that opened up onto the Mall. From here he was certain he could find the carousel, the two of them passing the bandshell, the statues of various artists, the promenade wide and pleasant, like flat water and they were perfect skipping stones.

"I'm reading *Ampersand*," Emmett told him. "Like I'm almost done."

"Oh yeah."

"It's the first A. N. Dyer book I've read. I don't know why I've waited so long, maybe because of my dad or something, didn't want to upset him, I guess."

"You like it?"

"Yeah, a lot. I'm a big reader, I mean, like I read everything, all across the board, but this book, I don't know, it's a really good book. Hard to believe he's my grandfather."

"I know what you mean," Andy said.

"He does the high school thing pretty well and it doesn't seem all that dated, you just sort of jump in and go along for the ride. And Edgar Mead, I like him but I know by the end I'm going to hate him. Like that scene where he loses his virginity to the Pudge?"

"Yeah."

"Cringeworthy but oddly honorable."

"Yep."

"Maybe that's the point."

"Maybe."

"You go to Exeter, right, like my dad did, like all Dyers but me."

"Uh-huh."

"I'm at public school, Oxford Academy, in Anaheim. It's why we live there, because of the school, otherwise, you know, it's fucking Anaheim. But it's a pretty good school."

"Excellent."

"Not like Exeter though. Is it weird going there?"

"Exeter is weird in general."

"But like with the book and your dad, is that weird?"

"Maybe a little. And it's Shearing, not Exeter."

"Right, right. But pretty close, right?"

"Exeter has girls now."

"Of course."

"And it's a lot less old-school preppy."

"Right."

"More foreign students, more buildings, but otherwise, yeah, pretty close."

"I'm just curious about the place," Emmett said, "and the whole family thing. Like I've been to the website and checked it out, you know, to see how it compares with the book and with my school. The place looks like a college. Looks like everyone has some superpower. I did the virtual campus tour and came across Dyer Hall and I wondered if that was like Dyer as in Dyer, I mean, of course, right?"

"It's named after your great-grandfather. He died in a car accident and his parents, your great-great-grandparents, gave Exeter a dorm in his memory. It's where I live, and it's probably where your dad lived too. Not very original. Let's put all the Dyers in Dyer Hall. In the book it's Moulder."

"No shit."

"Yes shit."

"Like where they all live?"

"Like where they all live."

"I'm at the part where Veck wants out of the prank, like he's been in the closet for seven days and he's whining about how it's not fun anymore and he wants to go home and have a bath and eat decent food and sleep in his bed and see his dog—all that crying about his dog—and the guys are like sorry but not yet, just a little longer, Veck, soon, Veck, okay, bud, and Veck tries to bolt and goes from being a pretend hostage to being a full-blown hostage, bound and gagged, and the guys find themselves in hard-core kidnapper roles, and poor Mead, or not-so-poor Mead, what with Veck and those perfumed letters from the Pudge, just about the saddest, most hilarious letters in the whole world."

"Yep."

"Is there really a used bookstore in a basement?"

"There is."

"And a secret closet?"

"Yep."

"The police are about to get called."

"What?"

"In the book."

"Oh. Don't hold your breath."

They came to the end of the Mall, or the beginning, depending on your starting point, where the statue of Christopher Columbus stood, arms outstretched, eyes heavenward, as if seeking forgiveness in the darkening clouds. The first few raindrops seemed innocent enough as Andy and Emmett took the path to the right. Andy was confident now, especially since a sign said CAROUSEL, with an arrow pointing, and in the distance they heard the confirming squeeze of Wurlitzer music, presently playing "The Blue Danube" though they had no idea of the name, only a familiarity from old cartoons. They half-waltzed up the slight incline. After the pretzel, they would definitely have a ride. But when they got up there, it was one of those moments, rare in the city, where the lack of people can fill you with apocalyptic dread, as if New Yorkers are always on the verge of extinction. Soon enough there was an explanation: those leaping horses were locked behind a gate.

"Fucking closed?" Andy went and pressed his face against the bars. "I'm the world's worst tour guide."

"It's open only on weekends during the winter," Emmett said, reading a sign.

The rain began to fall harder now, the wet eating the dry like a virus.

"Where the hell's the music coming from?"

A pivot and they spotted the source: a lone hot dog cart with a boom box fastened to the umbrella, like some mad Odysseus outsinging the Sirens, calling children to this false shore. The man behind the cart was squat and dour, suggesting the bitterness of a baker in a bread line.

"It's him," Andy said, in near-lunatic awe.

"Him?"

"Yeah."

"You sure?"

"Absolutely. It's you," Andy almost shouted, approaching with open arms.

The man grabbed a baseball bat from the bottom of his cart. "What you want?"

"Whoa, whoa. Just a pretzel." Andy turned to Emmett. "Two pretzels, please."

The man only slightly relaxed. "Sorry but you looked drugged up."

"No, we've just traveled a long way for your pretzel. I'm a fan."

The man seemed unsure if this was a compliment or an inside joke; either way, he reached into his bin and liberated a pretzel, and then another, handing them to these foolish, probably stoned kids. After paying the five dollars, Andy grabbed the mustard and showed Emmett the proper route around the knot, part peace sign, part heart.

"Why the music?" Emmett asked the man.

"Carousel closed, and I need to get people up here, so they think it's

216 · DAVID GILBERT

open, so they buy food for disappointed children, so the music, so that's why."

"It's bait," Emmett said.

"No, it's nice happy music."

Andy took a bite, and whether memory confirmed or memory insisted he smiled and proclaimed it easily the best in New York. As he ate it, he played the old game of imagining a person walking along the pretzel's snowy top and suddenly the path disappears in front of him, and he turns and heads in the other direction, but again the path disappears, the options disappearing left and right, until he's standing on the cliffhanger of the very last bite, wondering, What now?

"Tasty," Emmett said.

"Told you. You want another one?"

"Think I'm fine."

"Guess I'm fine too," Andy said, bittersweet at being full.

"Anything to drink?" the man asked.

The boys shook their heads but continued to stare at the man like he might pass along the next clue and continue their adventure, but the man just tucked himself under the umbrella, waiting to be activated by another dollar. Andy again wished that the carousel was open. It would have been awesome. He and Emmett could have gone for a couple of loops and laughed at the corny childish fun and the goofy innuendo of going up and down, the other children around them oblivious, just seeing big kids having fun, big kids laughing as hard as any little kid, all ridiculous and stupid and a tiny bit scary.

Andy dug into his pocket for his phone. "Before I forget, what's your cell?"

"I left it in L.A.," Emmett said.

"Why?"

"I didn't want to be bothered. I wanted anonimimity."

"Excuse me?"

Emmett grinned. "Anomininimity. Anoma . . . anona . . . anomi-nini . . . anomone." He shook his head.

"To be incognito," Andy assisted.

"Exactly."

"Who needs anonymity?"

"Certainly not me."

The rain before was merely prelude to the rain now, as the clouds unloaded in an almost thrilling acceleration, and maybe that's why the boys started to run, not because they were getting wet—they were instantly soaked—but because they were caught up in the velocity of the event and hoped to match its speed. They sprinted side by side without competition, laughing, whooping, sometimes jumping on and leaping from benches, pleased that the weather had conspired for more excitement. At one point they passed a street performer dressed as the Statue of Liberty, and though her toga was getting drenched and her green paint was streaking, she remained absolutely still on top of a lowly crate, dedicated to her oblique craft, her eyes breaking only briefly and following these boys who ran as if guilty of something, like mortals who had stolen joy from the gods' shitty day.

V

September 23, 1959

Dear Charlie,

Well we made it. The flight was endless and there was a moment after Los Angeles where the turbulence turned our 707 into one ugly duck but we flapped through and landed in Hawaii a full grown swan. If Maui is paradise, then Hana is its Eden. Isabel and I have tossed aside our fig leafs and gone native, shamelessness regained. If only we could have you sing Some Enchanted Evening again. That was quite a performance. Bravo. I must say the entire wedding was a blur, a pleasant blur but a blur nonetheless, though I recall a moment of you looking glum in the corner, rusting, it seemed. I hope it wasn't anything I said! Maybe it was too much drink and sweat — Christ it was hot. Did you have fun with any of Isabel's friends? They are a decent bunch, if horsey. Seems I always smell hay when I'm around them. I didn't see you on the dance floor except for that one turn with my bride — she said you were sweet — but perhaps that saved a few crushed toes. I still can't believe you got up there and sang a song. It was almost funny. But you have a good strong voice. Charlie, you're my oldest friend but we were bound to get older. I'm sure you'll meet somebody soon, somebody great. We can't do everything three weeks apart. And when you do get married I highly recommend Hana. I know you dislike the ocean and the beach but you would love this place. We swim all day long, the waves perfect rollers. I trust everything is tip top back in New York. Did my stepfather talk to you about moving over to Cravath? Is your Daddy down south for the dove season? I have nothing changes when you're away from the city but boy do you feel like you're missing scads. We move and yet stay still all at the same time. Did I tell you I got a very nice rejection from Gus Lobrano at the New Yorker? He wants to see more.

Don't think I am a natural short story writer but that's the place to start these days. I certainly could spin a tale about that wedding that would curl O'Hare. Anyway the surf beckons. Isabel and I bite the old apple in three weeks. I have no desire to return to the wicked east but return we shall as husband and wife. I must say I'm feeling quite lucky.

Your felled friend,
Andy

V.i

S HE MUST HAVE TAKEN THE TRAIN, the Harlem Line, probably drove from Litchfield and parked at the Wassaic station
and bought a *New York Post*, which she finished before the train even
arrived: the 8:30 A.M. to Grand Central, a trip of two hours, give or
take a few minutes. I myself did the ride a week ago. Despite what you
might think, I am trying to be accurate here. I forgot how much I enjoyed trains, their whistles and chugs, their storybook rhythms. When
I was very young my mother would take us to Florida by Amtrak, long-
distance train travel the lingering nostalgia of an earlier generation,
and we would stay in sleeper cars with their slick use of space, and she
would make the trip go faster by giving us a bagful of presents, just
small things, with specific details written on the wrapping paper, like
Four Yellow Schoolbuses, or *A Herd of Cows*, or *Children Playing Baseball*,
and when our window-pressed eyes caught sight of one of these things
we could finally rip open the present. It was as if my mother had gifted
the world into being. *A Red Volkswagen Bug. The Word SMILE. Any
Kind of Dinosaur*. While I rode along the Harlem Line I searched the
landscape in hopes of finding a sign of her, unwrapping *Lovely Green
Hills* and *Small Dying Towns* and *Seventy-six-Year-Old Isabel, Born Isles,
Once Dyer, Now Platt*.

She sat by the window, reading. The car was a third full. Isabel recognized the people by type—the suburban subspecies—every stop
adding a different variety. Most conversations cycled through cellphones, and she imagined "I'm running late . . . " swinging like Tarzan
from those ugly towers disguised as evergreens, swinging all the way
to wherever in Manhattan, throat full of yell. *Me inconsiderate asshole*.

Isabel was halfway through a new collection by Alice Munro. She had just started a story called "The Beauty Abishag"—started it again and again, a series of restarts, reliving Janice Killgard's fall from grace in the first paragraph. Something about age and crow's feet and plastic surgery gone wrong. Lipstick. A car wreck. An older half sister in Ottawa. The writing was typical Alice Munro clear-as-a-bell prose, though Isabel found herself skimming the surface, striding the gaps between words. What were those insects called again, the ones who glided over their pond? Skaters? Skeeters? Whatever their name, those are my eyes, she thought, as she read again about that red light in Rosedale and the visor drawn down, not for the setting sun but for the evening mirror:

> Had she imagined the light turning, the car behind her nearing its horn? She swore something flashed green beyond the mirror and windshield, something told her she needed to go. Of this she was certain. The crash came without impact. Life was lost elsewhere. Downstairs her nephew screamed and Janice checked her face a final time, her finger tracing the unnatural smoothness around her eyes and forehead. Do I look younger?

"A clone?"

"That's what he told us," said Jamie via speakerphone.

"He's not well, Mom," said Richard, no doubt jostling for position.

"Obviously," from Jamie.

"It's really sad," from Richard.

"More ridiculous than sad," from Jamie.

"Have some sympathy," Richard to Jamie.

Isabel had been in the kitchen putting together her famous boring salad when the boys called. Roger was outside throwing a tennis ball for the springers, Glass and Steagall, his little joke, which, in his defense, he regretted. Isabel watched him through the window as he fired the ball as far as he could and took delight in the dogs' competitive nature (Steagall was faster but Glass was smarter) and in his still-decent throwing arm (though he would rub his shoulder for the rest of the day until she finally succumbed and asked what was wrong). Roger was uncomplicated math, best suited to hearty hellos and fond farewells rather than the difficult middle, where he might drag. Baseball handsome is what Isabel's mother would have called him. Goodness, the beautiful girls he dated in his youth. Avedon models. Society girls. But he was twice divorced and in both cases he had no idea why except a vague sympathy that they wanted more from life. But more of what? Andrew would have hated the man with a passion incommensurate with the facts on the ground. A grilled-cheese sandwich could make Roger's day and sports on TV was his idea of heaven. But Isabel embraced this prosaic enthusiasm, crawled within this space and discovered she was happy watching the dogs sprint across the lawn, and cutting up tomatoes and peppers for lunch, and maybe tonight rubbing his shoulder by the fire, which he constantly poked as though its flame were personal.

Where was she? Something about a mistaken change? Back to the beginning:

Had she imagined the light turning, the car behind her nearing its horn? She swore something flashed green beyond the mirror and windshield, something told her . . .

"He had this whole story concocted," said Jamie.

"A Swedish thing," said Richard.

"Try Norwegian, a crazy Nobel cloning-conspiracy thing," from Jamie.

"Whatever," from Richard. "He's had some kind of psychotic break, that's obvious. And he talked nonstop about missing you and all the mistakes he's made and how he wished he'd never written a single book."

"It was medium-grade insanity, nearing full-blown," from Jamie.

"It was plain sad," from Richard.

"And what," she finally asked the boys, "do you want me to do about it?"

Brewster into Croton Falls into Katonah, where she once knew many people, thanks to her brother Jonathan, who lived in Pound Ridge, and her other brother, Peter, who lived the next stop down in Bedford Hills, plus the many New York friends who had fled the city for the sake of safer streets and sporty children and three-acre grabs of the great outdoors, all of whom developed a passion for ice hockey and drunk driving. That's not her line. That's Larry Macawber from *Tiro's Corruption*. Isabel remembered reading an early draft and telling Andrew he should go easy on Westchester and his fictional town of Cicero. "It's getting a bit mean, don't you think?" she said.

"How do you mean *mean*?"

"Don't be cute."

"I don't think I could be cute if I tried."

"Not true. When we first met you dabbled in cute."

"Really? That was cute? Must have been reflected off of you."

Isabel smiled more for effect. "Look," she said, "I don't care that we have a lot of friends there, some quite good friends, and family, nieces and nephews—"

"I've changed names. They'll all think it's the town next door, trust me."

"Like I was saying, write what you want to write, but you should know that it's coming across as angry and bitter, with easy targets everywhere. Instead of shooting fish in a barrel, you're using the barrel as a toilet."

"Maybe that's what I'm trying to do."

"But who wants to read a book like that?"

"I have no idea," Andrew said, sounding like a teacher who has taught the same course for too long. "But what if you forget the characters and their struggles, forget all the clever phrases? What if you sweep the fiction from the page? What do you have? An exposé of this A. N. Dyer character. And maybe that's the point."

Isabel went quiet. At the time Andrew was fifty-eight and she was fifty-five and they had been married for thirty-one years and had known each other ten more and over those years she had noticed him change from easy to hard, an unfocused irritation that began with the publication of *Ampersand* and after the birth of the boys grew into a general annoyance with loud noises and broad behavior, a defensiveness against possible attack, particularly when the subject was fatherhood, a growing incapacity toward anything involving joy, an aversion to live performance, a distaste for New York yet an inability to leave the city, a cheapness of the soul, a solitariness disguised as solitude that pushed the limits and if even gently confronted was denied with extreme prejudice. These men, as she often muttered to her friend Eleanor Topping, the two of them pressed together like sisters, their friendship filling in for the matrimonial gaps. These men, romantically isolated, secretly tortured, became like lighthouses flashing their treacherous shallows. Stay away! Stay away! Isabel was sure she had changed as well—of course—but mostly she thought she just looked older. Why did she stay with him? That was the question, sort of. Why did she let her life get so constrained by his company? Well, maybe she blamed herself. Maybe she gave him leeway because he was such a wonderful writer. Maybe after all this time together she was certain he was a decent man, particularly when measured against others in his line of work, even outside his line of work. If there had been affairs, at least he had been discreet. Until he wasn't. But really, when she thought about those maybes, when she was alone in bed and he was downstairs working, and she was debating the life you expect versus the life you get, she knew that leaving him would be like abandoning a helpless creature, and that seemed too cruel, especially after all their years together. Whatever his own feelings about the author of *Tiro's Corruption*, Isabel touched his hand and said, "I've always cared more about the man, who is much better than he thinks." Andrew ended up taking her advice and in the next draft humanized the characters and moved Cicero into Connecticut, probably not far from where she currently lived. It was the last book he wrote as her husband, Isabel going through the manuscript and flagging the *sofas* and the *drapes* and deciding to add *carpet* to the list of forbidden words.

Had she imagined the light turning, the car behind her nearing its horn? She swore something flashed green beyond the mirror. . . .

"He claims there was no affair," said Jamie.

"It's really bad," said Richard.

"He said the affair was just a story behind the story," from Jamie.

"A cover story," from Richard.

"Whatever," Jamie to Richard.

"And what do you want me to do?" Isabel asked again, exasperated.

These boys, these difficult boys. When do they become men? Early on Isabel was relieved at having only sons, frightened of the mother-daughter dynamic, of replaying her own mother, the famous swimmer, or so universally claimed since the fame was never documented in trophies or ribbons, never witnessed firsthand by any of her children. "Your mother could fly through the water," Isabel would hear whenever she found herself near a pool with a grown-up. You could glimpse some of that truth in those big, bony feet and broad shoulders, features inherited by Isabel and mostly awkward on land. "We called her the Eel," they would go on, as if eels embodied liquid speed rather than slipperiness. But then the Eel was better suited to men. She was the dinner companion who could keep up with the dirty jokes and the drinking and the smoking, who seemed to channel every role ever played by Katharine Hepburn. "Give me a straw and maybe I'll drink the goddamn pool," she once cracked during a Fourth of July party in Southampton, and the men laughed and Isabel, swimming with the other children but mostly staring up at her mother, laughed as well, which made the men laugh harder but embarrassed her mother. "Go swim between someone else's legs," she said, tossing an ice cube at her. Maybe Isabel assumed sons would be easier because of her own brothers, beloved by mother and sister alike: smart and charming, they tripped into every bad habit their generation had to offer yet rolled into their mid-fifties respected, admired even, for their recklessness. Those Isles brothers. They did have fun. Jamie inherited their smile, but he was too conscious of the resemblance and leaned on his uncles for maternal goodwill, his voice often dipping into straight-up impersonation, as if Isabel could be so easily snowed. Then there was Richard with his almost cannibalistic self-esteem issues. Did Isabel try hard enough with him? Had she let him go too quickly all those years ago?

"If he wants to be a junkie, let him be a junkie," Andrew had told her. "But he's on his own."

"I don't think he's a junkie. He's not shooting up."

"For God's sake, Isabel."

"Just to be clear. It's not heroin."

"To be clear, it's crack, and that still qualifies him as a goddamn junkie."

"I don't think that's technically true. I think a syringe needs to be involved."

"Is this really what we're going to argue about?"

"I'm just saying he's not a junkie."

"Whatever he is, there's nothing more we can do except step away."

Maybe Andrew was right, but he sounded so cold and dismissive, relieved even, washing his hands before they were dirty enough. But they had tried, tried hard and for so long. There were Phoenix House and Hazelden, there were the interventions, the experts, but Richard never budged from his desire and denied them even the chance to be proper enablers. Isabel would ask, "What did we do to you?" mostly to herself, even when Richard was drug-free and thriving in California, but the mystery of his descent and her possible role remained this other person shamefully locked within her, and she would imagine pushing that woman aside and kicking in doors and grabbing her son and dragging him to safety, flying him to an island, nursing him back to health. Richard once told her, "You did the right thing, letting me hit bottom like that," but she didn't believe him. That's not quite true. She didn't believe herself.

"You need to talk to him," Richard said.

"Yeah, maybe it will do him some good," Jamie said.

"Confirm that he's gone off the deep end," Richard said.

"We're just trying to figure out what we should do next," Jamie said.

In the backyard Roger tossed the ball one last time, then turned and waved at her, the dogs coming up behind, Glass with the ball, Steagall pushing for the inside track. Isabel wondered how she looked framed in that kitchen window.

"It's starting to rain," Roger told her, once she was inside.

"I have to go," she said.

"Really? Where?" He noticed the phone. "Oh, sorry."

"I'll come into the city tomorrow, in the morning," she said.

Roger went to the fridge and poured himself a glass of water, every movement slow and deliberate, like he followed a secret scoring system. The boys soon hung up, but Isabel remained on the line, even uttered a few listening noises. *Uh-uh. Uh-uh.* Roger gave her a pat. They had been together for two years and had no plans of getting married, but then he needed a triple bypass and Mr. & Mrs. Platt seemed easier. That was three years ago. Roger washed his hands, dried them through his hair, which was always perfectly composed. "Maybe we could have lunch as well," Isabel said to the dial tone. Why was she continuing with this pretense? She gripped the phone harder. A clone? How could he bring back up all of this heartbreak, and rewritten as science fiction, no less? Nearby Roger thumbed through the already thumbed-through newspaper, as if the headlines might change. At movies he ate popcorn one kernel at a time. He considered himself a passionate gardener when in fact he enjoyed bossing the real gardener around. "Melon's?" Isabel said. "That sounds great. I haven't been there in a long time." Roger grabbed two plates though what they really needed were bowls. "Okay, yeah, bye." What are you doing, you madwoman? It was as if A. N. Dyer were back in her head. "Love you too." Finally she hung up. Roger asked the inevitable question, and the truth was no big deal, or most of the truth, the going-into-the-city-to-see-her-sons part, but Isabel wondered if this might splinter into her first betrayal, if the buzzing in her head would infect the rest of her, because Roger didn't deserve this sort of brutal scrutiny, even as he went to the fridge and started the almost painful process of hard-boiling an egg.

Had she imagined the light turning . . .

Past Chappaqua, past Valhalla, Tuckahoe, Bronxville, Fleetwood, the train growing more crowded the closer Grand Central came and now a young black woman sat beside Isabel, two shopping bags crowding her feet, either recent purchases or soon-to-be returns. Isabel spotted a toaster oven. Before she could prove herself nosy she went back to "The Beauty Abishag." The title seemed familiar to Isabel, though her thoughts tripped from beauty to the hard edge of old age and how she was quite proud of her untouched face, a true face, she thought, her friends blaming her luck on genetics, having never seen her mother's post-op smile. The young black woman was full of argument on her phone. "You Tell Keesha I Do Not Appreciate Her Efforts On My Behalf As I Can Take Care Of Myself Especially In Circumstances Regarding Ronnie And His Love Life With Or Without Me Thank You Very Much." Isabel wished she didn't notice the voice, didn't hear the stereotype that was tinged with almost unavoidable racism. Maybe this girl was a lawyer. But probably not. From the window towns gave way to more concrete, the city glimpsed in the curve of the track, like a feudal past rising. "But Now You Are Making Just About As Much Sense As Keesha Who As I Have Said Has No Fucking Sense." Isabel turned to the photo of Alice Munro on the back flap. How old was she now? Roughly her age? They sported the same short haircut, though Alice had more of a shag while Isabel edged closer to pixie, a style she denied herself when she was younger, thinking it might be too mannish on her build. But she liked it. Anything to avoid the matron class. Perhaps that was why these new Alice Munro stories were more violent and lurid, like Hitchcock pushing Chekhov down the stairs. When she saw the book at Barnidge & McEnroe, Isabel muttered, Christ, another Alice Munro collection I should probably read, but these stories had nothing to do with dust and everything to do with blood. Browsing the bookstore Isabel drifted past the D's—DeLillo, Dickens, Dreiser—and noticed the snazzy edition of Andrew's books, a strange red slash on every spine. She tipped down *Ampersand*. For the new cover they used an early Diane Arbus photograph of a young man in a plaid overcoat, perhaps in Grand Central, and while the image was striking and it seemed a nice marriage of artist, writer, and era, she wondered why they would ever change the original with its Rothkoesque door. She opened the book to the dedication page:

To My Father
DOUGLAS ALTHORP DYER
(1892–1938)

In photographs Andrew was a dead ringer for his dad. They had the same dark eyes, repentant yet powerless to change, the smile, or lack of smile, a matter of contention. Isabel's mother called Andrew "the WASP," as in What A Smug Prick, though sometimes she amended it to What A Spectacular Prince, depending on her mood. At their wedding she gave a toast that began *Four score and seven years ago our fathers brought forth on this continent a new nation*, figuring if you had to give a speech you might as well make it a great speech. Isabel's father cried, but he was a Lincoln buff. What a disaster the whole thing was. Her brothers left a trail of broken bridesmaids, and Charlie Topping, oh so soused, sang them a song, tottering forward and gripping the microphone like it was the only piece of balance in the entire Waldorf, a couple of whoops from old classmates, hardly in support but in praise of humiliation, as Charlie sweated, positively defrosted back to his adolescence, his voice breaking against his choirboy training. *If I ruled the night, stars and moon so bright, still I'd turn for light to you. . . .* Thirty seconds in and people had to look away. Andrew dedicated *Tiro's Corruption* to him.

> *For Charles Henry Topping*
> *Amicus est tanquam alter idem.*
> —CICERO

Isabel turned *Ampersand* over. Despite everything, she was glad her photograph remained, right there on the upper left corner, no longer the entire back cover but the size of a postage stamp: Andrew posing in the middle of Sheep Meadow in Central Park.

"Now try smiling," Isabel remembered telling him.

"This is smiling."

"Very funny. Move your chin up a little."

"I don't want to come across as a buffoon."

"By smiling?"

"I want to look serious. A serious author."

Isabel lowered the camera. "Maybe you should get a professional to do this."

"No, I want you to do this. Plus you'll get paid."

"Keep it in the family, huh."

"The WASP thing to do, as your mother might say."

"What A Stingy Peter. Make your mouth less stern."

"Peter?"

"I couldn't come up with a good *P* word. Just smile."

"Pantywaist, Prig, Pissant."

"Please."

"Not even close," he said.

"Pretty please."

"This is what you get, Writer AS Peevish."

"Want A Sucked Penis?"

The shutter clicked, and Isabel had her picture, dissected by readers for the next half century, nobody ever guessing what had just passed through those ears. Andrew dedicated three books to her, starting with his second, *Pink Eye:*

> For Isabel
> *The girl in the ocean*

And then his sixth, *The Bend of Light:*

> Isabel
> *Where the Meanings are—*

And finally his eighth, *Eastern Time:*

> I.D.
> *My only clock*

By then she had accepted his faults, understood where his weaknesses lay, focused on the flow rather than the specific debris that came to the surface, and if she was often unsatisfied, sometimes downright depressed, she did this for the sake of the backward view, of seeing her younger self all those years married to the same man.

The train tunneled for the final stretch into Grand Central. Cellphones lost their hold and a dozen conversations ended in B-movie dialogue—"Are you there?" "Can you hear me?" "Hello, hello, hello?" Passengers collected themselves around the newfound dark. Isabel closed her book. Suddenly she was interested in the world outside, which was black except for the reflection of her face. Her mother once told her she was too handsome to be beautiful. "But I'm not worried," she added. "You've got a sharpness that will outlast the beauties in your grade. Trust me, doll, nobody cares how you slayed them at fourteen." It took almost twenty years for this slight to redshift into a compliment, for Isabel to stare into the distancing past and see her mother's drawn eyebrows as anything but desperate.

When did my life become a series of failed men? This thought came to her without specific ownership, and not terribly true, either, since she was more than her collective male parts, having done extensive volunteer work for various nonprofits and charities and sat on a handful of boards, including the ICP, and for close to fifteen years in her forties and fifties pulled down a mostly symbolic salary in the planning and development office of the NRDC. If this didn't add up to a career, it was good enough for Isabel and allowed her time to read and go to the movies—true passions—and to take long walks, whether in the city or in the woods, and let her mind wander its corners. The train doors opened and from platform into station toward the subway Isabel moved with the precision of a former urban athlete, eyes gauging the best path, chin balanced between no-nonsense and courteous, as though somewhere in the bowels of Manhattan a stopwatch ticked and a voice whispered "faster," and she continued to turn this thought in her head about men, her men, fathers, brothers, husbands, sons, how they all disappointed her even if she loved them with all her heart and suffered a deeper version of their own failure, right down to the roots of her teeth. The sleeplessness from last night came back into view. How would Andrew look? She hoped clean and well fed. But she had fears of long yellow fingernails. Thin white hair. Eyes so shrunken a blink might tear the skin. Later during that night he had transformed into a creature feeding on scraps of the past, reaching for her hand, famished. Toward dawn he became the last time she saw him seventeen years ago.

"I have a room at the Wales," he said, peeking in from the hall.

"Just until I find a rental," she answered from the living room couch.

"I should be the one moving out."

"I have no desire to stay here," she said. "In your mother's crypt."

"I didn't think this would happen."

"Really?"

"I've already told you how sorry I am."

"Yes you have."

"Ten thousand times sorry. I did a stupid thing. I made a terrible mistake. But it was just once, Isabel, after all these years just once. A single moment of weakness repeated only a few times. Just once."

"It doesn't matter," she said.

"It must matter a little."

"Your single moment of weakness wears diapers."

"I know, I know."

"And I'm not going to raise this child, not going to be reminded of it every day. I've put up with a lot but I won't put up with that."

"What can I do?"

"The gossip is already thick."

"I know."

"In the newspapers of all things. With pictures too."

"I have no idea why they care. There must be something I can do, something that'll bring you back to me, something I can say."

"And I'm left playing the fool," she said. "There goes Isabel Dyer, the fool."

"I don't think that's what people are saying."

"It doesn't matter," she said.

"If anything they're talking about me. I'm the fool, the old fool."

"It doesn't matter," she said again.

"I should have known better, me in particular. I got caught in the trap of youth, the desire for change without thinking about what's being changed. And now this absurd trope is a father again, ill-equipped, that's for sure. But"—and he tried to smile here—"the boy has a nice face. He's rather sweet and quiet, hardly cries, just stares and takes things in. For some reason I see you in his face. You have been nothing but an angel, Isabel Isles. I always loved your name, like a paradise somewhere between the Marshalls and the Gilberts, out in the tranquil Pacific. A shame to have ever mucked it up with Dyer."

Listening to this, Isabel wondered if actual sentiment was involved or if this was another extension of his fiction, something she would read a few years later and cringe, knowing what was real and guessing what was possible and being unnerved by the rest. She hoped he would remember that his zipper was down (though that memory broke her heart a little). But was she so blameless in this sense, feet propped on the couch, reading a fashion magazine? She played brittle cool to perfection, hardly a wet eye in the house. The injured wife of a writer. The hidden neurotic rage. Talk about cliché. And while she hoped this masked her sadness—and she was sad and hurt and humiliated and scared—beneath those core emotions present since childhood was an unexpected reaction: she was free to escape with her good manners intact, the wounded instead of the wielder of the axe.

"You should go," she said.

His last words to her: "You look lovely on that sofa."

Isabel surfaced from the subway at 68th and Lexington. She still had plenty of friends in the city and visited almost once a week, Roger and her going to dinner with other couples, the movies, the theater, spending the night at the Cosmopolitan Club. There was nothing wistful about crossing Park, crossing Madison. The number of strollers and limousines was always a surprise. And the construction. The city seemed to be pushing up a new set of teeth. The sly, enigmatic grin of New York with its cross section of stylishness, its promise of every stranger being something special, something unexpected, their passing light tempting your shadow, now simply mumbled math. Isabel realized she was being a crank—Manhattan from the beginning had been about money—but it seemed less fun nowadays, less sexy. Isabel had a peculiar relationship with money anyway. Her father was on the

Havemeyer tree but on a far less leafy branch, and he boomed but mostly busted throughout her childhood before hitting on the Acorn Press in the late fifties and publishing the I Can Draw That series, the Skedaddle books, the ever-popular Conrad Janus Mysteries, after which he divorced her mother and became spiteful of every cent, to the point where he actively ran the business into the ground. But it was during one of those early lean periods that Isabel was shipped to Southampton for July to stay with her cousin Polly. Isabel was fourteen.

"Fifteen in October," she told the boy swimming with her in the ocean. Polly was already back on the beach, complaining about the water being too cold, and the waves too choppy, and really they should go up soon and have lunch at the Little Place because she was starving and she had tennis at two-thirty and she needed her stomach to settle before running after a stupid ball all because her father was the constant runner-up to the ten-time club champ. Two days in and Isabel was already sick of Polly. "How old are you?" she asked the boy, glad for the new company.

"Seven-um, seventeen," he said.

"Oh." An older boy. He seemed younger except for the acne, which was well established, like a drought in its third year. She tried to glimpse his armpits for evidence of full-born puberty and perhaps as revenge against the obviousness of her breasts, which were small yet persistent in that sixty-five-degree water. But the boy was not a confident swimmer and Isabel felt bad for even looking.

"Can you, um, ah, touch?" he asked.

"Barely."

"Yeah, me neither, but you're a good-um, you're a good swim-swimmer."

"Thanks."

"I'm obviously not," he said.

"Well you're not sinking."

"Give me time. Trying to get used to-ah, to-ah rough water."

"It's not that rough." Isabel regretted the possible jab.

"Hence the trying-to-get-used-to part," he said.

She smiled and he smiled in return.

"Crazy thing is, I come from-ah, a family of fish," he said.

"Me too. But my mother's a shark."

They both floated in a congenial radius, half on tiptoes, facing the beach and the club in the distance with its brick terrace and gathering lunch crowd. Polly, arms crossed, posed for a statue called *Impatience*, annoyed yet incapable of leaving Isabel alone. She would make a fabulous stepmother someday.

"I should go," Isabel said to the boy.

"Yeah?"

"Yeah."

"Where-ah, um, where you going?" he asked.

"Lunch with my cousin."

"Polly Lash is your cousin?"

"Yep. Cut me and she bleeds." Isabel had no idea what this meant, but the boy again smiled and she thought he seemed nice, a safe introduction to the world of seventeen-year-old boys and what they might think of a fourteen-year-old girl with big feet. For the sake of curiosity and the two cats warring within her stomach, she asked if he wanted to join them.

"For lunch?"

"Only if you want."

"Um, okay."

Isabel thought of asking his name, but at this stage it seemed weirdly intimate, plus the moment had passed, and wasn't it the boy's job anyway? Instead she rode a small wave in, arms pressed back, shoulders arched, chin cutting through the foam.

Isabel missed swimming in the ocean.

At 2 East 70th Street the day-shift doorman recognized her—"That you, Mrs. Dyer?"—and with a certain amount of pride Isabel remembered his name—"Hello, Felix"—and chatted about family, his four children now all grown, the older two with children themselves, though time unarticulated was the truer subject, Felix following the doorman code and refraining from asking personal questions, but seeing Mrs. Dyer of the sixth floor gave him a passing awareness of the gap between when he was young and when she was old and how it had narrowed to a crack.

In the elevator Isabel counted the floors like beads on the rosary—please God don't let him be pitiful; deranged; irredeemably senile; muttering some nonsense; incontinent—until the sixth floor lit up and she found herself asking, Why am I even here?

Polly Lash had heard the same question years ago. "Why what?"

"Nothing," Isabel said with a weary shake of her head.

They were sitting at a table while the boy waited inside for his bacon burger. The Little Place crowd was nearing its peak though most of the adults were heading toward the Big Place with its finer selection of roast turkey and shrimp scampi and other dinner-like meals designed as an excuse for dinner-like drinks.

"Lunch with Charlie Topping of all people," Polly went on again.

"He seems nice," Isabel said.

"He's a lemon. Now his brothers—"

"Just because of his pimples? Have you looked at your forehead lately?"

"That's a sun rash."

"Well you have sun rash on your back as well."

"Are you his ah, um, ah, girl-um-friend, aah, all of a sudden?"

"That's just mean," Isabel said.

"All the older boys around here and you pick Charlie Lump."

"What do you call those blackheads on your nose, a moon rash?"

Polly's eyes sprouted fangs. "Why don't you go back home, oh yeah, you can't."

Isabel went quiet.

"I didn't ask you here," Polly said. "It's not my fault that your parents are in a state."

That was the winning blow. Even worse, Isabel wanted to ask Polly what kind of state she meant since the exact nature of her parents' situ-. ation was a mystery, like a magic trick without the magic, but things were definitely disappearing, starting with her brothers, who were spending the summer with relatives on a farm in Washington State. The dog was gone too. Even pieces of the furniture, that small painting by Greuze, were missing. But then Charlie Topping showed up with his bacon burger and a plate of extra bacon, and before sitting down he said an uncertain hello to Polly just in case she had over-turned her cousin's earlier ruling on lunch.

"Hello, Charlie." Polly relented.

Charlie sat down. "I'm Charlie-um, Charlie Topping," he said to Isabel.

"Yeah, I know. I'm Isabel Isles."

Charlie got up again for the introduction, his knees knocking into the table.

"Christ," Polly said.

"Sorry."

"Just do us a favor and sit back down slowly."

The three of them started to eat, glad for the excuse to avoid conversation. Every once in a while Charlie flicked a french fry to one of the sportier seagulls that scrounged the perimeter for food.

"Must you feed the flying rats?" Polly said.

"Gulls are useful birds and he's-um, he's caught three in a row."

"Wow, what a bird."

"The record is eleven."

"Boys and their games."

Charlie returned to his lunch. Isabel found something heartbreaking about the two dessert plates on his tray, the blueberry pie and the éclair, like this was where he grabbed his daily parcel of joy. Between that and his hair, which as it dried rose up like some earsplitting mushroom cloud, she wasn't sure if she could watch this boy finish his meal.

"Where do you go to school, Isabel?" he asked.

"Brearley," she said.

"Like in the, um, like in the city?"

"No," Polly jumped in, "the Brearley in North Dakota."

"Yeah, dumb question," Charlie said. "And you're here for the, for the summer?"

"Just for July, I think."

"Yes, just July," Polly confirmed.

"I'm leaving in a week for England," Charlie informed the two girls, "London, the Lake District, kind of a tour with my-aah, my-aah, um, grandfather." Charlie picked another french fry and chucked it extra hard and just out of reach for the seagull.

"Sounds nice," Isabel said.

Polly almost laughed. "Summer with um Grandfather. What a treat."

"He's a bit of a, of a, a Renaissance man, unlike my dad. I tried camp"—Charlie made a face—"and sports, well, I only like sports that are, um, barely even sports. If we were at a carnival, I could win a dozen, a dozen of those giant stuffed animals, I've done it before, the stupider the game the better I am."

"Yeah?" Isabel asked.

Charlie nodded, and then reconsidered. "Still can't swim worth a damn though."

"Fascinating conversation, you two," Polly said, her eyes picking up a bigger stick. "You know I just realized something: if you two got married, let's just say, that would make me related to you, Charlie. Imagine that. I mean we've known each other for so long. So many laughs together. Like remember the time you had that accident in the pool. An obvious kind of accident. Feels long ago but really wasn't. They had to drain the whole pool. No swimming for two days. And Isabel, your parents would have to pay for the wedding. Eek. That might be difficult. Don't worry, I'm sure something can be worked out. Maybe everyone could share a really substantial sandwich. Either way we should honor this moment, this spot right here where Charlie Topping and Isabel Isles first met and—"

That's when food went flying, two hot dogs with mustard and ketchup, an order of fries, grape juice, chocolate cake, the majority of which crash-landed on Polly's chest and lap. There was a moment of silence as all immediate oxygen rushed into Polly's gasping mouth, her lungs a kiln stoked by the tables around her, the heads tilting and straining, everybody feeding the silence until the silence was fashioned into something easily broken: Polly Lash, mortified.

In retrospect, poor Polly. Her life was far from easy.

Isabel stood in front of her old apartment door, its fire-code steel painted to resemble wood. Twenty years ago when the painter had done the faux finish—graining, he called it—she had watched him and thought she might enjoy this as one of those hobbies that could double as a casual occupation—a faux finisher—and she went so far as to try to marbleize the downstairs bathroom in Southampton, a look Andrew dubbed Cartoon Carrara. Isabel waited a second before ringing, like an actor between "To be" and everything else.

She could still clearly see that other boy in grass-stained whites, hands holding his now-empty tray as he presented his defense to Polly, that he had tripped, it was an accident, sorry, sorry, sorry, but Polly detected nothing but ugly intent in his apology, that he had done it on purpose. Charlie, ever helpful, tried handing her his napkin but Polly knocked it away in favor of yelling at the offending boy. "You really are a snake in the grass!" She stood up. Her beach dress was flavored with condiment, french fries tumbling to the ground, as well as a hot dog that rolled free of its bun and was quickly snatched up by the seagull. For a moment Polly, arms spread, was a canvas hung for all to see, but then she curled into herself and rushed away, turning back near the steps and beckoning for relative support. But Isabel didn't see her, or she chose not to see her, which was an unfortunate skill she had. Rather, Isabel remained at the table with Charlie and this other curious boy, who plopped down in Polly's seat and jammed a loose chunk of cake into his mouth, mostly to keep a safe distance from smiling. Who was he? The boy wiped his lips. His attention moved from sheepish Charlie and settled on Isabel with what seemed a purity of purpose, like whatever he had done, he had done for her. "So," he said through a mouthful of chocolate cake.

After a few more rings Isabel heard movement behind the door.

V.ii

WHEN THE DOORBELL RANG, Andrew was in his study and Andy was upstairs, while Gerd was outside doing her Gerdie things. And me? I was visiting my old apartment, since Ashley and the children were away. Okay, maybe I was snooping. Maybe I was imagining myself as a ghost, invisible in this world, trying to understand the family I would haunt for the rest of my life. Maybe I was being overly dramatic as I buried my face in my son's pillow and put a hand on certain stuffed animals like I could read their plush minds. I touched everything, photographs, drawings, the table in the kitchen. I was father as guilty fingerprint. Then I made myself a sandwich. I'd like to say that I left soon after but I didn't. I started to nose through my wife's desk, her closet, searching for something, a secret maybe, a letter to a friend in which an old boyfriend was mentioned or a crazy night in Marblehead or a skinny-dip gone wrong, something where she might open up to me. But I found nothing. That didn't stop me from going through her underwear drawer for the sake of more base privacies, which in their absence had become a mystery. That's where I was when the doorbell rang, fingers deep in lace, while Andy was upstairs and Andrew was in his study.

Both of them assumed Gerd would answer the door.

Andy stared into his closet, hand scratching his tummy, in particular the trail of hairs recently budded from his navel, which struck him as undeniably excellent, like a waterfall splashing down into a pool of pubes, his penis the dude floating on his back. This seemed big-time, stage-four man stuff, though the few hairs poking from his nipples kind of disturbed him, like filling coming through upholstery. Anyway, what to wear tonight? All of his pants looked like slacks and his jackets were either too blazery or too tweedy and uniformly too small. Usually he went shopping with Gerd, who pushed him toward the Nordic idea of American Preppy, which fell somewhere in Chicago, mid-1980s. But Andy never cared much. Except for tonight. Tonight he wanted to look decent even if he had a problem defining decent. Not hip. Not stylish. Not fashionable. He wanted to look older without looking like someone trying to look older. Jeanie's age. Hi, Jeanie. Hi, Andy, you look, you look, well, great. Yes, that's what he wanted, standing in front of his closet. Like something in a stupid movie, he supposed, except in a movie he would be the young girl and Jeanie would be the older man and he would be tempted—he as in Jeanie—and maybe she would kiss him—she as in Andy—but at the last second he would stop her and she would be hurt yet she'd understand, having dabbled in the scary messed-up world of grown-ups. But screw that. Andy wanted Jeanie Spokes riding down his waterfall, butt first and screaming. He slapped his tummy a few times. How dressy is this affair?

I ~~eased~~ slipped the key into the lock, ~~briefly~~ imagining that noises were sparks and the room was full of gas. The latch clicked. Nothing ignited. A few tiptoe steps ~~inside~~ into that familiar darkness. Though windowless, an inky light ~~seemed to seep through the seams~~ pressed through the brick and mortar ~~as if composed of collander~~ as if hand-pressed. I put the bucket down. The normal ~~musty smell~~ dank of the basement mixed with the normal mustiness of all those books ~~mingled with the fingerprints~~ once held by ~~the hands of~~ old students, some of them dead in Normandy, dead in Bastogne, dead boy eyes flickering against these pages, the words recording every tired blink, every eventual snore, of pimpled Shearing ghosts, their rotten teenage breath breaking over "This is the saddest story I have ever

heard" and "You don't know about me without you have read a
book by the name of The Adventures of Tom Sawyer" and all
the other worn-out beginnings. I have to admit, I always
liked the smell. It was like an old dried sponge, pleasantly
nasty. But today there was another smell ~~underneath~~
~~beneath~~ that dogeared those pages. I picked up the bucket.

Doom set in, the ridiculous doom of having nothing to wear, which
was a new kind of doom for Andy. He limped his wrist and lisped, "You
big old fag," hoping this might defuse things. It didn't. It just made him
feel like a pig. What was he looking for anyway? A suit? A velvet jacket
and leather pants? A cowboy shirt? He had no clue, but he knew it was
definitely not in here. He remembered how for a party last Christmas
he had borrowed a tux from his dad, the size a pretty close fit, the
early-seventies vibe a success with people who cared about those
things. In one of the pockets he had found two ticket stubs to *Don
Carlo* and he liked the image of his father in black tie sitting in the
audience, with his wife, he supposed. Andy had even downloaded the
music—it was by Verdi—and enjoyed "Dio, Che Nell'alma Infondere,"
though he could never tell anyone since he was unsure of its proper
pronunciation. But the song made him feel closer to the man. Andy
went down the hall and opened his father's closet, and as he browsed
through those clothes again, he was struck by the smell of cedar mixed
with shoe leather, the suits and jackets and pants dusted with his breath,
it seemed. There must be something in here, Andy thought.

I turned on the overhead light and whatever ~~precious~~
~~overwrought overrefined~~ dusky atmosphere disappeared -- it
was just books, walls of ~~fucking~~ old books on ~~rickety prose~~
cheap pine shelves. I was always bothered by the stains on
the carpet, ~~ridiculous me noticing this first~~ and thought
that when I was in charge I would ask for -- no, I would
demand, new carpeting. There must have been a leak or a

broken pipe long ago, and sometimes I draped a towel over the most offensive section, which resembled a litter of puppies consumed by fire. I would have moved a bookcase too if not for the effect on the flow. A new carpet was the only solution, period. ~~Why did I care so much about the carpet?~~ Then I heard the noise. You really had to listen, to the point where you might have guessed it was something else, ~~like regret,~~ like your own pulse sloshing through your ear. I am someone prone to hearing phantom screams in the shower and often catch songs in the hum of modern convenience, ~~"Double Crossing Blues"~~ "Goodnight, Irene" murmuring from behind the icebox. But I'm avoiding the present noise, ~~spent my life avoiding the noise~~. I went over to the far right side of the room, to the shelves with ~~Dumas Dostoyevsky~~ its Edgar Alan Poes, and reached between the books and slid free the bolts, one high, one low, after which I pushed aside three copies of <u>Poems and Tales</u> and turned the doorknob. ~~Talk about a bad dream.~~ It might have been a long forgotten janitor's closet, but it was our secret lair. On the other side of the door large gothic letters dubbed the 6x8 space ~~Malbolgwe~~ <u>The Wombat Cave</u> with all the previous emperors listed below, dating back to its founder, Dewer Darny, in 1924. Rogin was the present scholarship Caesar. For him, this was an exclusive club with a maximum occupancy of four, five if knee-to-knee. Once inside the door could be locked with another set of bolts leaving behind a sealed tomb of infinite possibility. A bare bulb hung from the ceiling. The walls were like the bathroom stalls of Lascaux. ~~But no one could get lost in here.~~ I flicked on the light. Timothy Veck looked up with wide desperate please-save-me eyes, obvious to see even if they were hidden behind a blindfold.

Suit after suit had that old Brooks Brothers label stitched inside, the Golden Fleece like a sheep being airlifted. There was the gray pinstripe. The every possible shade of navy blue. The herringbone. The charcoal. The summer weight or the winter wool. They seemed stuck in time, not timeless but timeful, like an old newspaper. None of the pants had cuffs or pleats, and the half-dozen khakis were all identical. There were two blazers. Multiple tweeds. A lone outlier of Italian design that still sported its price tag, its cost fifteen years ago. In general, no overt personality existed here, only a sober sense of purpose—to clothe—uncolored by opinion, unswayed by advertisement. All the news that's fit to wear. Andy tried on the pinstripe. He would need to cinch the pants with a belt but the length was good and the jacket was near bespoke. The mirror revealed a decent young man, perhaps a tad in costume, like he was starring in a high school production of *Adult! The Musical*. And while the pockets were void of Dad-like clues, the fabric seemed adrift in memories without content, a floating physical presence that despite everything was nice. Andy buttoned up the jacket. He had the feeling of something inescapably sad and fatally present.

    Matthews, the Eagle Scout ~~Nazi~~, had a background with ~~animal torture and~~ knots and had managed a doozy of loops and hitches so that Veck seemed upholstered to that chair. He must have tried to free himself because he had tipped over and was lying on his side. I thought of an animal in a trap. Not true. I thought of an animal dead in a trap. ~~I thought of me.~~ But Veck was alive. Where the rope found skin, the skin found blood. I bent down and ~~grabbed the chair and~~ tilted him upright. His head flopped over. I hadn't seen him in a few days, and they must have been slapping him around. His face seemed a few days fallen from the vine. Did they ~~butcher~~ cut his hair as well? Tears, snot, piss, drool scored a terrible path through the memory of dry and clean and comfortable. They had gagged him with a pair of dress socks that were held in place by the yellow and blue of the Shearing School tie. The blindfold I recognized from

Stimpson's ratty bathrobe. I still hadn't said anything yet.
I was mute. Edgar-free. Was that a cigarette burn on his
hand? ~~God, this is horrible.~~ I held this goddamn bucket with
a sandwich and a Coke inside, a chocolate chip cookie, and if
he needed I figured he could use it to go to the bathroom
in, but seeing him, ~~my oldest friend,~~ all squirmy and
miserable and hoping for rescue but fearing the opposite, I
wished I had a plan in my head instead of a meal for the
prisoner.

Andy finally heard the doorbell and in hearing it recognized that it had
been ringing forever. He went to the top of stairs. "Gerd! Door!" he
shouted. "Gerd?" Still nothing. "Jesus Christ," he said, taking the
stairs. "Yeah, yeah, coming," he said, pulling the jacket tight over his
bare chest, full of haste and annoyance, like he was a businessman, an
advertising executive, interrupted in the midst of coitus, like in a TV
show or movie, and he had a woman sprawled on his bed upstairs, a
blonde with a nice slope, and maybe the doorbell held the brunette
from the airplane who had wiggled past him in the aisle, her ass erasing
a dirty limerick. Imagine that, Andy imagined. The speed of fantasy
seemed faster than light, and he projected some decent velocity by the
time he hit the front door.

I removed the sash from Timmy's eyes and he blinked me
into existence, blink, blink, a friend. The gag was sopped. I
hoped the socks had at least gone in clean. Timmy uncramped
his jaw, like a snake swallowing a rat's worth of air. ~~A
snake? Hardly a snake. There was nothing snakey about
Timmy. It might be a worthwhile image but it is a poor
description of the boy. If anything he was sadder, like a
forsaken choirboy trying to comfort himself with a hymn.~~
The smell of piss mingled with perfume, probably the
Hypnotique that Harfield had swiped from Mrs. Willets'
bedroom. The jerk. What was next for Timmy? The stolen

brassiere and girdle? ~~Paint on some ruby-red lipstick?~~ The
combined odor was unbearable. Hypnoreek. They must have
really doused him and I pictured green smoke rising from
the first few splashes. "I want this to stop now," Timmy
finally said to me. I think it was his grab for bravery that
broke my heart.

As Andy opened the door, the sexy brunette crashed into a woman of
indeterminate age, though well beyond middle and short of ancient, a
wedge of human existence Andy hardly noticed. "Hello," he said. This
woman, she didn't move but rather stared at him like he was a distant
pinprick of light, perhaps moving forward. Did she have the wrong
apartment? Was she confused? Was she here for his father? Silence
started to push into the awkward extreme and Andy wondered if she
had Alzheimer's or something, if she had wandered from her floor and
had fallen into a mental hole, decades deep, if perhaps her super-cute
granddaughter was presently searching for her. "Hello?" Andy said
again, this time leaning in and trying to break whatever trance held
her. Something slotted within his consciousness, as if she was passing
through a similar adolescence. And he liked the short hair. Her sharp
nose. He had an intense desire to see her smile. "Is there anybody in
there?" he asked, his face like a flashlight.

Success. "Sorry," she said, shaking her head.

"Welcome back."

She nodded without much sureness. "You must be Andy."

"I must be."

"I'm Isabel."

She reached her hand forward, seeming embarrassed by the formality, her eyes creasing, maybe seeing more clearly through a blur. She
sort of flinched. Andy hoped he hadn't given her a weird handshake.

"I have a sandwich for you."

"I just wanna go home, Edgar," Timmy said, his lower lip
tapping a more frantic code.

"And a Coke."

"I don't like this anymore."

"It won't be for much longer."

"They beat me up, Edgar. I don't know why. I know I tried to leave but why are they beating me up? And other stuff too. I just want it to stop and go home. I want to see my dog. I don't want to be here anymore."

I showed him the sandwich. "It's bacon on bread." I had swiped the bacon from the dining hall that morning, no easy task.

"Why are they doing these things?"

"It's part of the prank," I assured him.

"It's not funny."

I opened the Coke. "Shoot, I should've brought a straw."

"I don't want a stupid sandwich, Edgar, I want to go home. They burned me. And my jaw. Everything hurts. I just want to go home. Please." Timmy could no longer control himself, the muscles in his face tightening around a pitiful center, eyes and nose and mouth draining what little courage remained. "I don't understand. Please help me. I won't tell, I swear."

"Have some sandwich. And a Coke."

"Please."

"It might make you feel better."

"I need to go to the bathroom," he whispered, like Huck Finn and Billy Budd and David Copperfield were listening. "I really need to go, and I don't want to do it in my pants. Please. I can't hold it much longer. I thought this was going to be fun, like camping, like an adventure. They burned me, Edgar. And I think they're going to do worse. And I need to pee."

I think I kneeled down close and said something like, "Calm down," and Timmy did calm down, briefly, an uncanny kind of calm, like adrenaline was involved, his breathing settling on a horizon, miles beyond me, to the edge of God knows where, and I thought of those smaller animals taken

down by their larger counterparts, how after all the
running and all the struggling, when those teeth finally
clamp down, they seem to slide into surrendering and wrap
themselves around what's happening, experiencing it fully,
like death is a different kind of birth, equally warm. ~~What
did he see?~~

"Isabel Dyer," she explained, "or once Dyer."

"Oh hey," Andy said, and he started to nod with growing enthusiasm, like a long shot possibly coming through—"Isabel Dyer"—and
though he hoped his reaction remained within the bounds of good
manners—"Wow, it's really, really nice to meet you. I mean, I've always been curious"—he feared he was blowing his cool and so retreated
to more familiar insecurities, touching his suit and saying, "I swear
this isn't my normal look."

"You look nice."

"I'm going to a party tonight. Imagine a shirt and a tie, my hair
combed."

"Devastating then," she said.

This woman had certainly aged better than his father, her face a
series of clean, strong lines, something Matisse might have sketched to
infuriate Picasso. As she stepped into the apartment Andy noticed the
smell that trailed behind her, pleasant if medicinal, similar to witch
hazel splashing against his pores and turning them taut. She must have
been beautiful when she was younger. They stopped near the stairs and
she took in the changes, or lack of changes, in the apartment. Andy
wished he could have somehow seen his own history in her eyes. Isabel
Dyer. The mother he almost had. In less than a minute he might as
well have belonged to her, and when her eyes returned from their brief
tour and fell back on him, he noticed tears, her hands quick to wipe
them aside, but they continued and soon she gave in to crying. Andy
wanted to comfort her. More than anything he wanted to wrap an arm
around her and squeeze, but he realized he was the likely source of this
emotion. Instead of long lost, he was bitterly found.

"I'm sorry," she said.

"No, I am."

"I wasn't expecting this," she said.

"I can only imagine."

"It's not you, I promise." She touched his arm.

Something in Andy fell, something like the feeling of feeling old.

"It's been a long time since I've been back here," she told him.

"Right."

"And I'm a little thrown."

"I'm sure."

"And I wasn't expecting this."

Before he could fall any further he was pulled back by a familiar voice.

"Isabel?"

They both turned and saw him standing there.

~~That's when I bent down and started to work on Matthews'~~
~~vicious knots, which were torturous and tight, every~~
~~intersection a car wreck of rope. A tug near the foot~~
~~tightened around Timmy's throat. It was like a string~~
~~instrument designed by Torquemada. A knife would have~~
~~really helped, but Timmy cheered me on, he was so thankful,~~
~~and while I could have been annoyed -- I mean, he was~~
~~raining thank yous all over me and I was reminded of what~~
~~a terrible pain he could be and how now I was his hero, even~~
~~if the hostage prank was my idea, but now I was the Timmy~~
~~savior, the emancipator of Veck, and I wondered how like in~~
~~some countries, those island nations in the Pacific, where~~
~~Gauguin lived the life and had his way with thick brown~~
~~girls, if since I freed Timmy our souls would forever be~~
~~conjoined, the saver and the savee, and I almost stopped~~
~~right there, said Okay, enough, because the knots were tough~~
~~as hell and the smell was beyond the realms of the real,~~
~~and in the movies I bet right now is where change-of-heart~~

~~Edgar Mead gets interrupted by either Stimpson or Matthews~~
~~or Harfield or Rogin or even better all four standing by~~
~~the door -- Well lookeehere fellas! -- and jump to the next~~
~~scene, where that sap Edgar is tied up as well. But nobody~~
~~was standing behind me. I was free and clear and Timmy was~~
~~slowly coming undone, and I thought of what my mother used~~
~~to do on my birthday when she spun these giant string webs~~
~~all over our house, rooms crosshatched and double stitched,~~
~~like a new visible dimension had opened up, and we the~~
~~players would grab our predetermined end and start~~
~~winding our way in, up, around, under, over, over, under~~
~~around up until a few rooms later we found a bow around a~~
~~cheap prize: Timmy Veck, piss-stenched but shit-free,~~
~~standing on his own two feet.~~

For the first time in a long time Andy was happy to see his father, the unexpected relief rendered as affection. He went over and guided his father forward, like a member of the audience pulled into action.

"Is that my suit?" his father asked.

"Yes it is."

"It looks good on you."

"Thanks."

"You need a shirt, though."

"Yeah, thanks for the advice."

"Seeing the two of you I thought for a moment I was unfettered from time."

"Stay with me here, Dad."

"What?"

"Just try to be normal."

"Do you think I'm crazy too?" his father asked this poor woman.

Andy shook his head. "Most people would start with 'How are you?' and then maybe move on to 'What brings you here?' and 'What are you up to?' That said, Mrs. Dyer, he really is crazy."

"Platt actually."

"Mrs. Platt then. It was nice to meet you. I hope I wasn't . . . "

"No," she said, picking up where he hesitated. "It was nice to meet you too."

There was no departing handshake, only a quick wave and Andy started back up the stairs, taking them by twos, speeding up the curve like he needed to remind himself of his youth, like regardless of where he was, he could be somewhere else in a flash, though halfway up he did glance back down and see that they were watching him with the same look on their faces, as if about suffering they were never wrong.

Timmy stared at me and I swear it was like he was trying
to bore sympathy into my skull, trying to steer me, to guide
my hands into untying the rope like I was controlled by
strings, like I had the choice and the choice was now --
challenging me, really, this royal pain, this lurker,
clueless of his effect on people, particularly yours truly,
greeting me from distances as great as a quarter mile,
Edgar! Edgar! Edgar! like he was going to jump up and lick
me, or worse kiss me, like I was Sarge back home from the war
and he was my three-cent Penny, and people would laugh
without him noticing and mutter -- "Here comes your gal" --
and I'd wonder what I did to deserve this, all because my
father insisted I should rise above the tide and show him
companionship, like I was his shadow of the war, the foxhole
chits scrawled in mud and blood, even if back home Father
Mead and Father Veck had almost nothing in common, the
insurance salesman and the snob, but regardless I was nice
to Timmy and treated him buddy buddy, a through-and-
through pal, or I tried to, I swear I tried to, but here he
was lips trembling and staring like freeing him was
already part of our history, and the more I absorbed that
future the angrier I got, like he held this secret over me,
this weakness on my part. I dropped the sandwich and the
Coke into the bucket with the resignation of a Civil War

surgeon. I kicked him in the shins. It was a half-hearted
kick. That was going to be the extent, a kick and then I'd
leave, but I kicked him again, harder this time, and I told
him he knew nothing, he was a fool, a laughingstock, a
terrible queer, I'm sorry as I jammed the socks back into his
mouth and retied the necktie tight, you probably like this,
I said, you inverted jackass, and maybe I slapped him, maybe
whenever a comma appears you should imagine my open palm,
and he probably still loved me even after I closed the door
and slammed those bolts home, probably still forgave me. I
restraightened the books on the shelves. The other Edgar.
I had baseball practice in ten minutes and I started to run
for the gym. The day was perfect, the green fields freshly
mowed, the few clouds in the sky the sort landscape painters
put in to deepen the flat blue nothing. A yellow birthday
balloon was snagged in a high branch of a tree. I made it in
time for fungoes.

The scene downstairs stayed with Andy for less than a minute before
he turned back to his father's closet and wondered if black wingtips
would go well with the suit and which one of the neckties he should
wear. But as Andy tonight took shape in the mirror, another part of
him came back with a different assessment, as he looped a Windsor
knot around his bare neck, that he was teaching himself something
important even if it might be something about failure.

V.iii

THE PLAN WAS for Richard and Jamie to meet their mother at J.G. Melon on 74th and Third, and over a hamburger she would tell them about her visit with Dad and they could discuss what they should do next. That was the plan. But Mom was twenty-five minutes late, thirty if going by the wedge of watermelon clock over the bar, and now the lunch crowd teemed and tables garnered a waiting list, the space between self and food growing longer by the minute. The brothers sat in the corner, the television overhead a thought balloon via ESPN. They were the missed free throw, the shot on post, the lipped putt. When they first arrived the host told them they could have their pick of table once their party was complete. How that word charmed them. "We are incomplete," from Richard, "You incomplete me," from Jamie, as they settled into the bar and ordered a club soda and a beer. It seemed a more innocent time back then, the good old days of a quarter-past-twelve. Their bartender was likely Bobby "Big Baby" Frizz, famous for his cantilevering stomach, but Richard and Jamie had no idea of his name. They knew Melon's, though. We all did. I can still see it on the northeast corner, its exterior painted green with a slice of red neon that seemed forever reflected in rainwater. Most of our childhood haunts had long disappeared, but Melon's still beckoned like a mirage miraculously real.

"It's like this place is preserved in amber," Jamie was saying.

Richard nodded.

"Same menu, same décor, prices certainly different, but essentially we could be those preppy kids over there. Nothing would be anachronistic. Same cash register even. It's timeless for as long as I've known time."

Richard stopped nodding. "You stoned?"

"Perhaps."

"And now you're getting drunk?"

"Drunk? Two beers doth not a drunk make."

"That's your fifth refill, Shakespeare."

"No way."

"Yep."

"In my defense it's a small glass." Jamie squinted and went all shaggy, the dimple on his cheek like a registered trademark. Fucking Richard, he thought, fuck Richard but fucking Richard, always determined to define himself in opposition to the world, like a linebacker, while Jamie was the running back slipping through the seams. But Jamie should be kinder. After all, his brother was showing impressive patience, though pity the ripped cocktail napkin and the mangled red straw. And Jamie himself no longer breezed through openings but stumbled and bruised easily. This morning he had gotten another call from Sylvia, quickly ignored and deleted, which made a total of three beyond-the-dead dials. And yesterday emails from old friends started to thread his mailbox with subject lines like *Have you seen this?* or *Sylvia Freaking Weston!* or *Oh my God!* All of them contained links to videos on various websites. Obviously something had happened; obviously someone at RazorRam, maybe Ram Barrett himself, had posted *12:01 P.M.* online and the video had metastasized. Goddamn Ram. Goddamn me. Eyes closed, Jamie could hear Sylvia's footsteps approaching. How are you? Scared shitless, thank you very much. His solution was simple: no more computer, no more phone. He embraced his own brand of Cartesian logic—I do not answer, therefore I do not exist. The pot helped as well. "I'm starving," he told Richard.

"Bet you are."

"Because it's lunchtime." Then Jamie added, "Asshole."

"Right."

"I'm not that stoned."

"Whatever."

"Seriously."

Richard turned toward the door, where a couple breezed in like a commercial for healthy promiscuity, the man and woman undaunted by the crowd or the thirty-minute wait or the man glaring from the vicinity of the bar. "This is getting ridiculous," Richard said.

"Getting? Gotten," Jamie said.

"Why does she have a cellphone if she never answers?"

"She's like God that way."

Richard considered his brother. "Good one," he finally said.

"I try."

"Sounds like something Dad would've written."

Jamie placed his hand over his chest. "Ouch."

"Sorry, low blow. Or high blow."

"Momma says 'Blow me,'" Jamie said, which was an old joke between them.

Richard smiled. "You remember *The Runaway Bunny*? Of course you don't, you don't have kids, but it's a great little book, for like small kids, two-year-olds, three-year-olds. It's about this bunny, duh, who wants to run away, or who threatens to run away, is actually asking his mother a totally different question, the way kids do, asking a far more abstract question, which sometimes you hear and sometimes you don't, or you don't hear until days later and you're like damn, that's what he was asking. Anyway, it's a great book, with amazing illustrations, truly beautiful, and maybe the best ending in the world. It was Emmett's favorite, read it to him a thousand times. Chloe preferred *Goodnight Moon*. There's even a reference in *Goodnight Moon* to *The Runaway Bunny* and vice versa. I mean, it's all kind of genius." Richard paused. "Why the hell am I talking about this?"

"I have no idea, man," Jamie said.

"There was a point."

"Something about Dad?"

"No."

"Something about a rabbit you once knew who ran away?"

"Ha-ha," Richard parried. He tried to keep himself within well-defined boundaries instead of letting his embarrassment poke through, you sentimental ass, talking about *The Runaway Bunny* like it's some masterpiece of literature. But there was a point, a humorous point, he swore. After a sniffy breath, Richard abandoned the thought. "I really need to go for a long run. I hate using the elliptical."

"Can I download this book?" Jamie asked.

"Enough."

"I'm being serious. It sounds interesting."

"Fuck off."

"I swear, this is me serious. At least tell me how it ends."

"The mother shuts the kid up with a carrot, okay, asshole." Richard checked his watch against the watermelon. "I can't wait much longer. I've got things to do."

"What do you have to do?"

"I have a meeting."

"There must be a meeting every five minutes in this city."

"No, not that kind of meeting," Richard said, yawning just to change expression. It was almost funny, this misunderstanding, if Richard could have given his brother the benefit of his own self-crushing doubt. Fucking Jamie. Stoned and drunk and deluded into thinking this was rascally and lovable. A long time ago that pleased-with-itself grin inspired the physics of a well-tossed apple, a helluva shot from Richard that slammed into Jamie's cheek and dented the bone into an adorable dimple. Typical, with his luck. But Richard tried to push aside old trajectories. Because it was funny, this misunderstanding, funnier still because Richard had gone to a meeting meeting earlier this morning, in a church basement on Lexington and 76th. The Manhattan brethren seemed so professional, so clean and well dressed, except for a few scrubbers in the back who appeared recently unrolled from a rug, kidnapped from somewhere south of there-but-for-the-grace-of-God. Richard ended up talking, as planned. He told those gathered about being back in New York after a long absence and how the last time he was here he was squatting in Central Park, finding a perch in an old elm that had his boyhood initials carved in the trunk. The cops shooed him away every so often, but he would circle back and climb higher and of course get higher—a nice laugh from the group—and he would climb higher still and get higher still until he found himself stuck near the top. "I was frozen," he said. "Because as we all know going up is a lot easier than coming down." A bit on the nose that. He told them how he pictured a hook and ladder screaming to the rescue, a crowd applauding as the fireman carried down this stranded crackhead kitty—no laugh here. But instead he unstuck himself when everything was smoked, practically flung his body from branch to branch and once on the ground again searched the surrounding leaves for any dropped crumbs. It was a decent story, if too well practiced from meetings in L.A., and maybe too L.A., too glib and too cute, too corny, desperate to be loved, sentimental—holy Christ, so fucking sentimental, Richard thought, *The Runaway Bunny* still in his head. For all his intense meaning, he was half-assed. Richard tossed the straw onto the bar. No, Jamie, this afternoon he had a different kind of meeting. "It's a business thing," he said, watching the straw go through its plastic death throes.

"I thought AA was your business?"

"My other business, movie business, screenplay stuff."

"Really?"

"Yeah." Humility flitted but Richard swatted. "I'm meeting with Eric Harke."

"Like the actor Eric Harke?"

"Uh-huh."

"Really? That's so fucking cool."

Richard went into immediate downplay mode. "We'll see."

"He did that young Albert Einstein thing, right?"

"You're thinking Thomas Edison."

"Right, right, right, as like a superhero."

"A super inventor," Richard corrected.

"Right, with those electromagnetic thingamajigs."

"That was the young Tesla."

"Right. And they lived in a giant zeppelin. What was that movie called?"

Richard picked the straw up again. "*The Steampunks.*"

"Very cool, very cool." A waggle of the mug and Big Baby poured a fresh one for Jamie, who took a sip, in hindsight a gulp. He was happy for his brother, hence the impressed nodding, a tight rhythmic loop, like his nose was keeping a small ball in the air, an appreciation of Richard's journey from miserable teen to terrible addict to successful husband and father and now what? screenwriter, all on his own terms, really impressive stuff, this nodding tried to convey, though the nodding also acknowledged all the years when Jamie depended on Richard's foundering since it made him shine in comparison, the healthy and presentable son, the charmer feeding his mother casual bits of brotherly criticism, like she was turf won or lost on a daily basis, like one of those hills in one of those wars in one of those countries. Jamie let the ball drop onto his lap. "What's the screenplay about?" he asked.

"It's a satire about the movie business."

"Sounds cool."

"About an old actor, sort of like Brando at his lowest."

"Okay."

"And he's starring in this ridiculous lowbrow comedy."

"Uh-huh."

"Not that I really know the movie business, except what I see in the movies."

"I'm sure it's great."

"It'll probably never happen."

"You're meeting with Eric Harke. That's huge."

A pause between brothers. Silence seemed written into the wood of the bar, which both of them traced with their eyes. Richard and Jamie hadn't talked much over the last twenty years. Mom was the usual intermediary, the wall through which they tapped, dependent on her dividing presence to keep them connected. Without her, the prisoners might riot before fleeing. But right now she was forty minutes late.

Richard thumped the bar. "Where the hell is she?"

Jamie suggested they just order some food.

"What could they be talking about?"

"I'm sure she wouldn't mind."

"You don't think they're rekindling the old flame."

"No," Jamie said, "she's just feeling sorry for him. What are Candy and the kids up to?"

"I think the Statue of Liberty."

"Can't say I've ever been."

"Me neither."

"They having a good time?"

"I think," Richard said.

"And Candy?"

"Sure."

"And how about you?"

"Despite Dad's behavior?"

"Yes, despite that hiccup. How's it been, being back?"

Richard thought for a moment. "I keep on expecting to run into people, you know, like people I've wronged one way or another. Or worse than wronged. I'm walking around with an apology speech running in my head, what with the way I left, you know, without a word to friends. Like if I see Ryan Swift—you remember Ryan?"

"Of course."

"I was kind of awful to him," Richard said.

"I thought that was one of the twelve steps. Amends, right?"

"He's one I missed."

"He lives in Denver anyway."

"Really?"

"Yep. Divorced. Has three kids."

"Wow." Richard propped his chin on top of clasped hands. A hundred old friends could have walked through that door—I could have walked through that door and Sal the host would have seated me ahead of everyone else, and Margie, who had worked there forever, would have put in my order without asking—bacon burger medium, cottage fries, Diet Coke—or maybe the Irish girl, Sheila, or even better the newcomer Kivi with those big glistening teeth like a wet T-shirt—but only strangers swung through. A few days in the city and Richard had bumped into just one old friend, Roger Braxton, who was hardly a friend, practically a sworn enemy since the second grade—Roger the crybaby snob, the weenie rich boy, the self-professed king of the club scene, there he was walking down Madison in his size-stout suit and balding pate that resembled the hair around an asshole, walking right toward Richard, who recognized this nesting doll of awful Braxton men, Richard letting this idiot pass with good riddance, but a few steps later he let go with "Roger? Roger Braxton?" and Roger turned around and seemed baffled until Richard identified himself, and they chatted for a minute, Roger dropping a few kind words into Richard's outstretched hand. Two blocks later Richard was back to hating the prick. Goddamn New York. Goddamn me. "I did run into Roger Braxton," he told Jamie.

"Oh Jesus."

"I was almost happy to see him."

"You used to beat the crap out of him," Jamie said.

"I did?"

"All sanctioned school violence but you made a point of it."

"I don't remember that."

"You don't remember breaking his leg?"

"Not really."

"He was the catcher and you barreled into him."

"Maybe I remember him blocking the plate."

"I can still hear the way he screamed."

"Oh shit."

"Now you remember." Jamie started to laugh, half-fake, half-real.

"He did seem sort of jumpy when I said hello."

"I bet he was."

Now Richard started to laugh, a third fake.

"Poor guy must have been petrified."

"I'm an idiot."

"He probably thought you were going to slide-tackle him."

The laughter continued to grow in percentages until its genuine form took over, the brothers giddy from waiting and relieved to find themselves in good company, perhaps even driving the laughter forward and riding its smooth wake.

"I almost hugged him," Richard said.

"He would've shat his pants."

Richard pulled a cellphone from his pocket.

"Is it Mom?" asked Jamie.

"No. This is Emmett's phone." On the touchscreen sweet Emma sported a fish face, her lips touching toward the infinite. She always called him Mr. Dyer no matter how many times he insisted on Richard. Brown eyes, brown hair, brown sunbaked complexion, so cute, so young. So persistent. This must have been her tenth call.

"Why do you have Emmett's phone?"

"Not really sure. I need to give it back to him."

"She's cute."

Richard turned the phone away from his brother. "She's sixteen."

"Even better."

"Perv."

"I'm just happy for Emmett."

"You can't believe how many phone calls and texts he gets."

"I bet. He's a good-looking kid."

"I mean, who has that kind of time to keep in touch?"

"It's all pseudo-connection, the device of the device."

"What the hell does that mean?"

"Not sure," Jamie said, finishing his beer.

"I think he's done something lousy to this girl, and she's upset with him, which is too bad because they've been friends a long time."

"You ever answer any of the calls?"

"Of course not."

"I would," Jamie said in a wicked tone.

Did Emma know that Emmett was in New York? Or had he just disappeared on her? Emma and Emmett. & Emmett. Already he seemed more of a man than a son, though Richard could still see the boy, even the baby, within those accumulated days. Like the universe, we are at our youngest and our oldest at the farthest edge. "He's reading *Ampersand*," Richard told Jamie.

"Well, it is a classic."

"I kind of hate that he's reading it."

"Why?"

"It's like what the hell have I done in comparison?"

"You're meeting with Eric Harke."

Richard made an uncertain sound, a sort of dubious groan.

"You've certainly crushed Dad in the fatherhood department," Jamie said.

"That's like getting a trophy for showing up."

"But hell, you showed up."

"Doesn't seem like much of a success to me."

"What, success like Dad's?"

"Nobody cares what kind of father he was."

"Except for his kids," Jamie said. "Ergo nobody really cares about him. When A. N. Dyer dies, he's dead. A thousand, a million people loving his books won't change that fact. They'll just read his obituary and move on to sports."

"You never had that big a problem with him," Richard said.

"Not like you."

"You just did your thing."

"What the hell was my thing?" Jamie asked. "Whatever it was, it seems so fucked up, what I did, what I do, did did, do do—I swear I'm not that stoned, but whatever the doing or the didding, it was all about other people's truth, that's what I wanted to capture. I hate that word. *Capture.* I don't trust anyone who captures anything except escaped prisoners. As far as I can tell I mistook misery for truth and spent a dozen years making the World's Most Horrific Home Video with me as the smiling host, stoned most of the time, weirdly suicidal but in the laziest, most passive-fantastic way, like I could die the good heroic death without doing anything good or heroic. Dirty little secret, half my time, probably more, was spent in hotels or bars or resorts decompressing. Hence my financial situation, which any reasonable person would be pleased about but is certainly not near what it was. I think I had an idea of what I was doing, back when I started, but I seriously can't remember."

"Seems important to me," Richard said.

"It was all self-serving."

"What isn't self-serving?"

"Somebody dying, to start things off."

"But you were there for them."

"Maybe the camera was but not me. I was too busy watching myself watch these things, and the whole time I swear I felt nothing. I tried, but I felt nothing. Maybe that's what Dad gave me. That ability, or inability, to see the truth outside my own head. Or maybe not. Maybe it's just me. But it drove me to scarier places, hoping I might see something that would finally prove that I was real and not some clever machine. It was like my own fucked-up Turing test. Even hearing me talk"—Jamie spun his finger like a wheel—"it's like, it's like hearing me talk. I am my own worst simile."

Richard thought about touching his brother's back but the engineering seemed difficult.

"I might as well have been smoking crack with you, no offense."

"None taken," Richard said. "But I see you more as the heroin type."

"I always did prefer my opiates." Jamie paused. "Myopiates."

"The crackhead and the junkie," Richard said. "We could solve crimes."

"Our own forgotten crimes."

"You do the drawing, I do the writing."

"I'm thinking stick figures," Jamie said.

"Yeah, but the world around them is like—"

"Vivid."

"Yeah, vivid," Richard agreed.

There was another head-lowering silence but this time the bar held a different grain, like the wood was a door and on the other side Richard and Jamie were boys again and free of the complications that were inconceivable at that age, their father perfectly fine, their mother just right, the brothers running around their homemade world and if they came within a few feet of each other shoulders would bump and they would fall into a grapple, like magnets always aware of the tug. When does that change? And why? Richard and Jamie sat at the bar and waited, and while the days of easy camaraderie were gone, they were for a moment content with the distance.

Five minutes later their mother showed up.

She strained against the crowd as if a train had just rolled in and she was the waving handkerchief. Richard and Jamie remained unmoved in the corner, letting her push forward, past the phone-booth-size kitchen and into the back room jammed with tables. They stayed brothers a bit longer, eyes mocking Mom, clueless Mom, fifty minutes late and with her desperate-to-be-young haircut and her almost annoying competence and hard-to-get-a-handle-on jumble of pride and shame, like she was constantly grading herself, though she did look good, their mom, the calm water in which the men in her life could admire themselves, never sick a day and probably the same weight as when she was twenty, a decent mom, better than most. Richard and Jamie played the same game without a word about the rules until their mother spun back and spotted them. She seemed caught between emotions. And the brothers straightened, reshaped as sons.

"Sorry I'm so late," she said, "but he didn't want me to leave."

"No problem," from Jamie.

Richard went to the host and told him their party was finally complete, the host consulting a slip of paper with all the focus of impossible math. Richard was ready to hate New York all over again, certain they would have to wait for—"Okay," the host said, "your table's ready."

"Really?"

"You used to come here, right, like years ago?"

"Yeah, yeah. Melon's was my favorite."

"I thought I recognized you. And your brother. Then your mother came in."

A sudden surge of unexpected belonging lifted Richard.

"Your father still writing?"

Even that didn't spoil the fine feeling. "Working on something, I think."

"Great." The host glanced into the back room. "Take the corner table."

The act of sitting down at Melon's involved a series of scoots from the people sitting nearby, the tables and chairs like the internal mechanism of a clock. Their spot was famous in a way: Dustin Hoffman and Meryl Streep had argued here in *Kramer vs. Kramer*. On the wall a small photo commemorated the scene, of Ted pointing his finger at Joanna seconds before he flings that wineglass against the wall. But in this scene Richard and Jamie patiently listen as their mother tells them about her visit, about this boy who opened the front door, shirtless in a pinstripe suit, funny and sensitive and maybe even a touch bold, like a fond memory, she says, and she knew, deep down, deeper than her bones, down in that, that, that small but sturdy hollow where your sense of self finds its rare, ineffable fit, down there she knew that Andrew was telling the truth, absolutely, that this boy was the boy she fell in love with, the boy she married, the boy who broke her heart, the boy who stood by her side, now impossibly old, as they watched the past bound up those stairs.

The brothers didn't know how to respond.

Isabel brushed a few imaginary crumbs from the tablecloth.

"I know how it sounds," she said, near tears. "Believe me, I know."

I imagine the brothers sitting at the table as if sudden participants in a séance, spirits entering the room and creating another world right there in Melon's where not only do you understand your parents as a combination of everyday delusions and misapprehensions, but now that you're older, as old as they were when you first glimpsed their flaws and foibles, you understand something else, something more as your eyes wobble on the gingham blur of the tablecloth: that without this deception the crystal ball reveals nothing but your own misshapen eye. So I say bring up these worlds. Worlds upon worlds. Let me sit at that table by the window with my mother during one of our Friday lunches before heading to Long Island. Let me be ten years old again with a solid construct of home. Let Melon's still stand instead of that artisanal Asian tea boutique now anchoring that corner. Let me glance toward that table where they filmed that sad movie about fatherhood and divorce and let me see the Dyer boys and their mother sitting quietly. Let me think about raising my hand hello.

VI

A.N.D.

November 3, 1959

Charlie, you devil,

Just got the tremendous news from a flightless old bird at Doubles — you knew this bird, rhymes with drunk and I'm being kind since she could rhyme a lot worse. So who is this girl you've been hiding? I hear she's from a good Boston family and might be a few years your senior. And a Smith girl. You know what they say. Actually, I don't know what they say though I'm sure they say something. Every Smith girl I ever knew fit me like a bruise. That's a lie. I just lied. I look forward to giving a congratulatory kiss to your bride-to-be, and Isabel tells me to tell you to tell her that she's landed one of the last decent bachelors in all of New York. Hope that doesn't mean you're thinking of staying in the Bean State. Caught sight of your father at the Racquet last week but he didn't mention anything so my guess is you're surprised us all. Then again he was afume about losing in court to Buffalo Knox. A funny game your father is playing, I suppose.

How am I? you ask. I'm pretending to work on the Floor while finishing this novel. Finishing? I mean finished. As in done. As in sent to a friend of my step-father's at Random House — at least I think Bennet Cerf works there. Of course THAT has to be his friend. I'll let him do me this favor. It makes him feel literary instead of pituitary. The novel is called <u>Ampersand</u>.

A.N.D.

Don't really know what the title means but I like what it suggests. Like Groucho Marx in type form. Or a drunk lemniscate a bit of broken infinity. Really I just like the word & the feel of the beach after a long hot day. What binds us, I suppose. Who the hell knows? Exeter has slouched its way onto the pages much more than I anticipated so I hope you've learned something about it 'cause I might need lawyering. Not really. I think the book is all right. I think I've made it true without once showing my face. More bludgeon than bildungs. But today is a better day. Tomorrow I will hate the goddamn thing. Who knows when old Bennett will get back, probably wrapping his NO! in a corny joke. Have you read A Separate Peace yet? Not bad, not great. Knowles hardly disguised his Exeter, I mean Devon. What a terrible name. Might as well have called it Dexter. I prefer my nom de schul— Shearing Academy. All of us were sheep and some of us got shorn worse than others. I could go on about the symbolic importance of wool and the theme of mohair but I will spare you. I do hope you'll like it, if it ever makes it to print.

    Will you be back for Thanksgiving and perhaps bring your fiancé to the table? If so we all need to get together for a proper dinner. Or will you be in Southampton, your father slaughtering geese? Let me know. Mabel and I would love to see you and of course meet this woman who has converted you. Now I can spoil your wedding. I'm thinking something from Elvis Presley. I'm all honesty — and never trust a person who says "in all honesty" — but in all honesty congratulations. I'm so happy for you. To Topping & _____ (I don't even know her name yet). Welcome to the club.

      Your friend,

        A.

VI.i

THE BOOK WAS CALLED *The Propagators*, though I have changed the title as well as the story and the name of the author—let's call him Christopher Denslow—who grew up in New York and attended Collegiate and then Williams—or those equivalents—and graduated with a five-hundred-page manuscript under one arm and under the other a half-dozen short stories written during a summer internship studying the western lowland gorilla. Physical anthropology was his true major and his absolute passion, or so he told *The New York Times* in an arts section profile. Young Mr. Denslow was photographed in front of the Congo Forest display at the Bronx Zoo, with Zuri, a twenty-six-year-old silverback, squatting behind the glass. The article was titled "Savage Beast, Meet Your Music," and it appeared soon after *The New Yorker* published one of his short stories—"Land Minds"—and *Harper's* published another—"The King Is Gong"—and Farrar, Straus and Giroux had won the bidding war for a two-book deal, a novel and a collection of stories, the price rumored to be in the high sixes, maybe even peeking into the magical seven realm. "I'm still in shock," he told the reporter, though Christopher Denslow was too young to properly convey shock, only good fortune as reasonable fate.

> *"I don't even consider myself a real writer," he said, shaking his head as if hearing the collective groan from a thousand MFA students. "I'm just glad people are responding to the work, but I'll be even gladder— see, that's not even a proper word—but I'll be happier when I'm back in Gabon studying the possible causes of fibrosing cardiomyopathy in these great apes."*

All of this happened a year earlier (and *gladder* is in fact a proper word), and now a fresh batch of publicity cooled the racks as *The Propagators* was hitting bookstores in less than a week. The early reviews read like a coronation.

From *Publishers Weekly:*

Starred Review. *After all the buzz generated by twenty-four-year-old Denslow's literary splash, finally we have a book to judge—*The Propagators—*not so much a book but a ripple that grows into a wave. The novel tells the story of Ana, a bonobo born in captivity and raised by Dr. Maurice Quine, a professor of behavioral psychology at the University of Wisconsin. Dr. Quine and his wife, Clarissa, treat Ana like a human child, teaching her how to eat with silverware; how to dress; how to act as just another member of the Quine family alongside the couple's two other children, Peg and Billy. Ana also learns sign language—she is a gifted student—and the mixology behind a perfect martini. But as she grows older, she becomes difficult to handle, uncertain of her place in this nuclear tree, and in one horrifying but heartbreaking scene, sexually aware. By fifteen she is no longer manageable and is sent back to the Congo for "rehabilitation." Denslow tells the story in alternating voices, from Quine to Clarissa to Peg and Billy, as well as Lucy Steers, the graduate student in primatology who takes on the task of reintroducing the chimp into the wild. All of this works as both a satire on postwar America and a thoughtful meditation on misplaced dreams, the pitfalls of conformity, of colonialism, the rise and fall of feminism. It is the human condition as seen through an ape. Every character is a wonder of creation, but what makes this book sing are the chapters devoted to Ana. Here Denslow limits her vocabulary to only a thousand words with basic grammar, but he wields those words and that grammar with a poetry that is a miracle to behold. We are Ana as she watches a college football game; as she befriends a stray cat; as she huddles in the jungle, clutching an umbrella leaf like a blankie. One thinks of* Frankenstein, *of* Born Free, *of* Ozzie and Harriet, *of* Civilization and Its Discontents, *but* The Propagators *is uniquely its own rare breed, a great book by a young writer.*

Magazines as varied as *Vogue* and *New York* and the *American Journal of Primatology* featured profiles of this writer with his moody good looks, his mouth a riff of late-night guitar, his nose a favorite line of W. S. Merwin, his eyes an old movie you stay up late watching, and always there was that shrug in his demeanor as if the camera were a game of chess and he was eight moves ahead. Christopher Denslow was the real deal. And if that wasn't enough, he was also rich. His father, L. F. Denslow, was the father of quant trading, which he helped develop as a faculty member at Columbia and then incorporated into an eponymous hedge fund started long before hedge funds became de rigueur for the ambitious. Fifteen billion under management, never a down year, even during the Great Collapse and its myriad aftershocks. All of this preamble is to say that Christopher Denslow's book party was not your normal book party, not in the era of book parties dwindling to a get-together in a friend's gallery, or a friend's loft, like resigned protesters protesting the death penalty, the cause bigger than any sad individual story. But tonight was different. Tonight *The Propagators* was getting its glass raised at the Frick, where the senior Denslow happened to be chairman of the board.

"I bet there's a list," Andy said, nervous.

He was lingering outside with Emmett, Andy smoking, Emmett taking in the architecture as if the masonry had a beat. The modest entrance appeared almost academic, like a door to a private school, and every few minutes adultlike people sprung up the steps with enviable confidence. Andy tried cribbing answers from over their shoulders.

"And I bet there's a cute girl checking the list, not like model cute but like interesting cute, unexpected cute, like a blond Italian, short hair, long neck, squinting like there's no way you're on the list but nice try, poppy."

"Poppy?" Emmett made a face.

"Whatever. Bottom line, there's a list."

"And we're on the list."

"I think we're on the list. I mean that's what she told me."

"Then we're on the list."

"That's my assumption. She's in charge of getting all the names, the who's coming, the who's not coming, the finalizing, the printing, the collating, the distribution, all the general list duties. Jeanie practically insisted I come. This Denslow guy has the same agent as my dad."

"We're definitely on the list then."

"I fucking hate lists. Nothing good has ever come from a list."

"Don't be so uptight, uncle."

Andy stiffened at the implication. "Am I being uptight? Shit. Maybe I am uptight. Under certain situations. Situationally uptight. Maybe this is a sign of my future uptightness, my total uptightness. Or I could just be easily nervous. Socially anxious. Does insecure equal uptight? Am I being uptight about the definition of uptight?" Andy rocked with near-autistic focus. "Sorry, I don't know what's wrong with me."

"No problem," said Emmett. "It's almost entertaining."

"That's because you're from California, dude."

Five twenty-somethings rolled down 70th like they had rehearsed every step, two women bookended by three men, all of them assured in their right to whoop away reality and triumph over doubt. They were like the new robber barons, entitlement their steel.

Andy lit up another cigarette. "Look at these assholes."

They walked into the Frick like a collective high-five.

"And look at you," Andy said to Emmett.

"Huh?"

"I mean compared to me. This suit I'm wearing is fucking ridiculous. I should have just gone the button-down and khaki route. Maybe a jacket. But this is like I'm auditioning for Nathan Detroit."

Emmett smiled. "I played Sky Masterson in our high school production."

"Of course you did. I was the one who painted the backdrops."

"Should I sing a little 'Luck Be a Lady'?"

"Don't you dare." Andy turned to his apartment across the street. "I could quickly go up and change. It'll only take a few minutes. We could smoke some pot."

"You look fine."

"I think you're closer to six two, by the way. And how big are your feet?"

"Size thirteen."

"Holy crap. That was probably a picture of your penis I sent to Jeanie." Andy had a final drag and—"Okay, let's go"—flicked the cigarette, a weak flick, more of a spastic twitch of pinstripes and dated lapels, possible bad breath, sweat like popcorn popping against his shirt, a zit sighted on his forehead with the steady intent of an assassin who any second could pull the trigger and eliminate this example of unglamorous youth, the only virgin within a three-block radius, this, this, this—"Andrew Dyer?" he said to the as-expected lovely girl manning the list, her finger falling down the page, lips muttering "Dire, Dire, Dire," until landing on "Dyer +1" and giving his name a purple check. The upstroke hit him like a defibrillating jolt.

Emmett patted his back. "We're in."

"Okay, okay," Andy said, newly invigorated with fresh anxieties, like he was an undercover agent in danger of being compromised by a wrong word, his superiors listening to his every move from an unassuming van—*Vito's Plumbing*—parked in one of the dark alleys in his head. Andy wanted to lift his arm and whisper into his cuff, *What's my mission again?*

"Quite a place," Emmett said.

"If you want to sound smart say it's your favorite museum in New York."

"Got it."

"Every painting is a masterpiece, that's what you say."

"Got it."

"Amazing the extravagance of the Gilded Age, that's what you say."

"But I think this is post–Gilded Age," Emmett said.

"What?"

"I read somewhere it was built in the nineteen-teens."

"Isn't that Gilded Age?"

"Technically no."

"Shit." Andy's nerve took a hit. He heard *Abort! Abort!* in his ear.

A cute woman seemed happy to see them, her hands offering a tray of Chablis.

They both took glasses.

"Cheers," Andy said. Holding a drink helped. It opened a small orbit of belonging, like the glass was his personal moon. Having Emmett here helped as well. When Andy picked him up outside the Carlyle, a tremendous feeling of relief hit him, like a long-forgotten thing suddenly remembered, the thing no longer important but the remembering a wonder.

"Where's this girl of yours?" Emmett asked.

"Don't know."

Most of the crowd was gathered in the Garden Court, with its vaulted glass ceiling and pleasing greenery, its purling fountain—a cool, tranquil spot advertised in guidebooks as a cool, tranquil spot. But its main pull this evening was the full bar. That was the sun to this solar system. Shoulders jostled for their own drinkable moons, people circling in various paths, some spinning into outer galleries, the Diet Cokes and Perriers, while Dewar's and Bombay never ventured far beyond the home star. Four distinct bodies seemed to travel around this party and we might as well continue with this planetary theme and start our stargazing with those who most resembled Venus. These were the people who worked in publishing: the editors, the publicists, the marketers, the agents, all of whom arrived on time if almost early, not just because this was a work event, but because this promised to be a rare work event that reminded them of when their industry burned bright in the New York sky, a place of true atmosphere instead of greenhouse gases. The excellent catering was also a draw. Dinner tonight came in a dozen bites. These people generally clustered in small groups, mainly so they could gorge without embarrassment—oh my God, the artichoke hearts with veal and ricotta is not of this world—but also so they could rain down sulfur on the contemptible around them, right out of Trollope or Balzac, they might mutter, gesturing with herbed cheese straws. For the most part they were the only ones who took in the art. It was such a treat to see these paintings without the, well, without the crowds, which was a kinder term than the actual humanity that amassed in their head. If they had to vote on a favorite, Duccio's *The Temptation of Christ on the Mountain* would probably win, even though they stood in front of the Vermeers longer. All of them had gone to nifty schools; all of them had chosen the love of books over straight commerce; and all of them realized, as every year their horizon grew shorter, not the mistake they had made, no—yes please to the sliced fillet on French bread with triple-grain mustard—but the miscalculation in terms of their place within the transit of passing times. Publishing would survive, they all agreed. It's not as if people were going to stop reading books. But then a stumped silence would follow as though they had been handed two pieces of wood and told to make fire. Better to shrug and grab the last scallop ceviche served in a delightful faux ice-cream cone.

Towering over Venus were those on Jupiter, also known as the friends of Laurence and Kitty Denslow, the proud parents, who could not help themselves and had to invite everyone, they were just so thrilled with their son. Laurence beamed as his hand reached out again and again, a Semper Fi squeeze followed by a gesture toward the table pyramided with books and a suggestion of buying a copy, or maybe three, "We need a bestseller to pay for this party!" while nearby Kitty laughed just like her serve in tennis, flat but precise, "Imagine what I'll do when poor Christopher gets married!" Most of their friends were rich, it just happened that way, like a baseball game attracts baseball fans. Wealth was the rocky core and provided a heat warmer than the sun. These people spun together in rapid rotation, the names other people dropped, wearing their ever-present satellites—the Hamptons, St. Barth's, Palm Beach, Aspen—like jewels on a necklace. The Frick, while grand, was within their realm of real estate and sometimes it seemed they browsed as if shopping. They were all happy to see one another even if they saw one another all the time, but their company confirmed in them a sense of depth, a surface without surface, that they were the good rich, the proper rich, the responsible rich, unlike the crassness this city now attracted. These people were hospital wings and museum courts. But enough of this tacky talk. They were here to celebrate Christopher. What a tremendous young man, they told Laurence, who towered over the crowd even if he was only five foot seven while Kitty boomed her good cheer down the line and mentioned how her father wrote a bit of poetry in his day.

Closer to Earth but no less assertive were the Martian-like friends of Christopher Denslow, mostly from New York, fellow grads from

Williams, summer pals from Nantucket, plus friends of friends who glommed on to the event, many in graduate school since a decent job nowadays was a reach. All and sundry grooved to the scene. It was like an indication of their own future triumph, which, from a distance, appeared hot but in reality was cold, as the ambitions of youth crashed into more adult terrain. The magazine articles. Those glossy pictures. It could seem as if their buddy Christopher had stolen something from them, their stomachs swelling with the rival of success, as they shimmered between arrogance and insecurity, grouping in packs of how-do-I-look? and what-are-you-doing-afterward? At their quietest they were cackling. The fabulous and near famous around them—there was even a rumor of a movie star—were the kind of New York company they hoped to keep, they expected to keep, deserved to keep for more than just a night, so they pretended this was no big deal. Just another Thursday. And really they preferred the Lower East Side. They watched Christopher sign book after book—kind of a pretentious title—and wondered if they should fall in line as well and get a signature. *To _____, Thanks so much for coming tonight. This book might be a better doorstop than read. Best, Christopher Denslow.* Four books had been signed this way, like the wunderkind couldn't come up with something original, his modesty belied by that encephalitic *C* and *D*. Then they heard he was appearing on *Charlie Rose* and their shields were pierced by the illusion of cheer. That's really great. Seriously. Super-impressive. They were on the verge of exciting things themselves, or so their parents promised.

Swirling between these various bodies were those always spotted when a good party was on the calendar. Some of these comets were familiar, like that artist over there who was in a few indie movies, Ariadne-something, Anastasia-something, or that minor face whose pride burned brighter than his career, the ice and dust of trying too hard not to care. They were omens of a possible future—Atatia-something?—the implication still uncertain. Then there were the striving society types who hungered for flashes and claimed membership by dint of proximity, like hyenas keeping company with lions, but hyenas never had to join the Racquet Club or the Colony Club, hyenas never had to get their children into Dalton. But here they were, dammit. And tomorrow they would be somewhere else. A handful of writers also reeled in this firmament, many from the Manhattan sky, but many more from Brooklyn spheres. Every three to five years they streaked with another book well received but modestly bought, their brightness mysterious even to themselves. Regardless, these writers trailed glances of vast amusement—Is that Amadellia-something over there?—while also maintaining stock-in-trade seriousness, discussing new novels or retreats or conferences, yeah, yeah, Amazon, yeah, ebooks, sigh, Franzen. They mostly preferred their own company, like the Perseids, in order to get down and dirty and gossip about outrageous behavior and how teaching was ruining their careers and they really should just write for TV. One of them had fucked Astrid-something years ago in a SoHo bathroom. These were the men. The women writers, they rolled their eyes like those girlfriends dragged to the beach in the postmidnight of August and instead of the promised light show watched a great big nothing scream across the sky. Give them the honest if unheralded Luna. And how about the younger writers, those proudly traveling from Greenpoint or Fort Greene or the newly created neighborhood of Stuy Heights? They were too focused on career to have any fun though they were all jazzed about MacDowell this summer and was that Remnick over there talking to Alita Masoon, the artist and actress, because they really should sneak over and say a quick hi.

"I had a story that came this close."

"Their fiction is crap nowadays."

"But this story would've been perfect for them."

"Because it's crap?"

"Ha-ha."

Andy and Emmett, their white wine sipped to death, shuffled through this galaxy and took their place in line for the bar, not really a line but a barely civilized evacuation, the two bartenders the only means of egress.

"I just need the job to last another ten years," they overheard a man say.

"Not sure that's going to happen," another man answered.

"Really?"

"It's going to get very lean across the board."

"Do you know something? Dewar's, please. Is there a plan in place?"

"Just what's floating in the air. Johnnie Walker, ooh Black please."

"I'll take the Black too."

Andy slanted toward Emmett. "What are you going to get?"

"A tequila sunrise."

"Um . . ."

"I'm kidding. Maybe a vodka tonic?"

"Yeah, yeah, yeah, that sounds good."

Andy puffed himself as tall as possible, brow creased with a coin slot of disdain, which he hoped made him look older, and he was prepared to tell the bartender how he had graduated from Bard with a degree in graphic design and the job market was shit and he was thinking of moving to Taipei to teach English, this image of himself a stereoscope in his head, Taipei Andy, and he was wondering how you'd order Asti Spumanti in Mandarin when he noticed the bartender staring at him as if the eyes were accessed via the nostril. "What?" Andy said sharply.

Emmett took over. "Two vodka tonics please."

"Oh yeah, that," Andy said, "please."

Without any question of age the bartender handed them their drinks and Andy and Emmett jingled the ice like a nest of exotic but short-lived creatures. They headed for the interior of the Frick, toward a Degas and a circle of men and women playing pass the nod. Andy took a sip. The vodka tasted as expected but the tonic was a revelation, as was the lime, and he relaxed a bit. "So . . . ," he said, the ellipsis like bubbles blown from a wand. His natural drift was to dislike these people; they could have been his fellow Exonians, smart and oh so exceptional, the promising future standing here in this room and Andy was their critical past. You all think you're so fucking special. Yes, that thought squeezed his insides, like a hand testing fruit to the point of bruising, but then he felt foolish because he was feeling good, special even. This was a happening party and he was here, on the list, sneaking a drink with his most excellent nephew, who was presently staring at the portrait of Comtesse d'Haussonville, his hands aping her pose, which made Andy the mirror behind her.

He was just about to mispronounce Ingres when he heard his name, clear as a bell.

"Andy!"

And there was Jeanie Spokes breaking through the crowd. She was wearing a dress that winked between hipster and prep, a vintage Laura Ashley number that was prairie on top and mini below her feet touching the earth in military-style black boots. She looked adorable. And the fact that she was obviously excited to see him made all trepidation dissolve into effervescence. "You're here," she said.

"Yeah."

"I've been looking for you."

"I've been here for a bit."

"To me you just got here."

"This is quite a party."

"Tell me about it. I've had the longest day, two days really."

"I bet."

"That's why I've been sort of out of touch."

"Oh."

"I'm totally exhausted."

"Sure."

"And buzzed."

"Okay."

"Whatcha drinking?"

"Vodka tonic."

"Excellent, excellent." Jeanie grabbed his arm. "I'm just so happy you're here."

Andy was prepared to dive into poetry concerning the pleasure of her company, but he refrained, knowing Emmett was likely eavesdropping from the salon. "I'm happy to be here as well," he responded.

"I love your outfit," she said.

"It's an outfit?"

"I just mean you look good."

"You look good too."

"This was my favorite dress in high school. I wore it in honor of you."

The unclaimed space within him shifted, everything tightening, both awkward and uplifting, as if a long-gestating adult were pushing against the adolescent membrane, trying on its body for size. "Oh," Andy said.

Emmett unstuck himself from the Comtesse.

"Hey, this is my nephew," Andy said. "Emmett Dyer, Jeanie Spokes."

Jeanie's expression shifted the way a pitcher will shift his grip from fastball to curveball.

"Nephew?"

"Yep," Emmett said.

"So your father . . . "

"Is my brother," Andy finished. "Or half brother. He's visiting from California."

"Really great to meet you, Emmett."

They shook hands.

"We got Dyers in the house." Then Jeanie gave them a raise-the-roof gesture, which in her dress played like Amish in the 'hood. "Okay, you two have got to come with me and meet some people." She took them both by the arm and half-guided, half-pushed them through the crowd, taking a sharp right into the oval room with those Whistlers, her mouth providing the screech of tires. They almost ran into a circle of older men and women, who stood in their own arrangements and harmonies. Andy was prepared to apologize, especially since he was sporting a slight battering ram, not that they noticed, hopefully, but boners in general made him contrite, but before he could say anything Jeanie nudged them forward. "Everybody, this is Andy Dyer and Emmett Dyer, his nephew from California."

A man clapped like a marvelous toy had been presented.

"Andy, old boy, it's Dennis Gilroy."

Andy had no idea who this person was. "Hello, Mr. Gilroy."

"Dennis, please. I work with your father."

"Oh."

"I'm his agent."

"Oh."

"Don't think it rings a bell, Dennis," one of the other men said.

"Oh shut your hole. It's so nice to meet you after all this time."

"Yeah, yeah. Same here."

Dennis Gilroy took the lead in introducing them to the rest of the group, all impressive people, Andy was sure, each name followed by a pause so the thrill could sink in, but Andy was too distracted by an overall sense of distraction to recognize anyone, let alone remember anyone's name.

"So how old are you now?" Dennis asked.

"Seventeen."

"Seventeen!"

"Oh to be seventeen again," this other man mused.

"But you still are seventeen," the woman near his arm said.

"I was actually much more mature at that age."

"God help us."

"I even respected women."

"Prick." She turned to Andy. "How is your father, by the way?"

"Okay, I guess."

"Still writing?"

"I think so."

"You know, I almost physically accosted him many decades ago," she said. "I was twenty-three and had just moved to the city—remember that crappy loft on Bond that's now probably worth five million? Why did I ever leave? Anyway one day I decided I was going to meet A. N. Dyer, that was my mission that week. Back then it was all about missions."

"Meet or screw?" the man said.

"What's gotten into you?"

"They're married," Dennis said to Andy, like this explained things.

"Jesus, with his kid right here?" she said.

"You're the one who said your MFA stood for—"

"Shut up, please. Anyway, back to your father. I was determined to meet him so I went all Mossad—I was wearing a lot of leather back then."

"Patti Smith wannabe."

"I'll see that and raise you a Ruskin," she said.

"That's mean."

"What about Ruskin?" asked Dennis.

The man crossed his arms, obviously accustomed to questions. "I've been wanting to do this mash-up of Ruskins, you know, *The Stones of Venice* but at Max's Kansas City, the pops as Impressionists, the punks as Pre-Raphaelites, Warhol as William Morris, Iggy Pop as Dante Rossetti, 'Lust for Life' meets 'The House of Life.'"

"Sounds wonderful," Dennis said.

"Could be. Maybe after the alien DNA novel."

"Oh yes," the woman said, "not until after that alien DNA novel, please."

"I've already sold it in a dozen countries," Dennis told her. "That's what a good agent does."

"And tomorrow Albania, I'm sure," she said.

"No offense," the man said, "but you're too old for such low-cut envy."

"Envy? For *The Heirs of Tippetarius.*"

"It's a working title," he said, "plus there's a deeper meaning."

"Yes. A not-so-subtle critique on the commercialization of literary writers."

"Sorry I'm not as smart as you are, honey."

"Smart isn't the right word, dummy."

While others seemed amused, Andy was unsure of his place within the conversation, a witness, he supposed, in this staging of a marriage, and though he assumed his last name was the carrot, his age was in fact the more effective stick, these older people pandering to his concept of a bickering couple, hoping they might entertain him and for a moment be less obsolete. Youth has a power often unrecognized by the young. It might land as a paltry blow but there is a vastness to its sting.

"What are you stuffing?" the man asked, pointing to Andy's near-empty glass.

"A Sprite," Andy said.

"That doesn't sound like much fun."

"Okay, a vodka tonic."

"Much better. And honey? Another?"

"Sure."

After the man departed the woman tried to wrangle her story back into the center, but Dennis Gilroy was talking gossip about this actor who wanted to take on the role of Ana in *The Propagators*—"Not like wearing a monkey costume but doing that motion-capture thing, with the green suit covered in Ping-Pong balls"—and Emmett and Jeanie were working on their rapport—"I have to say I'm tempted by the concept of L.A."—which left Andy as the only viable set of ears.

"With your father," the woman said, moving closer, "I waited outside his apartment, still his apartment, right, your apartment, right across the street from here, yeah, standing right outside the Frick and waiting, five, six hours a day for probably three days until he finally appears and I start to follow him. I have no idea what I'm going to do, or how I'm going to do whatever I'm going to do. I just want to thank him, as trite as that sounds. *Ampersand* meant a lot to me when I was younger. Something about those boys, that world, that time. And the writing of course. So I follow him and try to come up with a plan, like Lucy with Bill Holden." The woman paused, amused, it seemed, at her own expense. A splatter of freckles covered her face, almost joyful, as if she had gotten them as a girl racing her ten-speed through mud puddles. "I decide that I would trip into him and apologize, recognize him, say my piece, and then continue on with my not-quite-rational life." Dennis Gilroy, overhearing this, began to direct his attention toward her story and as a result directed the attention of others. The woman accepted their awareness with a mixture of jazz and neurosis, improvisation as a form of impersonation. "Three days of stalking and this was my genius plan. Raid on Entebbe this was not."

"This is A. N. Dyer she's talking about," Dennis told the newcomers.

"So I'm getting ready to do my little act when I see this other person, totally recognizable since he's basically me, and I realize this guy's following A. N. Dyer as well, and even worse, he has the lead. I start to walk faster. He sees me. He understands what's going on and increases his speed. Thank God neither of us is willing to run. Not yet at least."

"This is A. N. Dyer's son," Dennis added, smiling.

"So we're neck and neck, getting closer to your dad, but I could tell by the clench of this guy's jaw that he wasn't going to lose. No way. And not to a girl. Now people start to notice us—not your dad, he's just happily walking along, but the people behind your dad, the people coming in the other direction, they see these two lunatics nearing a commotion."

The man returned with drinks, and if he considered resuming his marital minstrel show, he stopped himself, seeing that his wife had a story going downhill.

"I was so much ballsier back then," she said. "Thirty years ago. Is that even possible? Terrible when time becomes a math problem. Anyway without thinking I very publicly grab this guy and push him away and scream, 'Get the hell away from me! I told you it's done! It's over! I can't take it any longer!' I say it just like that. Your father, he's like this close, he turns around and I damsel myself against his arm, near tears, and this poor guy doesn't know what's hit him. I mean, everyone is staring. His hero thinks he's a creep. He spins on his heels and runs away, screaming 'Crazy bitch!' which for my purposes is the absolute perfect piece of dialogue. Victory is mine. But I had been so focused on winning that I forgot about the prize: A. N. Dyer right next to me. I start to thank him and apologize for the scene. I'm shaking in real life. Nothing is pretend anymore. And he was so polite. An absolute gentleman. He took me to a bench and sat down with me and made sure I was okay. He seemed genuinely concerned. He asked if I wanted to call my parents. Told me he lived down the block and I could come up and get a drink of water and use the phone. He mentioned his wife, I think to put me at ease. And I was getting ready to recognize him and tell him how much I loved his books, but I couldn't, I couldn't stop what I was selling, maybe because he was being so accommodating and I was being so dishonest, and now I started to cry, this time for real, and I'm not really a crier. But I was new to New York. And I was feeling alone. And I had a history of rough boyfriends. And my loony parents back home. It all came gushing out. He gave me his handkerchief—a dying breed, those handkerchief men—and he must have sat with me for ten minutes as a stranger instead of a great writer. Finally I collected myself, got up, and thanked him. And that was it."

"You ever think of writing that down?" Dennis Gilroy asked.

The woman shook her head.

"Because it would be a perfect magazine piece."

"I have no desire to do that." She paused. "You really think?"

"Absolutely. You should talk to Remnick. Or your agent should."

"You know what would give the story extra kick," the man said, handing her her drink. "If the other guy was Mark David Chapman."

People groaned as if the mere mention made it true.

"*And I recognized the other man three months later,*" the man said in an unwise impersonation of his wife, "*when I saw who shot John Lennon.*"

"Asshole."

"What?"

"You're an asshole."

"Timing-wise it could be true. I'm just saying."

The man and woman carried on like this, her offense matched by his defense, like a tennis point trapped between smash and lob. The people in the circle started to lose interest, though they remained interested in Andy as a proxy to his father, the stories about the author continuing, often orchestrated by Dennis Gilroy, whose arm became increasingly attached to the boy's shoulder. Andy listened, nodded, smiled. He was polite to a fault and quickly getting drunk. All the stories were similar: letters sent and never answered; accidental encounters; a particular novel or character; the integrity of the great man. They all had kind words, if vaguely self-serving. It reminded Andy of the times he was with his father and a person might stop them on the street or come up to their table in a restaurant and say a heartfelt if embarrassed hello. "I'm sorry, but . . . " His father was pretty decent at getting these people to leave without being rude. "Thank you," he'd say, like he was disappointed that they pulled aside the curtain, like he expected more from his readers. But for six-year-old Andy it seemed as if Dad had all these secret friends and he'd stare at strangers and practically beg them to come over and say hi. You know this man. You can love him if you want. As Andy grew older he started to notice the toll these encounters took on his father, how his normal reticence grew more solemn, and by the age of ten Andy would try to divert their admiration by tripping on the sidewalk or spilling a drink, yelling in some cooked-up language, which his father once answered with "Is-chta nad und nachi-naught, fitti-nodd." Around thirteen Andy re-garded these fans as leeches and he took on the pose of bodyguard with an intuitive grasp of martial arts. I dare you to interrupt. And by his mid-teens Andy came to the conclusion that both idol and idolater were nuts. But tonight, maybe because of the vodka and the old suit and Dennis Gilroy applying pressure on his shoulder, he imagined these people here as mourners and his father was dead. Waves of loss and meaning tumbled through him. *My father seemed trapped in his own world and no matter how hard he tried to dig himself out—and I think he tried very hard—the rubble caved back in on him, leaving a bigger mess.* Dennis ushered Andy into another room, where more people offered him their unsuspecting condolences. *He was known yet unknown to me. He loved me. I know that. But I always had the sense of him hoping I would somehow free him from who he was.* The party was nearing its peak. Ev-eryone spoke in unison, conversation no longer requiring the oxygen of the outside world but circulating around news generated only ten minutes ago. Who was here? Who said what? It was like school assem-bly, those minutes before announcements began, when voices fed on the anticipation of their abrupt end. But what would silence things here? Andy, light-headed and in need of focus, steadied himself on a painting hung too far away to read the label. It was of a young man posed before a bright green curtain, his long-fingered right hand curled around a cameo that had the word *Sorte* visible. There was a resemblance between the sitter and Andy, in that large stylus nose casting a shadow across still-doughy cheeks, in that haircut, classically ragged, in that strabismic left eye, and perhaps this resemblance was what drew Andy's attention, like an elusive familiarity. That could have been me long ago. But what Andy noticed more than anything was the honking codpiece that breached his groin like the fucking hilt of a sword. Damn, he thought, his grin affecting his balance. He looked around for Emmett and Jeanie, hoping to share the visual.

"Andy," Dennis Gilroy said, "I would love for you to meet . . . "

VI.ii

T HE BLACK STRETCH LIMO was halfway over the Brooklyn Bridge, the traffic denying them any speed though Eric Harke whooped as if they were doing a hundred. "I love this fucking bridge." He rocked from window to sunroof to window again, like a dog sensing he was almost home. "How can you not love this fucking bridge? My absolute fucking favorite and I've been on some of the finest. The Alamillo. The Zubizuri. The Millau Viaduct. Great bridges, all of them, same with the classics. Ponte Vecchio. Pont Neuf. The Khaju—man, that's a beautiful fucking bridge, a really beautiful bridge, almost makes me reconsider. By the way I think the Golden Gate is totally overrated. It's a good bridge, an iconic bridge, and the color in that coastal light is genius, but it's not a great bridge. A great span, I'll give you that, but not a great bridge." Richard and Jamie nodded. Jamie was more amused than Richard, even with his front tooth missing and his nose likely broken, while Richard was more anxious about the state of his brother's face as well as Eric Harke's pupils, which pointed at them like a pair of shaky .38s. "I think half the greatness of this bridge is the full story of this bridge. Those poor Roeblings, dad dying of tetanus, son getting the bends, wife taking over the project, thirteen years of absolute heartache and loss, absolute family disaster, yet here we are, a century later, driving across this cathedral of industrial design, whatever suffering long forgotten. If I were an hour younger I'd open up the fucking sunroof and give praise to the Roeblings." Eric collapsed back onto his seat. Twitchy and sweaty, with a brand-new retro haircut, horn-rimmed glasses, a vintage suit, a bow tie, he had the vibe of early-to-mid David Byrne, and what with Richard's and Jamie's appreciation for New Wave music and their teenage days watching those first videos on MTV, what with the water flowing underground and this large automobile, what with the early evening sky and its remains of light, you may find yourself hearing the same song and asking yourself the same question: How did I get here?

Let the day reach back to lunch and their mother's confidence in their father's impossible tale, a hundred percent true, who knows how, who cares how, but the story was true, to the point where she started to tear up as if time no longer held her, and Richard and Jamie clamped down on their tongues and let reason go for the sake of mercy. Okay, okay, fine. Afterward, Richard walked Mom toward the park while Jamie cabbed it to Alice from Orso's apartment on Tenth and 56th Street. He had an hour and a half before his 4:30 P.M. class. For the last few days he had been staying with Alice, not only because it was a more convenient commute to the New School but also because it was free of any incriminating evidence. No Sylvia. No boxes of videotapes. No reflections of his guilty face on the smudged surfaces. He was also surprised to find himself liking Alice more and more, appreciating her unexpected naïveté for a woman so often burned, taking comfort in her realistic optimism, the way a cheesy movie could make her happy, how she defined herself by the day rather than the month or the year or the decade. In fact, as he approached her front door, he was getting visibly excited to see her again, his hard-on hoping for clairvoyance, but alas, she wasn't home. Jamie sat down and smoked a joint instead. *He is me.* That's supposedly what his father told his mother. Was he Flaubert now and Andy his Bovary? But Mom, previously sensible if dangerously patient, seemed fortified by this story. "You really don't have to believe me, I don't care, but I know that boy is your father." Yeah, yeah, yeah. Smoke entered Jamie's lungs via a grimace. It was like a tide flowing in and washing over a feculent shore. On the surface was general exasperation at his deluded parents, but deeper down were his own feelings of worthlessness, of disgust, of morbid obsessions, of lifelong fantasies about superpowers, of early promise versus present circumstances, all churned from under those rocks and stones before being carried into the ocean in which we all belong.

Then Alice came home.

Her face was still wearing her audition makeup.

"You look like a local newscaster," he said.

Alice pantomimed a microphone. "Jamie Dyer, stoned in my apartment, story at eleven." She reached for the joint in the ashtray. "I don't know if I should be offended or not since this is my hooker look. Seven lines. Not a bad part either. A once classy hooker but now she's older and desperate, mistaken for a cougar. It's tragically not quite funny enough. And this," she said, indicating her *Price Is Right* face, "is me trying to look like a young actress trying to look like an old hooker trying to look like a younger hooker who is really just an old actress. I tell you, it's exhausting." She plopped down onto the couch.

"So there are layers?" Jamie said.

"Like you can't believe."

"And how'd it go?"

"It's between me and fifty other whores." She tossed the lighter onto the coffee table and kicked away her high heels, her ankles showing evidence of blisters, the third eye for the disenchanted. "I think I did okay. But I'm dumb enough to enjoy auditioning."

"You're too wholesome to be a hooker," Jamie said.

"Oh wow, thanks." She sounded insulted.

"Don't get me wrong," Jamie said. "I'd pay good money."

"That's sweet."

"But you're more the nursery-school-teacher-who-dabbles-in-bondage type."

"I hate kids."

"That's part of your masochism right there. Hating kids gets you all hot."

"You've thought this through."

"I could go on."

"So you can't imagine me as a hooker?"

"I think that's a compliment, perhaps not my greatest."

Alice looked at him, her eyes starting to register the glassy effects, which to Jamie opened her up to girlhood, probably a tomboy with much older brothers, and a good Catholic mother who went to church every day, and a father who died when she was young, all of which Jamie knew was true but for the first time sensed the effects of this life on her face. "I bet you wanted to be a vet when you were younger."

"Never," she said. "Now whatcha got in your wallet?"

"What?"

"How much cash?"

A total of sixty-three dollars and forty-eight cents ended up on the coffee table.

Alice gauged the sum with a thinking *hmm*.

"You were probably voted most loyal friend," Jamie said.

Alice swept the money into her handbag. "What time's your class?"

The class in question was midway through a monthlong survey of docufiction, or cinema vérité, or fictive nonfiction, or narrative nonfiction, or any one of those terms as long as *mockumentary* was avoided. Over that time there had been discussion about the genre as a tool for satire, its effectiveness in this age of quote, unquote reality, its trickster role, its pitfalls of tired parody and lazy humor, its successful horror. They talked about what was true and what was camera true. *War of the Worlds* segued into *Nanook of the North* into *Land Without Bread* into *Forgotten Silver* into *Dadetown*. An entire period was spent on *David Holzman's Diary*. A pleasant conversation about *Zelig* turned into a much nastier one about *JFK*, which circled around to *Mao: The Real Man* and concluded with an agreement on the use of reenactments in *The Thin Blue Line*. "History as an act of fiction," Jamie riffed that afternoon, spent and woefully unprepared, "an insistence on a desired theme, a manipulation based on a series of plagiarisms." The students were actually taking notes. "Like memory itself," he went on, "which we know is far from truthful." Jamie almost laughed at this nonsense. "Who we are in battle with who we want to be and then throw in how we feel on that particular day. What does that make us? A dishonest construction? A manufactured truth?" He paused as if this deserved sinking in, though really he had nowhere else to go. "Which brings us to *Stage Fright* and how we buy into the opening flashback because it fits within the parameters of classic Hitchcock and our collective desire to sit in that theater and watch a movie about a man wrongfully accused." Best keep things short. "Hitch gives us what we want." Better. "Our memory, our identity, is satisfied. That's the beauty of genre. It's a conversation. But the flashback in the film is a lie. It even exposes that lie with the tracking shot that moves through the door and we hear the door shut without shutting on the camera. The point of view becomes untrustworthy." Wait, were they taking notes or texting? He really should have used *Dr. Strangelove*, but *Stage Fright* was a favorite (or a favorite of his favorite professor at Yale). "It's all mirrors and doors in this movie, the public and the private. Let's look at the flashback again." Jamie cued up the DVD. "Notice the use of, of—oh, just watch the thing."

He pushed PLAY, glad for the lull from his own bullshit.

He sat back and in the tired space between his eyes replayed an hour ago when he was with Alice on the couch and she had just finished her lovely show and Jamie was starting to move faster, chasing her orgasm, his toes curling until cracking, and Alice looked up and half-whispered, "I want you to finish on my face."

"Finish what?" he grunted.

"I want you to come on my face."

"Huh?"

"If you don't mind," she added, ever polite.

"Coming on your face?"

"Yes."

Jamie paused mid-thrust and propped himself on his elbow for a less pressing view. "Why would you want me to do that?"

"It doesn't turn you on?"

"Maybe a little, but still."

"No one's ever done it to me."

"And I think you should be congratulated for that."

"Maybe I want to break new ground," she said.

"You're stoned."

"It's what they do in porn."

"Oh yes, let us turn to porn for inspiration."

"But it all trickles down." Alice broke a bigger smile. "Poor choice of words."

"Very."

"Do you have a problem defiling my wholesome Midwestern face—"

"Ahh—"

"—with your world-weary spunk?"

"I never said Midwestern, that's your own paranoia."

"I've been thinking about this for a while actually."

"Jesus, you make it sound like a mortgage."

"I've done just about everything else."

"That I can attest to."

"And I like you, Jamie, a lot, and I want you to ejaculate on my face."

Jamie frowned. "That's so sweet."

"No, no, no," she said, restraining her smile, "I'm a hundred percent serious, or as serious as someone can be about this. It's like an experience without all the travel. So cast a few lines across this unspoiled pond."

"Please stop talking like that."

"It would turn on a lot of guys," she said.

"Call me old-fashioned but it strikes me as degrading."

"Would you mind if I came on your face?"

Jamie considered this for a moment. "Probably not. I'd probably like it. Maybe even love it. But isn't that about power or—"

"Shut up and fuck me." Alice rolled him back on top and maneuvered him inside of her, reaching for his ass to really kick-start things, her ankles wrapping for leverage, her back arching, her mouth alternating between biting and sucking, her finger doing that thing that Jamie liked, which he considered wonderfully dirty and accelerated him into another gear as she started with her lovely groans, God knows if real this time, and Jamie was getting close, closer, closest, pushing up on his arms. "I'm getting close," he told Alice.

"Yes, baby."

"You really sure?"

"Yes, yes, yes, baby, do it."

After a couple more rubs and grinds, Jamie pulled out and rushed up like he had an ember in his palm and Alice was the tinder. Straddling her shoulders, he perched himself over her chin; she was almost laughing now, mouth half-open, eyes squinting in anticipation, and Jamie would have laughed too but he was concentrating too hard, not only on coming but also on his aim, and here was his target, this enthusiastic woman, the audition makeup unable to conceal her decent good looks and honesty of character, that leaning smile that gamely said yes to whatever life proposed, and Jamie thought, I might love you, Alice, and more than anything this unexpected notion pushed him over the top.

"Oh, oh, oh, ahh."

Or some such embarrassment.

But instead of bursting forth with ropelike vigor, his shot sort of crawled out in the style of an exhausted old man escaping from a deep hole, sliding down the side and ending up in a hard-breathing heap, just happy to be free.

After a second or two, Alice opened her eyes.

"Um," Jamie said. "Maybe I could, I don't know, flick it on you."

And thank goodness she laughed, and his heart seemed to gain a door and became a house. Back in the classroom, Jamie blushed and covered his face with giddy shame as Richard Todd climbed that staircase, nervous about being discovered, carousel music chiming in the background, a nice touch. He let the scene play longer than necessary, both he and his students content with the use of time. Once the class was dismissed, he decided to subway to Brooklyn to pick up his mail and more clothes and maybe his laptop, maybe even his video camera, before heading back to Alice's for the night. An idea was taking shape in his head, just a title really, *Waiting*, which latched on to the people around him, on the platform, on the train, on the street, in the windows, the solitary man who sat on the stoop of his walk-up, who, upon seeing Jamie, stood up and revealed himself to be tall and bearded and waiting no longer.

"Do I know—" Jamie started to say when a burst of electric black caught him square in the face, the effect followed by the slower-dawning cause, a fist, a punch to be exact, that landed just south of his nose. Jamie staggered before falling ass-first onto the stoop. The great symphony of consciousness reconfigured around a single kettle drum, and after a few seconds of dumb figuring, he leaned over and bled onto the steps. It seemed his nose was giving birth. Jamie tried to stanch the flow with his sleeve but that just made whatever was being born angrier.

"I'm sorry," the assailant said.

"You going to hit me again?"

"No."

Jamie's vision was fuzzy but the voice spurred his memory. "That you, Ed?"

"I wasn't planning on hitting you," Ed Carne answered.

"I would hate to see you with some intent." Jamie's tongue brushed against his forever-snaggled front tooth, which was now indented to the point of weirdness, practically dangling, and Jamie, without much forethought, reached in with thumb and index finger and gave a tug. Ta-da! He showed the prize to Ed. "You knocked my tooth out."

"Shit, I'm sorry."

Jamie spat more blood. "How big is your goddamn fist, Ed?"

"I always had heavy hands."

"I think you broke my nose too."

"Looks that way."

Jamie tried to hold his head straight. "My calibration is all screwed up."

"I don't know what came over me," Ed said, whatever the coming long fled.

"I haven't been slugged like that since my brother."

"I like to think of myself as a nonviolent person."

"Hey man, I deserve it," Jamie said. "Probably deserve a few kicks as well."

Still looming overhead, Ed buried his hands in his pockets, perhaps in precaution. "I've been trying to call but you've been—I don't know where you've been. Not returning my calls. So I had to track you down and I've been waiting here, sleeping in my car, and I'm tired and I hate this city and I finally see you and with all the scenarios playing in my head not one of them involved me hitting you."

"It's okay." Blood started to shellac the back of Jamie's throat.

"No, it's not. It's just, I hated all that filming but Sylvia, she was insistent, and she was so sick, and I saw you and I don't know, I guess I just remembered all that stuff and I snapped."

"Like I said, I deserve it." Jamie spat some more blood onto the steps. He was almost thankful for the injury. It made him relax into the consequences, the abstract anxiety turning into concrete pain. And he was getting ready to apologize for jamming a camera into a place best left undisturbed. Her grave? What kind of ghoul does that? To give an otherwise decent project his own macabre ending, all because he was shallow and scared and had no idea what he wanted from life, death his only recourse. Before talking, Jamie pressed his tongue into the void of his missing tooth. The rawness was almost pleasant, like a childhood memory of being grown-up. "Ed—" he started.

"It's not your fault," Ed said. "You were just the cameraman."

"Mostly but—"

"And I'm glad she didn't tell me the whole plan, because I would have fought that for sure. Just too much. And the girls." Down Kane Street, the sun was nearing its westward flush, the shadows at their longest. Last week this conversation would have happened in unsaved darkness rather than the melodrama of this light. Ed Carne even turned west as if the time were spot-on. "I never cared about the video," he said. "Neither did the girls. We just missed her and wanted to remember her healthy and with us. Probably why I didn't contact you earlier. I'm still—we're still in mourning. I haven't shaved since she died. But then my oldest saw the video on the Internet."

"Jesus, I'm sorry. I'm still not sure how—"

"It's quite something," Ed said.

Jamie nodded.

"Just seeing her again. And the way it ends. Maybe you thought it wouldn't reach us rubes in Vermont. Maybe you didn't care. Maybe we never crossed your mind. But you stole her from us a second time."

Jamie wondered if under the sidewalk there was dirt. "I am truly—"

"Over seven million views on YouTube," Ed went on, "and growing a million every few days. Chances are right now someone is watching my wife die, watching her say that everything is fine, watching her, well, you know. And they have no idea who she is. She gets no credit. Not even a mention of her name. It's like the whole thing is anonymous, like she's just another woman with cancer. That hasn't stopped the reporters from tracking us down. Hollywood people too, looking for the rights to her story. Talk of a movie or something. A book. I don't know. The Carnes are suddenly the curiosities of Stowe. It's crazy. At this rate she'll die fifty million times by next month. I've talked to a lawyer in Burlington, a good one, and he said that since Sylvia was the primary creator of the content, we, meaning her family, are the ones in control, not you. You were just the cameraman, Jamie. So what I need from you is your signature on some papers and for you to hand over the original video, which is rightfully my property."

Jamie spat one last time. "Of course," he said. After pocketing his tooth and reacquainting himself with gravity, he guided Ed inside and up the stairs. It seemed like a flood had hit his apartment, a bureau's worth of clothes washed up on the floor, the furniture loosened from its moorings, the overall odor having only a brief memory of being dry. "I've kind of let things go," Jamie said, picking up an old newspaper in a gesture of tidying up.

"I've seen worse."

"Something to drink? Not that I trust what's growing in my fridge."

"I'm fine, thanks."

"Give me a second." Jamie popped into the bathroom and greeted his alternate self in the mirror: the Jamie who got what he deserved. A washcloth took care of his face but his shirt was forever ruined and his nose had a parenthetical bend to the left. But in general he liked this new look. He grinned. The gap was like a drunken tattoo.

"Really sorry about that," Ed said from the door.

"I think it makes me look younger."

"You should put ice on your nose."

"Probably." Jamie stepped past him and grabbed the RazorRam DVD and mini DV from the pile on the living room table. "I feel terrible that this ever got online. It was an accident."

"I should probably thank you," Ed said. "I would have locked it away in a drawer without ever watching." He slipped them into his satchel, his hand returning with two ten-page documents. "If you could sign these."

Jamie made a show of checking the legalese.

"Pretty standard stuff," Ed said.

Pretty standard stuff, Jamie thought.

"You're just affirming what is true."

What is true? Jamie stopped reading. "I have one condition."

Ed's beard curled in the vicinity of his lips. "What?"

"You have to hit me again."

"Huh?"

"You have to hit me again, as hard as you can."

"I told you, I'm not a violent person."

"I don't care. You hit me and I'll sign."

Whatever Ed's qualms, they passed—"Turn your head"—and soon he was out the door and back on the street while Jamie was back in front of the mirror watching his left eye shade from pink to purple. Pain echoed like a shout down a canyon, a curious hello rather than a cry for help. He couldn't help smiling. You doofus, he muttered. He threw a slow-motion punch at his reflection. Then he had a shower and was briefly unburdened by memory or imagination, to the degree where he washed his face twice, unsure of the first time. Fresh-scrubbed, he looked even more like a mess. He sat at his computer and typed *dying* and *woman* and *12:01 p.m.* into Google but held back from going any further. *How are you?* Jamie sat there waiting for an answer when the phone rang. It was his brother.

"Glad I caught you," Richard said in an odd tone. "I got a pal looking to party."

"Excuse me?"

"We're in a car, a limo actually, a stretch job, very sweet, and my friend's looking for a little boom-boom—wait, he says a lot of boom-boom—so I guess we're looking for boom-boom-boom and I thought of you, my Mr. Boom Boom."

"You haven't done anything stupid, have you?" Jamie asked.

"That's open for debate," Richard said. "But back to boom-boom."

"It's obvious you haven't bought drugs in a very long time."

"True."

"You with Eric Harke?"

"Yep."

"And what, you're doing coke with him?"

"No, just helping a friend in need."

"What a ridiculously bad idea, Richard."

"It's all good," Richard said.

"I thought you were a trained drug counselor."

"Oh baby, I am."

"*Baby* and *boom-boom*? Is this really how you went about your business back in the day, because frankly it's embarrassing."

"Look, I'll take what you've got."

"All I've got is some weed."

"Weed?" A pause. "Weed's no good. We need the boom-boom."

"Stop with the boom-boom, please."

"That's great. I knew you'd come through."

"Richard, I don't think—"

"Reminds me of our first deal. Remember that? An ounce of No Soap Radio."

Jamie sat up straighter.

"You remember that?" Richard asked again.

"We can't do that, and not to some Hollywood cokehead."

"Why not?"

"Because he'll know instantly."

"I'm not so sure."

"Look, I've had a rough few hours."

"Great, we'll be at your place in twenty minutes."

"Goddamn it." But Richard had already hung up.

No Soap Radio was a particular specialty for the Dyer boys. The first one they pulled on me was a standard game of hide-and-seek except they just watched TV while I sweated in the topmost shelf of the linen closet. "Oh, we looked," they swore. Then there were the times they ditched me in advance by making plans to meet somewhere, say a movie, and I'd save seats and they'd never show. "But we were at the theater on Fifty-ninth, where were you?" They would worship certain bands—Earth, Wind & Fire, Electric Light Orchestra, Styx—and when I would buy every album and memorize every song they would mock me for actually liking that crap music. No Soap Radio was always the taunt, the punch line to the non-joke, the two of them laughing until I laughed, which only made them laugh more. It seemed my fate to be in their crosshairs. The last No Soap Radio happened when I was fifteen and Richard and Jamie asked if I had any desire to come over and smoke pot with them. It was just after Christmas, and their parents were away for the weekend. It was a thrilling invitation. After a shower and a mad dash from Park Avenue, I found myself in their inner sanctum, in Jamie's room, *Discreet Music* on the stereo, Jamie and Richard paired with two girls who were pretty in that postpubertal, prefeminine way. Maybe they were already stoned. Richard, grinning, brandished a baggie and packed me a hit in his two-foot-long bright red bong, which I recognized from those magazine and tobacco shops along Third Avenue. I lied and told them I only had experience with joints, and they talked me through the process, almost sweetly. The water started to toil and trouble and smoke filled the tube like a special effect until I carbed and the ghost column rushed up into my lungs. My coughing was treated as a joyous inauguration. I passed the bong to my new compatriots and after four more conjurings with far less coughing, Richard and Jamie and the two girls began to swat giggles back and forth like a game of badminton. They mentioned, again and again, how stoned they were. "Are you feeling it?" they asked me, "Are you like feeling it, Philip?" with a wild flamboyance in their eyes. I remember not feeling much, if anything, feeling a profound nothing, like a natural disaster that takes place in Malaysia. I knew what they were doing, knew it was just another joke, let's get Philip Topping stoned on oregano. Just watch this loser, girls. And yet here they were watching, like they wanted me to sing, and in that moment I was both wise and all too foolish. It seemed the first time the Dyer brothers ever really cared. No Soap Radio indeed.

In the limo, Richard gave the driver Jamie's address in Brooklyn.

"So he has some blow?" Eric Harke asked.

"I believe so."

"And you think we've lost them?" Eric measured paranoid distances from the back window, his face a collection of minor anarchies. "Because this still feels pure," he said, tapping his chest, "but if I get photographed I'll just turn into another silly actor wearing another silly outfit." He turned away from the window. "How much blow does he have?"

"Enough, I think."

"Right on." Back to the window. "God, how I hate the ones on scooters."

As far as Richard could tell, Eric Harke was in the midst of a four-day binge, judging from the phase of half-moons under his eyes, as well as the overall state of his agitation, like a carnivore in a petting zoo, though Richard could have been reading his own history in that nervousness (there was a time when he believed every mirror was two-way). But regardless, paparazzi really had been chasing them when all this started.

Their meeting was scheduled for 3:30 P.M. After lunch Richard walked his mother to Central Park, checking his watch every few minutes. It was 3:17 P.M. when they crossed Madison. Every step was calibrated in terms of his own immediate timeline—twelve minutes now—which, while nerve-racking, focused him against the collective madness of his parents. He listened to his mother go on about how she's surrounded by nature in Connecticut and yet Central Park was what she missed most about the city. At one point she placed her hand on Richard's shoulder in a testing touch. "I know you hate being back here, but I'm glad Emmett and Chloe have had a chance to meet their grandfather, to lay down some memory even if that memory hardly does him justice." They stopped at the light at 75th and Fifth. "He does seem so old," she admitted.

Was she coming around to the obvious truth, that Dad needed help?

"Do I seem that old?" she asked.

"No, Mom, you look great."

"You get older but you don't realize just how old you look." Tears clung to her eyes and the word *meniscus* fell into Richard's head, an all-time favorite until he learned it was also part of his knee, the part he tore two years ago while fooling around on Emmett's skateboard. "You're still planning on Connecticut for the weekend?" she asked.

"Of course."

"Can't wait to spend time with the kids."

"It'll be nice," Richard said, dreading the trip.

"And Emmett's good, health-wise?"

Richard was weary of the question. "Yep. He's gotten really tall."

"That's great. Knock on wood."

There was always that apotropaic addendum.

The light turned green.

"I can't join you in the park," Richard said. "I have a meeting."

"Of course. One day at a time."

He didn't bother disabusing her.

"Well, honey . . ." She gave his shoulder a squeeze.

"I'll see you soon," he told her.

"You'll take the train to Dover Plains."

"Yes, yes, we've been over this."

"Saturday morning."

"Like we planned."

"And we'll pick you up at the station."

"Great."

"Any kind of food the kids want?"

"Whatever you have will be great."

"I'm proud of you," she said, without obvious reference but squeezing harder.

"Okay, Mom."

The light started to blink red. What does that mean? Ten seconds?

"You were a hard boy to love but you've grown into a wonderful man," she said.

Her eyes still gripped those tears, almost stubbornly, it seemed.

"Your father, he was the opposite."

How many more blinks? Two? Three?

"I should have been on your side more. That was my mistake and I'm sorry. But spend time with Andy and maybe you'll see what I saw all those years ago." The light was now solid red and Richard was ready to hold his mother back but she dashed across with just enough native speed and tiptoe charm that the cars and bus seemed to fall in behind her like dancers in a Busby Berkeley routine. Safe on the other side, she waved before heading into the park.

Why was it harder to love than to hate?

Or was that a stupid question?

Or worse, a naïve question?

A block from the Carlyle Richard's own phone for once chimed with a text. It was Eric Harke—Runnels late, be Thebes soon. Runnels? Thebes? And how soon Thebes? They were having afternoon tea at the hotel—I'm few in he afternoon—to discuss things, in particular *Ampersand*—Imam edge meat—though Richard was certain these things would angle toward an invite to meet his father—How's tour gather doing btw?—and while this gave Richard blunt-force indigestion—Need to Amir this happen—he was willing to entertain the notion—Gong to be awesome—for the sake of conversation. He scrolled through these texts while sitting in the upper gallery of the Carlyle—Still trapped—trying to appear at ease in a large velvet chair, sipping Earl Grey tea. The room appeared based on a Turkish bordello and the longer Richard had to wait the more he questioned which side of the exchange he was on. The entire Carlyle seemed a theme park where people paid vast sums of money to feel rich. At 4:27 P.M. Candy and Chloe strolled in, Chloe disappointed to find an empty seat instead of (insert scream here).

"Still not here?" she said as if she were Richard's boss.

"Maybe he's stuck on L.A. time," Richard said.

"And you've just been like waiting?"

"Yup."

Chloe shook her head like she was on the verge of giving him a pink slip.

"How was the Statue of Liberty?" he asked.

"But I really want to meet him."

"And hopefully you will. So the Statue of Liberty?"

"Smaller and bigger than expected," she said. "It's built on top of a fort, which is interesting. And Ellis Island was interesting too. It reminded me of like a concentration camp but like a concentration camp in reverse, like the immigrants were the bread that comes out of the oven." It was the year of Anne Frank and unfortunate analogies.

"Anyway," Candy said, smiling.

"But fun?"

"Sure," Candy said.

"And you?"

"Exhausted but good." Candy frowned. "Your meeting?"

"Who knows?"

He could see Candy trying to gauge the level of his frustration, which was always a concern for her and added to his own frustration, that he was so fragile in her eyes, which just compounded his impatience with himself.

"That's a movie star for you," she said.

"Yep."

"You okay?"

"Yes."

"You should just leave," Candy said.

"I will soon."

"But I really want to meet him," Chloe said.

"Chloe, enough." Candy stepped closer and gave the nape of Richard's neck a scratch. His constant stream of thoughts, never pleasant company, redirected into a single command: please don't stop. He lowered his head, closed his eyes. "I think we're going to walk to the restaurant," Candy told him.

"Long walk," he said.

"Too long?"

"Doable. Go through the park."

"Time-wise?"

"Should be fine."

"Good."

"Oh, keep going," Richard begged when she stopped scratching.

"We gotta go."

"Please."

"Emmett's up in the room," she said.

"Yeah, okay. Great."

The girls were having a girls' night out—Joe Allen, the musical *Wicked*, a carriage ride—while the boys had hazier ideas—maybe listen to jazz, or go to a comedy club, do something downtown, in the Village, near Washington Square Park—Richard wishing he had planned better.

"Have a good night," Candy said.

"Yeah, you too."

Chloe looked around. "So you really don't think he's going to show?" she said to nobody in particular, meaning her father. She picked up a spoon. "This could've been Eric Harke's spoon." Her voice had the pitched flair of her favorite TV shows, as if the origins of humor came from canned laughter. "I almost want to steal it," she said. "Oh Eric Harke's spoon." She kissed its oval shallow.

"Chloe?"

"Yeah, Dad?"

"Put the spoon down."

She smiled honestly, which was enough to forgive any behavior.

A kiss and a wave and Richard was back to sitting by himself, though *sitting* was hardly the right word, taking up space maybe, wasting space, judging by the waiters who circled. Richard stared at the crumbs on the tablecloth like they were evidence of a lost civilization. He took a certain amount of pride in his honest opinion of himself. I am bitter; I am competitive; I am cheap; I am proud to a fault. No blind spot here. I pretend to be pessimistic though I am secretly optimistic. I am tired. I am nothing. He thought he understood this better than most, which was a strange kind of arrogance. A wonderful man, his mother called him, a good father, said his brother, this for a person who often imagined Emmett and Chloe dying a terrible death, murdered, raped, missing forever, as if his redemption could only come via a tragedy. What a narcissist. As if his children were put on earth for his own absolution. And it was bullshit too. Because Emmett had been sick, had dipped into those mortal percentages, and Richard discovered no redemption whatsoever, just misery and fear and powerlessness. But really that was bullshit too. Because there is pride when the world aligns with your inner muck and another person's worst fear is your basic math. I have lived through your nightmare. I have survived. His posture turned into the slump of somebody lifting his limit in weights, and Richard thought about finding a meeting somewhere, a true meeting. He needed similar company. Because right now his only stance against himself was isolation masked as purpose, a scarecrow's attitude. This is who I am. This is what I do. I am frightening and I am alone. Richard shook his head. What bullshit.

"Dad?"

Emmett, nicely dressed, stood before him. God, how Richard wanted to hug the boy.

"Still waiting?"

"To be honest I don't know what I'm doing."

"You think he's still coming?"

Richard checked the time. "No."

"Has he called or anything?"

"No. You want some cold tea?"

"No thanks."

"You look well put together," Richard said.

"Yeah?" Emmett placed his hands on the back of one of the chairs and did the kind of casual stretching that usually presaged a parental request. Richard watched him with amusement. He could guess what was coming but he wanted to see how limber Emmett could get.

"So you excited about tonight?" Richard asked.

"Yeah, sure."

"We're going to have lots of fun."

"Okay."

"I was thinking we go downtown and hear this famous jazz violinist."

"Cool."

"And there's a wonderful Ethiopian restaurant I want to try."

"Um, Dad . . . " Emmett finally broke from the chair and went into solicitation mode, explaining how Andy had invited him to a book party nearby and how he had said yes without really thinking because it sounded interesting and Andy was a really good guy, like totally excellent, and well, Emmett wondered if maybe he could go with his uncle instead of doing the jazz violin thing, unless of course the jazz violin thing was a super-big deal and then absolutely no problem.

"Wait," said Richard, "you're turning down a night of jazz violin with your dad?"

Emmett straightened earnestly. "It's not that—"

"I'm joking. Go and have a good time with Andy."

"You sure you don't mind?"

"I'm sure. Just be back by, how does eleven sound?"

"Sounds good."

"And don't do anything stupid. Stupid can happen easily in this city."

"I won't."

"You have money?"

"Forty dollars."

Richard reached into his wallet and counted out sixty. This kind of generosity was not his habit. He wanted his children to appreciate their role as earners with chores and jobs, unlike his own upbringing, where he had a no-strings-attached allowance, his mother tossing him cash whenever he asked, even giving him a credit card in high school, just in case, those cases often involving dinners for him and his friends so Richard could pay by credit and collect their share and then go buy weed or blow. But Richard was determined that his children should avoid his path, that they should in fact wipe his path clean. But today he handed over the money. Maybe it was the Carlyle and its blithe wealth, or maybe it was a desire to see the boy's smile, an affecting piece of sleight of hand.

"Wow, thanks," Emmett said.

"Call me on your phone if you need anything."

"Yeah, okay." And before Richard could pardon the lie, Emmett came clean. "I sort of left my phone back in L.A. Probably stupid of me, definitely stupid, but I wanted electronic silence while here, New York without any L.A."

Richard nodded in total, if compromised, agreement. "I get that," he said, Emmett's phone giving consequence to his pocket, like a clapper to a bell. He could have handed it over right then and explained how he saw it in the car and assumed it was left behind by mistake, but the date on that particular explanation had gone past due, and perhaps more problematic, Richard liked receiving those vibrations from the faraway land of his son.

"I'm not looking forward to the emails and texts when I get back," Emmett said.

"A lot, huh?"

Emmett stared at the ground. "I hate to imagine."

"Girls?" Richard asked, instantly feeling like a foolish television father.

"A few probably."

"I always liked Emma," Richard pushed.

"She's okay. Kind of young."

"Isn't she your age?"

"She's just young. Her sweetness makes me want to act like a jerk."

"Yeah?"

"And so then I feel like a jerk."

"You're my son all right."

"Shut up, Dad."

"Okay," Richard said. "You can always call me on a pay phone or use Andy's."

"Yeah, yeah."

"And do me a favor and give me a tap when you get back to the hotel."

"Will do."

"Eleven."

"Got it."

"Eleven-thirty at the latest."

"Sure." Emmett turned to go but then stopped. "I just finished *Ampersand*," he said.

"Yeah. And what'd you think?"

"Not a masterpiece, but still great. The ending surprised me."

"I haven't read it in a long time," Richard said.

"I knew it was heading toward a dark place, but the way he twists the reader into being an accomplice, like you're the voice in Edgar Mead's head, that was pretty cool, like the reader affects what's being read, kind of a Schrödinger's cat-and-mouse game."

"Like I said, it's been a while," Richard said.

"Why do you hate him so much?"

Richard touched his chest as if accused. "I don't know that I hate him, I mean, I hated him when I was younger. He was a . . . " The right word seemed impossible. "Look, neither one of us was suited to the relationship. I would have hated any father, even the world's greatest, and he did his thing to the exclusion of everything else, which is probably why he's such a great writer. The only time I ever had that kind of focus was with drugs." This was what Richard wished he had said as he thought about this conversation later in his head, and weeks later, still thinking back, he would remove the drug reference and put in something about fatherhood. "Unlike him I'm happiest as a dad." Yes, that seemed perfect. But in reality Richard said, "We're just different."

"Oh."

"Very different," like this clarified his position.

"Oh."

"Two very different people," the final absolute clarification.

"Oh," Emmett said.

"You know what I mean?"

"Yes."

They both stood there, or Emmett stood and Richard sat, a pause opening onto a longer silence that grew in length and pulled at whatever briefly connected them, an uncomfortable force not rendered until goodbye.

It was 5:15 P.M.

Richard signed his room number to the insanely large check and wandered down to the lobby. Its slick black and white interior, its expanse of marble, begged for a Fred Astaire number. God knows the yearly budget on shine. People, mostly foreign, wandered in from the street with their afternoon purchases, the bags held aloft like they were crossing a finish line. It was also cocktail hour, so while the elevators carried the weary shoppers up, they also brought down the newly refreshed, their fog wiped clean. With nothing pressing and feeling conspicuously without purpose, Richard began to spot small housekeeping duties, like the lampshade that was crooked and the flower petals that had dropped on the table. There was a stubborn stain on one of the upholstered chairs. Richard often controlled his annoyance by cleaning things up. A joke around their house was that a screaming match with Dad often resulted in a reorganization of all the DVDs. But here Richard limited himself to straightening the lampshade near the fireplace. The gas fire briefly fooled him since the wood was strikingly real, right down to the embers. He imagined a forest of flame-retardant trees. In his jacket pocket was a small notepad for jotting things down, and he ripped out a page—*an office building in New York put under quarantine forever, the workers making a new life of this world*—and balled it up and was getting ready to feed it to the fire, to feed the whole notepad, page by page, into the fire, when Richard heard a voice nearby,

You can never really know something.

He turned and saw Eric Harke staring at him, hair tight along the sides, wearing horn-rimmed glasses and a dark suit with a bow tie. Before Richard could say anything, Eric squinted with self-engrossed schoolboy charm and continued:

My father was a bona fide war hero. He saved lives. He won medals. He got shot. Twice. He died eleven years after my Shearing graduation and a mess of unknown soldiers showed up at the funeral and gripped my hand like a handshake was an essential part of American industry. "A great man," they told me. How could I answer but yes? This great man who hustled insurance and never made a decent dime, not like the silver dollar dads of my classmates. I'm sure all those stooped GIs carried full policies, even flood. I think my dad wanted me to look at him the way those men looked at his coffin, with brief but undying love, like a drop of dye that colors an entire glass. But I wasn't in his war. When I was suspended from school he picked me up, a terrible expense coming all the way from San Francisco. In my room he grabbed my suitcase with a point of showing its lightness, either as a reflection of his strength or of my emptiness, I'm not sure. The man was hardly wider than his hat yet stood like the Lone Ranger. In the hallway all the doors were closed, pencils scrabbling math problems or dissecting lines from Tintern Abbey, but I knew ears were listening near the seams. I played up my footsteps and gave them my best Alec Guinness in Kwai. To the oven indeed. My father walked a few paces ahead and with clumsy effort unjammed the always jammed red door. I could see past him, to the quad lit by the moon and the desk lamps of studying boys. All was quiet for a second longer

until all was quiet no longer. The fire alarm sounded. Its endless echo
pulled us forwards and backwards as doors opened and heads turned in
speculation. All of those boys, my father included, none of them saw a
goddamn thing.

Eric broke character and grinned. It was obvious he was accustomed to
being happily seen. "Tell me I am not Edgar Mead."

"You're late," Richard said.

"That's being generous. Try really fucking absurdly late. I did get
here almost on time but I suffer from poor vestibular function, and I
needed some space to settle my head so I got a suite here, and the at-
tacks always drain me so I ordered room service for some protein and
my iPhone's dead and I don't have your info on my Droid so I couldn't
get in touch."

"You could've called the restaurant."

"You know what, I didn't think of that." His pupils bled like a felt-
tipped pen pressed too long on paper. "I try to do these everyday
human-function things all by myself but maybe I'm incapable. Just call
the fucking restaurant. Ridiculous."

"It's not that big a deal," Richard said.

"No, it's ridiculous. I get all excited about something—look, I got
dressed up, got a haircut, I mean I really got into it, you know, and then
I start getting all neurotic and self-conscious and vestibular and I drop
the fucking ball. It's a hell of a way to impress somebody. And I'm glad
you're calling me on it, Richard. Not many people do."

"You're just late, that's all," Richard said.

As they talked, Eric Harke, the famous actor, started to take magnetic shape, rearranging the compass of the lobby. People came up
with reasons to loiter. Checking phones. Inspecting guidebooks. Falling into deep conversation as if whatever they said Had To Be Said
Right There. A few bolder ones inched closer as if climbing a fraying
rope. All of this residual attention squeezed Richard and reminded
him of those enjoyable moments in thrillers when the veteran agent
realizes the room is a trap. Even the concierge seemed to be playing
along, leaving his station and marching toward them like he had a

pistol in his pocket. "Looks like we have company," Richard said to Eric.

"Excuse me, *Mr. Mead*?" from the concierge.

"Yeah?"

"Your car has arrived."

"Okay, great."

"And *Mr. Mead*, the doorman has informed me of photographers outside."

Eric wiped his mouth. "Shit."

"At both entrances, I'm told."

"Any other option?"

"Unfortunately, they know all the other options." The concierge spoke with extra formality, perhaps thinking his character should be MI6. "We could try a decoy."

Richard nearly laughed. "Really? The Carlyle provides a decoy service?"

"We get some boys from the kitchen."

"And dress them up?"

"To a degree. Not saying it's perfect."

A woman near reception brazenly lifted her phone to take a picture.

"Dammit," Eric Harke said, turning his back like the situation was getting hot, too hot. "I've got to get out of here. The longer I wait, the worse it'll get."

The concierge suggested an overcoat, or an umbrella, or maybe Mr. Roomer over there, gesturing toward an oversized slab of beef who stood near the entrance. "He's part of our security team. Very capable in these situations. That ring on his finger is from Super Bowl XXXI."

"Or you could just wave and leave?" Richard suggested.

Eric Harke placed his hands on the mantel and lowered his head, Kennedyesque. "I can't get photographed," he said. "It might sound stupid since my picture's been taken at least a hundred times today. What's a few dozen more, huh? Just smile. But I'm done. I've reached my fill. Those natives in Fiji, or wherever they're from, they were right about it taking away your soul, but it happens slowly, like a chisel." Eric turned his marmoreal head. "Let's go talk to Mr. Super Bowl."

The plan was for Mr. Roomer—"Pleasure to meet you, *Mr. Mead*"—to use his old offensive-lineman skills and peacock his three-hundred-pound frame into a shield, and Eric would hang on to the big man's overcoat and press his mug against the wool and rush into the waiting car. A celebrity sneak. Richard was unsure how he figured into the scheme, but somewhere in the discussion it was decided that he would join *Mr. Mead*—how they loved calling him *Mr. Mead*—in the car. Why not? He had nothing else going on tonight. On the count of three the doors of the Carlyle sprang open and Roomer cut a path toward the waiting car with Harke holding on and Richard covering the rear. Flashes lit like mortars. Voices yelled for *Eric! Hey Eric! Just one, Eric! C'mon, Eric! Fuck you, Eric!* Roomer slid into the back, then Harke, then—Richard saw Emmett leaning against the building, waiting for Andy. Richard waved, but Emmett didn't see him. A few pedestrians waved back, though, seemingly thrilled.

"C'mon!" Eric yelled.

In jumped Richard and the car sped away, stopping at the light.

Some of the paparazzi pursued.

A scooter pulled up and *snap-snap-snapped*.

Eric went near horizontal. "I appreciate the help, Roomer, but unless you're holding narcotic or know someone holding narcotic, I suggest you roll out before we go green." Eric handed him three bills, all hundreds.

"I can't help you there, *Mr. Mead*. Enjoy your stay at the Carlyle."

Roomer opened the door, blindsiding a photographer's knee.

The light changed.

"Where we going?" from the anxious driver.

"Just do whatever fancy jujitsu driving you specialize in."

The driver—"Yes sir!"—obliged but the traffic was heavy and it took nearly a half hour for him to lose the scooter, the scooter lampooning the concept of chase, pulling up alongside at every red light and giving them a wave. "Just one shot, Eric, please." Finally, either from boredom or other prey, he abandoned them with a playful *beep-beep*.

"Fucking scooters," Eric Harke said. Sweat collected along the ridges of his face, which he wiped away with extreme discomfort, and Richard thought of another scene from a thriller, where the hero tugs the skin around his neck and peels away the latex mask, revealing, well, in this case, an obviously coked-up young man. The particular humidity, the nictitating eyes, the sniffing about for deposits of binge-bundled snot, were all very recognizable. Words no longer tried to pollinate but tumbled into groans, gurgles, sighs, and his breathing was too loud, right, you could hear that, the heavy nose-breathing, which was way too loud—Eric suddenly held his breath as if all that noise was on the verge of capturing him. Yes, Richard knew this movie well.

"Gaaaaaaaaaah," Eric exhaled.

Richard nodded like *Gaaaaaaaaaah* summed things up nicely.

"My fucking iPhone," Eric said, holding up two phones. "My assistant said she was going to transfer my contacts to the Droid, but nobody's in here, so I guess not, and I'm not someone who knows phone numbers, not like that's a Hollywood thing, just a regular thing, I mean who knows phone numbers anymore, that's just a normal phenomenon, right, because my whole message is to stay away from—message? My whole goal, just goal, a goal, the goal, for me, is to be real, and not keeping-it-real real, just real real, a real regular person, particularly when I'm acting."

"Must be difficult," Richard said, thoroughly confused.

"Don't make fun of me."

"I'm on your side," Richard said.

"My side?"

"Yes."

"Well, I'm on your side too," Eric Harke said, offering his hand for a slap.

"Okay," Richard said, obliging.

"You and me."

"Sure."

"You're from here, right?"

"A long time ago."

"But you know people here."

"Not really."

"But do you know anyone who likes to have a good time, like go out and have a good time, like hey, let's have a good time and party, like—"

"You're looking for cocaine?"

A quick "Yes" followed by a relieved if guilty grin.

It was almost charming, Eric's timidness, as if he had no idea how to be famous. C'mon, man, the world was his drug dealer. Drive in front of any random club and ask the bouncer, troll any happening spot, just show up and in thirty minutes Eric Harke would find his nose kneeling and in an hour his Droid would be thrumming with news from a hundred friends who could provide whatever needed providing. But he was young. Richard thought maybe this was his first independent foray into lose-my-soul New York, alone and desperate and seeking the only known cure. And maybe it was his age, his dressing up as Edgar Mead, his celebrity that endeared him to Richard, who was maybe thrilled to be back in the old whirlwind, in a limo, like he was cruising his past, and maybe Richard wanted to try to keep Eric safe, or expose him as a hard-core fool, or maybe more than anything wanted to dabble in his nastiest fears and fall without consequence, maybe that's why he called his brother and put in an order of No Soap Radio. But as the limo stopped in front of Jamie's walk-up and Richard got out and buzzed the front door, he began to think this was a bad idea, maybe his worst ever.

Jamie finally came down.

"Holy shit," Richard said, seeing his face. "What happened?"

"Got into a fight."

"Yeah."

Jamie smiled, teeth first.

"Fuck," Richard said.

"Nice, huh?"

"How's the other guy?"

"Maybe *fight*'s the wrong word."

"About a girl?"

"In a way."

"You know you're not seven anymore. Teeth don't grow back."

"Aren't half yours fake?"

"Just three."

"And look at your lovely smile."

"Yeah, yeah," Richard said. "But seriously, are you okay?"

"I was going to ask you the same thing." Jamie showed him the baggie with an udder of whitish powder.

"What is it?" Richard asked.

"Good old-fashioned cocaine, like you requested. My neighbor had some."

Richard's pulse hit the gas instead of the brake.

"No Soap Radio," Jamie said. "What we have here is a mixture of Arm & Hammer, Advil Cold & Sinus, a handful of Ambien—I thought you needed some controlled substance in there—Altoids for their curiously strong flavor, a dousing of Anbesol dug up from the bottom of my dopp kit, all of it chopped up and mashed together. It's over the top. That's why I call it—wait for it—Michael Caine."

"That's insane," Richard said, pleased.

"In keeping with your request."

"Kind of yellow too."

"That's the Anbesol, possibly a mistake. Either way, this Michael Caine isn't fooling that Michael Caine." Jamie looked toward the limo. "He in there?"

"Yep."

"Why are you doing this?" Jamie tried to shoot his brother a look of genuine concern, which ended up hurting his head. "It's got to be a slippery slope. And do you really think he's going to do your movie if you supply him with pretend coke?"

"It's not that at all," Richard said.

"I realize you're the addiction expert here, but this"—Jamie shook the baggie—"cannot fall under any standard drug treatment practices, even by Hollywood standards. This shit ain't methadone, it's just shit with a minty aftertaste."

"I'll be fine," Richard promised. "It's not like it's real."

"Yeah, but we Dyers can get pretty fucked-up on imitation real."

"Don't worry."

"Just abandon ship and come up to my place."

"I can't."

"Why not?"

"Because I'm having fun."

"What, are you a star fucker now?"

Richard gripped imaginary lapels. "That's a stupid thing to say."

"Says the man pushing an ounce of Arm & Hammer."

"Shut up."

"Says the man with the history of profound drug abuse."

"Enough."

"Says the man hanging with the cover of *Tiger Beat*."

Richard shoved Jamie, an instinctive shove and without much force, but Jamie's balance was already compromised and he stumbled and fell, finding mostly humor in the fall, like he was on roller skates.

"Crap, I'm sorry," Richard said, reaching down.

"I'm okay, I'm okay." Jamie got up. "Like old times."

"I didn't mean—"

"It's no big deal."

"Seriously."

"Don't worry about it."

This minor piece of violence hardly registered within the history of their fights, but a certain nostalgia trailed behind, a mutual rhythm of regret and blame. One of the limo's windows rolled down and Eric Harke appeared like a worm eating its way through black fruit. "Everything all right? Because I've got a party I've got to go to."

"Everything's fine," Richard called back.

"Not to rush you guys."

"No, everything's fine."

The worm wiggled back.

"What's with the bow tie and the glasses?" Jamie asked.

"I have no idea," Richard lied.

"The Ambien might help."

"Yes, a genius addition."

"You promise you won't touch this stuff?"

"I promise."

"I can't help feeling this is bad news," Jamie said.

"Have you looked in the mirror?"

"Do me a favor and do not go near whatever party he's going to."

Richard patted his shoulder. "I'll call you tomorrow."

"Please do."

"You might want to see about your nose."

"You too."

The brothers shared a brief unsaid moment before going their separate ways, an appreciation of the long day and all the parts they had played and how they had looped back together again, here in Brooklyn, practically different people, Richard turning for the limo and breathing in a familiar odor, as if the eighties burned in an alley somewhere, while Jamie heard the reverb of a dozen more unsaid things as Richard opened the door and slipped in, but before the limo could pull away, the door opened again and in scooted Jamie, who took his place across from his brother, his smile a keyhole in search of a key.

"I just need a lift into Manhattan," he said. "If you don't mind."

"Not at all," from Eric Harke, a more-the-merrier kind of guy.

Jamie feigned astonishment. "Hey, you're Eric Harke."

"Shh, don't tell anyone."

"Very cool to meet you, man, very cool."

"And you are . . . ?" Eric asked.

Jamie turned toward Richard. "You going to introduce me?"

"Um, this is Jamie James."

Jamie frowned at his brother.

"Nice to meet you, Jamie James," Eric said.

The limo drove from Kane onto Clinton toward the Brooklyn Bridge. From Richard's unfortunate christening, Jamie mined a personality: lawlessly fey. And the busted-up face? That was the price of doing bidness in this town. It was no surprise that Eric Harke wanted to sample the product first thing, though Jamie begged him to go slow since this was like nothing he had ever snorted before. "This is haute couture for your nose," Jamie said, rather enjoying his persona, "artisanal shit." Eric dipped the corner of his American Express Black Card into the baggie, not before apologizing for having an American Express Black Card, something his manager got him, absurd but feel the weight, fucking titanium. The black gained a pile of ugly-looking white. Eric leaned over and the brothers parroted his body English. After a quick, hard sniff—always an amazing disappearing trick—the hand inside Eric's puppet face turned into a fist. Jamie James clapped his approval. "Tell me that shit's not something?" It took Eric a minute to recover before he agreed, his buzz helped along by the sight of the Brooklyn Bridge, hands down his favorite bridge, which bounced him from window to window, the suspension cables strumming like harp strings. "I love everything about this fucking bridge," he said as they gained Manhattan. "I even look like Washington Roebling."

"I can see that," Jamie went along, "in the eyes."

"Exactly."

"And the set of the jaw."

"Precisely." Eric exhaled. "I'm getting a weird taste in my throat."

"Yeah, right," Jamie confirmed.

"Almost refreshing."

The limo turned up Centre Street.

"You should have a drink." Jamie grabbed a bottle from the minibar.

"Maybe some water," Eric said.

"If by water you mean tequila." Jamie handed him a half-full glass.

"I was thinking water."

"It's Patrón."

Jamie clinked his glass and they both drank.

"You know what," Jamie said. "You'd be great in a western."

"You think?"

"Absolutely." Jamie refilled their glasses. "But you should be the bad guy."

"The guy in the black hat."

They clinked glasses again and drank.

"I do love me a good antihero," Eric said.

"Travis Bickle."

"Tom Ripley."

"Ooh, good one. Michael Corleone."

"Edgar Mead," Eric practically shouted.

"Edgar fucking Mead," Jamie seconded, his eyes raised. "How about you, Richard?"

"What?"

"Do you have a favorite antihero?"

"Um, Tony Montana."

"Tony Montana!" Eric definitely shouted this time and in went the Black Card. "You want some?" he said to Jamie.

"I'm good."

"Richard?"

"I'm okay," Richard said, sounding unconvinced.

Eric recovered quicker after this snort. "I have to say, this is weird stuff."

"Totally," agreed Jamie.

"Not much of a pop."

Jamie poured another shot. "It's all about subtlety nowadays."

"I certainly prefer"—down went the tequila—"subtlety."

"Hell yeah—fuck yeah."

The music, up till now a low-fi presence, bounded onto their laps as Jamie heard an old favorite and turned up the volume loud enough that Keith Richards seemed to be playing their lower intestine.

Let's drink to the hardworking people, sang Keith.

"'Salt of the Earth,'" Eric said, ever the eager student.

"That's right."

"Beggars Banquet."

"Exactly."

"Nineteen sixty-eight."

"I guess."

"Last song on the B side."

"Wow, that's some deep knowledge."

Raise your glass to the good and the evil.

"I do love this song," Eric said.

Jamie clinked glasses. "Because it's a great song."

"A masterpiece of ambiguous irony," Eric said.

"Okay."

"So crazy cynical too."

"You are wired, my friend."

"I suppose I am. It's all about the fucking subtext."

The song's slow open gained momentum, now driven by Mick, with

Jamie and Eric and even Richard joining in, not with singing so much, though there was some of that, but with a sense of ownership, like they were an essential part of its creation, members of the eternal present right there in the backseat—*They don't look real to me, in fact they look so strange*—the limo cruising up Park, climbing above Vanderbilt, curling around Grand Central, coming through the dark vault onto the more Technicolor aspects of Manhattan—*Let's drink to the hardworking people* in full chorus—and finally after a left and another left and a final left stopping somewhere between the past and the future.

"Here we are," Eric said.

Richard and Jamie knocked eyes.

They were in front of their father's apartment.

"Um, what's happening here?" asked Richard.

"A big book party at the Frick," Eric said, "hands down my favorite museum. It's for *The Propagators.* You heard of it? Because it's going to be huge." Eric scooped himself another Black Card bump of Sir Michael. "Fuuuck!" he said, pinching his nostrils. "It's like my nose is getting kicked in the groin."

"That's funny," Jamie said.

"I'm thinking of playing the gorilla in the film adaptation."

"Of what?"

"The book."

"A gorilla! No way!" Jamie was getting drunk.

"A bonobo actually. All CGI. It would be motion capture."

"How many movies are you attached to?" Richard asked.

"Just the ones I'm interested in. And the character's a girl too."

"A girl gorilla," said Jamie, impressed.

Eric took a deep minty breath, then said, "Let's roll."

Outside the entrance none of the smokers recognized the celebrity in their midst since they were too busy interviewing themselves with their tiny filtered microphones. Up the steps and the sound of the crowd inside pushed past them with the current of a single crowd creature, a giant luminescent jellyfish that floated and pulsed, floated and pulsed, tentacled by a hundred dazzling conversations, and Richard and Jamie had the brief sensation of being buoyant. The woman manning the list gave Eric Harke a wide, lovely smile that without question included Richard and Jamie. Into the Frick the three of them glided, or Eric Harke glided, though *glid* might be the better word, he glid into the Garden Court and accepted his position as the most famous person in a room already packed with self-regard, those nearby throwing down tongues instead of rose petals. Eric remained guarded while his watery baby blues signed autographs and shook hands, his smile smug yet warmhearted. Richard and Jamie wisely followed—or flid—close behind.

"You guys have got to meet Chris Denslow."

Whatever the actor's absurdity in private, in public blossomed into majesty, and Jamie was struck by the transformation and found himself smiling, which was like a palate cleanser for the crowd.

"Chris is a big fan of your father's work," Eric told Richard. "He thinks it's very cool that we might work on *Ampersand* together, fingers crossed. He has a couple of interesting ideas about how you might structure the screenplay, stay in Edgar Mead's head without doing the whole voice-over thing. Drink?" Eric had effortlessly guided them through the muddle and straight to the bar.

"Sprite," said Richard.

"What's this about working on *Ampersand*?" Jamie asked.

"You want a drink?"

"I'll stick with tequila. What's this about *Ampersand*?" Jamie repeated.

"You're a fan?" Eric asked, sipping a beer. "Because Richard—"

Richard put down the Sprite. "I'll have a bourbon actually."

"A bourbon?" from a whiplashed Jamie.

"Why not?" Richard said, taking the proffered drink and holding it close to his chest, like it was wired to that grenade tattoo. "It's a fucking party."

Eric tapped Jamie. "Do you know who his father is?"

Jamie James showed his street side. "Some asshole like his son?"

"No, man, he's"—Eric Harke yawned—"A. N. Dyer."

"Wow," Jamie said as flat as possible.

"And I'm"—another yawn—"I'm Edgar Mead. It's going to be

awe"—yawn—"some." Eric lifted his drink for a ratifying clink, and Richard complied without taking a sip, quickly returning the pin to his chest. He tried to intercept Jamie's glance before the full weight of criticism could fall on his shoulders, in hopes he might convey through a series of facial tics the whole story, and that maybe Jamie would understand, both from the inside and the outside, without clumsy explanation, and perhaps with this knowledge could forgive Richard, though *forgive* was too strong a word, especially since *Ampersand* was hardly his to give, but Richard, feeling exposed, yearned for those telepathic fantasies of youth.

"You'd be a perfect Edgar Mead," Jamie told Eric. He reached over and took Richard's glass and downed the contents in one gulp. "Fuck, I hate bourbon."

Eric yawned again. "Shit, I'm exhausted. I think I might need another bump."

"Good idea." Jamie gave his brother the empty glass, and Richard said thanks without saying a word.

Before Eric Harke could leave for the confines of the nearest bathroom stall, a pair of thick-fingered hands docked on his shoulders, part in greeting, part in massage. "Up past your bedtime, little boy?"

Eric turned around. It was "Krebs!"

Rainer grinned, his cheeks a curtain rising. "Look at this ragtag crew."

"You been here long?"

"Long enough to wonder where you've been. So this is the big surprise." Rainer sized up the new look. "I like it. Very then and now." Then he cast his eye on Richard. "Hello, Richard."

"Rainer."

"Nice to see you again."

"Likewise."

Rainer Krebs turned to Jamie, and before Jamie could decide between truth or fiction, Rainer thrust his hand forward. "And you are Jamie Dyer. I've been an admirer ever since Telluride all those years ago. *Lord God* blew me away, blew everyone away. I even have a bootleg copy that I push onto my friends. Why wasn't it ever released?"

"Music clearance issues," Jamie said.

"Of course, the songs he sings on the corner."

"That plus no one really cared."

"A shame." Rainer leaned his head toward Jamie. "Have you ever thought about putting it online? I have a site, a cult film site, and I think we could create a nice following. You were ahead of your time with what you were doing."

"Rainer's a film producer," Richard explained.

"*Lord God* would play very well in this day and age," Rainer said.

"You think?"

"I do. We should have a talk at some point." Rainer removed the mustard-colored pocket square from his suit jacket and handed it to Jamie, who regarded it like a new form of business card. "Your nose," Rainer redirected.

"What?"

"It's bleeding."

"Oh." Jamie dabbed his left nostril.

"Wait, you're a Dyer as well?" from a fading Eric Harke.

"We're brothers," Richard said.

"Why didn't you guys tell me?"

"You didn't ask."

"Are you involved in *Ampersand* as well?" Jamie asked Rainer.

"Well." Rainer turned toward Richard. "I'm not sure yet."

"Still in the preliminary stages," Richard said.

"So the three of you—" Jamie started to say.

"Could be the four of us," Rainer said. "What are you working on now?"

"Teaching mostly."

"Where?"

"At the New School."

An almost apologetic "Oh."

"Being brothers is just something you'd tell a person," Eric said to the growing void.

"We should find Chris." Rainer glanced around, and seeing no evidence of the man of the hour, became the prow for forward progress.

This kind of New York scene was familiar to Richard and Jamie from when they were boys and went to dances and coming-out parties, events where the Upper East Side groomed its young. Toss any of us into a benefit or gala and we can survive. We are all functionally charming. We all have decent names to drop. And walking with Eric Harke was almost an act of memory for Richard and Jamie. In their day they had the fame of their father. Maybe A. N. Dyer was a cold and distant light but he gave them a shine they parlayed into a swagger. Time, of course, is linear, but as they made their way through this crowd it seemed as if they were ants tunneling through an hourglass. In the packed East Gallery Krebs pointed: over there, Christopher Denslow, standing by Goya's *The Forge* with two other young men. The three of them seemed stuck in a fit of laughter, particularly the two other young men—not men, but Andy and Emmett, hunched over as if each might collapse without the other's support. Rainer and Eric Harke walked over, desperate to know what was so funny, but Richard, startled to see his son, held back, and so did Jamie, who was approaching drunk and was suddenly daunted by the idea that his father could be this son. Those eyes and mouth expressed a lunatic joy that he hoped once existed in the man. Christopher Denslow accepted the hellos and congratulations, but Andy and Emmett remained trapped in hilarity. Whenever they tried to surface—deep breath— they slipped further back. People started to notice. It was becoming unseemly. Nobody wanted drunk, perhaps stoned, teenagers at this party. The boys sensed this growing unease and repeated "Okay, okay, okay," as if propriety involved an act of daring. Finally, Andy and Emmett straightened, socially restored. Rainer and Eric and Christopher, Andy and Emmett, clustered into a tighter group. Introductions were made. This Dyer-rich crowd no doubt flabbergasted Eric Harke, who pointed to where the Dyer brothers stood. Jamie, thus identified, walked over, unsure of what he might say or do, but Andy was caught up in the wholehearted vibe of his family, greeted him with an extended "Hey man" that stretched his arms wide. Jamie perhaps accepted the hug a little too keenly after his long, strange day, his injuries standing as proof. Andy called him a madman, which Eric Harke seconded with a yawn. Richard watched this group like the last player to be picked. Richard could read Emmett's expression—*Oh shit, my dad*—no telepathy required. It was obvious the boy was buzzed. And so what? He was sixteen, a near-perfect student, vice president of his class. Christ, the life Richard had led by the time he was sixteen. But what with the combined genetic material of father and mother, Emmett was likely ill-suited to these effects, not to mention his already compromised medical history. Richard and Candy had had their conversations with Emmett, starting when he was twelve, about the dangers of drugs and alcohol and their own struggles with the disease (that word shamed Richard after what Emmett had been through). And here he was, drinking. And having fun. And let the boy have fun. Have fun, Richard wanted to communicate from across the room, but please be back by eleven. He decided to give Emmett an as-you-were salute and then turn and leave, but before Richard could raise his hand, he noticed Andy. It seemed like he was signaling him over. If Emmett was buzzed, then Andy was flat-out wasted. But something about his appearance shimmered. He wore a bulky pinstripe suit and a pair of scuffed wingtips, a gray and burgundy tie. A chill raised on Richard's skin. Think of a warm bath draining. The water removing and carrying away. A sort of tremulous blue haze. Andy swayed like the distance between them was a span, and Richard noticed the pimple burning bright between those dark anthracite eyes. A mirage of his possible father played. It wavered between the absurd and the slightly less absurd, the one and the same, as Andy made his way across the room, careful with every step as though a chasm loomed between the gaps. "Come on," he said after reaching Richard. His breath reeked. Just another drunk kid. He started to lead Richard toward the group, his grin forging its own truth. "We need you, man," he said.

VI.iii

THE SOUND OF TINY CLAWS SCRATCHING, a burrowing, Andrew decided. What started as a post-Vicodin, pre-dinner nap was turning into an aural investigation. It came from deep within the couch. A mouse maybe. A mouse family maybe. It was a comfortable couch and no doubt deluxe accommodations for a mouse. Hopefully just a mouse. Andrew scratched the cushion to test the sound against the sound inside the couch. After a minute he wondered if maybe he was trying to communicate. He stopped. The scratching continued. Gnawing might have been involved as well. As an experiment, Andrew screamed into the crevasse between cushions, rather like a loon. The scratching, and the gnawing, stopped. Silence. Or not quite silence. The pressure within his ear crackled with a cochlear snow, like an internal blizzard. He thought of New York, the sidewalks and streets flattened white, the park quilted. There had been a few heavy snowstorms this year. Probably no more on the docket. Winter was done. On the horizon another spring. Andrew shifted on the couch. He began missing the mouse-like sound. He pressed his ear harder to the cushion and held his breath. He'd always been good at holding his breath. Charlie Topping once stopwatched him at two minutes and thirty-three seconds, a tremendous length of time when underwater. The key was to give up some air early and then sink and pretend to sleep on the bottom. Like the water was your dream. Upon awakening, Andrew would burst to the surface, lungs burning, and Charlie would exaggerate the click like he was a crusty trainer who could hardly fathom this kid. Unbelievable, he'd say, playing every syllable. Everything was un·be·liev·a·ble that summer of holding your breath. Andrew scratched the cushion in his closest approximation of rodent. *You there? Hey buddy, you there?* Still nothing. He pictured the mouse peering from around one of those springs, his mouse family cowering behind him, a beam of flashlight scanning the upholstery's inner courtyard. Shhhh. Not a squeak, little ones. He always did want to write a children's book. Too late now, he supposed. *Ampersand* was likely the last book he would ever write. At least there was some decent irony in that.

Only the epilogue remained. Edgar Mead had saved Timothy Veck in the cruelest manner imaginable, though he did thwart the even nastier plans of Messrs. Stimpson, Harfield, Matthews, and Rogin. But maybe a baseball bat to the head and a shallow grave would have been more charitable. Regardless, the book was essentially done. The last page of the last chapter rested facedown on that pile of Eaton twenty-pound stock:

```
You can never really know something, at least that's my
absurd defense, that life is unknowable even though all
this time I've known the exact truth. But I pretend that my
own mystery bends along with the mystery of the universe.
My father wasn't a hero. He wasn't even in the war though the
war did do something to him. That confident vigor, that
Presbyterian aplomb, that square-jawed purpose thrust
forward in old team pictures, that bygone breed of
privileged American male, became unnerved once the
civilized world lost its spin. My strongest memory of him
was his funeral and all the kind if oblique words said as
my hand was cranked for water. A terrible accident. A real
shock. Yep, yep, and yep. His best friend -- and my godfather
-- Tommy Archibald Jr. cabled his condolences from England.
Most of his better friends were already in England or the
Pacific. It was women and older lesser men who gave me their
weak comfort. The good solid banker, Mr. Byers of Old
Westbury and the Lafayette Flying Corps, he was there, and
seven years later he would stand in my dorm as my
```

stepfather, eyeing me like a between-the-crosshairs Fokker
from the Luftstreitkrafte. He would let me live but with
the understanding that I now belonged to him. "This is not
how my son acts," he said, picking up my suitcase like it was
as light as my father's good name. He had negotiated a
suspension rather than an expulsion, and since he was a
Hotchkiss man, the name on the future dorm would have to be
my own. He led me into the hall. I should mention Alec
Guinness in <u>Kwai</u> and "Tintern Abbey" and the dissection and
the scrabble but is anyone listening? Does anyone care?
This will all get redacted, and those who do care will find
the proper business in the margins. I knew the red door
would stick. Put some dick into it, Nancy, was what the
seniors always told us. I strangled him a little. If I hadn't
stopped he would have died and I honestly don't know how I
stopped. A crack and the door opened. It was a cold New
Hampshire evening. I remember the distant comfort of
chimney smoke. And I remember imagining another fire, and
everything burning, the air silent of human suffering
except for the smell of boys going up in flames, my father
included.

Putting this down on paper was like rendering a carcass into tallow,
and Andrew was rather pleased with the light. Probably better than the
original, he thought. Of course tomorrow he would have to cross the
whole mess out, but right now he was satisfied and he was tired and
he wanted to lie down and close his eyes around Isabel and her unexpected visit from this morning. She was still so beautiful. Gravity's
tedious cousin had no effect on her good company. If anything her
aging was a move toward minimalism rather than his bombastic turn
toward the grotesque. Years of his life reeled behind those eyes and he
wished he could step in and understand himself in that context again.

"Andy," she said.

"What?"

"Are you listening?"

"To what?"

"Why didn't you tell me about Andy?"

"The boys talked to you?"

"Why else do you think I'm here?"

That hurt. Andrew remembered that hurting.

"They're worried," she said. "They think you're . . ." She left him undiagnosed.

"Oh I know what they think."

Did he sound like Nixon here?

"Why didn't you tell me from the beginning?"

"You believe me then?"

Isabel leaned back, which made Andrew realize he had pressed forward.

"Dolly the sheep was what, ten years ago?" she said.

"Longer than that," he said.

"But humans—"

"Yes."

"As far as I know humans have not been cloned yet."

"As far as you know, yes. They—"

"They?"

"The Palingeneticists. They've been keeping samples since Nobel's day but when the breakthroughs finally came, they had a much higher success rate with living donors, hence people like me. That's changed now. They've perfected the process. All they need for Keats is a strand of Keats's hair. Einstein. Mozart. Caravaggio. Whatever remaining shards they can get, they can use. No more ruin. In ten, twenty years the world will experience a new Renaissance, a new Enlightenment, a Golden Age of Golden Ages. I've even heard rumors of Shakespeare."

"The more you talk the less I believe you," Isabel said.

"I'll shut up then."

"Because . . . ," she said.

"Yes."

"Like with his smile."

"Yes, his smile," he said, smiling.

"And the way he stood and moved."

"Yes, the standing and the moving." He rocked on his feet.

"And the eyes."

He squinted.

"He's . . ."

"Me," Andrew said, like an enthusiastic toddler.

Could he take her hand now? Could he finally reclaim her?

"But why didn't you tell me from the beginning?" she asked again.

"You never would have believed me."

"So you let the world, you let me and your sons, believe that you had an affair?"

"It was the only reasonable explanation."

"Because I was devastated."

"Look at me," he said, in hindsight too defensively, "look at me."

Isabel's brow creased as if ready to rip along the line.

"It was a mistake," Andrew backtracked, "obviously."

" . . ."

"If I had known, I never would have done it. Of course not. If I had known. I do hope that's obvious. It must be obvious. I thought it would be a bump, maybe a hard bump, but then we'd recover and on the other side we'd have this boy—"

"We already have boys."

"Oh, I know, I know. But we would have this other boy and we could raise him together and maybe, and maybe . . ." His thoughts were sticking and the ones that crawled forth seemed malformed. "I thought maybe we could care for him."

"This takes narcissism to a whole new level, even for you."

"It's just—"

"He's not you, you know."

"I know that. Believe me. I certainly did better in school."

"This is sick."

"I had pure intentions at the time," he said.

"And what were those intentions?"

"What were they?" Andrew asked nervously, thinking a good answer might angle her into an embrace. "Maybe to give myself a chance to be happy. I know that's a silly word. What does it mean to be happy?

I don't particularly trust happy adults. But sometimes I find myself running into unexplained and unexpected happiness. Like a particular late-afternoon light. A song overhead in passing. A pleasant stroll around the boat pond. Brief moments where time and space seem to conspire for my sole enjoyment. Like childhood, I suppose, and I'm happy until it reminds me of what's been lost, the distance I've traveled from that point to this point. The bitter reason for the warm feeling. Better to go and lock myself in a room and focus on work and hope that might excuse my irredeemably shit existence. A shit father. A shit husband. A shit friend. Writing was just an alibi."

"You talk as if you had no control over life."

"I'm not sure I did," Andrew said.

"Oh please."

He was losing her. Again.

"If Andy had never happened, we would have stayed together, right?"

On this Isabel agreed.

"Even if you were miserable?"

"Yes, probably," she said. "But I loved you."

The past tense stung.

"I always saw you as that boy."

"And now?" he asked.

"You're just another man."

It was like he was falling. "I haven't been the same—"

"Please don't, Andy."

"I haven't written—"

"Please."

He must have sounded like a hand desperately reaching.

"I should go," she said.

"Don't."

"This isn't good for either one of us."

"I should've just killed myself," he said. "It was a consideration."

"Stop." Isabel started for the door.

"But Andy's a good boy."

"You should repaint the apartment."

"He's better than I am. Much better," he said.

She grabbed her coat from the hall chair.

"You'll check on him when I'm dead."

"You're not dying anytime soon."

"Don't be so sure. You heard about Charlie Topping?"

She stopped at the door. "Yes, and I'm sorry. I was at the funeral."

"You were?"

"I arrived late."

"In time to see me . . . "

"You were upset."

Andrew's breathing became stranded on the shallows.

"I need to go," she said.

After a few insufficient breaths, "Don't leave."

"I have to."

"I can get Andy. You can talk to him some more."

Isabel shook her head.

"Please stay." Every breath was a drawing of old smoke.

"I have to go."

"You're remarried now."

Isabel opened the door.

"You still look so lovely," he said.

"The boys are really worried about you."

"They think I'm crazy. You just think I'm a son of a bitch."

Before leaving she asked if anyone was taking care of him, her voice implying a soft touch to his cheek, a brushing away of a morning crumb, a rueful pout as she realized what a mess he was without her. But all of this was mere implication and possibly fabrication. It was more likely a technical question. Andrew told her rather glibly that there was nothing to take care of anymore. It was the doomed romantic reply. But a new effect registered as he lay on the couch and listened for the mouse or whatever it was to start stirring again. He imagined himself a lost boy. Not much of a leap really. It came quite easily. Andrew closed his eyes and unnested himself down to the most elementary scrap. A lost boy adrift in a strange world. He could practically close his palm around it.

"What the hell," he said.

He got up from the couch and put on a fresh shirt, wanting to appear decent, after which, already exhausted, he poured himself a preparatory drink. The floor was littered with random slough and he decided it was time to clean up. Or get Gerd to clean up. For the first time maybe in his life he noticed the fireplace's resemblance to a stage, the mantel its proscenium. A good detail, he thought. The hearth as family drama. He decided the mouse in the couch could put on plays here, the mouse fancying himself an actor. A mouse of virtue. It went without saying that a cat should be involved. It could be his next book. Why not? Andy could do the illustrations. He had the talent, if untapped. Before going upstairs Andrew stopped in the bathroom to get reacquainted with himself. His skin carried stains and specks that no matter the scrubbing remained intact. More than anything, getting old was just plain gross. Andrew splashed water on his cheeks, brushed his teeth, hoped there was still something recognizable in his face.

"I shall eat you up," said the cat.

"But what about my last words?" said the mouse.

"I'm imagining a tasty dollop of scream," said the cat.

"Aren't you, as they say, curious?" asked the mouse.

Gouaches would work well. Andrew shuffled into the entry hall and started up the stairs, the banister an essential friend. He would tell Andy everything. Sit him down and explain things. No more cock and bull. (A rest on the sixth step.) You are me and I am you. That sounded Seussian. The two of us are one. That sounded like a corny lyric. We are identical twins separated by some sixty years. That could work. Best to avoid the *c* word, he decided as he reached the top.

"Now that you mention it," said the cat, "perhaps I am piqued."

"What are you in the mood for," asked the mouse, "tragedy, comedy, history, pastoral, pastoral-comical, historical-pastoral, tragical-historical, tragical-comical-historical-pastoral, scene individable, or poem unlimited? I can sing as well."

"Too bad you're also a mouse and I'm a cat."

"A fable from Aesop then," said the mouse.

This fragile piece of inspiration was blunted by an odor that roved down the hall like a childhood game of blind man's bluff. It was both unpleasant and intriguing, pure unadulterated teenager. Ass funk and toe cheese and sneaker rot and armpit rank and various other effluvia rushed past him, laughing. And maybe he caught a whiff of me coming from the room across the way.

Andy's door was closed.

After a vain knock, Andrew peeked inside: clothes all over the floor, sheets in a heap, a glass half-full on the bedside table, a towel draped over the bathroom door, every dresser drawer open. From these clues Andrew tried to decode the boy, where his fingerprints might have clustered, why he had tossed a pair of socks into the corner, what he had seen from the window with the half-drawn shade. He pictured him with wet hair and a never-satisfying physique. A pinched sag of flesh for pectorals. A dartboard of pimples on his back that would resurface years later as moles. A belly button that caused unnecessary stress. How about the glass of water by the bed? Probably four days old, its potability debated every morning and night. Socks were an eternal frustration. Did he fear clothes in general, a shirt tipping into the same league as lunch, hence the future of grilled cheese with tomato every day and a bureau of plain white oxfords? In the smear of the bathroom mirror sat a smile that never quite clicked, even with practice, and frankly not the world's greatest teeth. Soon an unwavering frown would emerge as the primary expression and anxiety about being judged would hide behind eyes that acted like corkscrews seeking cork. A sudden memory dropped from the ledge of the long forgotten: Jamie's Exeter-era girlfriend, what's-her-name, staying in this room back when it was a guest room. One afternoon Andrew found himself drifting around and he poked in and discovered a pair of her underwear on the closet floor. He lifted them like a small dead thing and brought them to his nose, breathed in their plural tang. He remembered needing this indecency, hungering for the outlawed intimate yet having no stomach for the experience. Whatever the sin seemed absolved by putting it down on paper, hence that scene in *Eastern Time*:

> *There they were, discarded on the floor with the other tennis whites. An hour earlier Walter had watched Louisa tumble onto the red clay after*

running down his drop shot, her legs splaying like a swan considering flight, where upon he was given a quick contextual glimpse. The amber inner thigh. The shadow near elastic. The prickled cotton. Joan of course volleyed this miraculous return hard down the middle and they won the point easily. Another game for Team Shalott. For the rest of the match Walter found himself playing drop shots and lobs, anything to imagine that speedy little cunt, barely contained. Walter glanced toward the window. Everyone was cooling by the pool, Joan probably swimming her laps. He toed the whites, feeling their implied nudity. The skirt still held the blush of clay. "Nice running, très flash," he had told her, and Louisa panted comically before getting back to her feet and brushing her rear. Walter's foot tweezed the butterfly from its chrysalis. Their athletic plainness added a steeper angle to the thrill. There was no lacey effort, no seduction involved. A glance toward the door. The villa was empty but for the cook singing downstairs. Walter reached down. They were heavier than expected. Damp. His insides turned to echo—past, present, and future seemed to wrestle for the clock. He brought the front to his face, his nose pressing in. More than half the pleasure was this image of himself, Walter Shalott, secret pervert, but those percentages quickly dropped as he breathed in the fug and all that echoing found its fuckable source.

Andrew shut the door as if barring a fast-moving ghost. Back in the hall, he was unsure of his next move, but the desire to see Andy veered into anxious vicinities. Where was he? There's so much I need to tell him. The smell of teenage stink had faded, not really faded but become commonplace, as stinks do, and this caused further panic, like the boy himself was fading. Is he all right? What have I done? Andrew headed for the stairs. He must have seen the light under the door and thought maybe Andy was in there. But it was just me, the Druid of Dyer, sitting among that henge of boxes.

"Andy?"

The question was posed at eye level but I was down here, on the floor. "No, it's Philip," I said.

"Philip?"

"Philip Topping," I added.

"Christ, I know who you are."

He sounded upset. Did he notice the open boxes, the letters spread all around me?

"Charlie's boy," he confirmed to the universe above. It seemed my prying had no discernible effect as he asked me, rather pathetically, if I knew where Andy was. He needed to talk to him, very badly, his limited articulation compounded by his refusal to swallow away an air bubble that tweaked his voice into a higher register. I told him I had no idea but then said, "Wait," like a minor character in a procedural who casually remembers something vital, in my case something about a book party.

"A book party?"

"Yes," I said, slow-dealing my information. "And I think, I'm not sure but I think it's just across the street at the Frick, some young writer with a filthy rich dad. Andy was going with your grandson."

"My grandson?"

"Richard's oldest."

"Right, right," he said. "The one that was sick."

"I guess."

"And Andy was invited to this?"

"I really don't know," I said. Eavesdropping had its limits.

Andrew stared into the distance, as if seeing all the way to the back of his head. A goddamn book party. Another young writer. The publishing world. "And at the Frick," he muttered aloud. It seemed to me he was slipping away, which was certainly the case in retrospect. Sense had broken into too many parts too difficult to handle so he tightened his grip around the few small meanings that remained. "I need to go," he said, the recoil bigger than the blast. "I need to go find him and bring him back. Get him away from there. Yes, yes, we need to go right now, Philip."

I have no idea how *I* split into *we*, but he was eager, his face full of cajoling madness. All my life, or most of my life, I desired nothing more than this desperate invitation, but seeing him and feeling the way I did, I was past enchantment. "I don't think so," I said.

"It won't take long."

"I'm tired."

"Please, Philip. As a favor to me."

"I can't."

"I'm almost begging."

I said my final conclusive no and immediately regretted the decision, but the letters on the floor pressed with greater force and I let Andrew turn and leave and curse whatever was left of my name. He sputtered down the stairs, socks sliding. Another drink and another pill and on went the Wellingtons and the overcoat and the wool bucket hat. In the elevator, he almost reversed course for gloves, but once outside was dismayed to find the city benignly cool. I must look like a twit, he thought, prepared to ford a stream rather than a narrow street. But he was on a mission, whether snow or rain or pleasantly mild, and he passed through those smokers and breathed in their sociable exile before heading up the stairs. A young woman greeted him as if he were confused.

"Hello," she said gently.

"I'm just going in."

"Are you on the list, sir?"

"List?"

"It's a private party. You need to be on the list."

"Am I on the list? That's the question?"

"Yes," she said.

"In my day no one wanted to be on a list."

"But this is a good list."

"The nice-not-the-naughty list?" Andrew asked.

"Exactly," she said, smiling.

"Well then, Andrew Dyer."

She found his name with the earlier check. "You seem to be already here."

"Hence my presence," he said.

The woman, and she was young and attractive, and he was feeling old and nasty, but he was once young and attractive, as evidenced by what was inside, and to be honest the difference puzzled him, as embarrassing as that might seem, to be puzzled by aging, but back to the woman—she repeated his name and the relationship between name and face and literary occasion must have kicked in because she said, "You're A. N. Dyer."

"Yes," he said.

They both felt foolish.

"I'm so sorry, please go right in."

"Thank you."

"I love your books, by the way."

"And I think you're doing tremendous work as well," he told her. He was just trying to be clever, just giving her a taste of that old A. N. Dyer drollness, but he could see the injury the remark caused, his good intentions hiding a sharp stone. He continued in without checking his coat and immediately bumped into the mingling crowd, chattery and cheerful. It was hard to be in a hurry here. He envisioned a hundred small catastrophes of spilled drinks and apologies, sorry, excuse me, sorry, if he tried pushing through, overdressed in outerwear. He must resemble a senile farmer searching for his dog, and he was tempted to start calling for Smudge. The absurdity of this image gave him some armor, as everyone within elbow spar seemed to be from the same self-satisfied congregation, a particular brand of New York Calvinism that had strong opinions about predestination and free will, their existence justified by their own success, and while there were similarities with the ghosts of his era, the fundamental fervor burned more intense.

Where the hell was Andy?

Some lesbian offered him a tray of unidentifiable snack and then had the gall to explain said unidentifiable snack with a level of detail that bordered on the perverse. This scene replayed itself four times in five minutes, and there came a moment where Andrew wondered if active pursuit was involved. He waved away all offers until asking the last server if she had seen a dog.

"What's that?"

"My dog. He's lost."

"No, this is a green-market pizzetta topped with upstate micro-farmed vegetables and Old Chatham Camembert cheese drizzled with truffle oil and smoked salt."

"A shame. My dog would have loved that."

But Andrew did accept the white wine, which was too sweet and too warm. Arms raised, he waded through a narrow fracture into the Living Hall. Museums, the movies, the theater, when did these institutions become a form of air travel? The Frick used to be one of his favorites. The old director would let him wander around when the collection was closed. "You're our official writer in residence," he told him, and he presented Andrew with a laminated card. See, Andrew thought, I once did have friends. The most breathable air circulated near the walls, and Andrew recognized More and Cromwell, Jerome and Aretino. They all looked the same, More particularly well preserved in his fur and velvet, as was the Man in the Red Cap. They whispered to Andrew that paint was finer than flesh. He wandered deeper into the rooms. Nobody noticed him beyond his Magritte-like incongruity, which was magnified by his desire to have a rest in one of those THIS IS NOT A CHAIR chairs. In the next room, he gave a nod to Lady Peel and Lady Skipwith, inspirations for Samantha Peel and Valerie Skipwith in *I Saw Her, Waving*. The sight of Lady Hamilton as Nature clutching her spaniel saddened him—my missing dog, he thought, forever lost in art. The truth is, a number of paintings in the Frick show up in A. N. Dyer's fiction and perhaps being in their midst helps explain what happened next.

It started with an overheard snippet:

I told her, maybe because I was feeling soft from all our kissing, more stuck together than actual kissing, three minutes without a decent breath and I was chafed and recovering from the mugging, and she was saying how nice this was, the kissing, over and over again, how nice, her arm draped over my shoulder yet lacking any actual weight, just an impersonation of touch, but really, Penny was all right and pretty in a big-nosed way and her chest was there for the sacking, still all that talk of niceness made me want to push her to the ground.

Andrew turned and caught sight of the source not ten feet away. He was in horn-rimmed glasses and a suit with thin lapels and a bowtie gabbing with two women. There was a recognizable insouciance about him, in his easy if unreliable smile, in the sleepy shagginess, which enhanced his aura. Andrew stared at him, moving closer without moving, part push, part pull.

But instead,

he continued,

> *I told her about throwing that baseball at Bobby Hinkler during practice, I told her how I thought he was looking but he wasn't—he was looking at a bird, I think—and I didn't have time to yell and the ball smacked him right in the face. I threw it pretty hard too, more pitch than toss. I didn't tell her that. And maybe I did know about his interest in migrating birds. But anyway, he fellumphed to the ground, and I smiled. I definitely told her how my first reaction was a smile, because it was funny, Bobby Hinkler falling flat on his back, though I caught my smile in my mitt and ran over. He seemed dead to the world. A crowd quickly gathered. I started to shake with laughter and everyone guessed I was upset, even poor Bobby Hinkler, who was now sitting up and wiping blood from his nose, and I said, I'm sorry, I'm sorry, through the webbing, I'm so sorry, trying to break my unsettling glee. Even the coaches were concerned with my well-being. They thought I was wracked. I told Penny it was my biggest, most secret shame. Afterwards, I think she expected my hands to slowly travel to the upper decks, but I surprised her by sliding them home.*

It was Edgar Mead straight from chapter 18. Even in his muddled state Andrew knew this was too fantastic to be true, that there must be a good explanation, perhaps within the mixture of pills and alcohol, the overexertion, the long nights rewriting, the possible guilt and the goddamn gout. The last week had been fraught and he was likely hallucinating. Would any other characters drop in? All in all, he was amazed by the magic of his imagination, however delirious, and with curiosity he watched Edgar Mead beaver his teeth at this stand of long-legged women. What would he do next? Possibly something from chapter 23? Instead he spotted someone in the crowd and he went and dragged him over.

Andrew's gut reversed course.

It was Andy.

"Have you met my new best pal?" Edgar asked the swaying trees.

Before Andrew even considered the consequences, he rushed forward, moving as though properly dressed and every step was a slog through mud and rain. By the time he reached them he was soaked.

"Don't you touch him," he said, finger raised.

"Dad?" from a mortified Andy.

"You hear me?"

"Dad!"

Edgar Mead triangled his hands in front of his chest, like he had recently vacationed in the Ramayana. "I just want to say what an absolute thrill it is to meet you, Mr. Dyer." He gave a shallow bow. "I'm a tremendous admirer."

"Not another word from you," Andrew said.

"Dad, stop!"

Edgar played hurt in typical Edgar Mead fashion. "I honestly hope I haven't offended you. Because I know how annoying it is when strangers think they know you just because of your work. I feel that."

"You're not even real," Andrew said.

"Dad, please."

Edgar nodded. "I get it. Sometimes I wonder myself."

"You have to leave me alone," Andy pleaded.

"Am I just a product?" Edgar continued. "A faceless face?"

"I'm doing this for you, saving you from him," Andrew said to Andy.

"From him? I'm having like the best time in my life."

"I get it, the whole disdain for celebrity thing," Edgar said.

"I want you to be different," Andrew said to Andy, "a different person, the absolute opposite of me."

"That's not something you have to worry about."

"But I do worry."

"Trust me, I'm nothing like you."

"That's the problem. You're exactly like me."

Andy curled his hands into fists and seemed to pound on a willfully locked door. "Just shut up," he said. "Shut up and leave me alone. Please, Dad. People are starting to stare. Just for now, go home and we can talk in the morning."

"Or stay." Edgar suppressed a yawn. "We can have a drink. No hard feelings on my part."

"Please, Dad."

"I bet you're a scotch man," Edgar said.

Andrew removed his hat and wiped the sweat from his forehead. His skin clung to his clothes, and this compounded his sense of claustrophobia and introduced an element of vertigo. He needed something to hold. Whatever was in control of him was starting to abandon ship, jumping from a great height into a cold, dark sea. Basic function began to splash about and he thought, I might need help. Andy refused to look at him, while Edgar Mead maintained a freakish eye grip. Could a fictional character take him home? Reality, already taking on water, capsized even further when he saw Jamie approach, all beaten up, and Richard right behind him, along with his teenage grandson—Emile? Abbott?—and that girl who was friends with Andy, all of them appearing as if summoned. For a moment he wondered what he might conjure next.

"What are you doing here, Dad?" Richard asked.

"I'm not sure."

"I got hit in the face," Jamie said. "About time, huh?"

"Andy and I were just going home."

"I'm not going anywhere," Andy told Richard and Jamie.

"Nobody is going home," Edgar Mead pronounced. "It's early still."

"Does everybody see him," Andrew asked, "or am I the only one?"

"Have the two of you met?" Richard asked.

"I already know him."

"Don't believe what you read in the tabloids," Edgar said.

"Hence, horrible shadow!" Andrew nearly shouted. "Unreal mockery, hence!"

Jamie and Richard queered their eyes.

"That's from *Macbeth*, right?" Edgar said. "'You have displaced the mirth, broke the good meeting, with most admired disorder.'"

"Isn't that the truth," Andy said.

"You okay, Dad?" from Jamie.

Edgar was beaming. "When I was seven I played Macduff's son in La Jolla."

This bit of backstory Andrew was unaware of. He noticed Andy slinking toward the corner with his grandson, Dermot? "Andy, wait," Andrew called, his mouth starting to percolate something more sinister than saliva.

"Just let him go, Dad," Richard said.

"But—"

"They're having a nice time."

Edgar Mead put his hand on Andrew's shoulder and molded his expression toward the beatific. "He's a good kid. I imagine him someday walking with a limp, which will suit him, the way he'll scrape the ground with his injured iamb." This initially threw Andrew until he realized it was from the end of *Ampersand*. "Oh, man," Edgar went on, now in his own words, "everyone is just stoked by the chance of transposing this book onto film. With your blessing, of course. And with Richard doing the screenplay. Maybe we could get Jamie in on it too. A family affair. And with Rainer Krebs producing—where is Rainer? He's somewhere around. Anyone? You'll love Rainer."

Andrew grimaced. "I don't know what you're talking about," he said, the saliva situation turning every swallow into a sour meal.

"We can talk about this later," Richard told him.

Andrew swallowed again. "Strange things are in my head."

"You really are a *Macbeth* fan, aren't you?" from Edgar.

"Dad, you okay?" Jamie asked louder.

Andrew wished he could spit. "Where's your"—swallow—"tooth?"

"Knocked out."

"By what?"

"Like I said, from a punch to the face. You're looking kind of pale."

"I think I need to go home."

Edgar Mead waved. "There's Rainer. Hey, Rainer!"

A large head stopped and turned, towering over all other heads, the fellow guests appearing merely representational in his company, like the shallow end of a pool. He came toward them, paddling through well-coiffed water, with Dennis Gilroy and an earnest-looking young man following.

"Andrew"—Dennis's eyes went Wow—"great of you to come."

"I'm not really here," Andrew said between swallows.

"Mr. Dyer, Rainer Krebs. It's a pleasure. My great-uncle knew your stepfather."

"My stepfather?"

"Friends during the war, I think."

"War?"

"Andrew," Dennis said, "I'd love for you to meet Christopher Denslow. He's the young writer we're celebrating tonight. He's written a terrific first novel, which I really think you'd love. It's right up your alley."

This young writer stepped forward, obviously well bred and radiating a humble confidence, as though he were a force for good even if he occasionally found himself in offensive company. Like tonight. But you understand, Mr. Dyer, he seemed to say, shaking his hand like they were both privy to their own secret identities. "I met your son earlier, all three of your sons actually."

"Yes," Rainer said, "half the crowd seems to be made up of Dyers."

Andrew grinned, his lips a dam.

"Rainer's a producer," Dennis explained. "He's bought the rights to Chris's book."

"It's a very exciting project," Rainer confirmed.

"I might play the chimp," Edgar Mead said.

"A bonobo," Christopher corrected.

"In my defense, part of the chimp family."

Andrew wondered if you could drown in your own spit.

"And this punk is only twenty-four," Dennis said of Christopher.

"Almost twenty-five."

"Younger than you with *Ampersand*."

"If only there was a comparison to be made."

"Jeanie, do you have a book?" Jeanie Spokes at Dennis's command handed over a copy of *The Propagators*, which he passed on to Andrew. The cover was a crude but evocative drawing of a teddy bear scratched into dirt.

"Great cover, huh?" Dennis said.

The new-book smell and texture turned Andrew's stomach even more.

"Christopher designed it."

"I'm just glad it came out all right."

"What's the font again?"

"Dot Matrix."

"Christopher's also doing the screenplay," Rainer informed them.

"I'm sure he'll design the movie poster as well," kidded Dennis.

"I do have my ideas."

"I bet you do. Hey, you should sign Andrew's copy." Dennis took the book from Andrew and handed it to Christopher. "A passing of the torch moment."

Andrew was pretty sure he only had so many more swallows left.

"It's really something to be signing a book to you," the young man said. His earnestness, while honest, was without warmth, his eyes darkly calculating all his good deeds, even the minor ones, like being friendly to people and putting up with stupid questions, in general re-maining patient with those who were far less evolved, hoping this might excuse his other, faintly genocidal thoughts. "You were one of my heroes growing up," he said.

Andrew listed to the left.

"I'm not sure if Richard's talked to you about *Ampersand*," from this Rainer character.

"My all-time favorite number-one book," from Edgar.

"These guys do have an interesting take," from Dennis, "and a good track record."

Andrew listed to the right.

"*The Erasers* was brilliant."

"It's all about the script for us. That's number one."

Andrew turned toward Jamie. "I don't understand these people."

"Yeah?"

"I need to go home."

Jamie was swaying a bit himself. "Okay."

"Like now"—an uncertain pause after that last swallow—"I think I might throw up."

A party photographer had appeared and was positioning for a candid of A. N. Dyer with Christopher Denslow, his hand nudging Christopher closer, there, perfect, now trying to get the attention of the old man, right here, right here, his fingers snapping for focus, but Andrew was on the verge of collapsing.

"No pictures," Jamie said, stepping in.

"Hey, it's a nice moment," from Dennis.

Jamie took his father's arm. "We're going."

"Yes. Please. Fast," Andrew told him.

"Just one picture," Dennis almost begged.

"Richard," Jamie called.

Richard was busy watching Emmett talk with Andy, Emmett doing his best to cheer Andy up, which involved a series of animated gestures that Richard was desperate to understand.

"Richard, we need to go like now."

Richard saw his father's pallor. "Yeah, okay."

"What about Andy?" Andrew mumbled.

"We'll get him later," Jamie said.

"No, no, no, we should get him now."

"He's already gone," Richard lied. He took his father's other arm.

"Wait, Mr. Dyer," from Edgar Mead.

But the three of them were already hustling through the Library, through the Living Hall. Their hurried pace caused a small scene, these sons escorting their sick old dad toward fresh air. But the Dyer boys cut through the murmurs and the questions, steadfast with their guidance, no need for revisions or edits here; they were taking care, and with every step Andrew loosened and let his feet bounce along in a pantomime of walking.

"Faster," he said.

"Hold on," from Richard.

"Hang in there," from Jamie.

All this spit and Andrew was parched. *Water, water, every where . . .* The word *sequela* popped into his head. He had always wanted to use that word in one of his books. As the boys swerved through people, Andrew leaned his head back and imagined the ceiling starting to buckle, a few drops coming from the cracks, the mansion groaning as the flow from above increased and opened bigger fissures and linked the drops into a solid gush that inspired chunks of plaster to come down, revealing an unrestrained torrent. Screams would follow. The proactive would proactivate but to no avail. A foot of water. Now two. Now three. Rembrandt would sit back and watch like John Jacob Astor on the *Titanic*. Turner would slowly find his equal. There would be no escape.

"Almost there."

Andrew began to heave.

Through the vestibule and into the entrance hall and down the stairs, where the boys adjusted their grip and draped him between their shoulders in the style of soldiers removing the wounded, they got him into the cold, reassuring air and crossed the street, Andrew's Wellingtons no longer pretending to touch the ground.

Behind him, the Frick pitched and rolled.

"Can you make it to the apartment?" Jamie asked.

"Mmmhmm" was all Andrew could manage, which meant I think.

His head seemed to stir his stomach into ever-widening arcs, accelerating the contents within, the specifics of which he tried to forget though he knew cheese was involved. They entered the lobby of his building, the doorman quickly closing the door like an onslaught was coming. Whatever the gastrointestinal g-forces that had held the mess together seized up and Andrew realized that however bad he was feeling was about to get worse. He rocked like a jockey begging his ride to go faster. The boys rushed him into the elevator, Jamie removing his hat, Richard removing his coat, the two of them promising, Almost there, Almost there. Andrew for some reason thought of a sparrow caught in a garage. He could relate to the bird's confusion. Inside the apartment they hightailed him upstairs, through the master bedroom, into the bathroom, where they posed him in front of the toilet, unsure where their duty ended.

"Made it," Richard said, breathing hard but victorious.

Andrew stared into that stale hollow.

"You'll feel better afterward," Jamie said.

Was there anything more humiliating than an old man with his head in a toilet? He spat into the eye of that Cyclops. At least the cool porcelain was comforting and gave him a favorable anchoring to the floor. He looked over at Jamie sitting on the sink and Richard leaning against the wall and had visions of mobsters trying to get a rat fink to talk.

"Just let it out," Jamie said.

Andrew nodded, still baffled by the recent events. Poor Andy. He stared back into that clear cornea of water. Oh Polyphemus, look what you've done! He spat again. It seemed important to throw up, that not throwing up would somehow be a huge disappointment, perhaps even fatal. He closed his eyes. He wanted to cry but instead focused on the waves of nausea sloshing against his insides, like a careless boy running with a full bucket. All these metaphors. All these similes. A body trapped inside a body. Andrew gripped the rim tighter. You miserable fool. Just throw up. Snot untied from within his nose. He started to moan. Another wave formed, this one bigger than any boy, and Andrew let go and kicked for the gathering break, knowing he only had so much energy. The tide in his mouth receded as glands wrung themselves dry, and everything within him became liquid. Look out, look out, I'm going! It started small but grew larger, like a mouse chased by a cat.

Jamie went over and patted his back.

Richard wetted a washcloth.

"Is he all right?" I asked, peering into the bathroom.

I must have startled them.

"Get the hell out of here," Richard said.

VII

April 6th, 1951

Dear Andy,

I realize to get a letter from me, here and now, when I could just as easily pull you aside or visit your room, is bordering on lunatic, depending on my nerve of course and if I'll put a stamp on the upper right corner & let this piece of paper travel miles in order to gain a distance of a few feet. But speaking is not my strong suit — as you well know — & some thoughts are best put down using one's finest pen — as you well know again. So what are these thoughts? you might be asking now. In all honestly, I'm not sure. I'm just going to let the nib and ink guide me like a tattooist working on dear Queequeg. Savage sentiments, perhaps. I'm sure now you're curious so...

For the last month I have had terrible dreams, really just one dream in particular with a dozen different tails. In this dream you die. How you die changes but the manner of death is usually gruesome, I regret to inform you. Falling

through ice. Shot up on a battlefield. Throat slit
by a madman. Sometimes I find you collapsed
& bleeding & I have no idea the cause, only its
grisly effect. I seem to be having these dreams
every night & even on the few occasions when I
nap I awake damp with the horror of my oldest
dearest friend dead. For you are my oldest & dearest
friend, Andy. I cannot imagine my life without
you. You are an essential gear within my clockwork
jewels and without you I am stopped. That is the
sense I get in these dreams. An absolute stoppage.
I try to comfort you as you pass from this earth
to that great beyond that you have forever reminded
me in my earlier due. I squeeze your hand. I brush
the hair from your face — in these dreams your
appearance seems inspired by the Romantics. You are
Wordsworth to my Coleridge, Keats to my Shelley
And my lap is your final resting place. Forgive
the language. It is late at night and I seem inspired
by these poets as well. But it always seems so
real, this dream; I can tap into it even during the
most mundane moments of my waking day & turn
standing in line for lunch or pretending to play
right field into a threnody. Already I am laughable
enough at this school without people seeing me
wipe my eyes as a brace of drake mallards fly by.
Ridiculous —

The thing is, I haven't had a proper sleep for the last few weeks & I'm exhausted & featherbrained, certainly weary, possibly deranged, absolutely hopeless, constantly lonely & fearful that I'm a drag on you. I can sense that when you catch me staring. But you are the window with a view onto the ocean and I am the cripple, chin perched on the sill. I remember all the times you stood up for me & spoke for me & brought me along when Darwin would have left me behind, and I am certain much of that came not from clear affection or easy affinity but from the long haul of our time together, a rapport manufactured by parents & school & proximity. Yet buried in there was an understanding, I think. Your brave knight defended me. It was part of your code. But now, after seventeen years together, I must seem so weak. And you must be so sick and tired.

Which brings us to sleeping, which brings us to dreaming, which brings us to the point of this letter. I remember when your father passed away and my parents told me I had to say something to you, give you my sympathies, and I had no words & no voice, to properly entertain this notion. Yet I tried. I probably picked the wrong place & the wrong time, and you stopped me & told me my father would die some day so there was no point in bothering with the sorrys. We were all in the same boat

Fathers die. Mothers too. I think I cried because
I didn't understand the point. And you were
angry — of course you were angry. But we do die
some sooner than others, and we should try our
best to say the things that might mean something
before that day does arrive. After much thought,
I understand that you're not the one who's dying
in my dreams. I am. I sense it every night as I
try to fall asleep, the descent steeper and longer,
the landing harder. I am at Wit's End. But what
I need to tell you before I hit wherever I might
land is that I have a tremendous affection for you,
my friend. I always have. You mean everything to
me. I can scarcely define my life without regarding
you as the measure. I still remember holding hands
when we were toddlers on the march & feeling the thrill
as our arms swung. Even then I never wanted to
let you go. And as close as we are, or were, or have
been, or never will be again, I still yearned — yearn
to be closer. Those nights we occupied the same
dimension of sleep, whether camping or an overnight,
I wanted to reach over and touch you just to
confirm there was flesh to my feelings. I wanted
to show you the secrets of my devotion; its
tremendous volume. I wanted my chest to be a
door. I wanted you to see, if just for a moment, what
you mean to me within this small room. That's

what this letter is, I suppose, a coffin, in keeping with sweet strange Queequeg. Not that this paper will keep you afloat.

I wish I could say all of this was hastily put down in some fever dream, but I am knee-deep in nineteen drafts. Every word is the best that I can manage, even the ampersands. Particularly the ampersands. You & Me. I do hope the effort will help me get some sleep. Maybe it will do its job without ever having to pass through the mailman's hands. Regardless I do hope you take these words as what they are — a tribute, a whisper of my endearment. That said, after reading, please send this letter to the fire so that regardless of its content at least for a moment it might provide you with a bit of warmth.

Melville to your Hawthorne,
Charlie

VII.i

THE LETTER WAS SPREAD ON THE FLOOR, the sheets side by side. I could hardly bring myself to touch the paper but instead leaned over with the solemnity of a Muslim in prayer. The first thing I noticed was the cursive, a bygone calligraphy, and I remember thinking, This is my father's handwriting? The few notes he ever sent me were pure chicken scratch. Then I worked through the prose and discovered a beating heart. It was hard to reconcile my image of the man with the facts of this boy. Was this a Rosetta stone or just a piece of adolescent infatuation? But as I read further I began to push my own blood through its loopy capillaries and flesh took the place of harder, more impenetrable bone. My father only a minute reborn and already a new kind of mortality set in. This was the man he should have been. I leaned down closer. One part suicide note, two parts love letter, those sentiments often intertwined, I tried to imagine the courage and the fear, the hope and the dread, the great unburdening that must have been involved in its writing. That said, many of these empathies came later. Much of my initial reaction stumbled around Oh-my-God-my-dad-was-gay.

I see him walking across the quad in an overcoat, physically frail but intellectually limber, a boy often picked on though there's no begrudging the abuse. This is my fate. I am content. In his soul he understands that he was born a hundred years too late. He would have preferred a world of candlelight and coach rather than the brutishness of pure American power. I am a time traveler, he sometimes thinks, taking notes behind the lines. He heads toward that room, determined. All these years of loving Andy as a friend, as a best friend, an only friend, all these years of wanting to spend every minute in his company, his asthmatic lungs lacking any other need. As a boy this was just friendship. Whatever strong feelings could be explained away, like the small objects he stole, the red rubber ball, the gnawed pencils, as nothing more than practice love, the clutching of his hand an anticipation of more appropriate intimacy down the road. But the teenage Charlie guesses it might be something else, at least on his part, and while he can continue under the same set of rules, he needs to express his true self at least once, hence the letter. It is, he thinks, an honest, almost innocent rendering of his love. This is what you mean to me, Andy, even if I mean less to you. His biggest regret is the prose. Melville? Queequeg? Keats and Shelley? Hawthorne? My God please.

He pauses by the door, scared and thrilled but mostly scared, wondering if the letter has arrived or if he still has another day of anonymity. He knocks, pokes his head in. "Just return-um, just return-um, I have the necktie I borrowed," he says.

Andy is sitting at his desk, shoulders like frustrated wings. "Goddamn Halley," he mutters without turning around. "He's making me rewrite my Coleridge paper. How can something be too creative? I had all the facts in there, all of them. It was probably the best paper in the class."

"Probably," Charlie agrees.

It's just after dinner and most of the dorm is enjoying their brief freedom before study hall. Periodic hollers sound from the quad as whatever game takes shape and sucks in the passing boys.

Charlie fiddles the tie around his hand. "You, um, weren't at dinner."

"Maybe because I'm working on this."

"Right."

"What grade did Halley give you?"

"An A, I think," Charlie says.

"You think. That goddamn Halley."

Charlie steps into the room and either a draft or the slightest of prods closes the door behind him, the click of the latch causing Andy to jerk as if a trigger has been cocked. In that instant Charlie realizes his letter has arrived and he's socked with regret, worse than regret because the reasoning behind the letter now seems so misguided and self-defeating, even worse seems cruel and unfair to this friend he loves so much. I am one of those coward assassins, he thinks, and he starts saying, "I am, I am, I am, um, I am, sorry," the tears dropping like a too-late surrender of arms.

"Shut up and leave, I gotta get this paper done."

Charlie covers his face against the liquid parade. "I shu, I shu, I shu, I never why what I wrote, I should not have written what I wrote. I don't, I don't, it was a bad idea."

"Just go," Andy said.

"I just, I just, wanted to-um, to-um, just to tell you how"—perhaps I am overdoing the stammer here, overplaying the trope of those physical manifestations of our emotional selves, but I will slow him down and have him hum a song to himself, an old-fashioned waltz, so his voice can flow with a clear if eerie quality—"how much, I care, about you, after all, this time, together, that you, mean a lot, to me, that's all that I wanted to say."

"Charlie, what's wrong with you?" Andy backs from his desk, the chair gutting the floor. "You have to shut up about all of this." The air around him seems clamped tight.

"I am, so very, sorry."

"You don't have to provide me with the syllable count." Andy pulls a handkerchief from his back pocket. "No more crying, okay, it's almost study hall."

"I am an idiot," Charlie says.

"That might be true."

"I got carried away."

"We don't need to talk about it anymore."

"Okay." An intense relief, almost alchemical, opens within Charlie, and he grins. "Here's your tie." He presents the wet wrinkled thing like a booby prize.

"Holy mackerel, Kingfish!" Andy nearly shouts.

That line, timed with a bulging of the eyes, has been getting Andy decent laughs around campus, and Charlie grabs hold of the flimsy humor and possibly swings too far in the other direction, but he figures a laughing boy is better than a crying boy. And maybe for Charlie this release is tinged with pleasure, which carries affection, which he wants to share, and maybe he reaches over and puts his hand on the swale of Andy's shoulder and squeezes, something he's done a thousand times before, and maybe he expels a bit of nervous air, which might be confused with a sigh, or a moan, and maybe this cues Andy's own frustrations, pent up for so long, for so goddamn long, all these years of putting up with Charles Henry Topping, and maybe this anger breaks free, calved from the same substance as tears, and maybe that's why the violence is so sudden and upsetting, because Andy did love Charlie, but Christ he hates him now, the first punch just a probing jab to the chest, and Charlie seems to understand, and maybe this enrages Andy even more and the second punch comes that much harder and higher and Charlie falls to the floor and Andy wrestler-fast is on top of him, hands going for the throat.

Was that how it happened?

Am I even close?

From all these bits of information, both in fact and in fiction, I try to refashion my father, but the task is mostly impossible and just makes me feel sadder for the effort. After all, I was a part of that terrible acquiescence. His true life was to be borne alone. Thank goodness he met someone like my mother, who could push him forward with gentle purpose, like an usher seating a latecomer in the dark. By the time she met my father she was done with passion. Still, she created a tremendous amount of beauty with a cold heart. But I do think he was content. Or I do hope he was content. Mostly content. I remember once trying to tell him that I loved him. It was during my unsuccessful period of analysis, and I took him to lunch and we went through the preliminaries of catching up. I think he appreciated my desire to be a writer, even if failed, and in the middle of the meal I guided the conversation into unexplored terrain, our relationship, and said something like, I know you don't enjoy talking about these things, but I just wanted to tell you that I love you, and while I wish our relationship was closer, that takes nothing away from my deep feelings for you. It was almost word for word what my shrink told me I should say. "It's not about you. You need to give him the confidence to love you back." But it had the opposite effect. My father looked stricken, as if I had shoved into his face a piece of his home planet, long destroyed. I quickly slipped the conversation back into my pocket and moved on to other incidental topics. By dessert his color had returned and I was relieved.

I gathered up the letter from the floor and refolded its sheets into the envelope, imagining the DNA evidence on the glue. I tried to decipher some meaning behind his choice of stamp but could draw no connections from the sestercentennial of Cadillac landing at Detroit, the modern-day city rising up behind the explorer.

"You must be feeling something, right?"

The question came back like a taunt.

It was in this room, under the constellation of *FUCK YOU*, where Richard and Jamie tried getting me stoned on their brand of No Soap Radio. Rather than file boxes there were beanbags and tapestries and an absurdly large stereo system that seemed ludicrous even in its day and crates and crates of records—enough of Brian Eno, how about the second side of *Meddle*. Jamie and Richard nodded to Pink Floyd's endless "Echoes," coaxing me along with goofy smiles and these cute girls and the offer of an almost adult friendship. I knew they were tricking me, which in itself was a weird kind of power. I returned their smile and said, "I think I'm stoned."

Richard clapped. "Damn right."

"I'm wasted, for sure," Jamie agreed.

They started to giggle, and I joined in. Whatever my reaction, it was a source of hilarity for the group—"You are so fucking high, Philip Topping!"—and I happily put on the mask they handed me. I laughed uncontrollably. I comically zoned out. I riffed on alternate universes. I lost myself in the trippy music. Hooded and glazed, I stood up and danced like a far-out Gene Kelly, eventually grabbing the cuter of the two girls and twirling her around. Miraculously she went along with my clumsy moves. I pressed her close and gave her a tango dip and was amazed by the blond tuft that lived under her chin. For some reason this was an intense erotic thrill. I thought about losing my balance and humorously collapsing on top of her—my high was getting horny—

but instead I brought her back to her feet. "Your hand is amazingly soft," I told her, stroking her palm.

Richard and Jamie nearly blew snot from their noses.

I moved my hand up her forearm with its unharvested silk.

The girl looked toward Richard and Jamie.

"You, young man, are stoned!" Richard shouted at me.

I also had a tremendous boner, which I hoped was less obvious, but this girl's skin was a new frontier and I imagined the expanse unfurling from arm to breast to thigh, my hand a covered wagon heading west. "I kind of wonder," I started to say, "if this is like the real me, like me stoned, if this is the way I am without the hang-ups, you know, like free, if me stoned is me as I should be, and me not stoned, all screwed up and scared and insecure and paranoid, is really the fake me." I paused. "Sorry," I said to the girl, "I just really want to kiss you."

Her face buckled. "I don't think so."

The boys started to cackle. "C'mon, kiss him!" they both yelled.

"Um, no." She pulled her arm away and went over to her friend. "No offense."

"Prude," Richard said.

"Oh, shut up."

"Turn that toad into a prince," Jamie said.

"Not funny."

"I'm sorry," I said, "you're just very pretty." I turned to the other girl. "You too."

"Gee, thanks."

"You don't believe me?" I asked.

"No, I believe you."

"You seem dubious." I made a point of staring at them. "I can see it in your eyes. You think I'm like a joke or something. Maybe you're right, maybe I am a joke, a stupid joke. The real me. Ha-ha. I know I've fallen into your trap of let's get Philip Topping stoned. Let's see the dumb things he'll do. I'm your entertainment for tonight, girls, so go ahead and laugh." Jamie and Richard did laugh, but the less cute of the two girls gave me a sympathetic look.

"It's okay," she said.

"You want to hear what's really stupid." I now focused my attention on Richard and Jamie and struck steel to every word. "All I ever wanted was to be your friend. How sad is that? I'm like an abused dog. Maybe worse. I don't even know what I am anymore, the real real me. Just so stupid. And stoned. Too stoned." Maybe I was overly influenced by those After School Specials but I started to tug at my hair and search for a zipper near the base of my neck like I was on angel dust. "I don't even know if I'm a real person anymore. I can't breathe. Shit, I can't breathe." I sort of gasped and rushed to the window, throwing open its sash. Cold air instantly hit the room. I leaned far enough out to give the suggestion of a possible headfirst plunge.

The getting-cuter-by-the-minute girl came over.

"It's okay," she said, rubbing my back.

"I need to leave." I put tears in my voice. "Maybe take the express down."

"We all have our freak-outs," she said.

"C'mon, Philip," from Jamie.

"Yeah, man, close the fucking window," from Richard.

But I could hear that their voices were laced with concern.

Eventually I pulled myself back in and wrapped my arms around the less cute girl, who was now absolutely lovely, sweet and accommodating, a care in this harsh world. Her neck smelled of Noxzema. I squeezed against her giving volume. Perhaps they would laugh later—that goddamn Philip Topping—but the comfort seemed miraculous. And was that a bra clasp? I could sense Richard and Jamie's worry, or worry about the unknown repercussions. It was a new sentiment in regard to me. The wiser boy would have accepted this small prize, but I nuzzled that girl's beautiful skin and imagined it belonged to me and said from over her shoulder, "No Soap Radio."

"What?" the girl asked.

I widened my eyes on Richard and Jamie and repeated, "No Soap Radio."

Their faces went through a clumsy stop-motion.

"Mother"—Richard snapped to—"fucker."

Jamie dropped his stoned persona. "You knew the whole time?"

"Knew what?" from the girl.

"Knew it was a joke."

"Mother"—Richard flexed his arms—"fucker."

"Wait, what's a joke?" the girl asked, pushing me away.

"Of course I knew," I said. "You guys aren't that good."

"So are you stoned?" the girl asked, still confused.

"No. I do have a little headache, though." Which was true.

"Mother"—Richard got up—"fucker."

"This whole thing was an act?" the girl said, growing offended.

"You guys started it."

"That's just cruel," she said.

The other girl, in retrospect much cuter, laughed.

"I have to say I'm impressed," Jamie said.

"Mother"—Richard threw the baggie of fake weed to the ground—"fucker."

"Look, I'm sorry," I said to the girl. "I was just tricking you back."

"Asshole," the girl said.

"Maybe we were both being assholes to each other."

"No, you're the worse asshole. I really thought you were in pain."

The room tilted away from me.

"You got us, man," Jamie said.

"Mother"—Richard began to grin—"fucker"—which was surprising since he seemed pissed, but it was an honest grin, almost proud, like I was a little brother who finally stood up for myself. He came over and pushed me with affection, the way athletes do, and still tongue-tied on *motherfucker*, he put me in a headlock, motherfucker, and thwacked me a few times, motherfucker, this small amount of exertion priming the pump and bringing forth other words—"Fucking A"—though *motherfucker* still reigned—"you motherfucker"—until he rolled me to the floor, still under the auspices of roughhousing—"you funny motherfucker"—and I could feel my helplessness set in—"No Soap Radio my ass"—as he flipped me facedown and scooted onto my shoulders, his knees pinning my arms in a backward straddle. That's when he began tugging at my pants. Knowing Richard as I did, I panicked, which only doubled his determination. I started to kick. I begged him to stop. But his body had a scary leverage. I expected one of the girls to step in and calm things down but instead these other hands joined in, grabbing my legs and under four-part harmony shucking my shoes, my pants, even my socks, and now I was alternately pleading to the swampy carpet with its bong-water and chewing-tobacco pungencies and hoping for a burst of superhuman strength, like in those stories you hear, to bull-buck them from my back. But it was futile. I remember them mocking my underwear—"nice Fruit of the Looms"— before they gave a sharp pull. At that moment I knew this was easily the worst thing that had ever happened to me. It's quite strange when you grasp the immediate impact of something, its endless reach forward and backward, and the present becomes elastic, the tension always there. Jamie and Richard and the two girls took turns spanking me—"You've been a bad boy"—my embarrassing acne a source of hilarity and disgust. I was waiting for the inevitable escalation, and when I heard Richard call for a Sharpie, I thought, Oh shit, here it comes, sodomy with a permanent marker. I was so convinced of this, I started to cry, "Please don't, please don't," the promise of awful pain and deep humiliation filling my head rather than what came next: the almost ticklish scribble as one by one they drew all over my ass.

I remember running home and stopping a block short to collect myself. I was one of those people you sometimes see crying in public and you wonder what happened, what kind of disaster has struck? You want to comfort them but mostly you just want to know. When I got back to the apartment my parents were in the library. My father noticed nothing unusual, glancing up from one of the biographies he was always reading and approximating a smile, but my mother, she closed her book and came straight over and asked what was wrong, her hand touching my shoulder. She was regal yet casual, like an early graphite study for a masterpiece. We were close enough where I could've told her anything and often did, but that night the shame was too great and I brushed away the question. Perhaps I was open to a challenge. She tried to neaten my hair—she was always trying to neaten my hair—but quickly gave up and said, "Okay." Did she believe me or did she allow me my private misery? I remember feeling disappointed either way.

In my bedroom I took down the mirror from over the bureau. My backside resembled a bathroom stall. A cartoon penis spurted cartoon cum. Stink lines and flies radiated upward, likely the work of Jamie. Someone wrote I'M AN ASSHOLE with a helpful arrow. The four of them signed their names using their best Hollywood autographs—talk about leaving evidence—and I discovered the last names of cute Laura Handler and even cuter Jules Pierce. Laura and Jules. I could still smell the Noxzema. It started to seem almost innocent. They had written on my ass. So what? In the grand scheme of possible adolescent abuse, it was no big deal. Still, I was shaking. I jumped in the shower and scrubbed as if the victim of a far nastier crime, a victim of my imagination, I suppose. What kind of person jumps to such conclusions? I think I expected Richard to rape me.

I wonder if the two of them have forgotten this or if, like me, they just play along in forgetting. But how could my father forget his mistreatment at the hand of a Dyer without performing full-blown amnesia? After reading his letter I realized he was nowhere near some minor character, like Cooley, but was in fact Timothy Veck. What a cruel joke, to stick him in a closet, to tease and torture him, to twist his blameless love into the deformed heart of an ampersand. This part of my father I decided to liberate, a minor loss for the papers of A. N. Dyer but fuck him and his progeny. I was stashing the letter among my other stolen things when I heard that horrible sound coming from down the hall. It was as if someone was being turned inside out. I thought, maybe Andrew's dying, painfully, I hoped, and I went to go bask in his wretchedness, never expecting to run into Richard and Jamie. I'm sure I surprised them as well. And I wonder—or is this just pure fantasy—but I wonder if bundled within that surprise there was an image of me finally cracking and pulling a gun, holding the brothers at bay as I put my foot on their father's head and drowned him in his own spew. Did they fear my revenge after all this time? Did they see a muzzle flash before my old face slipped back on?

VII.ii

W E'VE ALL WOKEN UP LIKE THIS, in the tail end of a dream, where our bedroom is most certainly not our bedroom, the landmarks of doorway, window, bureau all turned around, the rug and furniture all wrong, these signs pointing to a different bedroom yet here we are, in our room and in our bed, and we shoot straight up, alarmed at what might have happened in the middle of the night. Are we no longer ourselves but instead this other person we always imagined, finally awake? We scrape against those fears of being misplaced, of being discovered and unknown. Our chest grabs. All of this happens within the span of an uncanny second before the room shifts, and the chair belongs in that corner again, and by God that window always faced east. You fall back into being who you were yesterday with an almost audible click. Well, the same thing happened to Andy except the room never shifted but remained misaligned, stripping the thread of memory. Where the hell am I? The easy answer—on a couch, sweating as if I had dengue fever—was quickly supplanted by a desire to remain as still as possible. Holy Christ shit. The headache, the dry mouth, the nausea, the replacement of body fluids with nitroglycerin, all these symptoms were in keeping with a very large hangover and could be explained by last night, but the ache in his legs, specifically behind his knees, that was something new. He was curious if he had been chased last night, by a pack of dogs, by a group of thugs? Or was he the pursuer, hoping to catch up, desperate to stop? Whatever the cause, Andy was clueless, like much about last night, and what the hell was that noise? Had he passed out inside a church?

His phone. It was his phone, Hallelujah no longer so amusing.

He spotted it within reach on the coffee table.

"Um, yeah, hello," he barely managed through the shag on his tongue.

"Andy? Oh great, it's you."

He didn't recognize the voice.

"It's Richard, Richard Dyer, Emmett's dad. I got your number from Gerd."

"Oh, yeah, hey, yeah."

"Do you know where Emmett is by any chance?"

"What's that?"

"Do you know where Emmett is? We're hoping he's with you."

"With me?"

"We're kind of frantic here, trying to find him. Do you know where he is?"

"No, I don't think so. Wait, give me a sec, okay." Andy sat up and heeled his hands against his eyes, which activated a swirl of nebulous light, like a mental screensaver, but there was no information behind this display. He looked around the room and tried to get his bearings. A bookshelf. A couple of IKEA chairs. A lime-green rug. A coffee table with piles of manuscripts, a few of them chimneyed with bottles of beer, and one with an ashtray like a pool, a dozen filters bronzing themselves along its edge. Where was his suit jacket? And why were his pants around his knees?

"Andy, you there?"

"Yeah, yeah, sorry, Richard. My brain's the size of a walnut."

"Well get it together, please. Is Emmett with you?"

A definite girl vibe wafted through the place, lavender based, and his suspicions were confirmed when he caught sight of the photograph on the side table: Jeanie Spokes posing with a few girlfriends around one of the New York Public Library lions. Okay, he was here, in her studio apartment. In all honesty, Xanadu fell a bit short.

"Andy?"

"Yeah, yeah."

"Do you know where he is?"

"What time is it?"

"Seven-fifteen A.M. I really could use your focus here. My wife is—"

"No, yeah, yeah, yeah, Richard, absolutely. We were pretty, well, I guess drunk last night."

"I know."

"Was I dancing?"

"I don't know. You guys disappeared."

"My legs are killing me. But I'm sure he's fine."

Where was Jeanie in this scenario? Did he lose his virginity here on this benighted couch, too wasted to remember, his unbuckled pants the only forensic clue? He peeked under his underwear and saw his prick huddled against pubes. What was he expecting, a high-five?

"Andy?"

"I'm on it. Just one second."

"Where are you at least?"

"The Upper West Side, I believe, way north." Andy used the couch and coffee table as parallel bars to pull himself up—the world's lamest gymnast. He tried to bolster his crushed spirits with the nearly magical concept of waking up tomorrow feeling fine but instead caught himself saying fuck you to that smug, smiling asshole. He buckled up his pants. A thought buzzed near his ear, of never feeling good again, of being stuck like this forever. Then a cement block dropped onto his head—

> It is not now as it hath been of yore;
> Turn wheresoe'er I may,
> By night or day,
> The things which I have seen I now can see no more.

—like he was standing in front of McIntyre again, his stomach similarly queasy.

> The Rainbow comes and goes,
> And lovely is the Rose. . . .

"Okay, okay," Andy said, hoping to motivate himself. "Yes, okay." And that's when he got his first full view of the apartment, a decent-size studio, with a raised section on the far end that defined the sleeping area in three steps. There was a mound of person under the sheets, a bare leg draped over the side, a female leg, pale and powerful, one of Jeanie Spokes's spokes. Was she naked under those sheets? As he approached, an odd sort of negative space opened up within him, the shape around her body pushing against his insides, like plaster into a mold. Feelings started to settle. All of this and I should stress that Jeanie Spokes was not naturally beautiful, with her pumpkin-shaped rear and boxing-glove breasts, but Andy was ready to awaken her with a kiss. Then he realized there was a bigger mound beside her, another species of arm and leg peeking free of the sheets. Andy instantly—you stupido, you sap, you schlemiel—understood the nature of this substrata. "I found him," he said to Richard.

"Oh thank God."

"You want to talk to him?"

"Please."

Andy went to where Emmett was sprawled, a pillow over his head as if bludgeoned by a sack of flour. He thought about ripping him from sleep with an angry pull or push, but after a few seconds of failed planning, he just nudged him. "Hey, Emmett." The pillow rolled away and Emmett did some basic intimate navigation, triangulating himself between Jeanie and Andy.

"Hey," he said.

Andy handed him the phone. "It's your dad."

There was only small pleasure in Emmett's discomfort.

"Hey. . . . Yeah, I'm so sorry. . . . No, I'm fine. . . . I should've called but the night got away from me. . . . I know. . . . Stupid. . . . I know. . . . It was bad judgment. . . . Just drinking . . . "

By now Jeanie stirred, her hands a washcloth on her face.

"Hello there," Andy said with faux cheer.

"Hi," Jeanie said.

"You have a good night's sleep or was it restless?"

" . . . Absolutely. . . . It was totally irresponsible of me and I'm sorry. . . . Yes. . . . "

"I'm not"—an ill wind blew against Jeanie—"I'm not proud of this."

"I think officially it's statutory rape," Andy said, as if his seventeen equaled thirty. "Plus he's my nephew and he's been celibate for almost, well, for almost forty-eight hours, so you fucked that up too. Good going."

"I don't know what happened."

"Really?"

"Seriously, I don't."

Andy was too fuzzy for sustained hard feelings. "My own personal history stops somewhere around Eric Harke—right? We were hanging with Eric Harke, how nuts is that. But even I can tell you how penis plus vagina times alcohol equals wash, rinse, repeat, but I thought it'd be me with the super-clean hair. I don't even know what the fuck that means. I just thought—did I like run somewhere?"

" . . . Uh-huh. . . . Right. . . . Right. . . . I will, Dad. . . . As soon as I can. . . ."

Jeanie winced. "I'm really sorry."

"The thing is I liked you," Andy said. "I probably still do. Is that totally pathetic? I should be righteously pissed, but maybe I'm not."

" . . . Okay. . . . Okay. . . . Yeah. . . . I will. . . . Okay. . . . Bye. . . . Love you too."

Emmett handed back the phone. "I don't think we had sex," he said.

Jeanie covered her face. "I'm pretty sure we did."

"You sure?"

"Yeah."

"And what was I doing?" Andy asked.

"You kind of passed out," Emmett said.

"Your dad pissed?"

"Why do they always assume you're dead?"

"Yeah, right, I know," Emmett said. "I'm sure I'm dead somewhere too."

Jeanie shook her head. "I feel like a high school slut."

"But weren't we all wasted or was I the only one?" Andy asked.

"We were all wasted," Jeanie said.

"I wouldn't be surprised if Eric Harke was hiding under the bed," Emmett joked.

Jeanie smiled—postcoitally, Andy thought.

"So I just passed out?" he asked again.

The other two had no answer except mutual agreement and Andy was hit with the awkwardness of being the only person in the room clothed and unscrewed. "I'm such an idiot."

"It's just a stupid thing that happened," Emmett said.

"No, you guys had fun. We all did. My fun just stopped on the couch."

"Andy—"

"I should go, totally the third wheel here," he said, starting to sense the lack of a future past, even if sex with Jeanie was always theoretical and whatever love seemed dubiously attached, still, it was love, if a lesser form, and the longer he stood by that bed the more he could feel how desire pushed back, often harder than the initial force, and whatever the gain could seem minuscule when compared to the loss. "Yeah, I'm going to go."

"I'll come with you," Emmett said.

"No, I kind of want—"

"Of course," Emmett said, looking injured. "Yeah."

Andy found his shoes and jacket curled near the couch. Everything seemed too big, as if a spell had broken after midnight. "I'll talk to you later," he said.

"We go to Connecticut tomorrow," Emmett told him.

"Oh, okay."

"So . . . "

"Yeah."

Near the door Andy turned around to give them another goodbye, so long, whatever. It seemed that his earlier awkwardness had crawled into bed with them, Emmett and Jeanie crowded by the gap sitting between them, twiddling its thumbs.

Andy closed the door.

Five seconds later he realized he should have gone to the bathroom.

In no mood to wait for the elevator, Andy took the stairs, which fell in twos, sometimes threes, a few leaps of four, until ten floors later he landed on the ground floor and emerged into the low hundreds on the most western edge of the Upper West Side. It was unfamiliar terrain.

But adrenaline beat against his hangover, humiliation and pride cheering him on, like he was a team accustomed to losing but losing well. In other words, he was feeling all right. Almost good. He headed east, into the dyslexic sunset. This brand of light was relatively exotic to Andy, as well as the quality of people on the street at this hour, walking dogs, going to work, jogging, all of them noticing this teenage glitch in haggard pinstripe, or Andy imagined they noticed him and perhaps remembered themselves in earlier incarnations, when they could break the night. Cross West End, cross Broadway, cross Amsterdam, and the fresh air and the rising sun and the oddly exhilarating shame made him want to run. He also really needed to pee. Faster across Columbus, across—what the hell?—something called Manhattan Avenue, a street he'd never heard of before. It sounded like one of those movie streets occupied by every New York type, extras dying to look straight into the camera. It was sort of creepy. Thank God good old Central Park West appeared on the horizon with its namesake green opening up behind. Andy sprinted in. He searched for a stand, a copse, a boscage of secluded trees—there, to his right, where he unzipped and mimed an interest in oak or elm, a mighty water rolling at his feet.

Then sing, ye Birds, sing, sing a joyous song!

What was it with these Bertram McIntyre hauntings? There was no way Andy was going to talk to his father about coming to Exeter. Imagine if he said yes, the embarrassing possibilities, the various opportunities for public mortification, Andy easily accessing the anxiety like a bruise that takes color before an injury. Finished, he slunk from the tree, and as an apology to the organic littering and to appease Mr. McIntyre, he opened his arms and proclaimed, "And let the young lambs bound as to the tabor's sound! We in thought will join your throng, ye that pipe and ye that play, ye that through your hearts today feel the gladness of the May!" which had its positive effect even if the dark side of his brain found Emmett taking Jeanie from behind.

It really is a beautiful park, Andy thought, walking south, and he wondered when spring did its springy thing. Late March? Early April?

The gladness of May? Concrete has no season and those trees along sidewalks are about as natural as lions in a zoo. Invariably there's a day in this city, one day when you bounce along the edges of Central Park without any mission and you—Hey!—realize that spring is here, just like that, the trees are lost in low hanging clouds of pink and white, and you're amazed, not just because it's thrilling, which it is, but because it seems to have happened without your noticing, without your participation, and that's the dumbfounding part, at least to Andy, how heedless he could be beyond the arrival of shorter skirts and thinner knits, and when he finally did notice, it seemed the blossoms were already falling and the whole miraculous shebang was already rolling away, like there was no spring, only sprung. But not today. Today the buds were just nibs on the trees. The terrain this far north was novel and every hundred yards or so an unexpected view opened up: a glade, a rocky outcrop, a wooden bridge over a stream, a lagoon, right there in Central Park, a fucking lagoon. Andy imagined nature heaving through pavement and insisting on itself, like the undead bursting through hard earth. Or maybe it was just the sight of fellow stragglers walking with dazed purpose and sneaky grins like they had just brushed dirt from their shoulders. Shhh, they seemed to say. Up ahead trees gave way to baseball fields with coquettish fans of infield. Screams were heard—a game of soccer bounded between two outfields, the players sprinting and leaping and tumbling and j'accusing. They were all so serious. That's what Andy hated about sports, its humorlessness after a certain age. The ball flying through the air was no longer about joy but about pursuit. And with this thought still in motion, when he came to the reservoir and commingled with all those joggers, he pictured them being chased. He dug a cigarette from his pocket. Look at this, people, but after a few drags he tossed the butt aside, his lungs charred from last night. Faker. And then he felt bad for littering. He wished that Emmett had come with him. So he and Jeanie Spokes had hooked up, so what? Well done, nephew. Because it would have been nice to compare notes from last night and commiserate over a greasy breakfast and maybe call up Doug Streff and the three of them could have gotten stoned. Andy thought he should apply to a few colleges in California, around L.A., maybe one of the Claremont schools, or USC, UCLA, whatever the difference was. Imagine the weather. The girls. Abandon the East. And did Eric Harke really mention something about having an awesome guesthouse and he should come and visit? Was that in the realm of possibility or merely the domain of the wasted? What would his dad say? Well, obviously no—Andy unhitched from the reservoir and started the meander around the Great Lawn—no, no, no, no, no. You can't. Please no. Not California. Not there. Too far away. He'd probably weep like a spoiled boy losing his favorite toy. What am I going to do without you? You can't leave. It's not fair. Even if I do send you to boarding school and over the summer ship you to Keewaydin; even if Gerd is more of a parent; even if when you're home I hide in my study and when I see you all I can do is blather about how special you are, about how much I love you, you know that, right, I love you very, very much. See, I say those important words. Those meaningful words. But if you leave, Andy, I swear I'll die. Christ, the drama. Andy pictured his father patting at his shoulders like he was putting out a hundred microscopic fires. Listen, please, listen, just listen. You have to know by now that you and I, we're the same. Andy jerked as if catching sight of an impending blow. We are no different. Maybe he was overhearing his own guilt, his own desire to be left alone. You are who you are, Dad, and that's cool, but I honestly don't need a big father-son thing. No offense. I just don't. And that's not to deny our decent times together. The Yankee games. The Disney World vacation. Skiing—actually skiing with Gerd but you tended to the fire in the condo. Those Augusts in that rental in Bellport where you knew no one and we would spend the day on the beach and swim in the ocean, you fearless in the waves even if your old-man flesh was like mold on bread. Pass a tree and you'd suggest a quick climb, cheering me on from the roots. I bet you can go higher. Andy kicked at the path. *You* climb the goddamn tree, he thought. By now he was getting tired but he could see that obelisk—Cleopatra's Needle—peeking, and he knew he was getting close to home. And maybe from exhaustion, from all the drinking last night, from the sight of Emmett and Jeanie in bed, from his stupid father and the coming apparition of spring and the innocent brightness of a newborn day, for whatever reason, Andy almost wanted to cry—actually was crying, crying those weird kind of tears you get from being so tired and raw, his axis aligned toward the sentimental, and he swore it was more performance than anything else, like an actor unfolding weepy beauty from a hangover. And maybe from somewhere deeper he was remembering his father at the natural history museum, years ago, Andy just a boy running from diorama to diorama, a box-shaped world that pressed against his palm, the cheetahs, the rhinos, the zebras, those elephants storming down the middle as though busting loose from this dead zoo, then up to the dinosaurs like dreams from the earth's unconscious, then down to the blue whale that transformed the swarming children into plankton, and it was in the creepy Hall of Human Origins that Andy reached up to take his father's hand and discovered a different man up there. You're not him. You're somebody else. It was like falling into a different life. He was no longer a son but just a boy. Andy quickly let go, ashamed, like he had somehow disowned his dad, and he circled around the exhibition with its various models of hominids, its skeletons and skulls. What if I'm missing forever? What if he's missing forever? What if I'm never what I once was? Twenty seconds bred multiple questions until he spotted his dad near the entrance, in front of the life-size display of early man and woman, more primate than anything else, upright and furry and naked, breasts and penis catching the light and putting a blush on a six-year-old. But what was most striking—and maybe this was why his father stopped—was how the ape-man touched the ape-woman's shoulder with a sort of primal sympathy as the two of them stepped forward, both distracted by possible dangers. Andy spied his father through the display. Was he crying or was that the natural warp of glass? Because he looked close to crying, like these stuffed things were old pets, a memory of what remained behind. Our meager link. Andy waited for his dad to notice that he was missing, but after a few minutes, he gave up. Dad? Yes. Can we go to the planetarium now? Sure, sure, lead the way. There were tears in his eyes. Not much but something. Did his father even remember this?

Andy entered the backyard portion of the park: Greywacke Arch—

hello-hello-hello—the glassed-in slant of the Temple of Dendur—where had Jeanie hid?—the toddler playground—this scar right here—down the decent skateboard hill toward Alice in Wonderland and the model-boat pond. It was too early for hot dog carts. Too bad. Even an inferior pretzel would be welcome right now. He passed a small crowd with an impressive array of cameras and binoculars gathered near the Hans Christian Andersen statue, their focus tilting east toward the buildings that canyoned the park. No doubt these were those birders checking on that hawk, or was it a falcon?

"I think, I think," Andy heard one of them murmur.

"Oh yes," another agreed.

"Get ready," from a man, his nose a zoom lens.

Everyone quieted, their eyes like listening ears, until suddenly they broke into a count, "One-two-three-four," and after five came up short, cheered and congratulated the world with their unmagnified sight.

"Way to go, stud."

"Seduced by a dead pigeon."

"That's three times this morning. You hear that, Herb?"

"Don't think you'd appreciate the technique."

"Perhaps not. But sheesh, the volume."

Laughter.

"What just happened?" Andy asked.

"Some lovemaking on the ninth floor." This Herb man pointed. "See that building there, two windows over, on the metal railing—that's Pale Male on the left, and next to him is his mate Paula. Above them is their nest."

"Above them is their nest," Andy repeated, liking how it sounded.

"They just had a diddle," Herb said. "We were counting the thrusts."

"Really?"

"Instead of fact checkers, we're fuck checkers."

"Oh, Herb."

"Is it a hawk or a falcon?" Andy asked.

"A hawk, a red-tailed hawk."

"Right, right, I knew that." From this distance the hawks were just a brownish quirk against the limestone, an impression of birdlike stature, but Herb of the huge zoom lens offered a peek and in an instant Andy was up close, like right there close, which first made him coo about the wonders of technology but was soon eclipsed by the sight of this kind of nature in New York, on Fifth Avenue no less. Andy had seen Pale Male before—they both lived in the same neighborhood, after all—but seeing him in such detail, with his bright yellow talons and barrel chest and eyes that seemed to question a non-birdlike existence, was thrilling.

"You think any eggs yet?" someone asked.

"Still too early. Maybe in a couple of weeks," someone else answered.

"Hopefully this year they'll take."

Chicks. Andy grinned. He knew the birder crowd went full paparazzi when a chick was born. He stepped back from the camera, his eyes still on Pale Male as if unsure how the distance translated. "Thanks," he said to Herb.

"Would you like to buy a picture?"

"I'm good, thanks."

"A key chain?"

"No thanks."

"Toilet paper?"

"Um—"

"That's a joke. Picture and key chain, that's for real."

"No thanks. What do they call the chick again?"

"A chick," Herb said.

"I thought it was like *eyeglass* or something."

"Eyas," Herb said.

"Right. They're funny-looking."

"Very. Hopefully in a couple of weeks we'll have one or two here."

"Cool."

"Come by again," Herb said. "We're always looking for young recruits. Or I am at least, first thing in the morning and last thing in the afternoon. A lot of birds will be coming through over the next few months. The great northern migration." Herb popped his eyes both ironically and earnestly, a pleasant tightrope walk. "It's quite a bevy of activity."

"Cool," Andy said, knowing he'd be back in school.

"Cool," Herb repeated, sweetly mocking. "Buy some binoculars and join us."

"Okay, maybe."

"Okay then."

Andy left Herb and his fellow birders and continued around the boat pond, his eyes still on the hawks and their aerie. There were starlings here too. Grackles. Ducks of course. Sparrows and robins. Andy remembered once hearing an owl late one night and going to his window and searching the trees across Fifth. The call was so clear. So close. *Hoo-hoo-hooooooooooo-hoo-hoo.* His ten-year-old imagination pictured the cartoon genus of the bird perched on a branch, wise and sleepy. He wondered if his father heard the call, if he was amazed by its presence as well. His study was right below. Andy could see the light bleeding into the darkness. Come and look, he tried to tap with his thoughts, but of course the window remained shut. Oh well. Andy even wrote a poem about that owl for his fifth-grade English class. It was good enough to get into Buckley's literary magazine and wound up (with my assistance) in a national scholastic publication, which I think was more embarrassing than anything else, particularly with the whispers of his father's name attached to the writing.

The Owl

> *A question of who wakes me*
> *And brings me to my window,*
> *To hear what only nature keeps*
> *Yet tonight asks what I do know.*
> *City-born I have no answer,*
> *My ears too in tune with noise,*
> *But I listen in hopes I might infer*
> *A certain wisdom and cheerful poise.*
> *How do I return this uncertainty*
> *Raised alone by its darkly call?*
> *Awake I dream you rise with me*
> *And as two we fly without rival.*

When Andy showed the poem to his father, with my bursting A++ circled and exclaimed on top, displeasure grew on his face as if the words spat back. "*Yet tonight asks what I do know* is a weak line," he finally said, "and I'm not sure the meter is very consistent. Or the form. Is there a form? And 'The Owl' is a terrible title. 'Awake I Dream' might be better, if pretentious, and there's nothing worse than a pretentious ten-year-old." He handed the poem back, his fingers leaving a damp mark. "I do like 'cheerful poise,' though. And well done on the grade, even if the double-plus business is silly." Andy smiled, not then but now, as he approached 72nd Street. He had worked so hard on that stupid poem. He wanted every word to somehow speak to his father. The memory of that desire came back stronger. We need to talk. I need to talk. There are things that need to be said, Dad. There are hawks in this park too. Walking onto Fifth, Andy passed a pigeon near the curb working on a piece of bread, and though he had seen a million pigeons before, this pigeon, with its formal gray attire and ascot of iridescence, struck him as maybe the first pigeon he had ever seen.

VII.iii

I'M DYING, A. N. Dyer thought, lying in bed, arms crossed, staring up at the ceiling, which, he swore, was slowly lowering, now only a few cranks from his nose. It was strange being back in this bed, a citizen again of this super-king-size island. As boys Richard and Jamie were awed by its expanse and would jump on board and play games of stuntman, tossing and leaping and tumbling. Isabel never cared, though all the roughhousing tightened Andrew's nerves. He constantly heard screams in their laughter. Split skulls. Blinded eyes. Stitches and scars. *Please stop, please stop*, he would whisper, begging for safety from all this spirit. Last night they brought him up here. They cleaned him. They tucked him in. The sheets on his left were still sealed, like a half-opened envelope. Seventeen years without Isabel but yesterday was on repeat in his head and how wonderful she looked and how seeing her reminded him how alone he was. His arm reached over. I'm dying, he told the chilly linen. This will be my deathbed. Articulo mortis. Richard and Jamie pooh-poohed him when he informed them of this last night—perhaps it was the extra tremolo in his voice and the vomit on his breath—the two of them looking down like death was a splinter and tomorrow they'd get the tweezers. In the middle of the night Andrew startled awake and tried to grab whoever was tasked with tending to his bedside—Richard, he believed—to pull him close, but it was just a sympathetic shadow, likely the curtain, the morning sun presently curling around its edge. We are all born twins, Andrew thought, wondering if the line was his, twins we only meet on the day we die. At least there's a companionable form in the end. The ceiling now seemed ready to squeeze. Andrew closed his eyes and attempted to swami his body toward that introduction, his pulse tapping softer and softer on that door until the door would finally open. I am dead, he thought.

And then he got up.

He still needed to type the epilogue for *Ampersand*. That would be his final act, his last words, Edgar Mead after college, a successful lawyer in the making, his future bright. A man spared. It was only a page and a half and it would take maybe an hour, including his patina of edits and scrawls, his illusion of life. Andrew was determined to change the tone so that when Edgar bumps into Timothy Veck in New York, he would at least reveal his eternal shame rather than express his glib apology, effectively splitting himself between the then and the now. "Christ, we were a disturbed lot, weren't we." That's what he said, smiling and shaking his head, a master of rhetoric. But this time pick up a damn spear, Andrew thought, and start poking. Put some blood on the page. Let sorrow run its endless course and try to wrestle that twist into a unity. "Not a day has passed . . ." Once this revision was done, Andrew would swallow every last Vicodin and exit either by razor or by window. Maybe that would set Andy free. So inspired, Andrew grabbed from his closet a bathrobe, paisley silk, circa unknown, and shuffled from bedroom to hallway to stairs, gimping carefully, desperate not to die until he had managed this last bit of creative reverie. None of his ailments mattered anymore. There was something to write. It was like he had stumbled onto a mysterious relic from his younger days and he cradled the charm close to his chest.

Near the bottom Andrew was struck by a thought: I haven't had sex in a very long time. This detour surprised him. Was it the feel of silk against his skin, its vaguely biological fabric? The bathrobe, tight and harboring a better quality of smell, seemed a stowaway from Isabel's wardrobe. But whatever the synaptic path, the above statement was true, and below loomed an even larger truth: I will likely never have sex again. This was no loss on the carnal front. Andrew would need multiple medications to merely consider a woman's hands in prayer. But it did strike him as metaphysically sad that he had no more of that game in him. Only doctors and dental hygienists and barbers touched him now. Sex had never been a huge focus for A. N. Dyer. Sure, his characters got caught up in the great congenital churn, but for Andrew personally it always played as too intimate, too clumsy to impose on anyone but his wife. A climax was more purge than pleasure, a banishment, and when finished, he wanted to apologize, like he had spilled something and sorry it's sticky. That's not to say he was a hundred percent faithful. I mean, who was? No matter how conservative a person might be, the seventies were the seventies. Funny, Andrew had no dream of ever being with another woman, yet he had his dalliances, while Isabel probably often dreamed of being with other men, more loving men, easier men, yet she never touched a soul. But occasionally Andrew could still park in fantasy. There was that particular bank teller he liked, her index finger ribbed in rubber. And there was a moment where he considered Gerd as a possible partner, but he could never muster the necessary energy. His bathrobe seemed to press harder. When was the last time? He remembered those wicked blue pills, diamond-shaped, like he might reclaim something.

Andrew opened the door to his study and headed right to—Richard, standing by his desk, papers in his hand, not papers but manuscript pages. "Is this the original?" he asked, his being caught red-handed shading toward innocent daybreak.

"What are you doing here?" Andrew's voice choked on outrage.

"I spent the night," Richard said. "I've never seen—"

"In here?"

"No, no, in the living room, on the sofa. I've never seen—"

"Couch," Andrew corrected.

"What?"

"It's a goddamn couch, and if you slept in the living room, why are you in here now?"

"I woke up early."

"And decided to peek into my study."

Richard squinted. "You feeling okay?"

"Do not patronize me. I will not have that. Not from you."

"Patronize? You were in pretty rough shape last night, Dad."

"I get dizzy, that's all. They think I might have Meunière's disease."

"Meunière? Are you seeing a doctor or a French chef?"

A grimace at this blunder. "Oh, aren't you clever?"

"I'm sorry."

"I meant the other one."

"Ménière's," Richard said.

"Yes, yes, Ménière's. Are you happy now? Anything else you'd care to mock? My labored breathing? My poor digestion? Trust me, the life inside this body is a laugh riot."

"Look, I'm sorry—"

"I'm in pain." A crack of emotion, as if forecasting tears.

"I know, I—"

"In constant pain," Andrew said, curious if he would tear up, "so much pain," but after the third try, he hobbled over to his desk, tearless. "You have no idea."

"It was a bad joke."

"It was a decent joke, cruelly timed."

When had he cried last?

"Okay, Dad, I'm a cruel bastard."

"I didn't mean that."

Richard kicked the ground with his breath. "Whatever."

Andrew looked for his Vicodin on his desk. It was normally right next to his typewriter, a small brown silo, *V* for *Vicodin*, ever stalwart but now gone. He opened drawers and moved aside papers, and finding no sign, opened the same drawers and moved aside the same papers. Where are you? You must be here somewhere. He was like a giant fee-fi-foing for a pill-popping Jack. He started to search in absurd places, as if this bottle had the wherewithal to hide. Under the phone. Inside the pencil holder. Within the antique inkwell. Once more with the drawers and the papers but this time with more flinging involved, and with nowhere else to go, Andrew went on all fours and investigated the clutter beneath his desk. It was a goddamn mess down here. All evidence of civilization had been lost below the knees.

"Is everything okay?" Richard asked.

"I'm looking for something."

"You need help?"

A quick "No" as Andrew panned through royalty statements and balled-up Kleenexes and mounds of opened and unopened mail, newspapers and magazines, haphazard socks, dozens of cast-aside books, piles of index cards with random jottings, some with enigmatic words or phrases—*ontogeny recapitulates phylogeny; the new Adam; the tonic key*—others with a sentence or two seeking a home—*This is not a story, this is a life*—one sheet of typescript giving him a minute's worth of pause:

On a flat green stretch of hard-tru the armies slowly amassed. There were only a few roads and they rippled white in the high summer heat, their route long and straight except for a few intersections where, as always, the greatest blood would be spilled. Only the weakest, most beaten-up stuck to the road; they had been kissed by other wars, wars that fathers and uncles lived through, grandparents mourning the cost. It was said that an older cousin once commanded a great deal of these assets, but nobody talked of those battles. War has its own mute nostalgia. The rest of the vehicles were relatively unscathed. Tanks and front loaders and bulldozers and police cars and fire engines and ambulances and a rag-tag collection of civilian cars, mostly slick and sporty, though a few taxis were thrown in as well as a stagecoach, none of these transports had a need for the civilized path. Not even the ridiculous limousine obeyed the road, its tinted windows hiding a squat billionaire who insisted on fighting. Nobody yet knew his car could turn invisible. And fly. The traffic was awful and the combatants were getting upset. Even before the war officially started there was a nine-car pile-up, an unexpected calamity. And a Tyrannosaurus Rex mauled a knight in armor. The uneasy truce between cowboy and Indian was almost lost when a Mexican bandit gunned down a Cherokee warrior, but luckily a spaceman stepped in and saved the day with his advanced knowledge of medical care. But this was only the beginning.

Andrew had no idea when he wrote this, for what purpose. There was a brief doubt that he was even its author since he liked the writing so much. Were there more pages like this floating around? It could have been a year old or thirty years old, a random start folded up and forgotten. Whatever its origin, its quality unnerved him. It was like coming across a photograph of a happy memory you don't remember, like your dad on the beach holding you upside down, your smile reflected in his face. Was that really you? Was that once your life? When did you become so dispossessed from yourself? Andrew tossed aside the sheet. Everything old seemed a rebuke. And with all that was lost and all that was unknown, goddamn if his big toe wasn't beating a war drum against his foot.

"You find what you're looking for?" Richard asked, peering down.

A tired sigh. "Why are you here?"

"You were in bad shape last night."

"As you can see," Andrew said, crawling toward the couch, "I'm fine."

"I'm worried about you."

"You can go home, my prodigal son. I thank you for your concern."

Richard stiffened. "I'm not prodigal."

"Don't be so literal."

"If anything Jamie's the prodigal son."

"Fine, fine. Then return to your hoeing, my bitter eldest."

"I just wanted to make sure you were okay."

"I heard you the first time." My goodness, Andrew thought, when did Richard become so straight and sincere, unlike the son of his memory who rubbed their noses in his foul behavior and had the frightening air of murder-suicide, a phrase Andrew almost used as the title for *Percy, By Himself.* This change in Richard seemed almost untrustworthy. In the good old days Andrew would have had confidence that Richard had stolen his Vicodin.

"Andy's not here, by the way," Richard informed him. "Don't worry, he's okay. He's with Emmett. The two of them spent the night somewhere without bothering to call. But they're both fine. I talked with them about forty minutes ago."

"Aren't you the universal father?" Andrew said from the vicinity of the coffee table.

"Just thought you'd want to know. He was pretty upset with you last night."

"Who?"

"Andy. But he was drunk, so was Emmett."

"Who's Emmett?"

Richard nocked a grin. "That would be my son."

"That's his name. Emmett. Emmett, Emmett, Emmett." Feeling embarrassed and defeated, Andrew gave up on the Vicodin and climbed onto the couch, allowing pain its full rout. The comfort of soon dying was replaced with the palpable unpleasantness of Richard staring at him. "He's sick, right?" Andrew said.

"Was sick, and that was a while ago."

"What was it again? Jamie told me but I forget. A kind of cancer."

"Leukemia."

"Right. Leukemia. That must've been hard."

"You could say that."

"But he beat it."

"So far so good."

Andrew grabbed a ratty throw pillow and placed it on his stomach for support. "Of course, avoid the definitive," he said, and then he coughed for a bit, trying to dislodge a hunk of awfulness from his lungs. "You know when you were, well, struggling, I used to have these fantasies—not fantasies, but daydreams, thoughts really, that flashed in my head, of you dead in a gutter somewhere, murdered, overdosed, another grim New York story of a wayward son, and I am the one tasked with identifying your body in that place where they keep bodies cold, not a mortuary, but a, a, a—anyway, I go and see you—morgue, a hospital morgue—I go and see you at the morgue and you're all ravished, no, I mean ravaged, and in that moment I truly love you, seeing you laid out on that slab, I can finally love you without complication, even though it's too late. But still I'm glad for the feeling, glad that I can, if this makes sense, mourn you for the rest of my life without guilt. How's that for insanity. I can only be a good father to a dead son."

Andrew wiped the perspiration from his forehead, checking his hand as if there might be evidence of blood. "I don't think I ever wrote that anywhere. Did I?"

"Don't think so," Richard said.

"Good. But you never did die."

"Sorry to disappoint."

"Don't be like that. I was going to add 'Thank God.'"

"Dad, I didn't—"

"I'm trying to tell you something, I'm not sure what, but it is something, and I would think you'd want to hear it, that this is what you want, Richard. I'm so easily overwhelmed by the basics of how to live and I think of you as being a tremendous adult."

"I hear you and I appreciate the honesty," Richard said.

"God, no validation, please. We're not in therapy."

"I'm just saying I can relate to being scared about your sick son, I know that feeling. It's miserable. Maybe I never really appreciated what you and Mom went through with me and my problems, but with Emmett I have those same exact flashes but instead he's dangling over an abyss—I know, crazy—but he's dangling and I'm holding him by the arm and trying to pull him up, but I'm not strong enough, and the horror in his eyes, it stops me cold, he's begging for me to make things all right, please, Dad, make it all right, and I can sense his hand slipping, I know he's slipping, I know my grip is loosening, I know that things aren't going to be all right, that it's about to get unspeakable fast, and even though I know it's just the normal craziness running around my head, thinking it I get a full panic attack."

Andrew considered his son. "This isn't a competition," he said.

"What?"

"Dueling dying-son stories."

"I was just telling you my version."

"Your version?"

"We all have our version, or I think we all do."

"Well in my version you're already dead, and in yours, you're doing something with your son, you're outdoors, in the mountains, rock climbing for Christ's sake."

"Now you're teasing."

"You're trying to save him."

"Please."

"I'm serious. No doubt about it, your dead son wins."

"Dead is dead," said Richard.

"Dead is dead," Andrew agreed.

Whatever the path, they had landed on a shared belief, after which they became quiet, the silence giving weight to the air, the seconds growing burdensome until they seemed to drop and cover every surface, including Andrew and Richard, who huddled against this increasing accumulation. Neither noticed the other, though there was the quality of mutual perseverance. Then, in a low tone, "Do you believe me?" and Richard knew that his father was asking about Andy and more than anything right then he wanted to please him, like a boy again, wanted to offer him his absolute blessing and atone for his part of the past. Why not let him believe what he wanted to believe? Where was the harm in that? And regardless of the facts, young Andy put a sweeter spin on the old man, especially seeing him last night with Emmett. Richard tried to tuck his father within that awkward adolescent shell, those milky eyes taking on the more identifiable gleam between desire and scorn, ignorance and certainty, the need to be loved and the need to be left alone. In that shudder Richard saw his son, saw himself. "I do believe you," he said.

"You think I'm telling the truth then?"

Was this a trick question? "Yes."

His father puffed his upper lip, testing its cubic limit, and Richard was ready for the final release, where forgiveness is exchanged with a simple gesture, apologies brushed aside, the mantle of father and son melting and leaving behind two flawed men trying to stay warm. But instead all he got was "Bullshit."

"What?"

"I think you're just amusing me."

"Dad—"

"I think you think I'm lost, that I'm a goner, in another world."

"Dad—"

"What's the harm, that's what I think you think."

"Were you just setting me up?"

"Tell me I'm wrong," he said, as though vengeful of Richard's faith.

"I want to believe you," Richard said.

"That's not the same as believing." Andrew sat up, newly energized. "I'm a pretty good reader of people and I think you think if you say yes I'll let you have *Ampersand*. I remember things about last night, Richard, the angling and the flattery, the downright sorcery. And when I walked in here, you were practically drooling over the manuscript. Tell me I'm wrong."

"Mostly I was excited to see the original, that's all."

"I had more respect for you as a crack addict. At least it was your own pursuit. What's next, Mr. Hollywood, *Here Live Angry Dogs and Brutal Men*? You could turn *Eloise & Tom* into a sitcom."

"Dad, I swear I'm on your side."

"My side?" said with a smirk.

Richard could sense the hopelessness of answering.

"None of what I've said is true?"

So instead he just pulled back—

"I'm out of bounds? You have no ulterior motives? Your intentions are pure?"

—and hoped he might retain his dignified whole, like a soul sacrificed to appease a greater irrational force. It was a thankless nobility. But rage would have only added to the show and he realized whatever he said could well be the last thing he ever said to his father, so best say something charitable, something worth remembering. "I like Andy," Richard started, surprised by his own calm. "And no matter the logic I like the idea that maybe that's you before whatever happened happened. To you. To all of us. You don't have to worry about him being alone."

"After I die."

"Yes, after you die."

"You'll take care of him?"

"He is almost eighteen."

"But you'll be there for him?"

"In whatever way he wants, sure." Richard shrugged at the uninspired view from the high road. "And I could give a shit about *Ampersand*. Honestly. I like the book and I'm proud I'm related to the man who wrote it, but I could give a shit about turning it into a movie. Those are other people's dreams."

"I think you mean you couldn't give a shit."

"What?"

"If you gave a shit, that would mean you cared."

"It's a shit we're talking about."

"Yes but—"

"And who cares about a shit except a lesser shit?"

"But it's still something."

"Something as seen by a turd." Richard rubbed his face instead of screaming. "I need to get back to the Carlyle and check on everyone. Really need to give Emmett an earful. But Dad, regardless of everything, I'm glad I came back."

"Regardless of what?"

"Regardless of your fucking insanity."

Andrew clapped. "Finally a straight answer."

"Glad I got one right."

"When are you leaving?"

"We're going to Mom's tomorrow in Connecticut."

"That's right, she's a country girl now."

"And after that, back to L.A."

"A Sharon girl."

"Litchfield. I could come over with the kids this afternoon for a goodbye."

Andrew frowned. "No, no, no, I have work to do."

"Really?"

"I'm close to finishing. Then I'll be done."

Richard was amazed but also thankful for the man's consistency. "I guess this is so long then." He went over and patted his father on the shoulder. "Silk," he commented playfully, "very nice. I'll call you next week."

"You don't have to."

"I'd like to."

"Fine."

"And maybe we'll visit again, over the summer."

"The house in Bellport is small, not like the Southampton days."

"Okay."

"I couldn't put you all up, even if I tried."

"That's okay," Richard repeated. "Seriously." He stood there and stared at his father. His face was no longer the fruit but the remaining pit. And Richard understood that his father, his dad—Didi, he used to call him when he was eight—was incapable of reaching across that divide, the distance simply too frightening, the chance of slipping too great, and to blame the man for this, to hate him for this, would be like blaming or hating someone because of what they feared. So Richard spared him the discomfort of his overflowing sentiment and just said goodbye with a neutral smile, closing the door behind him, which he did quietly and as a favor.

Where was I when all of this was happening? Walking back from the Hotel Wales, where I had spent a Dyer-free night. The police report puts the time at 9:12 A.M. when all that occurred occurred, which incidentally is my birthday and is a detail I didn't notice till now. Perhaps my role has been fated from the beginning. A dozen September twelfths have passed since the officer scribbled pen to paper, and while there is little joy in getting older, there is an appreciation of letting go and giving in. The cop was probably guessing the time, checking his watch ten minutes after the fact and approximating the chronology. That puts us in the same boat. Either way, on the sixth floor of 2 East 70th Street, in the Dyer residence, specifically the study, Andrew sat on that couch and suffered the aftereffects of Richard's departure. It was roughly the size of a fist in his stomach. He leaned back and pitched his mouth open, like a baby bird. Feed me, feed me. So helpless. So far removed from soaring. I'm an awful man, he thought from his nest, even though in terms of being truly awful he knew he was minor-league, which made him an imposter, which only reconfirmed his overall sense of bogusness. Except for the books. The books were real. Andrew bent forward and rocked. Those goddamn books. The reflec-

tion had replaced the man. How could he have crammed Charlie Topping into Timothy Veck? And Charlie never said a word, just played
dumb. We are connected, intertwined, a whorl endlessly repeating. It
came from love, this impetus to fashion a place in which they might
belong, in which they might confirm their humanity by invention. It
was meant as a kind of apology. How's that for failure?

Andrew wished he had a shotgun here.

He dragged himself over to his desk. The draft of *Ampersand* was
nearly two pounds of paper and still in need of an epilogue. Fifty years
ago there was the original and the corrected proofs, which Random
House had returned in two boxes. Back then this apartment was pris-
tine and entirely too big. "This is not for you right now but for you in
the future," his mother had told him, and Andrew joked with newly-
wed Isabel that they were living in pure speculation. "This is where we
are heading," he told her, his arms spread wide. Those boxes sat in his
study for weeks until he heard the heartbeat, cribbed from Poe, and
one night when drunk and ashamed and frightened, when life could no
longer be undone, he opened those boxes and started to stack the paper
in the fireplace, first with care but soon just dumping it all in. He knew
he was slumming in gesture, but sometimes you have to give in to your
baser symbolic impulses. When finished, the fireplace looked snow-
bound. Andrew pulled one of those red petals from the bloom of extra-
long matches and struck it against the bottom, the phosphorous
sparking—at least it sparked the first time, but fifty years later the
match snapped near the middle and Andrew had to pull another, which
snapped as well, Andrew gripping the third closer to the top and flick-
ing it more directly, skidding one . . . two . . . three times before snapping. "Fuck," he muttered. By now his younger self was back on the
couch and watching the fire cradle the paper in a weird kind of nativity.
There it goes. But the older Andrew tried another match, then another, then another—"C'mon!"—the two dozen matches remaining
like years in non-fire form. Heat rose on his forehead. He remembered
how the Eaton twenty-pound stock burned and let loose wisps of black
ash that took flight up the chimney as if commanded to give chase. It
was easier back then. Of course. Finally a match—miraculous!—lit!

Andrew noticed how badly his hand shook, a possible sabotage, so he used both hands to reach forward and carefully touch the front and back corners of the manuscript. The flame seemed to consider the prospect of its own combustion before nodding with agreement. There was no snap of wood, only the whoosh of industry. Maybe it was the cockled finish that gave it a blue-green hue. Maybe it was the ink. Andrew didn't recall the smoke from the first time, the speed of the blaze, sure, but not the smoke, which spilled up from the fireplace like a waterfall turned upside down. Rather than thinking this undesirable, Andrew thought it beautiful. A visible suspension of carbon, an entraining drift of warmth, from sierra to echo, pooling across the ceiling. Andrew breathed in without coughing. His respiration seemed rejuvenated. He breathed deeper. Who needed Vicodin? He lifted his hand and brushed at the smoke as if trying to glimpse the bottom. Or maybe the surface. It was everything but the epilogue. That would have to do. Another deep breath. Nearby a fleck of ash floated, its motion in league with his lungs.

VIII

Tell me please what he said.

VIII.i

JAMIE PROMISED HER THAT HE WAS FINE.

It was morning and he and Alice were in bed and she was staring at his face as if his eye and lip were a brutal scene from an otherwise sweet movie.

"Seriously, I'm okay," he said, "just hungover."

He had sneaked into her apartment late last night, after putting his father to bed and rehashing the evening with his brother, often with laughter, which was nice, until the effect no longer sustained the cause and the question of Dad was unavoidable. What to do about him? Call a doctor? Hire a nurse? Become—egads—dutiful sons? The laughter likely resumed when I poked in and gave them a goodbye wave. Why? I have no idea.

"It looks worse than it is," he told her.

Jamie had crawled into bed with ninja stealth, timing his moves against Alice's snores. The sheets came to his chin without a break in her breathing, which confirmed his ability to ease through the world undetected. But then she shifted and draped an arm over his chest, murmuring, "You're here," followed by a tired yet happy sigh. Jamie tightened, like a net trawling through the sea and sweeping up another poor unfortunate. Those looks of hope and confusion. *Please* and *No* and *Help* trying to squeeze through reticular gaps. Jamie closed his eyes. We are all trapped, he thought, and only those closest to freedom can understand the futility of escape. It was a decent line and he wanted to remember it, but by morning it was gone.

"Really, I'm fine," he told Alice.

That's when Alice noticed the tooth—or lack of tooth—and gasped.

"It's not a big deal," he said.

"Look at you."

"I haven't been to a dentist in a long time, it was probably rotten."

"So the guy did you a favor?"

"I think he did."

Alice probed her own front teeth as if confirming via contrast.

"Seriously, I'm fine," he said.

"You got attacked."

"I got hit. Twice."

"For no reason?"

"I don't know. Who knows? It happens. It's still a dangerous city."

"Were they drunk? Are we talking bar fight?"

"Just a him, and it was a random, on-the-street, *boom-boom* kind of thing."

"Did he rob you?"

Jamie tried channeling patience. "Nope."

"Did you call the police?"

"Nope."

"You should call the police. They should know about this."

"It's not a big deal."

"They would want to know about this, for their records."

"No they wouldn't." Jamie could hear his tone splinter. The post-injury giddiness had gone blunt, and he could glimpse himself through the advertising: love me, so I can have some power; care about me, so I can break your heart. Normally this is where he reached for the rolling papers. And if weed proved useless, he would start to thumb through newspapers for the latest upheaval and think about calling his buddies at Magnum Photo and add more vertical feet to his unwatchable monster. People, good and bad, naturally liked Jamie, and Jamie hated them for that. But Alice didn't deserve this. "I'm sorry," he said.

"About what?"

"My mood."

"I have no problem with your mood. I'm just worried about you."

"I'm fine."

"I know, I know, you're fine, you're great."

"I'll get a fake tooth."

"It's not about that. You're just so blasé."

"What can I do about it now?"

"I don't know," Alice said, "acknowledge that you got hurt."

"I hereby acknowledge that I, Jamie Dyer, got hurt. I also got drunk."

"No need to be a jerk."

"Now you're blaming the victim."

Alice aggressively moved to the other side of the bed.

"That was a joke," Jamie said.

"Hilarious."

"Look, I had a weird night."

"You could have called me."

"What?"

"After you got beaten up."

"I wasn't . . . You were at work."

"So?"

"I've never seen a waitress take a phone call."

"What, are we like surgeons? You could have left a message. A text. I can leave if it's an emergency."

"It wasn't a fucking emergency, Alice. I didn't need you." Jamie clenched his jaw and could feel Ed Carne slugging him all over again, the taste of blood seeping through. Alice, sweet naked Alice, his almost girlfriend Alice, she was simply asking for the minimum when waking up next to a swollen eye and a missing tooth, wanted to see her concern registered on his face, while Jamie was prepared to end the relationship, projecting years of misery within a single human need.

"I'm sorry," he tried.

"Don't be."

"But I am."

"I prefer the honesty," Alice said, swinging her legs over the side. Her bare back was pale and freckled, the ridge of her vertebrae hinting at those mysterious animal beginnings. "One day, when I'm older, like in twenty years, I'm going to think back on myself as being so young here, so young, my God I was young, but right now I feel really old."

Alice got up, resigned to whatever she was resigned to, but definitely resigned. Or resolved. The sight of her naked gave Jamie a terrible ache and added another complicating kink: no matter how familiar, her body always seemed newly hatched.

"Hey, sexy," he said.

"What?"

"I'm just saying you look good."

She balled up her eyes. "I'm taking a shower." She went into the bathroom, closed the door, and soon showery sounds came from within, water snapping against the map-of-the-world shower curtain, changing tones as Alice moved across its flow, tilting her head, running her hands through her hair, the sound sliding down her skin like light projected on a screen—Jamie could picture this as clearly as if he were standing in the bathroom himself watching her through translucent oceans.

"Fucking idiot," he said out loud.

He was doing her no favors by staying; in fact, he was doing her harm. Best put on the Dyer crown and disappear and let her avoid the creeping doubt and inevitable bitterness, the slow poisoning of the well until her pleasant existence became as tainted and barren as his own. Alice deserved better. She was probably realizing this as she watched the water drain. Pants, shirt, shoes, and Jamie thought he should leave a note, nothing serious but perhaps an ushering toward the future. *Sorry, maybe I'm more upset than I'm letting on, I'll call later.* Instead of trying to find a pen and a piece of paper and suffering through his hateful man-child cursive, Jamie went to her computer. He would email her. The computer awoke onto a website for an acting class: Jonathan Ray & the Art of the One Person Show. Alice in another acting class, perfecting another monologue. The endless endeavor. But he supposed nothing could keep the end from being hard. We're all trapped. The joint in his pocket tried to comfort him with a suggestion of a walk along the Hudson and maybe see that excellent tumbledown pier, a thing of beauty rather than a thing of ruin, and maybe he could continue all the way down to Battery Park, to where the post-traumatic skyline was being stitched. Jamie was in Jerusalem when all of that happened, waiting for random bombs while shacking up with an Israeli reporter, her name long gone but her backside memorable. He watched the whole thing on her television, shocked and envious, the envy worse than the shock. And when Hadara, or maybe Hadasa, when she got home from work and found him drunk on two bottles of Gamla red, she asked him, sounding unexpectedly sexy, "How are you?"

Within a few clicks he navigated through YouTube to the video for *12:01 P.M.* It presently had 5,356,389 views, about the size of a large city, he thought. The municipality of Sylvia Carne. It was strange to think of that number as a collection of individuals, to think of himself in terms of that basic math. Determined now, he hit play. It started with the title superimposed over a vegetable stand, a few seconds later a voice, his voice, off camera, asking the question, and Sylvia stepped into frame and commenced with answering, day after day after day, in the garden, at lunch, on a walk—*I'm fine*—Jamie watching beyond nervous and scared—*I'm okay, thanks*—his insides huddling like a boy about to be discovered, listening to those voices grow closer, wanting to be discovered so that the fear could end—*Good, and you?*—Sylvia hiking in the mountains, Sylvia with her dogs, with her daughters and husband, Sylvia painting—*Hanging in there*—Sylvia by Jamie's side, folding against him and forming into a memory of Sylvia, then Weston, when they had broken into the Exeter library after curfew—*Pretty good, thanks*—and climbed up to the Latin seminar room on the fourth floor and thrilled by their epic boldness started to fool around on top of the Harkness table—*Not bad, and you?*—their fingers tracing the seams, their youth embracing clothes as an essential part of the process, as heady as skin, jean grinding jean, the buttons and zippers and clasps, the constriction versus the slow release—*I'm doing okay, and you?*—Jamie and Sylvia by then familiar with fucking and fucking in just about every nook available, reckless with their fucking, notorious for their fucking, the faculty displeased with all their fucking like they were a gateway drug, a corrupting influence—*Good, thanks*—on the student body, Jamie lowering Sylvia onto the table and kissing her asterisk-like belly button and edging down her jeans, every inch a mile-long journey, occasionally glancing up and pretending to be in class, "I thought the scene where they boned in the classroom was quite excellent," which made Sylvia cover her face—*I'm all right, really*—her fluid beauty filling whatever volume you needed filled—*Okay, how about you?*—those eyes, even toward the end and particularly in the beginning, like when he first saw her crossing Front Street and she smiled, those eyes seemed bottomless—*Pretty good*—like you were a smooth stone forever sinking, and Jamie smiled at her in return—*Fine*—and for weeks looked for her in assemblies and on sports fields, in halls and quads, everywhere and anywhere—*I am well*—and when he did see her he drew her in with a series of half glances that he defined as love since up till then love had no definition—*Can't complain*—and pure hard attraction equaled fate—*I'm good, and you?*—as they found each other more often—*Hanging in there*—and no longer parted after hello but lingered, shoulders bumping, hands playing games of Indian wrestle, until a Saturday dance rolled around and when Supertramp played they ran outside and stumbled into the nearest shadow—*All is good*—and morphed from sculpted marble into messy flesh—*I'm okay, thanks*—and over the next few months transformed into couple, an exotic intermediary form of adult, in other words they fucked, which leads us back to the seminar room and the Harkness table and Jamie on top of Sylvia, pants around ankles, shirts pushed up, the two of them connected by the savory middle—*I'm good, I'm good*—when they heard the chatty approach of campus security, who preferred company to efficiency, and Jamie and Sylvia rolled to the floor and hustled under the table—*Just fine, thanks*—and crouched sweaty and unfastened and petrified, as the door to the neighboring seminar room opened, Jamie and Sylvia staring at their own door and the epic mistake of coming here, the pure stupidity, the definite suspension from school and very possible expulsion and likely wrecked future, and Jamie said, "We could run," and Sylvia whispered, "Shhhhh," and their door did its inevitable creak and the overhead fluorescents flickered on and two sets of comfortable shoes stepped in—*No complaints really*—these four legs seeming to stand there forever—*Plugging along*—Jamie battling intense crazy insane holy shit panic—*Okay*—while Sylvia held him calm by smiling and shrugging and being impish and cute with her eyes until one of the pairs of shoes came over—*Terrific, thanks*—and picked up something from the table and tossed it in the trash—*I'm basically good*—before leaving—*Ça va bien*—Jamie and Sylvia staying still for another half hour before regaining a modicum of nerve and getting up, drained and sore, Jamie going over to the trash—*I'm okay*—and removing the foil wrapper for a condom, the two of them forever unsure if their escape was determined by luck or charity or institutional laziness—*Not bad*—though charity seemed the more likely cause and made for the better story.

I'm all right.

Sylvia was now answering from bed, her voice clotted, her eyes dim with palliative care. Over the course of two months she had time-lapsed from sick to brutally sick, her complexion chalky and mottled. Jamie had no sense of the transformation while filming. Back then it was just another day, just another awkward interruption. "Sylvie, how are you?" It all seemed ineludible yet gradual. But watching now, the daily loss staggered him.

I'm good.

Even toward the end she answered without pretense. Never had so much effort gone into such banalities. But again, something had changed. The social pleasantries had taken on weight, and not just the easy weight of juxtaposition but the harder weight of pressing on and crafting meaning from meaninglessness. It was like Sylvia was holding our hand and giving us permission to die.

I'm okay.

That was her last reply. She was gone by the next morning. After a bit of interstitial black, Ed Carne and his daughters appeared and that painted coffin was lowered into the earth as if next spring a mother might bloom. The funeral section lasted about a minute but after all the previous cuts it played like an hour. And this was where Sylvia would have ended things, probably with her name and dates, but instead the fade to black gave way to the briefest breathings of muted light and there she was, definitely dead and in the coffin, in the midst of cycling through decay, but Ram Barrett had done a masterful job with the postproduction, blowing up the film to its grainy limit so that

Sylvia seemed shaped by dust, her face dissolving within the dissolves, focused only on specific, near-abstract details, like her nose, her pierced ear, her lips, her eyebrow, these parts passing through to the reconciling whole.

Then it was over.

And how did Jamie feel? Sad, certainly. But less sad than expected. If pressed, hardly sad at all but genuinely moved. Or generally moved. Yes, moved. I am moved, he said to himself. But how much of that movement was based on relief, on being liberated from this morbid yoke? I am free. No longer liable. That seemed closer to the truth, if narrowly defined. I can move on, he tried. Start fresh. All those boxes of videos in his apartment, maybe he could construct something from them, a piece of art in high-def relief, a lava flow of magnetic tape. He rose to the idea of lava. The hot and the cold, the liquid and the solid. I am lava, he half-joked. From the bathroom he heard the shower stop, the map of the world screeching aside, the toilet seat banging down to make a platform for drying legs. Lava from the *Lavare*—funny how his Latin stuck—to wash. Larvae, Jamie riffed. Pupae. Imagos. The lessons of holometabolism from high school biology with Mr. Schwank, which a few kids twisted into homometabolism and tossed at various students, like a faggot maggot might emerge from Steve Lowenthal's head. Jamie imagined his father hollowed out. Hallowed out. It was coming, of course, maybe soon, the great decomposition. The meaning of life is that it stops. Who said that? Was that from one of his novels? Jamie shut his eyes. His head seemed a weary ravel of interconnections. He wondered how much of him was the empty space left behind by his father. Like those poor plastered souls in Pompeii. The Garden of Fugitives. Is that who I am? A placeholder? A representation of something lost? The bathroom was quiet now. Alice was either plucking her eyebrows or waiting for her nerve to reenter the bedroom. Jamie opened his eyes and watched the door. Was it too late to leave? He wasn't sure what to do, but he watched that door with absolute conviction, putting all of his squirmy shame onto the wood, the knob, the light between rail and sill. I should go, he said to himself as he waited.

VIII.ii

W HERE AM I? Do you even care? Or am I blocking your view? Sit down, sit down. Okay, I am sitting, on the curved bench of the Robert Morris Hunt memorial on 70th and Fifth, my eyes tinting toward yellow, my ears ringing a low-fi buzz. I have no idea who Hunt is beyond this recognition of his services to the cause of art, as the inscription on the pedestal reads. The bronze bust shows him with a Vandyke and a penetrating, mildly annoyed gaze, like he's just caught someone passing gas on 71st Street. Standing guard on either side of him are full-blown statues of women in togas—muses, I suppose, one holding a chisel and a palette, the other holding a small building, which I recognize with my present eyes as the administration building for the World's Columbian Exhibition in Chicago, part of the famous White City. Why would this temporary structure be chosen as Robert Morris Hunt's crowning architectural achievement? Either way, sitting there, I regard these muses as aloof, the one with the hammer ready to brain me.

Unsure of the effect, I swallow another Vicodin, and again take pleasure in reading A. N. Dyer's name on the prescription label. That's eight pills in twelve hours, not including the one I offered Bea when she visited at the Wales and the ten I handed her upon her leaving.

"Please stay," I told her.

"I can't."

"Please." Her skin was so smooth, it seemed unfair.

"Sorry," she said.

I had already given her all the money in my wallet, because it was late and she was heading back to Staten Island and needed to take a car service, and though I was probably being too generous, I needed to prove my worth, especially after making a fool of myself with all the I-love-you's in bed. That's when she mentioned the Vicodin.

"How about some for the road?"

"Why?"

"Because they're fun," she said, "and I like having fun."

"You have to be careful, you know. They can be very addicting."

What a joke.

"You know what else is addicting." The ball of her foot started to till my lap.

I shook my head. "Man, I was nothing like you when I was your age."

"What were you like?"

"Not so put together."

Bea stopped. "I just wear the clothes 'cause I get them half-price."

"Yeah, but you're so confident."

"I live at home. My career is folding shirts and finding right sizes."

"You're young."

"I've never felt older." Bea got up and put on her clothes.

I loved watching her get dressed. "You ever wear a bra?"

"You know the second I leave here I feel totally out of control."

"Then stay."

"You don't understand."

"Hey," I said, "I've ruined my life for you."

"For me? I never asked you to do that. That was your fault, your screw-up. Don't put that on me." Bea zipped up her dress, made a few adjustments in the mirror followed by a catalog pose. "I like this one," she said. "It's part of the Creatures of the Wind collection. You know what my brother calls my place of employment? B.J.Crew."

"Sounds like a typical brother."

"I think I'm going to go to a club," she said.

"I'll come with you."

"That's okay. But how about some more Vicodin?"

She went from distant and hard to wispy and soft, my downfall and my revival, and I was helpless and tapped a pile onto her palm, her hand closing before I could get a proper count. Then she gave me a kiss and was gone. I imagined her dancing with friends, all of them hardly noticing their own sweat. Did I mean anything? Two more pills went down my distressed gullet. It warmed me to think of A. N. Dyer in pain somewhere, the man who locked my father away in a novel, even worse, in a cheap, cruel joke. Of course the irony, the Dyerian irony of the whole situation, is that without Andrew and his ugly reaction, maybe Charlie would have become brave and migrated down to Greenwich Village, and maybe I would have never been born. I had A. N. Dyer to thank for my crap existence. A decent wife gone. Two sweet children broken. A job lost. A sense of purpose squandered. A father misunderstood. A mouth insanely dry and nothing to drink.

As I sit on that curved bench and catalog my present difficulties, I feel small and lonely, like the world will never understand Philip Topping, like I hardly understand him myself. I'm sorry, is this boring? Well, luckily for you I see Andy Dyer in the distance. He's about a block away, coming home from a night that has stumbled into day. As if from another era, he wears a grown-up pin-striped suit, with his shirt untucked and his necktie draped like a skinny scarf. I lift my head to be seen, but he doesn't see me, like all those goddamn Dyers. He doesn't even see me when I wave. Rather he's looking up toward the sky. In that moment I no longer see Andy but see his father and the past he's written for me, my grim future a glint in that impenetrable eye.

Andy stops near the curb; he turns south, still looking skyward.

Sirens sound in the distance, the harsh sonic bleat of fire engines.

I don't follow his gaze or the gaze of anyone else on the sidewalk.

My eyes are focused on the old man's back.

All I can say, and this is hardly descriptive and a real literary chestnut, but what follows is like a dream, and like most dreams is probably best left to the dreamer. I remember how my muddled head floats and carries my reluctant body along, and though I've barely moved, I'm standing right behind him. I notice moth holes in the suit jacket, the left pocket slightly torn from its flank by decades of burrowing deep. From the wool I smell hints of cigarettes and booze, Chanel No. 22 mixed with Speed Stick by Mennen. Those teenage shoulders are as manly as a coat hanger. Andy, still looking up, totters on the edge of the curb, leaning like he's trying to grasp something with his chin. The first fire engine approaches with its staggering *bwaaaaaaaa*. I take note of the bus in the bus lane, not traveling fast but traveling fast enough, the driver yielding to the emergency on his left. A pigeon kicks up. A pedestrian shouts, "Over there!" The rest is a blur. Chestnut meet saw. I know I yelled his name. But did I push or try to pull him back?

The bus hits him square on the shoulder and spins him. I can still clearly see the driver's face going from Oh shit! to Oh no! to Oh God! and if I had the talent I could draw him in near-perfect detail though even a child's crayon could capture those eyes. The rate of speed is almost slow enough and the driver is almost quick enough on the brakes to provide a sense of blessing. Tires never touched Andy. He wasn't run over. But the impact is strong enough to send him flying. He lands back-first followed by his head whiplashing against the curb. Between bus and body and head, it is a fugue in three notes, the last the tragic strike, and where Andy once stood, a pair of wingtip shoes seem casually kicked away.

I am the first person on the scene but others quickly follow. One man screams, "Don't touch him!" which I read as accusatory. Andy's eyes are—how much of this do you want? Do you want to hear the sound he was making? Do you want to see the bus driver weeping? Do you want to know about the ridiculous advertisement plastered on the side of that bus, which would give ironic counterpoint to what was happening? Do you want to have a sense of how pale Andy was, how he stared up like a giant beast was descending? Do you want—a blink, another blink, until his eyes narrow onto mine and he asks me more bemused than broken, "Did I just get hit by a fucking bus?"

I nod.

"I just got hit by a fucking bus," he repeats now as a statement of wondrous fact.

I try to grin, but this resurrection seems scarier than the accident.

His tongue rolls around like he's working taffy from his teeth.

"Are you okay?" I ask, an absurd but necessary question.

"Remember the times in school when I pretended to trip and fall?"

I nod again. Blood starts to trickle from his left nostril.

"This would've gotten a huge laugh."

I don't know what to say, so I just nod some more.

Suddenly Andy sits up, like he's overslept. "Shit, he's going to think I'm dead," he says. "Tell him"—he wipes his nose and scrutinizes the blood—"tell him that I'm fine, okay." He pauses then lies back down and closes his eyes, no longer believing the dream, it seems.

Do you want to know exactly what happened next?

More sirens, like they were chasing this tragedy down Fifth.

Do you want to know how he began to convulse?

A crowd has gathered around us.

"I don't think he's breathing."

"Someone should do CPR."

"Oh Jesus."

"Don't touch him, that's like the first rule."

"But he's not breathing."

"He seemed okay."

"Give him room."

"Hang in there, kid, it's going to be all right."

Do you want to know if I buried my head on his chest?

"You need to do CPR. I don't think he's breathing."

"Here come some firemen, thank God."

"Hit by a fucking bus, man."

"Is he okay?"

"Just a kid."

"Give him room."

Someone reaches around my waist and I am lifted into the air, my arms and legs flailing like a child removed from his stricken father. These arms carry me back to the Hunt memorial and sit me down and hold me half for comfort, half for restraint. They belong to a young fireman who tries to calm me down by saying, "It's going to be all right," and then yelling, "Where the hell is EMT?"

Space opens up around Andy, a resigned ripple effect.

I see two firemen working on him.

"Just hang in there," the fireman tells me, though his attention is clearly elsewhere, and I see where he's looking, toward the building on the far corner, where smoke streams from sixth-floor windows, not the black heavy smoke of consequence, just the cloud-like haze of easy combustion.

"I know them," I say.

But the fireman isn't listening. His wedge of a face, Hispanic in shade but all-American in cut, presses forward, taking in the action around him. He only eases up when a fellow fireman leans from one of those smoldering windows, more interested in what's happening on the street below. Soon an EMT and a policeman come over, and I am guided to the back of an ambulance, where I am draped in a shiny metallic sheet, the type marathoners wear after finishing their race. I have no idea how long I sit there. Nobody questions my part beyond the heartbreak of coincidence, the general sentiment being one of thankfulness that an old teacher and family friend had chanced upon the scene. I was the familiar face, the loving touch, the unlocked door offering a bit of shelter. According to Lenox Hill, Andy's official time of death was 10:25 A.M., but I am the real keeper of that last minute.

He just tottered on the curb and sort of half-stumbled, half-stepped.

It all happened so fast.

It was surreal.

Total slow motion.

Boom, ba-boom, like that.

And for a second he seemed fine.

I can still see him, clear as a bell.

Do you want to know if there was much blood?

Do you want to know if his mouth was ever so slightly open?

It became one of those stories, never told honestly.

Do you want to know if he said anything?

Do you want to know if the bus driver handed me his shoes or if I just took them?

VIII.iii

N ORTH ON PARK to 96th Street and down to the river and onto the FDR, the merge always an ordeal, waiting for the opening and then gunning into the lane, but by now the natural aggression of driving—*Fuck you, cocksucker*—in New York is flowing, a relief since those first few minutes behind the wheel are always doubtful, as if today might be the day you lose your nerve, but once blown free onto the FDR you can sit back and trust your mirrors again and play three moves ahead, pinching the son-of-a-bitch Civic trying to cut in for no real gain, and after the Triborough, forever the Triborough regardless of the RFK rebrand, you can flip on the radio, as I did now, and almost relax. Brian Lehrer on WNYC. Something about the hidden dangers of the federally mandated lightbulb. Everyone was outraged. It was ten in the morning and the traffic was light relative to the normal mess. The potholes, the amount of crap on the shoulder, the state of the bridges, suggested a fresh topic for Brian. The roads seemed war-torn. Or maybe that was just my mood. I-278 East to I-95 North and I no longer cared because gray was starting to give way to rudimentary color and driving became a pleasant kind of drifting. The GPS guided me, her sexless charm trumped by her seductive knowledge. Here was a person, a woman, on my side. A wrong turn was merely recalculated. We would never get lost. The two of us had hours together, long gaps between her commands, and while my eyes focused on the basic chore of moving forward, the rest of my thoughts roamed without direction.

It was Richard who smelled the smoke. He was talking with Gerd in the kitchen, voicing his concerns about his father and asking her opinion, if maybe they should hire a nurse, if Gerd had any experience with senior care, and Gerd was saying she thought she could handle the bulk of the issues, at this point at least, when Richard interrupted her and asked if she smelled something.

"What?"

"Like smoke."

"I have a cold," Gerd apologized.

Richard followed the smell from kitchen into foyer, pulling himself forward like his nose was on a string. Definitely smoke, he thought. Definitely a something-burning smell. It seemed more cigarette than straight-up catastrophe, like any sidewalk outside an AA meeting, but also heavier, especially the closer he got to his father's study. The string was now a rope. A cigar? A hundred cigars? Or worse? He dropped speculation and burst through the door, his imagination prepared for a possible blaze, the curtains crawling, the walls engulfed, like one of his all-time favorite movies as a boy and he would sprint in, part Steve McQueen, part Paul Newman. But instead of *The Towering Inferno*, Richard was greeted by a roaring yet relatively cozy fire in the fireplace. The rest was just smoke. A lot of smoke. "Jesus, Dad." Richard waved his hands and headed for the windows.

"You still here," his father said from the couch.

"You forgot about the flue, Dad."

"Don't you think I know that?"

"This is a mess."

"It's my mess and you can leave."

"All this smoke can kill you."

"Just leave."

"C'mon, get up, get up."

"It's not that bad."

"It's bad. Now get up."

Gerd poked her head in. "I called 911."

"It's just the flue. Help me get him out of here."

Gerd and Richard lifted Andrew to his feet, no small ordeal, and Gerd took charge of leading him into the living room while Richard rushed into the bathroom and soaked a few towels. Before smothering the fire, he noticed what was burning, the manuscript pages blooming in reds and blues and greens before withering into a thin film that fluttered in the newly introduced draft. The paper made for quick kindling. Here and there a few lines poked through—~~Sometimes the only way to free yourself from one of those ruts is to do something awful, really disgraceful, and I was in a terrible rut, the deepest ever, and I~~—which toyed with Richard's thoughts. You want *Ampersand*? Well here you go. The fire said Fuck you and Richard said Fuck you back before he laid the wet towels on top and there was a hiss and a mini mushroom cloud that choked the room. He imagined charred flesh on the other side.

The building's super appeared with four firemen.

"Only a closed flue," Richard said, sounding almost demoralized.

Thirty minutes later they got the other news from a policeman.

During the service, I wondered if Andrew still had the smell of smoke in his nose as Richard and Jamie brought him down the aisle of St. James. I was standing near the back, uncertain of what I had done exactly, if I was the dreadful cause. Richard and Jamie led their father forward like sympathetic guards to the gallows. Whatever their burden, the prisoner seemed already dead. People assumed his downcast eye and general slump confirmed his absolute devastation—*oh, to lose a child*—but Andrew stared down mostly amazed that his feet still touched the ground. Let go and he was certain to haunt the rafters. Unlike my father's funeral there was no procession, no boys' choir, though the church was filled with teenage boys and girls, classmates getting their first taste of peer mortality. The boys wore their solemnity like rented formal wear, their emotions as hard to pin as a detachable collar, while the girls tried on this sadness for size, as if the deceased had taken something more precious than virginity. Fellow Exonians Felicity Chase and Harry Wilmers held hands in their pew, though Harry's palm was prickling with sweat and Felicity was trying to remember the last line of *The Great Gatsby*, something about a green light and the snow falling faintly. A few pews closer Doug Streff had gotten stoned in honor of his pal, which was an epic mistake, the entire church pressing in on him like he was responsible for every breath.

Parents and teachers, old family friends, the usual funeral and wedding crowd, sought comfort in their shoes, ashamed of being in the presence of an Almighty who could allow a seventeen-year-old to get hit by a bus. Once again a handful of A. N. Dyer fans showed up but none of them brought books; they only offered him the communal readership of their tears. What bullshit, Andrew thought, as he was steered to the front of the church, half-expecting Richard and Jamie to shepherd him all the way to the coffin and tuck him inside. But that was bullshit too. He knew exactly what was going on even as his mind was roiled by the Prelude and Fugue in A minor, the organist's favorite since he was a child growing up near historic Williamsburg. How did Andrew know this? Because at this moment he insisted on omniscience. Like passing Gerd in the third pew he knew that years ago she had answered an advert in a Stockholm newspaper—*Surrogates needed, 100,000 kr.*—and went to a grand Gothic estate where five-year-old Einsteins day-dreamed about time in that slanting Nordic light. Her new employers informed her that a couple in the United States needed help, and after a thorough medical exam and signing a thick contract, she was taken to a dorm to live with other young women, none of them realizing the future they carried. Nine months later, Gerd was forever reshaped into mother and she begged to remain involved with the child, even if just as a nanny. Yes, Andrew knew everything about everyone as the caden-zas in harmonic minor decorated his mind with ribbons of synaptic light worthy of the Grand Illumination. Richard and Jamie positioned him in the first pew. What was the point of this? Death had rendered the story moot, and as in a fable, Andy had transformed from fantastic puppet into plain old boy.

Reverend Rushton spread his arms, and Andrew had him say, I am the resurrection and the life and all the rest, but this time he recast him as Professor Serebryakov, arrogant and ineffectual, and if Andrew had a gun he would have taken better aim than Vanya. He would prob-ably still miss. Our roles might change yet we are fated to the same lines. That sounded fine, but what the hell did it mean? What was his role now? What were his lines? No doubt Edgar Mead, sitting with Christopher Denslow and Rainer Krebs, could jump in and tell him, Edgar Mead who hated himself when he was alone. "This is all bullshit,"

Andrew muttered, and Richard and Jamie tried to quiet him but he was ready to push them aside and leave this ceremony, as artificial an ending as anything lowered on a rickety crane. "Total bullshit," Andrew muttered again. From behind a pair of hands reached forward and rubbed his shoulders with a forgotten yet not forgone touch. "Get through this and we can go home," Isabel whispered, the word *home* settling him down, making the infinite local.

Reverend Rushton said his amen and we all sat. There was no eulogy, since no one was in the proper frame of mind to talk, and frankly, Reverend Rushton preferred it this way, having witnessed over the last decade an overabundance of eulogies, some families insisting on as many as three speakers, which turned the whole affair into a grim retirement party. He had a solid homily prepared. He had worked the theme of fathers and sons into the flow from Job 19:21–27a to Psalm 121 to 1 Corinthians 4:14–21 to Psalm 23 to John 6:37–40. And this time around he insisted on a communion. The ritual had its healing place, plus it was an opportunity to introduce the power of the Real Presence to a younger, less sacramental generation. In other words, he had a good crowd. It reminded him of his early missionary days, the best of his life. "Why do you, like God, pursue me never satisfied with my flesh?" the Reverend read. "O that my words were written down! O that they were inscribed in a book! O that with an iron pen and with lead they were engraved on a rock forever!"

Enough about books and iron pens, Andrew thought. Andy should be the one sitting here, trying to muster some pity with Richard and Jamie, who might glimpse their father before he turned forever into rock. A wave of mourning broke toward the altar, and Andrew sensed Jamie getting lost in turbulent water. He was the one who went to the hospital after Richard had called him and told him what happened, Jamie jumping into a taxi with Alice, who insisted on coming. In the emergency room they were escorted into a smaller waiting area that seemed reserved for the particularly dire, inside which another couple sat, their bodies wringing the air. Thankfully Gerd showed up and could tackle the questions on all the forms. A doctor eventually appeared and he crouched in front of them and with a gentle voice, like he was reciting a grim but thoughtful tale, told them how Andy had suffered multiple traumas, the first being the impact of the bus to his body, the second and far worse being the impact of his head to the street, and between the swelling in the brain and the cardiac arrest, they could never get him properly stabilized, and despite their greatest effort, he unfortunately succumbed. Gerd covered her mouth as though blocking the news from getting in, and Jamie grabbed Alice's hand and squeezed. He remembered being thrown by the word *succumb*. He pictured Andy being attacked and no longer fighting but standing firm and letting go, like Sean Connery on the bridge in *The Man Who Would Be King*, a movie he loved as a boy. The doctor asked if he wanted to see his son before they moved him, and Jamie was in no shape to correct the mistake and simply accepted the promotion. Son, brother, father, what did it matter anyway? The boy was dead. Before leaving he turned to the other couple and wished them good luck, which he hoped was a decent thing to say but later feared the opposite. Good luck? The doctor guided him through the ER to a nearby trauma room, en route describing what Jamie would see, the body and its effects, the bruising, the procedures, the extreme measures taken, which frightened Jamie. Suddenly he was scared of misery and its hollow question. "I just want you to be prepared," the doctor told him. Jamie went into the room alone. The floor had been recently cleaned, the supporting machinery unhooked and pushed aside, avoiding eye contact, it seemed. Under the normal hospital smell lingered incongruously the first few drops of summer rain on hot pavement. Jamie thought of turning around and leaving, but instead stepped forward like he was fessing up to stealing. Only Andy's head was exposed, his face less scathed than Jamie's; the rest of him was wrapped snugly in a blue sheet. The body possessed an uncanny stillness while everything else in the room resembled a whirlwind. It's nothing like sleep. It's the opposite of sleep. And please no using the word *peaceful*. Jamie stared for a long minute, his feet sensing an edge, whatever emotion overcome by the vastness of the fall. Unsure what he was doing exactly, he reached down and touched Andy's chest and with his other hand touched Andy's forehead. Again with the stillness. The skin was damp. A few sharp hairs anticipated an eventual need for a razor, and a cluster of pimples embarrassed his chin. There was that sundial nose, fully formed and recognizable, and those thin lips, forever sphinxlike. This was his last face, already foundering. "I'm sorry," Jamie said. He placed his thumb on the faint worry line that over the years would cut a deep trench and he tried to draw up from the boy via a mystical kind of energy he never believed in all the memories from his young life. He offered it space in his own body, to fit wherever it might fit. He performed this improvised ministry and when he came to the end, or the beginning, he said once again, "I am so sorry," not quite grasping the apology though sensing somewhere the reason. It was all too much to bear, right up to the moment in the church when his father surprised him by wrapping his arm around his shoulder and pulling him close.

From Job 19 on to Psalm 121. And from I-95 to I-91 to I-84 to I-90. Trees and farmland grew more prevalent, the sense of space near bursting, as if these roads were rope holding together an overstuffed suitcase. Past Worcester. Past Lowell. As a longtime trustee my father did this same drive four times a year for twenty-four years, alone and probably listening to his cherished Bach cantatas. He loved to drive though we his children considered our mother the far superior driver, the three of us nervous in the backseat whenever he slipped behind the wheel, only because he was so careful and exact, unlike Mom, whose roadster moves we took as confident rather than reckless. She measured success by time whereas he graded himself on every turn, every press of the brake, apologizing for every unanticipated action. We never noticed his driving, only the other cars passing by. But on those quarterly excursions to Exeter no one judged him. I signaled for every lane change, even when there was no one behind me, in honor of him. I always hated these returns to school. And my mother drove so fast, desperate to break her record of four hours and two minutes. But if there wasn't a chance of notching a new best, and if I struck her as particularly despondent, after turning onto 125 she would stop at Eggies Diner and I would order a bacon burger deluxe and a vanilla shake—my last meal, she always teased, her eyes wanting to wipe the unwipable grease from my chin.

"Do you love Dad?" I once asked her on one of these occasions, my tone leading the question toward an obvious No, perhaps feeling the sting of our imminent parting and sensing in our closeness something that must've trounced any love she had for my father.

She squinted, which at my cynically earnest age I took as politics, and said, "I do love him. He's a very sweet man. The secret is you have to adjust your expectations, Philip. Don't get trapped in other people's opinions and how they view things. You are in charge of your own happiness, even in high school."

"Well, I'm not happy," I told her.

"I know," she said. Was she sick by then, even if in the early stages? So many of my memories have her undiagnosed and leave me wanting to tell her to please go to the doctor and insist on a CT scan of your abdomen. "Just do your best," she told me while applying lip gloss. "Shower every morning and every night. Keep your sheets and towels clean. Remove all clutter from the floor. Control what you can control and try to take pleasure in it. Make one decent friend. Avoid wearing too much brown. Always keep in mind that there is life after this, Philip, you just have to die a bit to get there." Her compact snapped shut and she smiled. "And so ends the lesson. Thanks be to Mom." How do we survive being so loved once?

But today Eggies was closed, forever, it appeared, and I would have to press on. My father's ashes were in a duffel bag in the backseat. Almost two hundred pounds had been rendered down into an intimate five, though I still imagined a complete man inside the box, like a genie who would appear in a furl of smoke, a captive to other people's desires. To my brother's and sister's relief I had taken charge of the New Hampshire half of the scattering, and later this summer, early August, we would gather at the beach and as a family would conclude the rest into the ocean. It had been more than twenty-five years since my graduation from Exeter. The number boggled. Those intervening years, if a person, would be old enough to get married and have a family while my legal separation from Ashley was a colicky two-month-old and Bea was a few weeks away from giving birth to straight-up extortion. In death my father and Andy could share the same crib, with my mother babysitting as a high school senior. Time is a form of propagation. It takes from us its cuttings and strikes the stem into the earth. Here! When we look back the shape bears a resemblance but is possessed by a different spirit, as if a third person has grown between the then and the now, memory's holy ghost.

When Exeter appeared, it looked the same, if quainter and more idyllic, a well-crafted old-fashioned New England boarding school rather than a stockade in Federal brick. The students walking along Front Street came across as both younger and older than the boys and girls in my day, almost parading like they were performing their daily accomplishment. The natural striving unnerved me. I tried to warn them against me, this cautionary tale rolling by in a Land Cruiser. I imagined Andy here, the vision chilling me, like a cold drip from the back of my mind. "I got hit by a fucking bus." Sometimes I continued the story for him. In college. At cocktail parties. On a first date. I got hit by a bus once. Yep. Like a bus bus. Like a big bus. On Fifth Avenue. Slammed right into me and sent me flying. Swear to God. Shoes off and everything. Standing on the curb, tired and hungover, and I guess I leaned forward, or stepped forward, probably just lost my balance and *bam!* this bus, this fucking bus, hits me. No question the story would evolve over the years, versions where Andy would stretch the truth for the sake of a cute girl's smile, where he would blame his forgetfulness on the whole being-hit-by-a-bus thing, where he would tell people that every day since was a gift, maybe over dinner and too much wine, claiming that it had changed him, that something in him had been jostled clear and he became, well, lighter and heavier, if that made sense. And then Andy would go mum, seized by a thought no longer within reach. Amazing how a whole life, a thousand complicated emotions and regrets, can boil down into a single ache. The GPS cheered my arrival, her voice revealing a hint of surprise, like she had doubted me all the way.

I parked in front of Jeremiah Smith Hall. The headmaster wanted me to say a quick hello, and walking up those stairs and into that building, my old insecurities returned stronger than ever but now with the added pleasure of being chained around the ankle of a middle-aged man. Awkward past, meet disappointing future. By the time I lugged myself up to his office, I was apologetic with sweat.

"Philip Topping," he said, as though instilling truth into my name. He was a year into the job and younger than me and already had the bearing of a man who represented the beloved George Stone era. He absorbed my humidity with an unflappable smile. "How was the drive?"

"Fine."

He crossed his arms. "Too many sad occasions lately."

I nodded.

"First your father, and then Andy Dyer. Just terrible. How is Mr. Dyer doing?"

"Okay, I suppose," though I had no idea. The only contact I had from A. N. Dyer after the funeral was a short letter asking if Andy had said anything right before he died, and since I had already misled him once with my father, I didn't quite trust myself again. That's not true. Maybe I wanted A. N. Dyer to suffer over the unknown facts, to turn his imagination against himself. Either way, not a word had passed between us.

"The whole school is in shock," George Stone said. "We had our own memorial service, and Richard and Jamie Dyer came up, which was nice, to have them here as part of the Exeter family, and they stayed on for the A. N. Dyer Award, what with it being the fiftieth anniversary of *Ampersand*, and we decided to have no Veck, just Richard and Jamie announcing the winner. It was very moving. And I think it helped. There's going to be a scholarship in Andy's name."

Did he expect a contribution?

"Tough, tough times," he continued. "You know your father co-headed the search committee that hired me. I got to know him before his health turned. We had lunch in New York, the two of us. Such a wonderful, dedicated trustee. His kind is always missed."

When was the last time I had lunch with my father? The early nineties maybe. "I appreciate you letting us do this, with the ashes. I imagine it's out of the ordinary but I'll be discreet, I promise. It's more of a gesture than anything else."

"Are other family members coming?"

"No, just me—well, Bertram McIntyre will be there."

"Oh, that's wonderful." George Stone grinned despite himself, like he had trained over the years to be a sober and all-encompassing citizen, a good, solid man, when in reality he was still stuck in high school. "I'll be thinking of your father—what time?"

"Sunset."

"Perfect."

We shook hands and I left, relieved to be rid of his young authority. It was only four o'clock, so I drove to the Exeter Inn and tried to have a nap and failing that tried to call my children. I had taken on twice-a-week responsibilities. But Rufus and Eloise's innocence only made my guilt seem more pronounced and I stumbled near tears whenever in their company. Who needs a father like that? So after almost dialing, I put the phone down. Around 6:15 P.M.—I was very focused on that digital clock—after thirty minutes of five-minute deadlines, I got up and showered, stirred only by the last second.

Bertram McIntyre was waiting outside the main entrance of the church. In blazer and tie, he was schoolboy immemorial, though with a stylish accent of blue scarf. He appeared older but essentially unchanged since my days, more pinched around the shoulders perhaps, as if plucked from the earth by a giant. But when he saw me he let loose with a smile that flicked his age into the nearby bushes, like growing old was a nasty habit. Not only did he take my hand but he squeezed my arm. For a moment I thought I was his favorite student. "Philip Topping," he squeaked.

"Hello, Mr. McIntyre."

"Bertie now, please. So good to see you, Philip, so good." His enthusiasm was notched with an emotion that students only heard when he read certain passages aloud, like the living wall of whales in *Moby-Dick* with their endless circling during the slaughter—Mr. McIntyre, Bertie, would choke up and we students would jab our tongues in unison. "You look well," he told me.

"I wish I felt better," I answered, my honesty unexpected.

He pointed to the box. "Is that him?"

"Yes." I made a show of weighing its heft.

Mr. McIntyre nodded, his mouth trying to maintain an unbiased grin. He placed his right hand on top of the box and proclaimed, "The words of Mercury are harsh after the songs of Apollo," and then turned toward the church entrance and said, "Shall we?"

Among all the surrounding brick, Phillips Church stood its neo-Gothic ground, a piece of humble geometric granite: rectangle, triangle, square. It seemed the sole survivor of an apocryphal past. The church's squat tower was defensive in nature and I could imagine archers firing into Exeter's civilizing horde, every arrow espousing an equation from below. Inside, the vaulted ceiling ribbed with wood and the lung-like organ pipes gave the impression of being swallowed whole by a living creature and you were satisfied to be its bait, a different feeling from St. James, which had me fighting all the way. During communion at Andy's funeral, I remember shuffling down from those last rows and Jeanie Spokes sidling up to me. "Hi," she whispered like she was uncrumpling a note.

I frowned hello.

"I've been wanting to talk," she said.

I continued frowning.

"You were there, when it happened."

"Yes," I said.

"I'm sorry, but did he seem upset?"

I tried to shush her with my eyes.

"I just, I need to know," she said, her eyes red-rimmed, as if she had exhausted her supply of tears and had now moved on to blood.

It was taking forever to get to the front. Reverend Rushton must have been thrilled with the turnout.

"Before it happened," she went on, "did he seem upset?"

"I'm not sure," I responded. "But this isn't the place."

"Like do you think it was totally an accident?"

Was there an accusation in her tone? I turned to gauge her expression, but she was busy matching her pace to the shamble on the floor. Did she recognize my scuffed wingtips? They were three sizes too big, my feet almost embarrassingly small, and with every step my heel lifted and chafed, lifted and chafed. "I'm not sure what really happened," I said.

"But do you think he could have stepped out on purpose?"

The people in front of us approached the altar and kneeled.

"The body of Christ."

"The blood of Christ."

"Do you think he could have . . . "

On my left the Dyer boys clutched their father like brackets, trying to hold him close without taking complete ownership, while in the pew behind, Isabel seemed to study them as though diagramming a simple yet complicated sentence. *These men are my boys.* Space opened up and I went ahead and kneeled, my ankles popping free. Jeanie soon joined me. It was obvious this was her first communion. She cribbed my pose and loudly chewed the wafer, her eyes expressing only the wonder at not being struck down by lightning. And maybe this gave her the boldness to pause in front of A. N. Dyer's pew and say, "I loved your son," in the tone of a blameworthy bride. But she was innocent and later I told her so. Repeatedly. I probably told her too much. But we all told Jeanie Spokes too much, even Andrew, who in exchange wanted to know everything about Andy. Eventually she disregarded our basic comfort and insisted on greater guilt, crafting her memoir *Ellipsis* around the biography of A. N. Dyer. It was something she called memeography, a term that thank goodness never took. Walking back to her pew, did she even notice Emmett staring at her?

In Phillips Church Bertram McIntyre gripped my arm with a sweet senior touch and led me to a heavy wooden door. "I have my own key," he said proudly. "Not that I can climb those stairs anymore. But in my more devout days I had a regular habit of going up for a drink and a cigar. My own secret clubhouse. And when your father visited, he would join me. It's a humble yet lovely view." Mr. McIntyre flicked on the lights and peered up a narrow stone stairwell. "At the top is a trapdoor. You'll need this key"—he specified which one—"to unlock it." The keys were ringed around a pocketknife, its weight and smoothness instantly enviable.

"Up there?" I asked.

"There's no nun waiting, I promise," he said.

"Let's hope not."

"I'll go and watch from the street."

"Okay."

"And maybe afterward we can get a drink."

"I'd like that."

"Excellent," he said. "I'll be standing to the east, appareled in celestial light."

"Wordsworth," I said, as if being challenged.

Mr. McIntyre seemed taken aback. "Good for you."

I stood up straighter, like I was taking position in front of his class. " 'It is not now what it was before, wherever I may turn, by night or by day I learn, the life I once saw I see no more.' "

"I am impressed," he said.

"I can still recite the whole thing," I told him.

"Maybe after a few drinks," he said, turning to leave.

I started the corkscrew climb, my father in one hand, keys in the other, and after passing a small room on the second floor, and on the third floor church bells I vaguely recalled hearing on Sundays and Wednesdays, the spiral ended and the remaining ascent came via ladder to the aforementioned trapdoor. I tried to imagine my father's tassel loafers clambering up those rungs. Maybe he was giddy with adventure, pushing through the hatch like he was sneaking into another world. I pulled myself up. The roof was solid but I feared the small square opening in the floor, as if making someone fall was every trapdoor's fantasy. The view gave the campus an intimacy that was contradicted on the ground. To the north the huge academy building with its white bell tower and clock face lorded its hour in every direction, but from this particular vantage the weathervane, a triple-masted sailboat, stole the show, its bow pointing toward the Squamscott and the Great Bay beyond. The sun still had some time before hitting its rosy stride. Shadows stretched, and my eyes saw the work required in keeping this world still, the mortar troweled for every brick, the mansard slate dealt in solitaire rows, the game of tic-tac-toe on the other side of Louis Kahn's scrim. My past blurred into the students walking back to their dorms after dinner and I gathered them up and told them everything would be fine.

I spotted Mr. McIntyre, towheaded in this light.

He waved.

I waved back.

Inside the box the ashes were sealed in a plastic liner that proved impossible to rip or pull apart and left me quickly defeated and angry, all this travel and time, all this good-son determination, and I couldn't open the stupid bag, curses coloring my effort as well as the threat of old childhood frustrations brimming into tears. Then I remembered the key chain and its pocketknife. Along with its vintage brassy excellence there was an engraving on the handle—WE THIS WAY—that continued onto the blade—YOU THAT WAY—its meaning secondary against its ability to cut through plastic, which it did nicely. I widened the gap with my fingers, releasing a talc of dust. Here he was. My father. The ash was finer than expected, soft gray sand from a beach of pulverized bone. I dug my hand in, to feel the mass give way through my fingers, a gesture that seemed far from creepy, if anything seemed mandatory. I went to the edge of the roof. A slight but helpful breeze blew to the east. I lifted the box toward Mr. McIntyre in a gesture of cheers. I should say something, I thought, something beyond "I love you." I tried to picture my father standing up here taking in this view with Bertie, the old poets on their lips, and a strange but familiar awareness came over me, like when you sit in one of those tiny chairs in kindergarten and knead Play-Doh with your son or daughter, or when you read them a book you once cherished, those moments where you live on both sides, the life already seen but today differently met, and it seems like time becomes, I don't know, becomes more physical, I guess like on a cellular level, the great goddamn understanding trickling through your blood, from top to bottom, bottom to top, the journey knotted in the vicinity of your stomach. As the shadow of Phillips Church hinged forward, I looked over Exeter as both a fiction and a fact, and using my father's runaway eyes I stared down at that old teacher staring back up, his scarf a thin blue flame. He waited for the ash to fall this way or that, and I opened my father's heart and as if descended from the sun let him live another story, a story free of A. N. Dyer, free of his family back in New York, his own private story put to rest right here. I saved nothing for the ocean and hoped a kind and helpful wind might blow Charlie Topping toward Bertram McIntyre.

Back in St. James, Reverend Rushton faced the coffin and spreading his arms said, "Into your hands, O merciful Savior, we commend your servant young Andrew. Acknowledge, we humbly beseech, a sheep of your own fold, a lamb of your own flock, a sinner of your own redeeming. Receive him into the arms of your mercy, into the blessed rest of everlasting peace, and into the glorious company of the saints in light. Amen." And on that cue the pallbearers appeared. They hoisted the coffin and started down the aisle, the organ launching into "Immortal, Invisible, God Only Wise," which, though long forgotten, was familiar from my younger days.

> *Immortal, invisible, God only wise,*
> *In light inaccessible hid from our eyes . . .*

Hands reached out from both sides of the aisle, in some cases stretching awkwardly just to touch the coffin, classmates and friends leaving their final mark on notions of immunity while those older paid respects to their worst fears and the relief of being spared.

> *Unresting, unhasting, and silent as light,*
> *Nor wanting, nor wasting, thou rulest in might. . . .*

The Dyers followed close behind, Richard and Jamie helping their father along, Isabel minding them as if they were moving an heirloom through a narrow hallway. Emmett and Chloe and Candy completed this family tableau. Richard would go back to California soon, and Jamie and Isabel would take on the bulk of the caring for Andrew, though Gerd did most of the work. Her loyalty grew even stronger after Andy's death, verging on devotion. But eventually a full-time nurse was required and a hospital bed would replace the desk in his study. Isabel had lunch with Andrew a few times a week and would sometimes read him crime novels and always accept his apologies, which toward the end were a near constant and hard to bear.

> *To all, life thou givest, to both great and small;*
> *In all life thou livest, the true life of all. . . .*

No longer of sound mind or body, A. N. Dyer put Richard and Jamie in charge of his literary estate, and though the Morgan Library was disappointed in the lack of *Ampersand* and insisted on a price reduction, in late April they happily took possession of his papers and started the labor-intensive process of cataloging the material. Richard surprised Jamie by maintaining his father's aversion to film adaptations, rather vociferously too—"We are doing what he wants, no questions asked"—but after he died, and Andrew lived for another five years, four years longer than anyone anticipated, Richard contacted Rainer Krebs and Eric Harke, who was now too old and battered to play Edgar Mead, but he wanted to direct. In fairness the movie wasn't a disaster—it had moments of true inspiration, particularly the invented scene along the Cornish-Windsor Bridge—but for the most part *Ampersand* the movie hewed too closely to *Ampersand* the book and revealed a flaw that many people had always suspected, specifically that the book was emotionally claustrophobic. Richard and Jamie had better luck three years later with *The Spared Man*, which Richard wrote and Jamie directed. It was a small movie, done extremely well, with Eric Harke playing the lead. For their next project they're reviving one of their own earliest collaborations, *The Coarsers of Bedlam*.

> *Great Father of glory, pure Father of light,*
> *Thine angels adore Thee, all veiling their sight. . . .*

The coffin approached its final stretch. A black man in a white robe opened the church doors in anticipation of its continuing outside, and the air pushed in. The day was sunny but cold, a reminder that winter still had its role, and I was amazed by how fast I could feel the chill. It's like in the theater when an actor lights a cigarette and instantly you smell the smoke. Are our senses that keen? Is it the smoke we smell or the memory of smoke, our anticipation of what's to come? How much of experience is merely filling in the blanks from earlier experience? I was near the last pew, likely singing too loud. But I once had a decent voice. The coffin passed by, and it was incomprehensible to think of Andy personified within that wood. I thought about reaching over and adding my handprint, but as my tone suggests, I refrained. The show of emotion seemed distasteful. Then again, maybe I worried that beneath the dead lay the undead waiting for an excuse to burst through. The Dyers struggled to keep up with the coffin's pace. Andrew resembled Oswald right after he was shot. Did that make me Ruby? And Richard and Jamie avoided eye contact but I could feel their scrutiny like a phantom limb around my throat.

> *All laud we would render; O help us to see*
> *'Tis only the splendor of light hideth thee. . . .*

We choose what we see. Or what we don't see. I hated them yet I loved them, knowing that they knew me in full. I thought I heard Richard whisper to his father, "Pay no attention," and I wondered if I had some sway on its meaning, or was he making an unconscious, possibly conscious, allusion to the last line of *Ampersand*, in the epilogue, after Edgar Mead bumps into Veck?

> We said our goodbyes. Veck walked south, and I walked north, and I decided that after all these years it was good to see him again, damn good, that he had turned into a good man, a good solid man, that this good solid man had stepped nicely in front of the boy, and if you didn't pay attention, well, you could miss a lot about someone right under your own nose.

Did the ghost of my father haunt these proceedings as well? There are so many possible meanings, victim or villain, son or father, me or you. The Dyers were outside now, heading toward the waiting limousine, and while a reception was to follow I was certain Andrew would go back to his apartment with Richard and Jamie. *Pay no attention.* But to what? The hymn finished and the organ tiptoed into the postlude. People started to move from pew to aisle, red-eyed and unsteady, slowed as if their mourning were as deep as chest-high water. What happens now? Where should I go from here? My concern was mostly focused on the next ten minutes but it also stretched into the coming week and month and year. I saw Ashley alone and was glad she saw me, her anger briefly subsumed by a sadness I dared wrap myself in. While talking was out of the question, I did manage the merest opening of my hand, and I hoped she recognized something in that wave, whether a glimpse of my children or of my father or of just plain me, something in that code that was worth keeping, even if only from a distance. There were other familiar faces as well, old students and friends. After a certain age you have to pretend that people care about you. For a moment I imagined rushing past them all, my shoes going *clock* against the limestone—*clock-clock-clock-clock* as I hustled down the steps outside and ran toward the limo, my imagination uncertain of what I would do or say when or if the window rolled down, if the limo was still parked or already heading home, if the Dyers would hear me or notice me chasing behind, if they would let me continue with this dream for a while longer before I had to return to my small room. But in my defense, I remained where I was, head lowered and in tears, and I would remain in place until the whole church emptied. But do you even care? Who are you anyway? Somewhere, I swear, I think I heard bells.

O NCE UPON A TIME *the moon remembered having its own moon. But that seems like a long time ago, when fathers told stories before bed and sons would listen and give themselves over to every word before growing sleepy. Their father, just hitting his stride, would have to end in the ecstatic near middle, pleased with his improvisation and feeling like he really should write these things down.* The Moon's Moon *by A. N. Dyer. A book for the boys. He even told them his plan as he kissed their foreheads good night. The next book I write is for you, he said. And their faces lit up, and as always his wife was thrilled. Yes, yes, that's a wonderful idea. But when where-were-we came, too much had been forgotten, the names, the details, the magic of that made-up moment. The story was lost, part of that vast unfinished library, the dreams of books within books. Sad, of course, because he was at his fatherly best in these moments, perhaps his writerly best as well, his imagination acrobatic and able to weave ridiculous requests without complaint, the words streaming into the ears of his most appreciative, if underserved, audience. But sometimes he feared he complained like this was a chore, like Daddy's tired, and enough of the interrupting, and do you even realize how good this story is? Do you understand the privilege of this performance? You have quite a father, he wanted to inform, and at times he resented their lack of astonishment. If you would just shut up and pay attention, I could show you something amazing. Well, boys, I am here to apologize for that man, and while he was looking for praise, I'm merely looking for sweet dreams. To be honest, I'm not sure how we become what we become, whether it's the ground or our grip. Either way, I am sorry. Nearing my end, I try to trace back to the beginning, but beyond the obvious wordplay, I have no idea where the beginning ends. Honestly. I am as much a boy today as I am an old man. And while I no longer believe in stories per se, stories are all I am, like the one about the father and his sons. I do wish we had properly finished* The Moon's Moon. *Maybe our collaboration would have worked as some kind of ligature rather than the open wound of my own name. But please, if you can, tonight or tomorrow, try to imagine that moon without its moon and think of that one remaining soul up there who after all these years still holds on, convinced he is free, dragging himself across the ground in search of—who knows? But his roots slowly turn that cockled surface into a misshapen reflection of his own face, all in hopes that those looking up might remember him and kindly return him to where he once belonged.*

Acknowledgments

MANY THANKS to everyone at Random House for all their time and effort: Caitlin McKenna, Beth Pearson, Tom Pitoniak, Robbin Schiff, Gabrielle Bordwin, Sally Marvin, Simon Sullivan, Carole Lowenstein, Laura Goldin, and in particular Susan Kamil, for her infectious enthusiasm, and David Ebershoff, for his keen eye and confidence, his eternal patience in the face of pathology.

A thank you to Marcy Drogin for her cheerleading.

Lasting thanks to Bill Clegg, friend first, everything else second.

Lifelong gratitude to my parents, Parker and Gail, as well as to Lynn and Parker.

A hug for my children, Max, Eliza, and Olivia.

And to Susie, all my love.